M000086284

A Promise for
TOMORROW

A Promise for TOMORROW

MICHELE PAIGE HOLMES

Mirror Press

Copyright © 2017 Michele Paige Holmes
Print edition
All rights reserved

No part of this book may be reproduced in any form whatsoever without
prior written permission of the publisher, except in the case of brief passages
embodied in critical reviews and articles. This novel is a work of fiction. The
characters, names, incidents, places, and dialog are products of the author's
imagination and are not to be construed as real.

Interior Design by Cora Johnson
Edited by Cassidy Wadsworth Sorenson and Lisa Shepherd
Cover design by Rachael Anderson
Cover Image Credit: Brekke Felt, Studio 15 Portraits
Cover Model: Kara Moore

Published by Mirror Press, LLC
ISBN-13: 978-1-947152-24-3
ISBN-10: 1-947152-24-6

Other Books by Michele Paige Holmes

Counting Stars
All the Stars in Heaven
My Lucky Stars
Captive Heart

A Timeless Romance Anthology: European Collection

Timeless Regency Collection: A Midwinter Ball

Hearthfire Historical Romance Series:
Saving Grace
Loving Helen
Marrying Christopher
Twelve Days in December

Hearthfire Scottish Historical Romance Series:
Yesterday's Promise
A Promise for Tomorrow
The Promise of Home

Forever After Series:
First Light

Power of the Matchmaker series:
Between Heaven and Earth

Dear Reader,

The book you hold in your hands is the second installment in the Hearthfire Scottish Historical Romance series. While *A Promise for Tomorrow* is an exciting and romantic read all on its own, it begins with the hero and heroine already having become acquainted and having gone through several previous adventures. May I strongly suggest that if you have not done so already, you read the first book, *Yesterday's Promise*, in the series before beginning this one.

Yesterday's Promise is the story of how Collin MacDonald—a Scottish laird—and Katherine Mercer—daughter of an English soldier—meet and marry. Starting at the beginning of their story will make this book a more fulfilling read. *A Promise for Tomorrow* begins immediately after the last chapter of *Yesterday's Promise*. *The Promise of Home*, the conclusion of this trilogy, will be available in spring 2018.

Originally, I had hoped to keep this series to two books, but the Scottish Highlands in the late 18th century is a time period rich in both historical significance and tragic events. In the aftermath of the failed Jacobite uprising of 1745, stringent laws had been enacted and English patrols were present in the Highlands to enforce them. Many of the events in this story are based in fact—men's bodies really were left on the gallows for eighteen months, as a warning to others who would think to defy the crown. The penalty for a Highlander caught in possession of a firearm was fourteen years indenture in the Colonies.

Perhaps most tragic of all, the clans themselves were changing internally. With their abilities to lead and rule stripped from them, clan chiefs or lairds began thinking of monetary gain rather than the care of their people. Sheep replaced families who had lived on the land for generations. The Highlanders driven from their ancestral homes fled to the coast and cities looking for work. Others immigrated to the Colonies. It was a time of great upheaval and change for Scotland, and she was never to be the same.

It is my hope with this trilogy, to capture a small bit of that time—the story of a resilient people who did their best to hold onto the past while forging bravely into an unknown and vastly different future. Amidst the records of my own Scottish ancestors, I've read of tragedy and hardship, yet also seen glimpses of love and joy . . . family. Katie and Collin have become like family to me, throughout the telling of their story. I hope you will feel the same and enjoy every page of their journey.

Happy reading.
Michele

Prologue

The Scottish Highlands, October 1746

Collin

I curled in a ball on my side. This night was colder than any I'd had at the old Campbell keep thus far. The thin blanket did little to protect me from the hard stone floor, and I shivered uncontrollably, from pain as much as from the temperature. I had welts and would feel them for days.

Squeezing my eyes shut, I grimaced, imagining the taunts I'd receive. Nearly everyone who worked in the castle had witnessed my punishment for planning an ill-fated escape. I imagined that long after the pain subsided, many would still remind me, the enemy MacDonald, of it.

Behind me Katie's door creaked open. My four-year-old charge had attempted to get past me before, but I wouldn't have believed she'd try it tonight—not after I'd been both beaten because of her and then taken an additional beating *for* her.

I waited, not moving, for the right moment to catch Katie at her mischief. Laird Campbell was right; there would be other times I felt like strangling her.

The hem of her sleeping gown brushed the tip of my nose as she stepped over me. Her familiar childlike scent, all innocence and flowers—or so the soap she washed with implied—wafted down. I wasn't fooled. In the few weeks of my captivity and our acquaintance I'd come to know her as an impish waif. Another second and I'd reach out and grab her ankle before she could cause any more trouble.

"I'm sorry, Collin." A blanket fell across my shoulders, and she dropped to the floor beside me. "Please don't hate me. I didn't mean for you to be hurt. I just didn't want you to leave." She curled up beside me, as if intending to sleep right there.

"Go back to bed, Katie." I tried for a stern tone, but the pain interfered.

"I'm sleeping here tonight. And I've brought you my pillow." She thrust the ball of fluffy cloth at me, inadvertently plunging a stray feather up my nostril.

I held back a sneeze and shoved the pillow back at her. "You can't sleep here. Your grandfather would do more than beat me for that."

"He would?" She sat up straight, and in the dim light I caught her horrified expression.

"Aye. He wants you safe, and that is behind a locked door."

"I don't like being kept in there. Or guarded."

That made two of us.

"No one likes being confined," I said as a shiver passed through the lass and me at the same time. I leaned up on my elbow and nudged her. "You should go back to your room before more trouble finds us."

She made no move to go. "*Do* you hate me?"

I closed my eyes in frustration. "I might, if you don't go back to bed." Whether or not she slept wasn't my concern. Just so she was on the other side of that door.

"I don't hate you." She leaned forward, groping through the dark for my hand.

2

"Could've fooled me," I grumbled.

"I'm sorry I told Grandfather you were planning to escape." Her small fingers curled over mine. "I don't mean to be awful. I'm just—scared. Do you ever feel that way?"

More often than not lately, since my father's death and my subsequent landing in a hot bed of Campbells. But I didn't tell her that.

"Everyone is afraid sometimes," I said, hoping that would be enough to appease the lass and send her back to bed. "What are you afraid of?" Still grasping my hand, she knelt beside me and leaned in, as if anxious to hear my answer. *You.* I didn't say it aloud—didn't need to. Katie reared back as if struck. "Me?" she whispered, sounding amazed rather than hurt. "You feel it too, what happened when Grandfather said those words over us. It scares you."

There was no point in denying it when she'd read my mind anyway. "Aye. It does worry me." More than anything else had before or since. I'd take a lot more beatings like the one I'd endured tonight if that meant I could be free of the burden I felt, the very real knowledge that the future was no longer mine to command—entirely. Laird Campbell had said I might have some choices. But always, they would be governed by the thought of the lass. Our lives were entwined now, whether or not we wished it.

"I'm sorry you're afraid." Katie apologized for the third time in as many minutes. "I'm sorry you have to stay here with me. But I'm also glad that you are." She leaned over and pressed a quick kiss to my cheek. "Goodnight, Collin. I won't come out of my room again. Even when I have nightmares." She jumped up and was gone quicker than she'd appeared.

I waited until I'd heard the door close and she'd turned the lock before laying my head down again—on her pillow.

She'd left it. Her blanket too. I guessed she really was contrite. Perhaps things would be different between us now, the days not quite so difficult as they had been.

Part One

A day to come seems longer than a year that's gone.

Chapter One

Campbell lands, Scottish Highlands, July 1761

Katie

We didn't have to knock. Liusaidh waited as I had seen her, standing in the open doorway of her small home, her face turning slowly to and fro, as if searching for someone. She was not watching but listening. Liusaidh was blind.

"Hello," Collin, my husband of two weeks, called out when we'd dismounted Ian's horse and tethered it securely a short distance from her front door.

Her mouth opened, but she said nothing at first, though she turned in our direction. "Collin? Collin MacDonald, is that you?"

"Aye," he called and strode toward her, into her open arms. I watched as she hugged him the way a mother might hug her grown child.

"And who've you brought with you?" Liusaidh asked when they had parted and she wiped at her wet, sightless eyes.

"My bride." Collin straightened and puffed his chest out proudly, though she could not see it. I felt grateful she could not see me either, or she might have doubted his show of boasting. I was not looking my best.

Avoiding the chickens pecking about the yard, I walked over to them, every part of my body aching. Our unconventional wedding trip had consisted of traveling from my home in England to the Highlands of Scotland, to my mother's people, the Campbells. Along the way I had come to understand the dangers my new life was to entail, including a brother-in-law who wished me dead, and my own clan chief who wished my husband dead. Collin and I had not had an easy time of it.

In spite of this, or perhaps because of it, we had grown close over the past several days. He held his hand out to me now, and I clasped it, grateful to be at his side, grateful to my grandfather who, years before, had the foresight—literally—to betroth me to Collin.

"Hello." I curtsied before Liusaidh, then straightened to find her reaching toward me. Collin nodded, and I stepped forward, allowing Liusaidh to run her fingers over my face.

"Katherine's lass," she whispered.

"Aye. It's Katie. I've brought her home at last," Collin said.

"Bless you both. Bless us all," Liusaidh exclaimed, pushing past me to stretch her neck in either direction once more. "Come away in." She ushered us inside, then closed and barred the door behind her.

She stood there a moment, emotions flittering across her face with surprising rapidness. Her hands twisted with nervousness and perhaps fear, even as her face held a deep sorrow. But she seemed to push past each as she greeted us once more.

"Goodness, Collin. It's been years. And you, lass, you were just a wee thing the last time you crossed my doorstep."

"It is good to see you again," I said politely, though I had no recollection of ever knowing her.

"Wish I might say the same." She laughed at her own joke.

I sent a despairing look at Collin. "I'm so sorry. I didn't mean—"

"Not to worry about it." Liusaidh waved away my concern. "Collin knows I like to jest with people. I've been blind my entire life and don't know anything else. It is no bother to me and no shame at all."

"The name Liusaidh comes from Saint Lucia," Collin said, "the patron saint of the blind who was a fourth-century martyr, said to have had her eyes gouged out."

Liusaidh clasped her hands together. "You did listen during your lessons."

"Of course," Collin said. "Laird Campbell would have taken the strap to me if I didn't." To me he said, "I came here for my church learning. Seeing as I was a MacDonald, your grandfather feared services once a week weren't enough to make me into a good, God-fearing, man. Liusaidh made certain I learned the name and story of every patron saint there is, along with the stories in the Bible, the commandments—"

"And basic manners." Liusaidh frowned at Collin. "Why have you not removed your muddy boots? Do you think I can't hear them squishing across my floor?"

Collin looked guiltily at his boots while I directed my smile toward Liusaidh. "I have you to thank for gentling him, then."

"Och, aye. And what a task that was." She boxed Collin's ear as she walked past. "I imagine the two of you are fair starved. I've some fresh fish the lads brought me today. I'd be happy to share with you."

Collin and I exchanged looks of dismay, and I covered my mouth to keep from laughing—or possibly crying. *Fish again?* We had eaten little else as we'd made our way through the Highland wilds.

"What I would really love is a bath, if that would not be too much trouble. I can heat my own water and—"

"By the smell of you, you're both in need of a bath and a change of clothes." Liusaidh carried a tea tray over to us and placed it on the lone table in the room. "I've nothing much for you, Collin, but Katie, I'll wager you'll find something useful in that trunk over there." She pointed to a large, ornately carved chest near the hearth. "Your grandfather brought it to me for safekeeping many years ago—said you'd stop by for it someday. It belonged to your mother."

I sat near the fire, drying my hair, when Collin returned with an armload of wood. "I've enough cut to last a good month or more, assuming you'll not need much in the summer." He stopped abruptly, peering around the dimly lit room for Liusaidh.

"She's gone to sleep," I whispered, pointing to the blanket that hung across the room, dividing her bed from the rest of the tiny house.

Collin nodded sheepishly, then carefully placed his load in the wood box. I rose to help, but he waved me away.

"You're all clean."

"You are too." He'd bathed after me but then, realizing Liusaidh had no wood, had gone out to cut some for her.

"Aye, well, that never lasts long." He smiled ruefully.

I returned to my spot near the fire and continued brushing my hair, using the silver brush and comb set I'd found in my mother's trunk. The trunk promised many more treasures, but for tonight I had located a sleeping gown only, happy to have something clean to wear. The bath itself had been heavenly, but equally divine was the thought of never wearing the filthy dress I'd arrived in again. Whatever else I found in my mother's trunk, it would surely be better.

Collin took one of the blankets from the pile Liusaidh had laid out for us, then handed me another. I took it reluctantly, feeling somewhat disappointed that circumstances would not force us to huddle together for warmth. The past few nights, while not the most comfortable sleep I had ever enjoyed, had been entirely pleasant in their own way. Collin's chest at my back and his arm securely around me had been comforting. I loved listening to his deep and steady breathing as he slept. I enjoyed waking each morning, my first sight his face close to mine.

Was that not to be now that we were on Campbell land? Would we even share a bedchamber? In the house I'd grown up in my parents had two chambers that connected to one another. The night before my sister Anna's wedding we had all slept at her bridegroom's home, while he stayed at his parents' town home. Anna had shown me the room that was to be hers, also with a connecting door to her husband's.

Somehow I doubted the Campbell holding would be that sophisticated or modern. The castle itself was centuries old, and in need of repair, if what my cousin Alistair had told us was true.

"Thank you." I placed the blanket at my feet as my eyes met Collin's. I recognized the inner struggle raging in his that I'd seen so many times in the previous days. "Thank you for keeping me warm all those nights and for bringing me safely here."

"There's a bit of a question as to who was warming who," he mumbled as he turned away.

"What?"

"Nothing." Collin spread his blanket out near the door,

well away from me and the warmth of the fire. He removed his boots for the second time, then stretched out on his back, hands behind his head, reminding me of that first night we had slept under the stars together.

It had been a terrifying night, between his twin brother's attempt on my life and then an attack by a member of my own clan. But I would go through both again for the opportunity to relive the past week at Collin's side. Something had changed between us during that time, and I feared losing it now that we were no longer alone.

"It will be warmer sleeping here by the fire than near the door with its draft," I suggested casually.

"Near the door is where I must be," Collin said. "Lest anyone tries to break it down."

I pulled the brush through a particularly stubborn tangle. "And did they, it could fall on your head and render you unconscious. What good would you be to us then?"

"I would hear them before it came down, and I would be ready the second they tried to enter." Collin sounded almost enthused about the possibility, as if he was looking for a fight.

"Let us hope so," I said, giving up the idea that he might sleep nearer me. Finished with the brush, I knelt before the fire, leaning my head close so my hair might dry.

The room grew silent, save for an occasional snore from Liusaidh on the other side of the partition or the crackle of the burning wood. I stared into the flames, wondering and worrying over what tomorrow would bring. I was here to claim my grandfather's inheritance and to take my place as leader of the Campbells. The present laird favored neither option. And I did not favor our inevitable confrontation.

"You've grown up bonny, Katie."

I turned to look at Collin. "Thank you. You cut a fine figure yourself. I cannot tell you how relieved I was when I realized it was you whom I was to marry—and not any of my Campbell relations."

Collin chuckled. "You've no preference for red hair, then."

"It is a fine color," I said, thinking how well it seemed to suit Alistair. "But I prefer your dark." *I prefer you.*

Emboldened by his unexpected compliment, I decided to be direct and ask what I wished. "Will you sleep beside me, Collin? Or may I sleep over there by you?" My request tumbled out in a rush of words as I leaned forward slightly on my knees, exhilarated by my boldness and anticipating another night in Collin's arms.

He hesitated, then shook his head. "It would not be wise."

Why? I wanted to ask but felt too hurt. I turned myself from him, focusing my attention on the dying flames and trying to keep my promise to be done with tears. I could feel Collin pulling away from me again, and I didn't understand or like it. I needed him. I thought he needed me.

Grandfather had said we needed each other. The only way we were to succeed in our quest was together. But I was only a few paces away from Collin, and I felt the gap between us widening as it had been before.

Chapter Two

Alistair, Finlay, and another Campbell clansman arrived first thing in the morning, before dawn had pinked the sky. Collin had woken me minutes before, and I had barely enough time, even with Liusaidh's help, to dress before the knock at her door.

"Edan has been the keeper of your grandfather's records for many years," Alistair explained by way of introduction to the short, thin, white-haired man. "As such, we've been the keeper of Edan these past years, secreting him away shortly after your grandfather's passing. He's come today so you can sign for ownership of the estate."

With a slight bow, Edan stepped forward and placed a sheaf of papers on the narrow table. "It is a pleasure to meet you, my lady, and to see all unfolding precisely as your grandfather predicted." He cast a quick glance at Liusaidh, preparing tea at the stove. "And thank you, Liusaidh, for sending word so quickly."

We gathered around the table, Edan and I using the only chairs, and he proceeded to untie the bundled documents. For the next half hour I listened attentively as he explained my grandfather's will and the process by which he had enabled me to inherit.

"Typically the laird of a clan is the male who holds title to the castle or dwelling on the property owned by a clan. While not an official requirement, it is always a male to whom this honor passes, as is the case with the Campbells at present.

Your grandfather died without a male heir, as did his only child. Therefore the lairdship has been claimed—note, I say *claimed*—by your grandfather's great nephew."

"None of this sounds very hopeful," I said, though part of me found it very much so. What did I know of this people and land? Who was I to claim anything?

"Ah," Edan said, his lips twitching. "But there are ways for women to circumvent some of these restrictions, or at least to vary them."

"Do tell," Collin said, growing impatient, I could see, given his frequent glances toward the door.

"You are the male standing to benefit from this lady's inheritance, are you not?" Edan turned in his chair and gave Collin a shrewd look.

"If you consider being co-owner of a pile of ancient stone and having the responsibility of ousting its current occupant a benefit, then yes," Collin answered. "Neither Katie nor I do this for money. I have my own keep to manage, and Katie's dowry was substantial enough that the two of us would be well provided for without her grandfather's estate."

The two of us . . . I wondered briefly if that was Collin's fantasy as well—that we might simply forget both of our ailing clans and start a life together without those burdens. If so, it was only a dream. In the fortnight of our marriage I'd come to know he was too good, too loyal to walk away. And strangely, I was starting to feel the same myself. As much as I didn't want this responsibility, I felt I must accept it and do what I could to help my mother's people.

Edan continued his fixed stare at Collin, as if judging the truthfulness of his words. "Bold and defiant, aren't you? I suppose that's why the old laird liked you so much."

"Collin's all right," Alistair vouched.

Living up to the labels Edan had just given him, Collin

pushed farther. "I should like to sign for Katie's dowry today. It needs to be claimed and distributed to the MacDonalds as soon as possible to avoid further complications." He made eye contact with Alistair over Edan's head.

Alistair seemed almost to flinch and looked away quickly.

Odd.

"There is a time and place for everything," Edan said. "The time now is for filing these documents. Time enough later for searching out Lady Campbell's dowry."

He referred to me as if I was not married, had not the given name of Mercer, and certainly was not a MacDonald. Perhaps that was the way of things in the Highlands—that a woman retained her maiden name even after marriage, though I'd not held the Campbell name in that regard either. More likely it was that the Campbells—or at least this one— did not approve of my match to a MacDonald.

"What do you mean, *searching*?" Collin asked, his calm voice belying the concern I knew he must feel. "Do you not know where the dowry is?"

"Where it is or is not, is none of my concern." Edan waved dismissively. Alistair clasped his hands behind his back and pressed his lips together.

"Search high and low, where not all planted therein doth grow," Finlay said in his poetic lilt. "There you may find what you seek."

"Or may not," Alistair mumbled. "No one was ever told. And many years have passed since—"

"This is no game," Collin interrupted. "Lives depend on that money. If Clan MacDonald doesn't receive it soon, they'll come for it themselves."

"That is *your* problem," Edan insisted. "Mine is ensuring your wife has the legal right to the property left to her. Which—if not swiftly accomplished—poses a great threat to you both."

"Best be hurrying," Liusaidh said, bringing tea to the table with a practiced hand.

"Not here, please." Edan flung his arms protectively over the papers. "No offense to you."

"None taken." She poured a cup each for Collin, Finlay, and Alistair to hold where they stood, then returned the kettle to the stove.

"As I was saying." Edan cleared his throat and glanced at the documents before him, as if uncertain exactly what he had been saying and where we had arrived at in the process. "The Campbell land belongs to the entire clan, so it is impossible for you, legally, to be named proprietor of such."

"Then how is Brann able to evict tenants from it?" I asked.

"He can't. Not legally, anyway," Collin said. "A laird has only as much power as his clan affords him." For now, at least, he appeared to have abandoned the subject of my dowry.

"Fear has afforded Brann a great deal," Finlay said.

"Time enough to speak on those matters later." Edan shot both Collin and Finlay a look that clearly said he did not wish to be interrupted again. "Now then—Salic law says that if there are no sons to inherit, the descent passes to daughters rather than to more distant male relatives. Most often this refers to moveable property—livestock and such."

"Because a woman cannot own land." I'd become very aware of this since Father's passing and my stepmother had lost nearly everything.

"Correct," Edan said. "But since we are not speaking of property—land, that is—only the dwelling upon it, your grandfather was able to deed the castle to you. And your husband, if you so choose." He added this with an undertone that suggested he would not choose such a path, was he in my position.

"Signatures will be required here, here, and here." He began shuffling papers in front of me, pointing with a dry quill snatched from his pocket. "I've prepared multiple copies of each document. Ink, please."

Finlay uncorked a small bottle and handed it to him. Edan dipped the quill in the ink and held it out to me. With a feeling of dread, I accepted it.

There were places for two signatures on each copy of the document—mine, and my husband's, if I so chose. With a steady hand I managed to sign my name, feeling a tangible weight settling upon me with every letter. I passed the documents to Collin for his signature as well. It had never been a question. We were in this together, and I wanted him by my side in every way.

"Are you certain, Katie?" he asked. "It is not required. Your grandfather set this up so you alone could have ownership."

I handed him the quill. "I'm sure he wanted this. I want it too."

Still Collin hesitated.

"Go ahead," Alistair urged. "We haven't much time. Brann may have heard you are here. He's spies everywhere."

"Brann is the reason you *should* sign," Finlay spoke up. "If these papers are safely filed, he's going to contest this. It's less likely he will win if a man has been deeded ownership as well."

Collin held the quill poised above the paper. "Or would the court be more likely to return the holding to Brann, rather than give it to a MacDonald?"

"The law operates outside of the clans; it should take into consideration your gender more than your name or affiliation." Edan spoke with some reluctance. "Under coverture husband and wife are one person, and that person is the husband. Finlay is correct. Katherine will have a better chance at her claim if your name is also on the deed."

"Very well," Collin said.

I watched as he penned the same fine signature he'd given on our wedding certificate. When finished he handed the packet to Edan, who divided the parchment into three piles and handed the first to Finlay. I watched as he tucked it carefully beneath his shirt.

Finlay is to deliver them? "I thought—"

"Thinking is all well and fine," Alistair said. "Just take care what you speak from here on out." He clamped a hand on Finlay's shoulder. "And you take care in all things."

"That I will." Finlay's smile did not reach his eyes. "It's not me you've need to worry over." His gaze landed on Edan a second before turning his attention to me. "A moment, if you please, Katherine."

"Of course." I stood and followed Finlay across the small room, feeling Collin's gaze upon my back. He might have joined us. Anything one of my clansmen had to say to me, they could say to my MacDonald husband as well.

Finlay stopped near the pile of wood Collin had brought in last night. "I've something from your trunk that was left behind. I imagine most young ladies might have wished their gowns saved, but you are not most, and I supposed you might want these more."

He seemed almost to trip over the words, and I felt a rush of familial affection as Finlay reached into his sporran. No matter what he'd brought, I was touched that he'd thought of me at all.

He withdrew two of my paintbrushes.

"Oh, Finlay, I could kiss you!"

"Wait. There's more," he said almost shyly, as a blush surpassing the red highlights in his hair crept up his face. He stuck his hand in the sporran once more and this time delivered charcoal and three jars of paint to my anxiously waiting hands.

"Now I shall definitely kiss you," I exclaimed, giddy at the prospect of being able to paint again.

"Probably shouldn't," Finlay said. "Not with your husband standing right behind."

"She *has* professed to enjoy kissing. Go ahead, Katie." Amusement, not jealousy, tinged Collin's words. Taking his suggestion, I leaned forward and kissed Finlay's flaming cheek.

He brought a hand up, covering the spot my lips had touched. "Good luck is certain, receiving a kiss from a bonny lass before a long journey."

"So you *are* the one going to deliver the deed?" I looked to his shirt, beneath which the papers were concealed.

"Aye. I'll not fail you."

The pressure of Collin's hands on my shoulders ceased my questioning. "We need to go, and so do these men."

Why three copies of the documents? Where were the other two headed?

"These will make it safely to Edinburg," Finlay promised. "That much I *know.*"

Something about the way he spoke the last gave me pause. I looked back at him.

He gave a slight nod and spoke softly. "Painting, poetry, a ballad or a dream, any of these of the future may speak."

I gasped. "You're a—"

"I am nothing." Finlay pressed a finger to his lips. "And most certainly I was not here." He walked past us to the door. "Take care of our little lass, Collin. Take care of each other." He pushed open the door, ducked beneath the rafter, and disappeared into the early fog.

Questions swirled inside my mind, but I held onto these for later. Finlay's startling revelation demanded my full attention. *Another Campbell seer—and a male.* Why was he not chosen to lead the clan instead of me? How many others were among us? Was my strange ability perhaps not so strange after all?

"God speed, friend," Liusaidh said as Edan, too, rose to leave.

Their eyes met across the distance of the room, and it seemed to me that they saw one another, though she had no sight.

"God speed," he whispered.

Chapter Three

M y first close look at the castle neither endeared it to me nor stirred any memory. The stone was dark, grey, crumbling in many places, and stacked so high I had to crane my neck to see the top as we rode into its shadow. I'd known I wasn't to be welcomed by its primary occupant, but I'd hoped to find the castle itself somehow more inviting.

"It's ugly," I declared, feeling less than thrilled with the prospect of living there.

Behind me I felt Collin's shoulders lift in a shrug. "It was designed for safety. It's done its job well enough through the ages—never conquered that I know of."

"Until now," I said, half under my breath. We hoped to conquer, or at least reclaim it for the Campbells . . . though what they saw in such an ancient edifice was beyond me.

"See the battlements spaced precisely along the top." Collin inclined his head slightly but did not look up as I had. I supposed he knew the structure well, every nook and cranny perhaps. He'd lived here far longer than me.

"They've defended your clan numerous times over the years," he continued. "It may not look like much now, but with some effort I've no doubt the keep could be restored and stand many more centuries."

"Mmhmm," I mumbled noncommittally, my mind already racing with the obstacles and dangers to be faced in order to repair the weathered stone, particularly the top tiers.

"It would have pleased your grandfather to see it as it used to be." Collin's arm tightened around me, as if in reminder of our purpose here.

"I wonder why he did not attempt the task himself." My grandfather had passed away a few years earlier, before I could return—before I'd even *known* of him. Until the last week or so, I'd not recalled anything of my younger years in Scotland.

"Who says he didn't add fortifications?" Collin hinted in that intriguing way of his. "Maybe he only wished it to look weak, when really . . . "

"He'd strengthened it other ways?"

"Not *it,*" Collin said, "but those who would defend the clan. A castle is only as good as the people inside. Right now both appear lacking, but Campbells have a history of strength and resilience. God willing, we'll help them return to that. We promised your grandfather we would try."

The towers loomed ominously as Collin and I rode through the gate, flanked by Alistair, Donaid, Ruirdairh, and a half dozen other clansmen I'd just met this morning.

I hadn't wanted to ride, not while wearing my mother's gown. The fabric and stitching were delicate now from the years spent aging. As I noted the state of affairs within the keep walls, I realized Collin's suggestion that we ride had been a good one. Unlike the grassland outside, thick mud made up the ground here, much of it wet and oozing as tradesmen and launderers alike discarded their excess liquid with little thought or care.

We only narrowly avoided getting wet ourselves when a boy, no older than six or seven, flung a bucket of slop across our path, intended for a litter of piglets on the other side.

"Take care," Collin called. "You've almost soiled the lady."

Instead of offering an apology the child pulled a face at us and ran off.

"Hmm," Collin said. "Reminds me of a lass I once knew. Must be her relative."

I thrust my elbow back toward his ribs—not hard but enough that his chuckle turned to an *umph*.

"Not much has changed," he grumbled good-naturedly.

I happily accepted his teasing, felt grateful for it, even. It was a welcome, if momentary, respite from the tension building between us since we had entered Campbell lands. I cherished these exchanges that felt almost normal. Seconds in time afforded us to act and speak, to jest, as any married couple might.

"Actually, it *was* different here when your grandfather was alive." Collin directed the horse around a pile of manure. "He'd no tolerance for idleness; his keep was a place of order."

"Be glad you've not been here to see all that has befallen this place and people," Alistair said.

I found the order Collin described difficult to imagine. How could so much have deteriorated into chaos and filth in such a short time? Aside from the castle itself, seemingly on the verge of collapse, tall weeds grew up around it, giving the appearance that it had not been cared for or inhabited for some time.

"Perhaps I should not have signed those papers so quickly this morning. I don't think I want this place after all." Nothing about the scene before us bespoke of home—the home I had dreamed of the past weeks, since learning of it.

"Leadership is never about what you want," Collin said. "And if it turns to that, often the one in charge is no longer fit for leading."

"Like Brann," I mused.

"Aye," Collin said solemnly.

As we drew closer, people stopped their work to stare. One woman gasped and brought a hand to her mouth. Another fell to her knees as we passed. One very old man doffed his hat. Children scampered off, rushing around carts and dodging barrels as they hurried, I supposed, to tell others who had not seen us. Apparently a man and woman, freshly bathed, dressed in clean clothes, and riding a horse was a rare sight.

If nothing else, it smelled as if we were a rarity.

I sat sidesaddle in front of Collin, feeling much like the prodigal who had returned home, though I'd done no wrong. The one left behind was the one who had wronged these people. The evidence was everywhere. We'd heard the tales from Liusaidh and Alistair and had seen it yesterday and again this morning.

Many of the homes Collin remembered from my grandfather's time were gone now, reduced to piles of ash, covered over with grass and the tracks of the sheep Brann had purchased to graze on land previously farmed by tenants.

"Where have all the families gone?" I'd asked on our way here this morning. "Have they new homes built elsewhere? Were they taken in to live at the keep?"

"Nay, lass." Alistair had scrubbed a hand over his face as his mouth turned down. "Burned out, many of them. Often while they slept in their beds. Others managed to gather a few of their belongings and leave. Where they've gone I cannot say."

Liusaidh, too, had shared tales of sorrow last night. "When Brann told the widow Ravigill that she must leave, she tried to pull down her house, so she might have something to rebuild with. Her husband died at the mill six months past, and other than her ten-year-old son, she hadn't a man to help

26

her. While trying to salvage the roof, she fell and lost the babe she carried, then died herself shortly after."

"What of her son?" I'd asked, dismayed for the boy who'd lost both parents.

"Children," Liusaidh corrected. "Four—little more'n bairns, two of them. Taken in by her sister, until she was forced from the land as well. I've no idea where they are now. No one does."

"Whole families just disappear." Her expression had been grim.

The expressions of the people watching us ride up to the castle were grim as well. Hopelessness seemed prevalent, the mood of the people as dreary as the fortress I had inherited.

Collin guided us to the stable. He helped me down, his hands lingering a moment at my waist. "Courage," he whispered before stepping back and handing Ian's horse off to a man he seemed to know.

"Can you stable him for me, Willie?"

"Aye." Willie nodded at Collin, though I noted his eyes kept straying to me. "Good to see you again, MacDonald. You as well, mistress. You've the look of your mother and grandfather both."

"Thank you." His welcome seemed genuine, and I offered him a smile as I curtsied, my hands lifting the hem of my mother's gown to keep it from the mud at our feet. In spite of the disheartening sights, it seemed I could almost feel my mother's presence and my grandfather's too, leading and guiding me to do things I couldn't have done on my own.

Help me. I was starting to understand what Collin had meant about heavenly assistance—from both God and those who had gone before us. I certainly needed it today.

Willie led Ian's horse away. Donaid and Ruaridh collected the other horses and followed.

"Here we go." Alistair pressed his lips together, gave a quick glance to our fellow clansmen, and started forward.

Collin reached for my hand, squeezing my fingers reassuringly. He started to take a step, but I held him back. "Wait."

He did not ask why, but his free hand slid to the pistol at his waist, hidden poorly beneath the loose folds of his shirt. He'd insisted upon keeping it with him, though in truth I think it brought little comfort to either of us. Home or not, we were in enemy territory. Declaring ourselves and our intention so openly, while perhaps the only possible way to avoid bloodshed, also seemed it might be the exact way to invite it. We were—

Outnumbered. I turned around, staring at the ivy growing along the corner of the stone, seeing clearly who was on the other side, as if the stone was not there at all. Brann appeared a few seconds later, flanked by four other men. Collin and Alistair had followed my lead, and we stood our ground, facing Brann as he approached.

He was exactly as I remembered, though taller and broader now. Sandy hair hung shaggily over his ears, not quite long but neither short, and his face looked as if he'd attempted a beard unsuccessfully, with odd patches of hair growing at different lengths along his jawline. His shirt was filthy, and his smile revealed a set of teeth that looked as if they belonged to a much older man. I suppressed a shudder.

"Dear Katherine." He held his arms out as if to greet me with a hug. I made no move toward him.

An awkward few seconds passed before he lowered his arms and turned his attention to Collin and his pistol—in his hand, I was alarmed to see.

"MacDonald, is that any way to greet the laird of the land you're trespassing on? Hostility is apt to get you into trouble."

"Not hostility," Collin said. "Precaution. And trespassing seems a strange choice of words, given what you've unlawfully claimed."

Brann's smile stiffened. "I've done nothing but comply with every requirement of English law. Unlike yourself." His gaze slid to Collin's pistol once more. "You would do well to be careful who sees your weapon and whom you point it at."

"There aren't many I'll feel the need to," Collin said. "I know my friends here."

"You might have at one time," Brann returned. "But the old man is gone. Things are different. You've been gone a long time."

"Your services as laird are no longer needed." I'd remained silent long enough, and their circular conversation could only lead one direction that I could see.

"How so?" Brann asked. His eyes were a brilliant blue and might have been pretty had they a particle of kindness in them.

"I've signed the document accepting ownership of this castle, deeded to me by my grandfather, and it is, at this moment, being registered in Edinburg." It was, in fact, only just on its way to the clerk, Finlay and Edan having left no more than a few hours earlier. "I appreciate you *filling in* during my absence," I continued in an even tone.

A flicker of surprise registered in Brann's eyes but was quickly gone. "I've seen no such deed."

"Perhaps not, but it exists. I've no doubt my grandfather made you well aware of his wishes." Alistair and the others had been wise, hiding Edan and his records the past years. No doubt Brann would have destroyed both at his first opportunity.

"You'll understand that I'll be staying until I see proof of such legalities." He cocked his head to the side slightly, and two of the men with him stepped backward and moved swiftly away, no doubt to stop the transfer of the estate before it happened.

I swallowed my concern and attempted a look of calm acceptance. "Of course. But *you* understand that we will also be staying here. You are welcome to remain as well—for now." He wasn't really, but there was only so much I could do with just my word—and Collin and a handful of clansmen—to back me.

Brann nodded, a false smile upon his face. "My home is yours." He stepped aside and swept his hand out, indicating that we were to precede him inside. I started to take a step, but this time it was Collin who held me back.

"After you, *Laird*." His tone was needlessly mocking, causing me no little alarm. We didn't need a fight right off. Or at all, if it could be helped.

"As soon as you put your pistol away," Brann said, looking pointedly at Collin's hand.

"I prefer to keep it where it is," Collin said.

Brann scoffed. "There's no love between us, MacDonald, but do you really think I'd murder you in the middle of the day, in front of your wife?"

"Probably not," Collin said. "Seeing as you're more the type to set fire to people in the dark of night." He tucked the gun away. "Still, I'll be keeping this ready."

"Have it your way," Brann said, turning from us. "For now."

I heard his muttered words, certain he'd intended just that.

We followed him to the main entrance and up wide steps to the great hall. I felt a vague stir of familiarity, either from my dream or recently recalled memory.

"Best watch yourself," an old man warned as we walked past. From his tone I couldn't tell if he was friendly or not. And therein lay the problem.

If it was just Brann who was our enemy, it would be possible to be rid of him. But we'd no idea how many of the Campbells were on his side, or how many might be on ours.

Chapter Four

The immense fire in the wall-sized fireplace was doing its best to lull me to sleep. For the third time I straightened in my chair at the banquet table and tried to focus on the conversation. Collin sat beside, instead of across from me, with two of the clansmen who'd accompanied us from Liusaidh's hut this morning sitting on either side of us. Hugh was a giant of a man, and Lachlan, his opposite, had a tall, wiry body. Alistair and the others had gone home to their families, but it had been agreed that Collin and I should have at least two trustworthy clansmen with us throughout each day and stationed outside our door each night.

It wasn't much compared to the supposed army of men loyal to Brann, but it brought a little comfort.

Donaid, one who had journeyed with us from England, but from whom we had been separated the last week, sat directly across from us now, in the midst of Brann's council.

The tension in the air was a palpable thing. Collin and I asked questions and were given mostly unsatisfactory answers regarding the current state of affairs with the Campbells. Little of the council, if any, would side with us, we determined, from the answers they gave.

This made sense, of course, as those eating with the laird and enjoying the benefits of castle living were no doubt in league with him. I suspected these were the men who did his dirty work. No doubt taking care of Collin and me was on their list. I had never enjoyed a tasty meal less.

Collin and I had decided—prior to our arrival this morning—to drink only water at the keep. Three members of my grandfather's council had become ill and then died in rapid succession shortly after his death. According to Ruaridh, many of the clan suspected Brann had poisoned them, though no one had been able to prove it. But as it was more difficult to conceal poison in water than wine, Collin and I had deemed having water as our only beverage the wiser course.

I found it wiser for other reasons at the moment, as no doubt my heavy eyelids would not have been able to resist the relaxing effects of the dinner wine.

Given the threat of poison, we'd also had to eat with utmost care, following Brann's lead—serving ourselves only from platters he'd taken from, then taking a bite, only following one of his own.

Collin leaned forward in his seat now, his gaze intent as he came as close to pleading with Brann as I guessed he would. "Katie's dowry *must* be delivered to the MacDonalds within a fortnight, or I predict significant trouble from my brother."

Brann appeared unfazed as he leaned back in his seat, one leg propped casually across the other, a glass of amber liquid in his hand. "So the MacDonalds are still scraping by—if that—when you, at least, could be much better off. I cannot understand why you're so keen to preserve the poverty of the Highlands. It's a fool's errand—as is your request for this supposed dowry. I know as little of that as I do of the deed you claim entitles Katherine to this castle."

"That you don't know of the deed is your own fault," I said, irritated by his denial and more so by my inability to provide the one material thing Collin needed from our marriage. I believed him when he said he hadn't married me for my dowry, but I also believed he'd expected to receive it—

not for any personal gain, but to keep the MacDonalds from starving another winter. "Obviously Grandfather felt he couldn't trust you with either the important documents or the clan's funds," I said to Brann.

"Liam didn't trust anyone in his last years," Brann said, not denying my accusations. "He didn't do much to lead this clan either—cooped up in his room most days. They were all but begging for leadership when he finally died." Brann paused long enough to take a drink. "You'll see the wisdom of my decision yourself in the coming months—if you're here that long." He stole a glance at the right side of the table, where his council was still seated. "When once again the harvest is worth less than what it cost to plant."

"Of course it's worth less." Collin's tone had turned angry, whether at Brann's unspoken threat or his cold-hearted assessment. "When you hardly plant enough to feed the inhabitants of this castle, let alone extra to help the other tenants or any to take to market. Income depends upon volume."

"*My* income depends upon sheep." Brann said. "Though you are correct. Volume *is* important, which is why I continue to grow the herds." He was still defending his position, as he had been all day, for clearing away so many of the crofts and the farming families who had lived in them. "The moors that make up the land are more fertile in weeds than grain. Only a fool would try to farm them."

"Several centuries of Campbells would disagree with that opinion," Collin countered.

"Certainly the ancestors of the families who lost their homes would," I added. "To say nothing of the families themselves." It made me angry, too, thinking of the Campbell men, women, and children who had already been driven from the land. These were relatives I would never know, people whose lives had been stolen from them, people my grandfather had expected me to return to and care for.

Collin glanced at me—one of the few times he'd taken his eyes off Brann all evening. "Katie is tired. We can talk more of this—and her missing dowry—tomorrow."

"Tires easily, does she?" Brann's eyes narrowed as he looked at me.

"Not at all," I said, rising before Collin could offer me assistance. "It is the company I find wearying." It had been a long, anxious afternoon in close proximity to Brann. I swept past them both, across the hall to the foot of the stairs where Bridget, a fixture in the castle since before my birth, led us to our room.

Candle in hand, she began a brisk march that left no question as to her abilities in spite of her age. I followed at a slower pace, with Collin a step behind. His pistol was concealed once more, but still within easy reach. Hugh and Lachlan followed.

Collin's senses had been on alert throughout the entire day, taking in everything around us, even as he listened to every word uttered by Brann and the others near to him. Now as we walked he kept his hand close to his pistol, and his eyes darted this way and that, trying to scope out the dark corners.

"Here you be." Bridget forced the key in the lock and pushed the door open. "Your old room, the one you shared with your mother." Lowering her voice she added, "I'd have cleaned it for you earlier today, but I didn't want Brann knowing I'd found the key until the last minute, when it'd be too late for him to get in here—not that he was likely to ask. I've had it for years, but he never cared to go in here, never even asked about this room. It was your grandfather's chamber he wanted, your mother being dead long before Brann became laird."

Dead by his hand. I wondered if Brann was afraid he might find her ghost in here. "Thank you, Bridget." I had vague memories of the older woman from when I was a child and felt at once that I might trust her. Though Collin knew her as well, he was more cautious.

He held his hand out. "May we have the key?"

"Of course." She surrendered it without hesitation. A maid carrying a stack of clean linen came up behind her.

Bridget stepped aside. "Strip the bed, then make it up," she ordered.

The woman hesitated, as if loath to cross the threshold.

"Don't be all night about it." Bridget took hold of the woman's arm and pulled her into the room. Collin and I followed while two other maids trooped in behind, one with an armload of firewood, the other struggling beneath the weight of two full buckets of water.

Collin hurried to relieve her of them. She gave a squeak of thanks, then hurried off.

Odd. I wondered if the maids were wary of Bridget or us, or something else entirely.

Collin watched all carefully as the women bustled about doing their work. I had eyes only for the bed. It had been so very long since I'd slept in one. And there was only *one.* Collin and I would be sharing this chamber. I could only assume we would be sharing the bed as well. After the trying day it had been, I needed the comfort of his arms around me tonight.

Bridget hurried about the room, removing sheets draped over the furniture and the paintings on the walls. "We'll come back and do a thorough cleaning tomorrow," she promised. "But we can at least make it appear normal tonight."

It looked better than normal to me, more so as the furniture and rugs made their appearance. Who knew that such an eyesore from outside could harbor a quaint room such as this?

"How long since this room was last used?" Collin asked.

"Since Katie left," Bridget said. "Laird Campbell said it was to be kept for her, and there would be a curse upon any who attempted to stay here in her absence."

"Brann really is superstitious," I mused as I stopped before the fireplace and gazed up at a painting two of the maids had just uncovered. "Collin—"

"What is it?" He came to stand behind me, one hand resting lightly on my shoulder as he looked up. "Bealach Druim Uachdair. It's almost the same as *your* painting."

"Your mother was quite the artist." Bridget arranged two chairs in front of the fireplace. "That painting was one of your grandfather's favorites. How he loved his mountains."

"I never knew," I murmured, feeling the connecting threads of my past weaving through me. I didn't remember my mother working before a canvas, though it seemed as if I ought to, ought to have questioned, somewhere along the line, where my own abilities came from. "Do you suppose my painting was created from a memory of this?" I asked Collin.

"Maybe. The likeness between the two is astonishing." He reached past me to retrieve a small wooden horse from the mantel. He smiled wistfully as he held it out to me. "Happy sixth birthday, lass."

I took the horse and ran my fingers over its smooth planes and curves. Like my wedding ring, the details were incredible. The mane could have been real, and the eyes made the toy seem almost alive. "It's beautiful."

"One of my first attempts," Collin said, returning it to its place.

I moved slowly about the room, studying the other artwork. The last to be uncovered, also the smallest, was a portrait.

"I remember when your mother painted that one." Bridget clucked her tongue. "Had to hold you on my lap so you'd be still enough. Took us weeks upon weeks, as you'd no patience for it."

I stared at the portrait, studying my younger self, and felt my heart might burst. I'd never thought to question where my talent came from, but knowing it had been my mother's first, and that I had that of her within me, filled me with bittersweet joy.

At last the maids finished and Bridget ushered them all out, with a promise that she would return with our breakfast tomorrow morning. "No point in eating at table with that horrid man any more than you have to," she whispered loud enough that I worried Brann—or someone allied with him— would hear.

As if she'd read the concern in my face, Bridget patted my hand with affection. "No need to fret over me," she assured. "He knows I loathe him, but he likes his comforts, and this house doesn't run itself. If he wants good food and clean sheets, he'll keep me around."

"Nice to know he has *some* sense." I shared a con- spiratorial smile with her, hoping Brann would have sense enough to leave once it was proved ownership had transferred to me and Collin.

Bridget left. Collin consulted in the hall a moment with Hugh and Lachlan, then returned to the room and closed and locked the door.

"I'll install a bar tomorrow. Until then—" He dragged the bureau closest to the door in front of it.

"Are you certain that's a good idea? Brann *is* known for setting fires while people sleep. We might need to get out quickly."

"I doubt he'd try that in his own castle."

"It isn't his anymore." I moved to a chair and sat, more than ready to be done with my shoes.

"True," Collin agreed. "But he'll act as if it's his. Besides, you'll know beforehand if something's going to happen."

"I'm not certain I share your confidence." I finished removing the first shoe and started on the second. "It would seem that a seer should know more of the future. But I cannot see if Edan and Finlay are safe. I didn't see you coming to England. I hadn't any idea that Malcom would try to hurt me."

"I don't have an answer as to why you're able to know some things and not others," Collin said. "For your grandfather it was the same. He believed he would be shown what he needed to, as will you." Collin dropped into the chair opposite me.

"He described his sight as a game of chess. He might be shown some of the moves but not all. He might know which pieces would eventually be eliminated and the outcome of the game, but it was up to him what to do with and about that knowledge. He warned me once that the things you are able to see may not seem helpful at first. Sometimes you may see a clear path, as you did on our journey here. Other times, you may feel helpless to do anything about what you are shown."

I dropped the second shoe to the floor with a frustrated sigh. "If I'm unable to do anything with what I know, what good is this ability at all?" I recalled Finlay's cryptic revelation this morning. "How many other Campbells have a similar gift?"

"I don't have all the answers. I'm sorry your grandfather isn't here to speak with you. He'd know better than I." Collin slumped in his chair, his eyes closing.

My frustration with my unanswered questions and lacking abilities, Brann, our situation—everything—came to a grinding halt as I looked at my husband's weary face. Collin had done so much for me. He needed me. He believed in me. That would have to be enough. We would figure this out. All of it.

"Sometimes your gift may not seem useful," Collin continued. "At other times, it might save your life. And it is those times I most care about and am grateful for." He opened his eyes, to look at me tenderly.

I couldn't disagree with him about the usefulness of my sixth sense and hadn't forgotten the danger I'd felt on our way here when faced with the decision of which route to take. I'd known exactly what both Brann and Ian had been thinking, and I still knew what the consequences could have been had I not known and acted accordingly.

Collin must have mistaken my silence for continued argument. "Why didn't the Campbells side with the Jacobites in the rebellion?"

"Because Grandfather knew they would lose." I remembered Alistair's explanation and how I'd thought his statement rather pretentious.

"He did," Collin said, "but he desisted for more reasons than you might suppose. It was not simply to be on the winning side or to gain favor with the crown. Your grandfather saw what was coming for Scotland—he saw *this*— people starving and homeless, families being thrust from the land they'd farmed for generations, lairds turning against their own. He told me he saw the end of the clans—unless the war could be prevented. And so the Campbells refused to aid in the prince's cause and did all they could to be prepared, hoping, against hope, that they could be strong enough after the war to preserve not only their families but the Highland way of life as well."

"But here we are seeing all that Grandfather feared come

to pass. What good came of his knowing? You said yourself that he— *we*—are powerless to change the future."

"Life was better for your family—for a while anyway," Collin said. "There's that, and Liam was also in a position to save me from the same fate as my father. And in turn for me to then save you, when Brann would have done you harm."

"Something very good came of it," I said quietly, repenting of my earlier arguments. The thought of Collin being taken and killed made my stomach churn, as did the memory of Brann strangling my mother. If Grandfather hadn't known the future and acted as he had . . . neither of us might be here.

Even the tiniest decision I made might have significant consequences. A shiver passed through me with the weight of such responsibility.

Respect your gift, I could almost hear my grandfather saying. From now on I must do more to both heed and understand it. We were going to need all the help we could get.

Chapter Five

"**K**atie, you've fallen asleep."

A hand brushed the top of my head, and I looked up to see Collin standing in front of me, nearly swaying on his feet himself. I uncurled my legs from the chair and held my hands up to him, hoping he would take them.

Instead Collin reached down and lifted me into his arms.

Not so tired, then? I wrapped my arms around his neck and felt my own weariness fade as he carried me over to the bed.

"I ought to have carried you into the castle today, as this is to be our home, but I couldn't exactly do that with Brann walking beside." Collin frowned as he set me gently on the bed. "Concerning ourselves with evil spirits seems foolish, though, when we've the evil bodies themselves in residence."

"Carrying a bride over the threshold keeps evil spirits at bay?" I knew the Scots were superstitious, but this seemed a bit of a stretch. "Just how is that supposed to work?"

Collin shrugged. "The spirits cannot follow where you haven't stepped."

"So . . . you'd need to carry me in and out of the castle every time?"

"No." Collin rubbed his forehead, as if puzzled, then shrugged once more. "I never said it made sense, but it's tradition."

"And Highlanders are all about tradition." Our wedding

ceremony had been steeped in it. I patted the bed beside me. "Tell me more. What other marriage customs are there?"

Collin hesitated, then sat, but not close enough that we were touching. "We ought to sleep," he said. "Tomorrow is likely to feel longer than today."

"Sleep might restore my body, but *you* restore my spirit." I sucked in a breath for courage, then placed my hand over his on his leg. Likely no wife had ever been so bold and assuming. My stepmother would have been appalled at such behavior. I glanced at the painting over the fireplace and wondered what my real mother would have thought or done. What *had* she done to not only capture, but keep, the interest of an English soldier, my father?

"There are some things about our marriage you ought to know," Collin said. "Not customs or traditions, but things pertaining only to us."

"All right." My gaze flickered to his serious one. Then I pulled my hand away and turned on the bed, so that I was facing him in close proximity. "What is it?"

Collin swallowed slowly, his Adam's apple bobbing. He wore a look of discomfort, from the lines creasing his forehead to his pursed lips, yet when he looked at me his eyes sought mine.

"On our wedding night, you were surprised at the room arrangements."

"I was," I said, equally surprised that he would bring that up. "I was also *relieved.*" The rejection I'd felt was still fresh in memory, but also was gratitude at his consideration. Over two weeks later, I was beginning to wonder if not having consummated our marriage meant something else, something more. *Something bad.* "It *was* considerate of you to get me my own room, given the trying day it had been and that we were literal strangers to one another."

Collin nodded. "I'd hoped you'd see it that way, though I could tell I'd hurt your feelings."

"I was far more relieved than offended." I couldn't exactly say the same now. While I might not feel ready for all the particulars of the marriage bed Anna had described, neither did I wish to have a marriage without affection. Alone, in the wilds of the Highlands, Collin and I had gradually discovered that affection. But since our arrival on Campbell land, he'd been pulling away, distancing himself from our trek toward intimacy. I both wanted and dreaded to know why.

"Last night, at Liusaidh's, you asked if I would sleep near you."

"And you said it was not wise." Now we were getting somewhere.

"Aye." Collin tugged at his collar as if it bothered him or the room had become too warm. "It is not a good idea for us to be too close—for me to sleep beside you, or to—" He paused, his mouth moving oddly, as if it did not wish to form the words.

"Yes?" I prodded, wanting to hear the *why* of his explanation more than what else it was that we should not be doing.

"Katie." He angled his body toward me, then took both of my hands in his and held them firmly as he looked me squarely in the eye. "It is imperative that we don't—" His chin dipped as he cleared his throat.

Is he blushing? "I will not get you with child," Collin blurted, then released my hands and scooted away.

"What—why?" It was not what I had expected him to say, and I felt *my* face redden at the boldness of his statement and my uncensored response. "Is it that you cannot?" I asked in a hushed tone. Was that even possible? I'd heard of couples being barren, but somehow I'd always thought that had more to do with the woman than the man.

"I *dare* not," Collin clarified. "It is too dangerous."

"Oh," I said stupidly as my mind scrambled for comprehension. *What is dangerous about making a baby?* In spite of the things Anna had told me I couldn't believe there was any real danger in that. Childbirth, on the other hand . . .

His mother. Of course. Collin had told me she'd died birthing him and Ian. I should have realized what that might mean for him, how he might feel.

Hope that Collin really did care for me, that he didn't want to risk losing me, competed with the idea that he took his duty to protect me and my *gift* this seriously.

"I understand the dangers of childbirth." Perhaps the risk was greater in the Highlands than in England. Nevertheless, I found the idea didn't frighten me. Neither did the thought of having a baby—of being a mother—seem unappealing. Before I met Collin I had been convinced that a life dedicated to my art was far better than one as a wife and a mother. Now that argument didn't hold. I had survived without paint and canvas, but I did not think my heart could survive without Collin.

How would it be to have a child created of our union? A son with his eyes, or a daughter with his dark hair. Something new and foreign took hold inside of me at these ideas. How precious such a child would be; how much I could love him or her. I had never before considered such possibilities, and no doubt my face betrayed the emotion skipping joyfully across my soul. A yearning I'd not even realized I had sprang to life— one of those moments in time where you are forever changed and cannot return back to the person you were before.

I chose my words carefully, knowing I was about to argue for something I still wasn't entirely ready for. "It would seem that the decision whether I wish to risk carrying a child ought to be at least partially mine."

"It is not the dangers of childbirth of which I spoke." Collin still wouldn't look at me. "Though certainly the risk is real, and indeed you ought to have a say."

"Then I suggest that we pretend we did not marry for the sake of our clans, or prophecy, or any other such thing. Let us pretend that we began as my sister and her husband did, that our marriage came of our feelings for one another. And let us see what happens."

"I do not have to pretend to care for you, Katie." Collin turned to me at last and brought his hand up to touch my flaming cheek.

I tilted my face, leaning into his touch. "Nor I you."

He bent his head close to mine, so our foreheads were together. "It is enough to hear that from you. To know."

It wasn't enough. Not nearly so. I craved Collin in a way I'd never dreamed of. I wanted to be with him always, every second of every day. I wanted him close, to be in his arms, free to love him as I pleased.

I remembered our near kiss at the river and the foolish decision I had made to push him away instead. I would make up for it now. I would show Collin that loving each other was worth the risk.

I pulled back a little, and Collin lifted his face so that our eyes met. I hoped he saw determination and desire and love reflected in mine. "I do want you to know," I whispered as I leaned in. Our mouths brushed against each other lightly, and I found that wasn't enough either. I raised my hands to hold his face and pulled him closer, this time allowing my lips to linger on his.

"Katie." Collin's eyes closed on a groan. "We mustn't."

I pretended not to have heard, keeping my mouth just barely against his. I sensed the inner war within him and saw that the part of him who wanted to kiss me was going to win.

I was about to smile with certain victory when he deepened our kiss.

My lips parted, and my arms slid around the back of his neck, holding on tight, as if I'd climbed to the top of a mountain and would surely fall if I let go.

And oh, the height! My heart soared when his lips continued to caress mine, his hands cupping my face and sliding to tangle in my loose hair. I was out of breath but didn't care. What better way to perish than being kissed by the man who consumed me?

Collin's lips roved over mine possessively, as if he wished to know every part of them. I wanted him to know everything, and I gave it freely. *I love you* thrummed through my mind and body. I was in love with my husband, and this kiss all but proved he felt something for me—other than a desire to protect.

With a last, almost playful tug at my bottom lip, he pulled away—breathing as hard as I.

"Katie, we mustn't—"

I silenced his second attempt at protest with my mouth, shifting my weight so I knelt on the bed beside him and grasped his shoulders. "Kiss me, Collin," I ordered, my lips brushing his as I spoke. "Show me what you feel for me. Telling me isn't enough."

He groaned again but complied with my request, cradling my face in his hands once more and crushing his lips to mine. What could only be passion had burst to life between us and seemed bent on consuming us in its fire. The world fell away so that it was only Collin and I who existed. All else ceased to matter or even to be. *I love you.*

"I love you, Katie." That he spoke the words first brought tears to my eyes. I stopped kissing him and threw my arms around him.

"I love *you*, Collin. Thank you for coming all the way to England for me, for bringing me home. I'm sorry for being difficult, then and now."

He gathered me—bunched skirts, petticoats, and all—on his lap and held me there, my face pressed against his shirt and his heart pounding loudly beneath.

"I would go to the ends of the earth for you," he said solemnly.

"Let us pray you do not have to," I said.

"Aye." He kissed my forehead.

Our breathing slowed gradually, the passion turning to something deeper. I simply wanted to hold him and be held. Forever.

"I have robbed you of sleep," Collin said at last, as he looked toward the moonlight coming through the shuttered window. "Morning will be here before we know it."

"Morning is hours away. I want to spend every one of those as we've spent the past few minutes."

"We cannot." This time he sounded as if he meant it. Collin lifted me from his lap. He stood and took several steps from the bed before turning around to face me.

I smiled at his serious expression, made less so by his mussed hair and collar. No doubt I showed signs of our tryst as well. I scooted to the edge of the bed, smoothed my skirts, and folded my hands demurely in my lap. "Was there something you wished to say?" Now that we had established that we both cared for one another and that I was aware of the dangers and willing to risk a child coming of our union, I could think of no argument he might make against our continuing on that path.

"Aye." Collin clasped his hands behind his back and began pacing before the bed. "There is to be no more kissing, no more anything."

"No—"

He held a hand up, silencing my protest. "I am most serious. The danger to your life—and to any child you might conceive is real. And while kissing does not a child create, it leads to more temptation than I can promise to withstand."

This admission ought to have pleased me, but I could think only of what came before it. *No more—anything.* I was not surprised when Collin next announced that we could not share a bed. He said he would make a spot on the floor so no one need realize our arrangement.

"I shall realize it," I said, forming the lips he had thoroughly kissed into a full pout.

"This is not what I want, Katie." He ceased pacing and knelt before me. "It is what must be done to keep you safe."

"You mean my gift safe," I muttered.

"No." He took my hands. "I mean *you.* That morning Ian found us together in your room at the inn, he assumed we had lain together as husband and wife. I fear he would kill you, should that circumstance ever occur."

"Why? He witnessed our marriage, so surely he ought to have realized—"

"Ian believed the marriage was solely for the purpose of obtaining your dowry." Collin gave my hands a light squeeze, then released me and stood once more. "I had to convince him of that, because were it to be anything different—were you ever to conceive and bear a child, that child would be in line to be a MacDonald laird."

"And Ian could not stomach anyone with Campbell blood having that position." I finally understood. No wonder Collin had been upset that morning, and no wonder I had hardly seen him in the two days that followed. He had been keeping Ian away from me, trying to convince him that all was not as it had seemed.

Exactly what Alistair had tried to tell me. *All is not always as it seems.*

"Ian already tried to kill you once," Collin said. "I'd prefer not to give him another reason to try again."

"Very well." I admitted defeat—for now. But surely we would find a way around the Ian problem. Problems. All of them—sooner or later. Our life could not be spent thusly—near one another but not permitted to truly be husband and wife.

"Brann is equally dangerous," Collin said. "Did you see the way he looked at you tonight when you said you were tired? He is already speculating about whether or not you might be with child."

"We've been married but a fortnight." I threw my hands up in exasperation. It seemed everyone was interested in the intimacies of our marriage.

"Time enough." Collin gave me a wry grin. "Brann wouldn't see you killed for it, but he'd want you—and the child—for himself more than ever. It is highly possible that any child of yours will carry your gift, and therefore be in danger as well. But even if that were not the case, Brann would know he could use the child to get what he wanted from you."

I stood and followed Collin across the room. "Even if a child was conceived tonight—"

He turned sharply to stare at me. I willed my blush away and continued, eager to make my point. "Even then, it would be months before the baby was born. Brann won't be here."

"He will have to be more than away from this place for me to feel you are safe." Collin paused near the door, pushing the bureau so that it was more squarely in front.

"What do you mean?" A sick feeling started in my stomach where only a minute or two before had been the most pleasant sensations.

"You know as well as I." Collin faced me once more. "You don't really believe that simply because your name is on the deed—if that even stands—that Brann will go peacefully? He'll want a fight."

"As do you." I'd sensed it this morning, this change in Collin, before we'd even met Brann. This was about more than the present or our future. He was carrying the past with him, bent on exacting retribution.

"What did Brann do to you?" I folded my arms. "When you were both younger, when you lived here before, what happened?"

"Isn't it enough that he strangled your mother?" Collin demanded.

I winced at the reminder. The anger I'd felt in him earlier had surfaced easily with the change of subject.

"Will killing Brann make anything better? Will it bring her back?" It felt like I was defending Brann—the last thing I wanted. Neither did I wish to see Collin consumed with hatred. This side of him was new—and frightening.

"It will ensure he never does the same to you." Collin moved to stand before me. "Brann is the reason you were taken from me. He betrayed your grandfather and went to the English—told them I was here. Told your father you were with me. Brann took you from me, and he won't do that again."

"He can't. He *won't*. I'm grown now, and I won't allow it." I reached up, taking Collin's face in my hands, forcing him to look at me. "He has *no* power over us."

"Not now he doesn't." Collin's voice quieted. "But if there was a bairn involved . . . " He took my hands from his face but pulled me close, into the solid security of his embrace. "A parent will do a lot for a child—anything, really. Even give up his life if necessary."

He was thinking of his father, who had willingly faced a

firing squad to ensure that Collin lived. I squeezed my eyes shut, hurting for him, that he had such a terrible memory to live with.

"All right," I conceded—truly conceded. I would do anything not to bring Collin more pain or worry. I would sleep alone, keep my desire for kisses to myself, forget the notion of having our child.

"Brann would know you would do anything to keep *our* child safe," Collin said. "You would be at his complete mercy."

As I could be already. There didn't need to be a child for the threat to be real. I would do anything to protect my husband. If Brann discovered just how much I cared for Collin already we would both be vulnerable.

Chapter Six

"The Campbell lands begin here." Collin placed his finger on the map, over a blue swathe labeled *Loch Tay.*

"Which side of the loch? Is our clan permitted to use it?" On our journey here I'd learned just how valuable bodies of water—and access to them—were when traveling in the Highlands.

"Both. Campbell land surrounds it." Collin traced the faint line running higgledy- piggledy around the lake and spread out in various fingers beyond. "Though the MacNabs, Menzies, and even Murrays lay claim to it too."

Meaning they felt it worth the risk of encountering Campbells to reach the water. We'd taken a rather circum-venting route from my home in England to the Campbell holding, in part to avoid crossing the land of other hostile clans. And also to ensure that we had food and drink—fish and fresh water—the duration of our trip. For us the many lochs scattered throughout the Highlands had been the difference between life and death. Seeing no other sizeable bodies of water nearby, I could understand why those other clans laid claim to the loch as well.

I sipped from the mug Bridget had brought with our breakfast while Collin finished the last of his porridge. We'd awoken this morning to discover that Brann was no longer in residence. He'd disappeared sometime during the night, and no one knew—or would admit to it, at least—when he would be back or what he was up to.

His absence had done little to ease our strain, as three members of his council, his brother and two cousins, were still milling about. We'd spent the morning avoiding them while meandering the main floor of the castle, reacquainting ourselves with the place that had been our beginning. We had ended our tour here, in one of the small chambers adjoining the great hall, this one containing maps and having been used for plotting defensive strategy in times past.

Collin's finger continued its progress along the map. "To the south the border goes here, all the way to The Firth of Clyde. And further west, this belongs to the Campbells as well." He outlined a finger of land jutting out a considerable distance from the main body of Scotland. "Loch Awe runs through Campbell lands here." Collin's hand moved north over the parchment. "And finally, the whole of this belongs to the Campbells as well." He spread three fingers out across a large portion of the map.

"That's enormous." I sucked in a breath, feeling more than a little overwhelmed by the vastness of what he'd just shown me. I planted my palms on the table and leaned forward over the parchment.

Like a goddess looking down upon my kingdom. That was hardly the case, and instead of feeling thrilled at what Collin had just shown and described to me, I felt terrified. People were spread out all over that land. Campbells, looking for a leader, someone to save them from poverty and displacement. Where and how were we even to begin?

"There are some other Campbell clans in the Highlands as well, though not associated directly with your grandfather's line." Collin pointed out a few more places on the map, distant to those he had just described as ours.

"Well, that's something at least," I said half-joking. "If we fail to save *our* Campbells, at least the name will still exist somewhere in Scotland."

"We won't fail." Collin glanced sideways at me and took a step away, instead of coming closer and placing his hands upon my shoulders as he used to. I made a pretense of studying the map a moment longer to get my bearings. While I finally understood the reasons for his reticence to be close, it didn't lessen the hurt such actions caused. I needed him and his affirmations of love. He really was the calm to my storm and the comfort to my fear. I wasn't certain I could do this without his arms around me as we stepped forward—blindly it seemed, in spite of all Collin was doing to help me understand my history and what we were up against.

"So, that is the land Brann has been filling with sheep." I pushed off the table and stood, arms folded as I thought. "It appears there should be plenty of room for both—people and their farms, *and* sheep."

"One would think so," Collin said, bitterness in his voice.

"Where is your land?" I asked, scrutinizing the map once more as I realized he had neither mentioned nor pointed out the MacDonald holdings.

"Here." More bitterness. Collin used his little finger to trace a slim line bordering a northwest corner of the Campbells.

I said nothing but swallowed painfully as I stared at the thin strip of land labeled *MacDonald*. It was no wonder I had missed it, tiny as it was and sandwiched between the sprawling Campbells to the south and a good-sized Cameron parcel to the north.

"Reconsidering your marriage vows?" Collin's mouth twisted in an ugly, unfamiliar way.

"I didn't marry you for your land," I said quietly, uncertain how to tame the beast I'd sensed growing within my husband since our arrival.

"Nor for my money, I hope." Collin snorted. "As I have

none." It was not an exaggeration. He'd used his last guinea to get us here.

I turned away from the table and the troublesome record spread across it, the written evidence of the downfall of the clans who'd been Jacobite supporters. "You know I don't care about either land or money." I'd married Collin because I'd had to, because I was honoring a promise made long ago by my father—and my much younger self, it had turned out—and because I had believed it would provide a financial benefit for my stepmother. Those reasons didn't really matter now. I wanted this marriage and Collin, no matter if he came only with the shirt on his back.

"Well, that is good," he said shakily. "As I've not much of either." He ran a hand through his hair, making it stand on end and causing a sore temptation for me to reach out and smooth it down for him. *To soothe away his hurt.*

But we had made another promise to each other last night, a vow to avoid touching one another, insomuch as possible. I'd never hated a promise more, or believed I would be so challenged to keep it, but at the end of Collin's explanation, I had been unable to argue with the wisdom of such a decision.

Anytime we came within a stone's throw of one another, some sort of flame seemed to ignite between us, bursting to life with a passion Collin did not trust himself to control. If anything, I was less trustworthy than him in this regard.

I kept my hands to myself, clenched in the folds of my skirt, and let his hair remain as it was.

"Who determines the borders?" I asked, forcing the topic to safer waters.

"Used to be the clan with the most weapons." A wry grin made a brief appearance on his face. "In the past dozen years the boundaries have become more or less settled, changing only when the English take land from one clan and give it to another. That's not as common now. Most of the Jacobites' lands were forfeited immediately following the rebellion."

Including Collin's father's. So much for the change of topic.

"Would you like to ride it?" Collin asked. "Some of it, anyway. We can't cover the entire Campbell holdings in one day."

"Take our leave of this charming edifice?" *The castle of gloom,* I had come to think of it. I could hardly contain a grin.

"Aye," Collin said. "You ought to see the land and meet the people who live here."

Those who are left. "I'll ask Bridget to pack a basket for us." A ride to inspect the dismal state of affairs of my clan wasn't exactly a picnic outing, but it almost felt like one. The prospect of being away, and at least somewhat alone with Collin, lifted my spirits as possibly nothing else could.

The sun was directly overhead before we made our first stop, near a worn-out-looking stone cottage with a thatched roof that likely invited more rain in than it kept out.

Collin dismounted and left Ian's horse to search out what he could on the moor. The ground here was not particularly flat but seemed fertile, lush with green and purple, albeit at a constant slope, a gradual climb toward the snow-capped mountains to the east.

"You're a good girl." With affection I patted the neck of the mare I'd ridden. Though I'd been disappointed to realize that Collin intended to carry our no-touching policy so far that we would no longer ride together, I could not deny that

I'd enjoyed the freedom of controlling my own horse and flying across the heather.

Or the illusion of freedom, at any rate. Two of our Campbell guards—Moreiach and Quinn today—slowed their horses to a stop behind us. They'd kept pace all morning, staying just out of earshot so Collin and I might have a conversation, a constant reminder of the danger we were in.

"Do you know who lives here?" I asked, leaning forward into Collin's arms as he helped me dismount. At least he'd deigned that much contact appropriate and allowable.

"Used to be Eithne and Gavin Campbell. I hope it is still the same." Collin set me on the ground and promptly released me. "They were kind to me when I was here. Eithne and Gavin never had any bairns of their own. Gavin's hands were crippled, so your grandfather sent me here to work for him, shortly after you'd left."

There were dozens of other stories between the lines he'd just spoken. Of a pain-filled and difficult time for both of us, and perhaps for this couple as well, who'd not been blessed with a child of their own. That Collin had found a place where he'd been treated kindly filled me with an instant liking for these people before I'd even caught first sight of the woman at the door.

Wiping blackened hands on an apron then smoothing the kerchief tied in her hair, she stepped from the cottage and made her way toward us.

"Her husband's appearance is somewhat different," Collin whispered to me. "Try not to stare if you can help it."

"Of course."

"He can't farm the land as other men, so instead they make the soap for most of the clan, in trade for their sustenance."

Halfway across the yard Eithne paused, her eyes lifting to Collin's.

"Mercy. Is that you, lad? Have you grown even taller now?"

"I don't think so. Perhaps you are shrinking." Collin's voice was lighter than at the castle, lighter than I'd heard in days.

"That may be." She took a step closer, and Collin beckoned me to come with him to meet her.

I smiled, liking her more already as I caught the tears glistening in her eyes.

"Here you are, looking as fine as can be." She waved a hand in front of Collin. "And I'm a pure nick."

A what? I looked to Collin for an explanation.

"Eithne is concerned about her appearance," Collin said to me while smiling at her. "But she's as bonny as ever. Still making soap?" he asked.

"Aye. And what a mess it is." She inclined her head toward a great black kettle hanging over a fire in the yard. "The lye is boilin', and Gavin fetched another load of ash and lard this morning. I was just filling the barrels." She held her blackened hands out as evidence.

"Eithne makes the finest soap you'll ever use—has for years." A teasing glint came to Collin's eyes. "Her soap's nearly as famous as MacDonald whisky."

Eithne pulled a rag from the waistband of her apron and swatted at him. "One'll clean your outside and one your insides, right? Same troublesome lad, I see." Affection shone through her words, and my gratitude for her deepened. At least a few Campbells had cared for Collin.

"Eithne, I'd like you to meet my bride, Katie." Collin introduced me proudly, as he had to Liusaidh, and I felt grateful to be looking a bit more worthy of his boasting today.

Living in the gloomy castle had some benefit, including the regular use of water for bathing as well as my mother's trunk with its supply of pretty, if older, gowns.

"Spitting image of your mother, you are." Eithne reached out, as if to clasp my hands in greeting, then apparently thought the better of it and began to withdraw her blackened palms.

Already tired of Collin's avoidance, I decided to have none of this and surprised us both when I snatched her hands quickly in mine. I raised them to my lips and kissed the back of both, over her bony, weathered knuckles. "Thank you." I lifted my face to hers. "Thank you for caring for my Collin while I was away."

I'd never before called him *my* Collin that I could remember, but it described perfectly the way I felt. He was mine, and nothing was going to take him from me. Not Brann or Ian or anyone else.

Eithne squeezed my hands as a smile blossomed on her wrinkled face. "Bonny in soul as well as body. You're blessed, Collin." She released me and planted her hands on her hips. "So, have ye ousted the imposter from the castle then?"

"Not exactly." *Imposter* seemed an interesting choice of words and too lenient a description of Brann. Charles Stuart was known to most English as the imposter, having sailed from France to Scotland, intending to take over the English throne. Certainly the fighting he'd caused had resulted in bloodshed, but from all I had learned of him, he had not been an outright murderer—as was Brann.

"We've filed Katie's claim to the keep and await news of its acceptance," Collin said.

But it's not likely Brann will leave without a fight. I read the unspoken words in his stiff posture and defensive stance.

"We are here, and that is a start." I sent a look of displeasure Collin's way. Could we not have one afternoon free from the tension of the castle?

"Aye. It is." Collin's smile was apologetic, and he wrapped an arm around my shoulder in a brief squeeze. "Katie's sight saw us safely delivered. No doubt it will see us through what is to come."

"I expect no less," Eithne declared. "Now, I suppose you'll be wanting to see Gavin."

"Aye," Collin said, eagerness expressed in that one syllable. "Is he about?"

"Oh, yes." Eithne rolled her eyes. "Drove to fetch the ash, and now he's good for nothing the rest of the day."

"I'm pure done in, woman." A man who appeared much older than Eithne emerged from the doorway of the little house. Leaning heavily on a cane, and moving at an odd angle on twisted legs, he shuffled toward us with a slow, painful walk. "Kicked me out of bed in the middle of the night, she did. Telling me I must be off to collect the ash. As if it couldna wait until morning. I'm fair puckled now."

"You ken well enough yourself it couldn't wait," Eithne returned with a shake of her head. To me she explained, "The lye has to cook slow all the morning. Until it's very strong. If I start too late in the day, I'll be working alongside the moon." She waved me to come with her, and I followed, leaving Collin to his reunion with the fair-puckled Gavin.

We crossed the yard to the enormous kettle, even larger close up, and she leaned forward, face scrunched, sniffing at the rising steam. "Not strong enough yet."

Truly? I held a hand to my face, in an attempt to cease the pungent aroma's assault. It seemed impossible the smell could *be* any stronger.

"We're behind, see!" she shouted across the yard to her

husband. "Should have pushed your sorry hide out of bed sooner."

Gavin raised his cane in the air and shook it at her in response. It was only when I caught Eithne's quick smile, followed by a loud snort, that I realized they were teasing one another. Relief swept over me, and my feelings of concern for her obviously ailing husband dissipated.

"He's been that way for years," she said, catching my curious look between them. "Hands started to twist soon after we married. Knees don't like to work. Everything that's supposed to bend doesn't want to. Pains him terrible, but he doesn't complain. And he loathes sympathy."

"So you don't give him any."

"None at all." She winked. "A man's pride is sometimes all he's left. I give that to Gavin each time I expect more of him and harp like any other woman would on her man."

I wasn't entirely certain I agreed. *Do I harp on Collin?* My stepmother had done so only in my father's last years, and it had not been pleasant for any of us. So while that method-ology might work well for Gavin and Eithne, I had no desire to put it into practice myself.

"Once the lye is strong enough, what must you do then?" From a distance I had watched, a time or two, as our household servants made soap. I'd never had much interest in the process, and neither had my stepmother. She'd taken to ordering it most of the time, instead of having it made at the manor. But now I supposed this might be one of dozens of skills I ought to have at least a cursory knowledge of—on the off chance that Collin and I were ever to live our lives alone, somewhere peaceful and beautiful like this, somewhere no one would threaten or bother us, and where we could work together creating everything, from our home to the children who would fill it.

This thought stimulated the new feelings that had been inspired by our talk last night. My stomach tingled pleasantly at the idea of carrying a child there. *Collin's baby.* Our eyes met across the yard, and a flush warmed my cheeks as I imagined the kisses and what else would have to precipitate such an event.

"You have it bad for him, don't you?" Eithne said with a knowing smile. "How long have you been married?"

"Two and a half weeks." I felt my blush deepen.

"Ach." She clucked her tongue. "And out of bed already. Surprising, knowing that lad. When he puts his mind to something, he sticks to it until it's done right." She nodded at the delicately engraved wedding band on my left hand. "Cannot tell you the hours and days and months he worked at that. And now I'd guess he wants a bairn to carry on his name. I'm surprised he's allowed you out of bed at all until that's well and accomplished."

I was certain my face was positively flaming now, in spite of the fact that Collin and I had not actually been in a bed together yet. As that was not a discussion I wished to have with such a new acquaintance, I returned to my earlier question. "Will you teach me how to make soap?" The idea did interest me, in spite of the smell.

Collin had already proven he was good at providing for and protecting me. I wanted to be able to perform my part of the marriage tasks as well. Learning to make soap seemed as good a place to start as any.

"Roll up your sleeves, lass," Eithne instructed. "You'll be an expert in no time. We'll make a mild batch, one good for cleaning that bairn you'll soon be carrying."

Chapter Seven

"Haste ye back!" Gavin called, lifting a gnarled hand in farewell as Collin, Quinn, Moireach, and I turned our horses away and left the yard.

I fell into line between Quinn, out front, and Moireach, lagging behind, with Collin riding beside. Because of the late hour, Collin had asked them to stick closer to us on the ride home. The sun was no longer visible, but neither had dark come upon us yet. As I'd learned during our travels from England to the Highlands, summer here was different, the daylight some two hours longer, due to our northern location. It wasn't just my imagination that made each day feel like it lasted forever.

But today had gone too fast, and I felt reluctant to take leave of our delightful and amusing hosts to return to the confining walls of the castle, and possibly Brann. Earlier I had suggested to Collin, in private, that we might stay the night.

Collin had not deemed it wise to linger. Our escorts for the day were long overdue to return to their families and other responsibilities. And now that we had confronted Brann, he felt we needed to pursue that course of action—before Brann formulated some other plan to be rid of us. I think we both had no doubt he had been away doing just that. But while I would have been content, for the night at least, to ignore and avoid that threat, Collin wanted to meet it head on.

Taking the lead now, he increased our speed from a canter to a gallop, glancing back at me as he began. "Can you ride faster? Dark will eventually come, and I'd just as soon be in our room when it does."

"I can," I assured him, kicking my heels into the side of the mare. This morning I had relished our brisk ride, but now I felt exhausted. Soap-making required significant labor.

Eithne had assigned me the task of taking a paddle to the large kettle, stirring and scraping continually so that the fat would not boil over. Initially I'd believed this the more agreeable of the duties, as I'd watched her unload the meat scraps and lard Gavin had collected and cut and mash them before adding them to the pot.

If I'd believed the smell bad before, it was nothing to what she had to face, working with animal fat that was who knows how old. The steam rising from the kettle into my face wasn't exactly pleasant either, and I began to understand my stepmother's reasoning for putting soap on the "to be purchased" list of household goods.

Around four o'clock Eithne had finally declared the concoction done, at which point I'd felt done in as well. My arms—both of them, for I had traded off stirring with each— had never felt so sore. I would be fortunate to be able to lift them enough to put on a clean shift tonight.

But I had treasure in my basket to show for my efforts. The batch I had stirred still had to sit overnight, but Eithne had let me help her finish what she had begun the day before. I'd used the last of my arm strength to grind dried lavender with mortar and pestle, and this we had mixed in before pouring the soap into molds. The two bars she'd given me to take had still to cool completely. I'd never felt so proud of anything I had made.

A sense of accomplishment and even exhilaration always accompanied a completed painting, but there was something different and satisfying about having created something useful. I only hoped I'd have the energy to draw a bath and make use of the soap tonight.

"You look a mite more puckled than poor Gavin." Collin slowed Ian's horse to keep pace with mine. Apparently I wasn't moving as fast as I'd believed. I felt a bit guilty at this. Collin, Quinn, and Moireach had to be tired too, having labored in Eithne's garden all day, catching up on all that she and Gavin could not possibly manage themselves.

"Don't you mean plucked?" I asked. When Gavin had used the term this morning, I thought I'd either heard him wrong or perhaps it was a joke between he and Eithne.

Collin shook his head. "That would be a chicken. Do you feel like one who's been caught and had your feathers pulled?"

"Caught and plucked clean." I giggled, for some reason finding this amusing. I squawked like a chicken and urged the mare to go faster.

"Maybe I shouldn't let you ride on your own." Collin steered Ian's horse closer as sporadic bursts of laughter continued to spurt from my mouth.

"Maybe tomorrow I shall learn to make quills with all those feathers." I laughed harder.

Collin cocked his head to the side and narrowed his eyes. "How much did you drink today?"

"A lot. Of water. It was terribly hot out there at the fire."

"You're certain that was all?" Collin didn't sound convinced.

"Of course." I sat up straighter and twisted in my seat to better look at him. "We agreed to only water while we are here. I keep my promises."

"I know that. I'm sorry, Katie." He sounded sincere.

"It's all right." The giggles had fled as quickly as they had come. "No wine, no touching." No joy. Today had been a brief and welcome interlude from the heaviness of our lives. "I'm tired is all, and I've the tendency to become giddy when that happens. Anna and I used to see how late we could stay up. We believed we needed to practice, so that when we were old enough to have a season and attend balls, we would be used to staying up all night."

"Did that work? Were you used to it?" Collin's tone was mildly curious, and I wondered if he had somehow forgotten that there had been no season for me. No balls or late-night parties of any sort. I'd attended a few events with Anna prior to her wedding, but by then my role was that of the older sister, and it was not required that I flit about and socialize at all hours of the night.

"It worked for Anna, perhaps, but not for me. I never made it much past midnight without getting a fit of giggles. We would both be laughing so hard, we'd be crying, all tangled up in the curtains of the bed, bouncing around like a couple of children." I could almost feel the bed beneath me now, instead of the plodding horse.

"I can see that in my mind," Collin said. "Can imagine that along with laughter, you are given to bouncing and other boisterous activities when in a bed."

I snapped my head around in time to catch his grin.

He is teasing again. Teasing Collin was the Collin I adored most. If only he would appear more frequently. Being privy to the sparring match between Gavin and Eithne today might have inspired him.

I continued my story. "I would laugh until I simply couldn't anymore, and then the next thing I knew it would be morning." I smiled to myself, lost for a moment in the pleasant memory. "It's probably a very good thing I never had a season. I can just imagine it now—I'd start giggling during a dance and would either offend my partner or have him thinking that I was raving mad." I closed my eyes, imagining for just a moment, and a second later felt the jerk of my head as it bobbed in sleep.

"That's it. You'll ride with me." Collin leaned closer, pulling back on the mare's reins as he ordered Ian's horse to a stop. "Quinn," he called. "Will you come take this beast and lead it with you back to the paddock? Katherine isn't fit for riding at present."

"I am too," I argued only half-heartedly as Collin transferred me in front of him and wrapped his arms securely around me.

Quinn circled back to us, then led the mare away.

"There now," Collin said when Quinn had moved away from us once more. "You can lay your head back against me and sleep if you'd like. I'll not let any harm come to your basket of soap cakes."

"Thank you," I murmured, grateful for this new arrangement. "Isn't this considered touching? I don't want to break my promise and make it difficult for you."

Collin snorted. "I think I can keep my desires in control while seated upon a horse."

"You desire me?" I'd never heard him put what was between us in those terms before.

"You know I do," Collin said, a bit of a growl in his response.

I accepted his invitation to rest and leaned back against him, snuggling into the warmth of his chest. "I desire you too," I said sleepily.

"It would be easier if you didn't." A definite growl this time.

"Why?" I turned to look at him.

"I would never force my intentions upon a woman," Collin said. "But you're so . . . willing."

Yes, I was. And becoming more so by the minute, as it seemed, was Collin, given the way his hand lingered over my stomach, his fingers splayed, caressing in a manner that threatened to make me go mad.

"Shouldn't a wife feel that way about her husband?" I asked. "It would seem most unfortunate if desire did not run both ways."

"I have no idea how it should be between a husband and wife," Collin said. "My mother lived perhaps minutes after our birth—not long enough for me to ever know her or to observe her relationship with my father."

"Did he ever speak of her?" I asked.

"Aye." Collin's chin rubbed against the back of my head as he nodded. "Only in terms of the greatest reverence. He never remarried, never considered it, that I was aware of. It was plain he loved her very much, even to his dying day."

I'll love you until my dying day. "That is terribly romantic." I sighed dreamily, lulled to a state of utter contentment and bliss in Collin's arms.

"It's tragic," he returned sharply, startling me fully awake. "For a woman to die young, without even knowing her children, for a man to spend his life alone. There is nothing of romance or fantasy in that."

"No. You are right." I sat up straight and leaned away from him. "I'm sorry. I only meant that your father's enduring love was—"

"I know what you meant." Collin wrapped an arm around my middle once more and pulled me back against him. "Sleep, if you can," he said gruffly. "It will be another long day tomorrow, and I need you to have your wits about you if we're to enjoy a longer life together than did my parents—or yours."

Chapter Eight

Memory is a peculiar thing, given to appearing suddenly, randomly, when stimulated by the other senses. Mine had seemed wont to do that at the oddest times since my marriage to Collin and my return to Scotland. Our fifth day at the castle it arrived in full force, wreaking havoc on my taut nerves while at the same time fine-tuning my developing feelings for my husband.

Our morning began as usual, or what had become so the past three days, with breakfast alone in our room. Collin and I sat opposite at the small table, devouring a plate of bannocks prior to discussion of the day's strategy.

We'd decided to trust Bridget with our meals—it was either that or starve while Brann wasn't in residence for us to mark carefully what he ate before partaking of it ourselves.

In our wanderings about the keep we had discovered a poison garden, made entirely of plants with the ability to seriously harm or kill. Wolfsbane, baneberry, white willow and many others flourished under the care of a most attentive gardener—Brann.

Bridget had told us the garden was his passion, and he was not beyond experimenting on others to see what effects each plant, its bark or berries, leaves or even its scent, might induce. Collin had declared that would be the first thing to go, once Brann himself was gone.

His absence had done little to ease our strain, as members of his council still watched us closely. After our day spent with

Eithne and Gavin, we had continued our excursions, though none had been as pleasant as the first. Instead we had seen just how much damage had been done—how many lives ruined—by Brann's expunction of the tenants. Two families Collin had wished me to meet were no more. Their homes, their livestock, they themselves were simply gone, vanished from the land as if they had never been there.

Collin guessed that roughly half of the Campbell families had suffered a similar fate.

"Poor odds," he'd said, "should Ian decide to show up and start a row over your missing dowry."

Poor odds if we needed support to unseat Brann from the Campbell keep. Some remembered Collin, though with much skepticism and suspicion. I, notwithstanding my Campbell heritage, was still a stranger here. Having been raised in England, the daughter of an English soldier, I wasn't likely to gain anyone's trust right away.

"All the more reason to find the money before Ian decides to come for it himself," Collin said. "Better to keep the devil at the door than have to turn him out of the house."

It wasn't the first time Collin had referred to his brother as the devil. The description didn't seem far off.

Yet if Heaven was represented by the clan's priest, it didn't promise to be much better. We'd met Father Rey the previous day, in the kirkyard while visiting my mother's and grandfather's graves. He'd come out from the kirk to see us, or more precisely, to persuade us that we should not interfere with God's will, insomuch as it included clearing the sinful Highlanders from the land. Our encounter had left me feeling little better than I did after a confrontation with Ian.

All these thoughts and concerns swirled about my mind as we ate in silence. Instead of looking forward to another day with my new husband, in our new home, I felt only mounting pressures.

Collin lifted his mug and drank deeply.

I waited until he'd finished before speaking. "We've questioned everyone we know and many we don't, searched the castle as much as we are able, and explored a good portion of the Campbell lands for that place Finlay alluded to where what is planted is not apt to grow. What else do you suggest?"

"A peek at the clan records. A visit to the treasury wouldn't hurt, either." Collin picked up another bannock and began buttering it. "If we are to run this place we need to know what we have to work with."

"And you believe the council will allow us access?" I didn't. Not for a second.

Collin took a large bite and held his up his hand, indicating he would answer in a minute.

Even if the dowry did still exist and Collin was somehow able to claim it, I felt strongly in favor of *not* turning it over to Ian, given his penchant for thinking of none but himself. It was one thing for Collin to see the money justly dispersed among his people but quite another for Ian to have it to use as he pleased.

"Who says we need permission?" Collin's sly smile didn't quite cover his underlying anger, which led me to believe he still itched for a fight.

"I do." I folded my arms across my chest as we faced off, staring at one another across the table. "We have to play by at least some of Brann's rules until he is gone. Then you are welcome to explore whatever you want."

"He's gone this morning." Collin finished off the bannock and licked his fingers. "I realize you're frightened of Brann, and wise to be, but it's Ian I'm most concerned with at present. If not appeased—and soon, especially given his unfortunate *accident . . .* " Collin's brows rose as he looked at me pointedly.

As if I needed reminding that I had shot and wounded his brother.

Collin continued. "I fear it will mean contention between the MacDonalds and Campbells, which would devastate both our clans. We may not have many weapons between us, but there's plenty of harm that can be done with a hayfork or bare hands."

The morning of our wedding it had certainly seemed like both the MacDonalds and Campbells had plenty of weapons, but I had since learned that so many had been present only because of the circumstances. *Because of me.* Collin and the Campbells had wanted to see me safely home. The MacDonalds had wanted to see that, too, so they might collect the dowry. And of course, with both clans highly mistrustful of the other and traveling together, they'd armed themselves well.

I was not likely to ever see so many pistols and swords again in the Highlands, as the 1746 Act of Proscription and its thorough enforcement by English patrols had effectively stripped the clans of their weapons and any right to bear arms. Collin had told me it had taken years to acquire those present at our wedding, and that each represented nearly the sum total of weapons for both clans.

The thought of *any* pistols or swords being used against each other was terrifying. I'd never intended to stir up the old contentions or start fighting between our clans. But what else was I to have done the night Ian threatened my husband? Collin might not be here, had I not acted.

"Would you prefer I hadn't shot Ian?" I asked, very aware of just how *here* my husband was, how fine he looked this morning, clean-shaven and wearing a new suit of clothes, a gift from one of the clansmen still loyal to my grandfather, and now to me. Our hands touched over the plate of bannocks, and equal hints of yearning and accusation flashed briefly in Collin's eyes.

I snatched my hand away quickly, to show him I hadn't touched him on purpose. Not that I didn't want to. Our agreement to avoid intimacy had only seemed to deepen our desire, or mine at least. I could not speak for Collin, and he had refused to speak of it again. But I, at least, thought of it. Of him. The nights in the forest we'd spent curled up together, the passionate kisses we'd shared.

At the moment it was all I could do not to reach out and brush a lock of his dark hair aside. It had untidied itself already and swept low across his forehead, giving him a very devil-may-care appearance.

If only. There was nothing light or amusing about our circumstances—any of them.

"I am grateful for your intervention that night," Collin said around another bite of jam-laden bannock. "Though your aim could have been better."

"It was dark, and the trigger didn't want to budge." I didn't care to consider or discuss the particulars of Ian's injuries, which had rendered him unable to ride a horse for some time. "You had a pistol aimed at your chest. I thought only to remove it." Collin would have to see Ian again if my dowry was to be delivered, and it was that I felt most strongly against.

"I thank you for that—truly," Collin added, as if he felt I might not believe him. "But we must still attempt amends of some sort. I know my brother, and if not appeased, he'll stir up trouble, which we've plenty of already at present." Collin dabbed at the crumbs on his lips with a cloth napkin and tossed it on the table as he stood. "Let's see what we can find today. If not the money, maybe some record that will lead us to it or give us a clue as to where it's gone."

I stood and followed him to the door. "I'd say it's out grazing the fields."

"I don't think so." Collin shook his head. "Your grand-father was too clever to leave the dowry anywhere Brann might easily access. Brann may have depleted the clan's other funds, but I actually think he's telling the truth when he says he doesn't know anything about the dowry. Alistair, on the other hand, might know something, or did at one time." Collin lifted the newly-installed, heavy crossbar from its place and pushed the door open.

I paused in the doorway, glancing back at the cheery fire and comfortable bed, wishing we could simply spend the day ensconced in the quiet peace the room afforded. It had become our sanctuary in this unwelcoming place.

By contrast the chilly draft that hit us as we stepped into the hall seemed to warn of the day to come. There would be more frost from the council, more treading lightly and peering around every corner with care, lest an unknown and unseen enemy surprise us.

I rubbed my arms briskly, thinking that for July, the castle was terribly drafty and chill. Winter here promised to be miserable. *What* had I inherited—besides trouble?

Collin pulled the door shut and inserted the key. "Let us not speak our speculations here in the open," he whispered.

I nodded agreement. Our guards had gone down to breakfast a few moments earlier, but that was no guarantee we were alone. The dark corridors of the castle could easily hide eyes and ears spying for Brann.

"I'm sleeping better at least, now that we've a crossbar." Collin pulled at the key, but, as on previous days, it didn't want to budge. "Next to fix the rusted lock."

"Grandfather never wanted a bar on my door." A long-ago conversation stirred in memory. "He felt you were a better guard than any piece of wood."

"I should hope so." Collin gave the key a final tug, and it slipped from his fingers, spinning toward the floor and landing with a ping of metal.

I crouched to retrieve it, and as I touched the stone felt myself wrenched back in time, to cold winter nights when a gangling youth curled up here—to protect me.

Collin. I saw him as he had been. I felt his absolute misery, from the desolation in his heart to the chill in his bones. My eyes filled with unexpected tears.

"Katie?"

I looked up at him, grown now. Here, in the present, with me. *Still sleeping on the floor because he believes it's the best way to keep me safe.* "Grandfather wanted you to be able to get inside my room quickly if needed. So he made you sleep here." *Like a dog,* Collin had said.

He nodded. "Aye. Though in all the months I did, I never once had to enter your room." His gaze strayed to the floor, and I wondered what he was thinking—wondered anew that he didn't hate me and every single Campbell. Few treated him well, I realized, as voices and conversations from the past unleashed and rampaged through my mind.

. . . look, it's the MacDonald nursemaid . . .

. . . this apple is for the lass, and this one is for you . . . I saw a cherry red apple beside a rotten one.

. . . should've shot you full of holes like your da. Maybe we will . . .

. . . we'll slit his throat one night when he's sleeping in his dog bed . . . The last voice I recalled was from Brann. He and his band of followers were near Collin's age and might have been his friends, but hatred runs deep. Jealousy did not

make it any better. I saw clearly in Brann's mind how envious he had been of the attention my grandfather gave Collin. I saw now that his jealousy had only multiplied.

My fingers had grown cold where they touched the stone. *Over a year, spent here night after night—for me.* I grasped the key, accepted Collin's outstretched hand, and stood facing him, nearer than we had been to one another since our ride home after the soap-making.

"Thank you," I whispered as the tears that had hovered wet my cheeks. "Thank you for everything." Until a moment ago I had not remembered this particular sacrifice. What else had I not yet recalled? How great was my debt to my husband? What could I do to pay it back, to give as much as he had given—and was still giving—to me?

With reluctance, it seemed, Collin turned me from him, his hand light against my back.

"You are welcome." His voice was gruff.

Dashing my tears away, I forced a smile to my face and started toward the stairs. "Let's see about finding that dowry."

Our arrival downstairs was met with the news that Brann had returned. We waited for him to appear, Collin anxious to discover what he had been up to and equally keen, it seemed, to take advantage of a few more baked goods from the tray Bridget had just deposited on the sideboard.

I'd little appetite. My stomach was tense with worry over so many things, not the least of which was Brann's return. Donaid and Hugh—our guards this morning—joined Collin, and a few members of Brann's council lingered near the fire, waiting for him as well, I supposed.

I walked the length of the now-vacant tables slowly, running my fingers along the smooth grain. I remembered doing this as a child, walking circles around my grandfather and his council as they met.

I came to the head table and paused, my fingers resting lightly on the back of the chair that had been Grandfather's. The room shifted, and he materialized before me, seated proud and tall—though a glob of spittle slid down his cheek. I gripped the chair harder as the younger Collin appeared once more. His ribs shown through his worn, filthy shirt, and his arms were pulled back at what had to be an uncomfortable angle, as he was led outside by two strapping men.

They were intending to hurt him badly, perhaps even kill him. My stomach lurched, and then my younger self was rushing forward, demanding that Collin apologize even as I wiped Grandfather's face. My words came off as angry toward Collin when really all I could think of was that I must not allow him to be hurt anymore.

The memory passed, leaving me limp and dizzy. I pried my fingers from Grandfather's chair and forced my footsteps away, down the other side of the long table. A quick glance at Collin showed him hale and hearty and still eating. I smiled to myself, grateful for his appetite that could finally—hopefully—be appeased. He must have been continually starving, the past weeks, subsisting on little more than oatmeal and fish during our journey here.

I passed twelve chairs down this side of the table, with another two at the far end. *Where Collin and I used to sit.* I made the mistake of touching one, and memory assailed me once more. Only this was a vision of a time I'd been unable to spare Collin a beating—one I had caused. I saw Grandfather's face, stoic with resolve, and then watched with horror as he brought the strap down. I saw Collin's flinch and felt the sting as the belt struck.

Gasping, I fell forward over the chair in front of me.

"What is it?" Collin was at my side in a second, his hand on my elbow, concern etched in the lines of his forehead. "Do you see something?"

"The past," I choked out miserably. "Us—you—here. Beaten because of me." I couldn't look at him, I felt so ashamed. I let go of the chair, and the vision ceased, scarcely a second before Grandfather's belt struck a second time. I jumped a little anyway, expecting to feel it again.

Don't touch anything. The floor, the chairs . . . it was as if the castle had been waiting to share its secrets. It had seen all and remembered. And now it wanted me to as well.

"That was not our best night." Collin's tone held no reprimand. "But as the past cannot be undone, there is no point dwelling there. It's the future we must concern ourselves with."

"I can't seem to help myself remembering." Neither could I help myself from leaning toward him, wishing he would put his arm around me, though I deserved no comfort. "I was a wretched child."

Collin chuckled. "You were a *gifted* child." His tone sobered. "One who suffered much, I think, under the weight of guilt you felt from the things you saw and from witnessing your mother's murder."

Brann's untimely arrival collided with the memory. I felt his presence before I saw him. Collin stiffened and stepped away from me, though not too far.

"Unwell again, Katherine? Do mornings not agree with you?" Brann's gaze roamed over me as he strode toward us.

"If I am ill it is because of past recollections. The Highlands, and particularly this castle, have brought to mind many less-than-pleasant memories."

"Oh?" His tone was casual, but I thought I detected a flicker of concern in his cold blue eyes.

My next words were reckless. "Watching a twelve-year-old boy strangle my mother the first time was horrifying enough. Seeing it again as an adult is even more troubling."

Brann stopped mid-step. Our eyes met as we each acknowledged what this meant. He had killed my mother, and I not only recalled that day from childhood memory but had seen it again in vivid detail as an adult. I knew what he was capable of and the evil that ruled him.

And I was not afraid to confront it.

Brann's look hardened, his gaze sharpening, knifelike. His lips curved. "That was not my first murder, or my last."

I am not bothered that you know, he might have said.

"Though I must say that with your mother I took particular pleasure in—"

Collin's fist smashed into Brann's mouth. With a yelp, I jumped out of the way as their bodies collided and wrestled one another to the floor. In a matter of seconds Collin had the advantage, his fist pummeling Brann's face. Beneath this commotion, I heard another sound.

I whirled around and faced five members of Brann's council advancing on us, three with knives aimed at Collin, one already drawn back in an attitude to take aim.

"Stop," I cried, then flung myself between Collin's back and the men. I threw my hands out wide, as if that might somehow increase my chances of blocking their attack.

"Katie, move!" Collin jumped to his feet and pushed me aside, making himself an even easier target. Behind him Brann started to rise.

"Stop it! All of you," I commanded. "Put those blades away," I ordered. "And you—" I turned my attention to Brann, who staggered and wiped his split lip with the back of his hand. "Are you such a coward that you can't fight one man to another without having half a dozen men at your back?" More foolish words, but bravado was my only weapon.

Collin had other ideas. One hand moved slowly toward his middle and the pistol hidden beneath his shirt.

"Touch your weapon, and my men plant their knives in Katherine's chest." Brann's voice was deadly, certain. This was no bluff. He still wanted to use my abilities, but he was also willing to be rid of me if it came to that.

Collin's hand froze where it was as three dirks swiveled toward me.

My heart pounded beneath my dress, and a sheen of sweat broke out along my forehead. My mind scrambled frantically for what I might say to get us out of this impossible situation. Slowly I turned from the men and their knives and faced Brann.

"Haven't you been haunted by my mother's ghost enough?" I'd no idea where the words had come from but did not mistake the brief flash of terror that crossed his face.

A tense silence followed my question. Behind me I sensed five pairs of eyes on Brann, awaiting his command. Collin stood motionless, his clenched fists hinting at agony and frustration. If his purpose was to protect me, I could imagine how helpless he felt being unable to do anything in that regard. It was the perfect opportunity for Brann to kill us both, and I couldn't see why he would not. It was all I could do not to squeeze my eyes shut and wait to feel the metal pierce my flesh.

Instead I forced my gaze to Brann's and held it firm. And, as with his flicker of discomfort a moment earlier, I felt his unease. *I* was making *him* nervous.

"Witch," he whispered with venom. "Just like your mother. I should burn you at the stake."

"You would curse yourself more." More words before I'd fully formed the thought. My voice sounded surprisingly calm, though my insides clenched with dread. I kept my gaze locked with Brann's, knowing somehow that if I broke mine first, he would break me.

"Put your knives away," he ordered suddenly. "All of you. You too," he shouted to Donaid and Hugh, who stood off to the side. I'd forgotten they were here, that Collin and I were not completely on our own. Inwardly I sighed with relief while wishing for a chair to drop into.

Now what? The danger was far from over. I felt I must say something more. Nothing came to me this time, so I did the best I could on my own. "Collin and I have come here to help, to—"

"*Liars,*" Brann shouted, his voice reverberating off the high stone and timbers of the hall. "You're little better than thieves, trying to convince me to hand over money from some imagined dowry."

"It wasn't imagined." Breathing heavily, Alistair charged through the doorway. "Though it is missing." With a canny eye he took in the scene and slowed his pace and joined us, not so discreetly replacing his own dirk at his waist. He looked from one person to the other, his gaze lingering on Collin, Brann, and finally me. "Heard from one of the servants there was some trouble up here."

"No trouble." Brann readjusted his shirt and ran his fingers over his split lip. "I was just about to offer to show Katherine the accounting of the past few years. If the MacDonald still wants to trail after her like a lost pup, he can come too. You can see for yourselves that Liam left you nothing."

I placed a restraining hand on Collin's arm, lest he lose his temper again. If he did, I was bound to lose mine as well—

with him. Now that the moment of danger had passed, my fear transferred rapidly to anger, fury even, with Collin that he had been so careless.

"Follow me." Brann led our entourage toward the back of the hall.

I cast a fleeting look at Alistair, wishing we might talk to him, or that he *would* speak to us of the dowry, other than to acknowledge that it had existed.

Brann marched down the steps to the castle kitchens. Collin and I followed, a few of the others trailing behind. We made our way through the long, narrow room to the gardens outside.

"If it's records you're after, you'll see the truth soon enough," Brann declared.

Collin muttered what I supposed to be a Gaelic curse beneath his breath. "As you'll soon see what it's like to have MacDonalds beating down your door."

Chapter Nine

B rann led us behind the castle across another muddy path to a cluster of stone buildings that showed the centuries that had passed since their creation.

"Edan was your grandfather's solicitor," Brann said, explaining what Collin and I knew already. "He left around the time your grandfather passed away—rather suspicious," he added. "Who's to say he didn't harm the old man and then take off with the money himself—if it was even there to begin with?"

Neither Collin nor I responded. It felt too much like Brann was baiting us, hoping we'd make a mistake and say something about Edan or his whereabouts.

After a moment had passed, Brann continued. "At one time we'd another man who had taken over the position. If he's still around, perhaps he will know something of this supposed dowry. Though should you find it, there would be conditions, as with any dowry." Brann threw a look over his shoulder at me. "As laird it is I who should have had a say in your choice of a bridegroom."

Again, Collin and I let his comment slide, though there were any number of responses we might have given, each of which would not have been well received. Brann was not laird.

For the moment, there were more pressing worries. I knew Edan was definitely not anywhere nearby, it being impossible for him to have traveled to Edinburg and back in just five days. No doubt his replacement would profess to know nothing of the dowry. So why was Brann bringing us here now, on this fool's errand?

Perhaps we were heading for some carefully laid trap. I reminded myself that Hugh, Donaid, and now Alistair were here with us. And it was the middle of the day. If Brann hadn't done anything at the castle, he was unlikely to try anything now. Still, the feeling of unease persisted.

What is it? I begged my subconscious to make known any danger, but my mind remained frustratingly blank.

As expected, when we reached the building, Edan was nowhere to be seen. His replacement was also not to be found, with no notice left of when he might return. The door was locked as well, with weeds growing up around the front and a thick layer of grime on the window that made it appear the building had not been in use for quite some time, years perhaps.

Brann shrugged as if to say, "I told you so," then turned from the grimy windows.

"It is apparent no one has been here for a while. Your grandfather was careless that way, allowing his estate to be poorly accounted for. He didn't leave me much to work with, so I've not bothered with precise records myself." Brann kicked at a loose stone near the door and cast a derisive look toward the shoddy building. "Something else really ought to be done with this."

"Aye. Burn it to the ground and bring in more sheep," Collin said.

Brann chuckled, an evil laugh that showed he found little amusement in Collin's jest. "Too near the castle. Not good grazing. But it might make a decent home for the two of you when it is proved the castle still belongs to me. While I'm not keen to have a MacDonald living among us, Katherine's talent might be worth negotiating a place for you here." Brann paused, shifting his beady eyes from me to Collin. "Then again, why should I have to negotiate at all when you're not welcome with your own clan, especially with your wife's promised dowry no longer part of the bargain?" Brann gave a dark laugh, then turned and left us, standing in the mud in front of what appeared to be a long-deserted dwelling.

I waited until he was well away before speaking.

"What now?" I asked, my gaze swinging around the tight circle from Collin to Alistair, Donaid, and Hugh.

Alistair spoke first. "It's doubtful you'll find any answers here."

"Where *will* we find them?" Collin's tone was as angry as I'd ever heard, though directed at our greatest ally here.

"If I knew, I'd tell you." Alistair scratched his head. "Brann was truthful when he said the old laird was sequestered most of his last years. I heard tell of the dowry, but I wasn't the one he trusted with its whereabouts. Trouble is, I'm not sure who was."

Finlay. He knew something—whether from a conversation with my grandfather or from a vision of the future. He was our best hope for finding the money anytime soon. And he was gone.

Collin let out a frustrated sigh. "We might as well go through what records are here."

"I'll leave you to it." Alistair clapped a hand on Collin's shoulder. "Keep your temper. It'll help you keep your head attached."

"Thanks." Collin sounded anything but grateful.

Impulsively, I stepped forward and gave Alistair a hug. "Your arrival was timely, and I thank you for it."

"Thank ye, lass." He didn't blush as Finlay had when I'd kissed his cheek, but he smiled so that I could tell the gesture had pleased him. "Watch each others' backs, the both of you."

He raised a hand in farewell as he walked away, reminding me of when we had parted at the moor on our journey here.

"We will," I promised. Collin gave the usual Scots' grunt. He was already busy trying to get inside, fiddling with the doorknob.

"Isn't it locked?" I asked. Brann had gone so far as to lift his hands to the filthy window and peer inside.

"Keep away." Collin took the stone Brann had kicked from the path, then stepped back and threw it at the window. The glass shattered easily. "It's not like Edan is going to be coming back here," Collin said. "He's been gone since your grandfather's death. Finlay said to search high and low, so we'll try here as well."

"Finlay?" Hugh's brows rose, and he perked up. "What else did he say?"

"Many things." I gave what I hoped was an enthusiastic smile to Hugh. "The man is a brilliant poet. He regaled us with tale after amusing tale during our journey here." I prattled on, feeling the need to cover Collin's blunder. Had he forgotten that no one was to know of Finlay's presence at Liusaidh's, or of his part in transporting the documents to Edinburg?

"The very first words he spoke to me were about my hair—'like a field of dry heather,' he said. I wasn't quite certain it was a compliment, but the words, at least, sounded lovely."

"Eyes like the sky afore a storm." Collin, busy removing broken glass from the window frame, paused long enough to glance at me.

You have no idea. There was a definite storm brewing inside of me. From the moment Collin had leapt past me to launch his attack on Brann, from the way he'd pushed me aside and made himself an easy target, to his careless words endangering Finlay, my fury had been building. Even his continued obsession with finding the dowry was starting to grate on me. Ian and the MacDonalds simply might have to live without it.

As our gazes locked, I inhaled deeply, reminding myself that Collin wanted that money not for himself, but for his people. But what about my people? Who had we come here to help?

Finding it will *help the Campbells,* Collin's look seemed to say.

Perhaps, I answered silently. I still didn't like the idea of appeasing Ian, but neither did I relish the possibility of seeing him again, if what Collin feared was true and he intended to come here. We had our hands full enough with Brann.

Our wordless conversation over, Collin returned to his work, and I to mine.

"Finlay is my uncle," Hugh said. "We didn't realize he was going to bring you home. It was all done in secret, you see."

Mostly in secret? Someone outside of the group of loyal clansmen had known of the plans to bring me back. Malcom, the man who'd kidnapped me on our journey here and had then been killed by Collin, had been in contact with Brann and likely working with someone else among our group. That we still didn't know who was yet another worry.

"Your uncle added levity to our journey," I said. "He has a verse for everything. 'Marry in June when the roses grow and oe'r land and sea you'll go,'" I said, doing my best Finlay imitation.

Hugh barked out a laugh. "Not bad. But don't be too impressed by the verse. That one is an old proverb. There's one for each month of the year. Not much truth to any of them."

"Of course not." But we *had* traveled far, over land and loch at least, if not the sea itself.

Collin broke out the last of the glass and crawled through the window. A minute later he opened the door.

"Come inside, Katie." He held his hand out, helping me over the buckling threshold.

Hugh and Donaid started to follow, but Collin stopped them. "I'll feel safer if you both wait outside. Donaid, go around back and keep an eye out. Hugh, if you'll watch the front, Katie and I will have a look around here."

"I'll give a low whistle if there's trouble." Donaid puckered his lips, making the sound we were to listen for.

"I'm not much for whistling," Hugh said. "But I'll cough loudly or rap on the door if trouble's coming."

Collin nodded his appreciation. Having dispatched our guards, he closed the door to Edan's deserted quarters behind him, leaving the two of us alone in the dusty, cobwebbed room. No sooner had the door shut than he rounded on me.

"What were you thinking, throwing yourself in front of me like that? I'm the one who is supposed to protect you, *not* the other way around." He flung his hands about, nearly shouting.

"You won't be able to protect anyone if you're *dead*," I countered. He'd no right to be upset with me. I, on the other hand, had every right to be angry. "What were *you* thinking, attacking Brann like that?"

"How could I not? He was speaking of your mother." Collin began pacing footprints across the dusty floor. "A subject you ought not have mentioned."

I cringed inwardly, recognizing his point as valid. "I am sorry about that."

"Mmph," Collin muttered. On his second turn around the room I caught his sleeve and stopped him.

"Brann won't kill me. You know that as well as I. He'd rather use my gift, and for some reason he's wary of it—or me.

But you . . . he'd be more than happy to dispose of you. You mustn't anger him. *Just* as you told me not to raise Ian's ire, you must do all you can to appease or at least avoid Brann—for now."

Collin lowered his voice to a whisper. "I should like to kill him and be done with it."

"Was that what Grandfather asked of you? Was that what he foretold? To begin here with murder?"

"I don't know what he'd planned." Collin pulled away from my touch. "Only that I must protect you at all costs. Forgive me if I felt that included sparing you from hearing the details of your mother's death. Though you all but asked to hear them, bringing that up to Brann as you did."

"I *said* I was sorry." How many times did Collin expect me to apologize? "And I know the details. I was there."

"That doesn't mean you have to relive them over and over." Collin stepped closer to me once more. He grasped my arms in a way that seemed anything but loving. "And you're wrong. Brann would kill you. He would have when you were a child, had I not been there to protect you. He will now, if he feels you are more trouble than you're worth."

"He wants—"

"Yes," Collin agreed. "He does want to use you, in more ways than you can likely imagine or should. I've seen the way he watches you. His greed is about more than your gift for knowing the future."

"Then let's leave this place," I pled. "We are up against too much here. Even if I'm granted ownership of the castle, what reason do Brann and the council have to leave? None. And every reason to do away with both of us."

Collin released me and took up his pacing again, one hand held to his head. A bruise was starting to form on his left cheek, where Brann had landed a punch. Other than that,

Collin appeared unscathed from the incident. I, however, felt shaken to my core. The thought of something happening him, and then of being left alone in this wild and dangerous place . . .

"I don't want to lose you, Collin." I waited to speak more until he was the farthest away from me on his track around the room. "I can't imagine my life before you came or see any future without you. I want to help my family, but more than that, I want to be with you."

"Don't you think I feel the same?" He crossed the room in half the steps it had taken him before. This time when he took my arms it was to pull me into his and crush me against his chest. "Dear God, Katie. I was so frightened. Three knives aimed at your heart—"

"Then you understand how I've felt twice now, seeing your life hang in the balance."

"Aye." He kissed the top of my head and held me tighter. Neither of us spoke for a long minute, content and grateful to be feeling each other's heartbeats.

Collin lessened his grip just a little, leaning back to look at me. "I don't see how we are to accomplish all of this, just the two of us."

"We've more than the two of us. Heaven is on our side and will be so long as we are trying to do the right thing, for the right reasons. I'm just not certain killing Brann falls into that category."

Collin grunted. "I'm fair certain it would feel right to me. It would mean you're safe."

"From Brann, but what about his council? What about Ian?" I wrapped my arms around Collin's waist and held tight, lest he had any ideas about releasing me. He'd reached out first, so I felt it all right to call a temporary halt to our vow not to touch. Our argument deserved remorse and apologies with at least as much passion as the words we'd flung at one another.

"Ian." Collin sighed. "I've half a mind to take you from this place and leave Brann to face the consequences for your lost dowry."

"He and Ian might take care of our problems themselves. They might kill each other."

"A possibility." Collin nodded, rubbing his chin across the top of my head. "But Ian is still my brother and the MacDonalds still my clan. I cannot abandon them."

He practically had already, choosing to come with me to claim my Campbell heritage, instead of returning to lead the MacDonalds. Leaving them in Ian's care did not sit well with either of us.

"We are right back to where we began with our problems."

"It does seem that way." Collin took my shoulders and held me away from him. The lines on his face relaxed, and the hard look in his eyes softened. "I am sorry to have frightened you, Katie."

"You're the one who said you were frightened." I tried to tease away the moment or felt certain I would either kiss him or burst into tears from wanting to so terribly and having come so near to losing that privilege forever.

"Back in the hall you weren't afraid?" His brows arched in disbelief.

"There are not enough words for how afraid I was." Reluctantly I allowed my hands to slide from his waist. I shook a finger at him. "And if you ever scare me so much again, I'll kill you myself."

Collin's mouth quirked in the slow smile I so rarely saw. "Is that a promise?"

"You're not amusing." I put my hands on my hips and mustered a fierce glare.

"No? Well, you are." He was still smiling. "There is more than one way to die, you know. Some, I hear, are very pleasant." He brushed his thumb across my lips as unmistakable desire flared in his eyes. Then he spoke words I'd longed to hear. "If we survive long enough, I'll fully expect you to make good on your word."

Chapter Ten

Pinching the tip of my nose, I stifled yet another sneeze. Two hours in the musty room hadn't led us to much except dust. Careful not to stir up any more than necessary, I opened another ledger, this one from 1752, nine years earlier, when my grandfather had still been alive and I had been living in England. Starting on the first page, I ran a finger down the columns that recorded how much and what had been planted that year. A dozen pages further and the entries changed to amounts harvested, monies earned at market, and rent collected. The ledger was just like those I had already looked at, with profits down from the previous year.

"Nothing in this one," I said to Collin, seated across the table from me. "Barley, rye, potatoes, turnips and the like, none of which seemed to provide much of an income for the clan."

"That seems to be the pattern of it." Collin didn't look up from the book in his hand, his own fingers busy tracing the ledger. "Yet from this accounting, more was planted every year."

"Supply and demand?" I guessed.

"I don't think so." Collin shook his head. "Most of what was grown was used for the clan itself, but some was traded or sold in town or with other clans. Those numbers should have remained consistent, or at least fluctuated up and down, depending upon the year."

"Apparently 1752 was a poor one. Rationing must have

been so strict that they even recorded some of the game they shot. 'Red Fox shot a week past.'" I read the entry of the twentieth of February. "Is fox good eating?"

"If you're hungry enough." Collin gave a derisive grunt. "Had it a time or two before. It makes for a long meal—lots of tough chewing. Soak it in brine first, if you're ever unfortunate enough to have to prepare it."

"Thanks for the advice." *No fox meat.* I catalogued this with the other culinary tidbits—*uncooked oats are disgusting,* and *fish long dead are not good eating*—that I'd picked up from Collin over the past weeks.

He looked up suddenly, a peculiar light in his eyes. "What year did you say that was?"

"1752. Here." I pushed the volume toward him across the dusty table, accidentally tipping an inkhorn in the process. I jumped back in my chair, anticipating the spill.

"Not to worry. It's dried." Collin picked up the bottle, shook it, and tipped it upside down. Not a drop came out. "Whoever Brann found to replace Edan obviously did not care much for the position."

"I'd be surprised if he came here at all." Instead of propping my elbows on the table and leaning forward, eager to hear what Collin might have discovered, I sat primly in my chair, taking care to touch as little as possible.

After a moment of studying the book he looked up. "Red Fox was no animal, but a well-known and unpopular Campbell."

"What has that to do with declining profits?"

"Perhaps nothing—or maybe everything. Like your grandfather, he worked closely with the English. He was a frequent visitor here, and the two were great friends. Red Fox had the unfortunate responsibility of collecting taxes from clan leaders. And it was often he whom the English tasked with removing Jacobite families from their homes to make way for those who'd supported the king."

"No wonder he was shot," I said, half feeling sorry for the man, and half loathing him.

"The interesting thing," Collin said, "is that the English suspected he was a Jacobite sympathizer. Your grandfather was suspected as well. If the English were right that may account, in part at least, for the decreased profits."

"How so?" And what had that to do with our search for the dowry? After staring at so many entries and figures my head was beginning to ache, and nothing Collin was saying seemed to make sense.

Instead of answering, he began reading the 1752 ledger. "Amount planted, date, harvest . . . " He mumbled to himself as he scanned the pages. "Clan allotment, taxes, sent to market—" He pushed aside the other books, then used his finger to scribble numbers in the layer of grime on the table.

"Just as I thought." Collin circled the bottom number of his calculations with flourish. "It's *not* all accounted for. There's a difference between the total amount that was harvested and the sum of what was used here and what was sent to market. It doesn't add up."

"You're saying Grandfather did something else with some of the crops, but there's no record of it?"

"Aye." Collin sounded excited. "The English suspected Red Fox of helping those families he had to displace. If he did, someone would have been supplying him with the means to do so."

"Grandfather."

Collin nodded solemnly. "He wasn't a Jacobite sympathizer; he was a human sympathizer. It didn't matter to him which side of the battle you'd been on, only that you were a good Scotsman and did what you could to further your country and people from then on. If those suspicious of Red Fox were right, he was doing both of those things, and it makes perfect sense that your grandfather would have been in league with him." Collin bent his head to the book once more. "According to this, Red Fox was shot on St. Valentine's Day. Another martyr, perhaps. I doubt anyone will be memorizing *his* name and story through history."

"I am glad to learn of it," I said. "The story of a Campbell who perhaps gave his life while helping others lessens the sting of the horrible things done by my family."

"As should knowing the man your grandfather was." Collin closed the book and set it aside. "If he was indeed aiding those displaced families, it was at great risk to his own life."

"Why would the English be bothered that he'd helped?" I asked. "It wasn't doing anything against them."

"No?" Collin's brows arched. "They didn't want another uprising. Anyone or anything associated with the Jacobite cause had to be removed. Bonnie Prince Charlie and his Jacobite army had made it all the way to Derby—a little too close to London for the king's comfort.

"Though the English suspected Red Fox, he had been an agent for them, working for the crown—on the surface at least. They didn't take his murder lightly. To prove their point, James Stewart, the man believed to have killed Red Fox, was hanged, and his body left on the gallows for over a year as warning to anyone who thought to rebel against the crown."

"That's barbaric!" I grimaced at the thought of the hanging and a body left out to rot like that.

"That's English," Collin retorted. "No offense intended regarding your father."

"None taken," I murmured. My father was still a touchy subject between the two of us. He'd been one of the men to fire a musket at Collin's father and end his life. That alone seemed unforgivable. But it was the violent way my father had taken me from Collin when I was a child that Collin had the most difficulty with.

"Did you see it—the body?" I asked.

"Aye. What was left of it. Your grandfather took me. At twenty, I was grown and ready to be on my way in the world. He was of a mind to let me go, but first he wanted to make certain I fully understood the dangers, and what hardships I— and the MacDonald clan—would face if I acted foolishly." A wry grin twisted Collin's lips. "I cannot say I was always fond of the education your grandfather provided."

"It sounds . . . unpleasant," I agreed.

"He was a hard man." Collin's gaze grew distant, traveling again to a time I was not privy to. "But a fair one as well. You did not want to cross Liam Campbell, but there was no better man to have on your side."

I brought a hand to my mouth as I considered Collin's theory and what it might mean for our quest. My mother had married an English soldier—and instead of killing the man, Grandfather had allowed the marriage. He had taken in a MacDonald boy, seen that he had a proper Papist education— in spite of the climate against such—and betrothed him to his only grandchild. Grandfather had charged Collin and me with the care of both of our clans and seeing that our families and the Highland traditions were preserved. It made perfect sense that he would have used some of the clan's means to help displaced families or those struggling to survive.

He was a laird to more than just Campbells; his concern for others extended beyond the needs of his own people.

And he wished Collin and me to carry that on. He would have realized we would need money to accomplish such a goal. "Instead of discouraging me about finding the dowry, this makes me feel more certain than ever that there was one and that we'll find it."

"Not likely here." Collin set the book aside and leaned back in his chair, stretching. "Edan had to know what was going on, that your grandfather was, in essence, siphoning off some of the clan's income. He's probably the one, if any, who knows what's become of your dowry."

"Pity he's gone for at least the next few weeks." I rose from the table. "If you don't believe we'll find anything here, can we go?" After all this dust I was eager to return to the castle and make use of a fresh pitcher of water, a wash basin, and my lavender soap.

"We'll have to leave," Collin said. "Now I've no choice but to go to Ian—before he ends up here—and try to stall him."

"Not alone, you won't." My heart raced at the suggestion of facing Ian again. But neither did I wish to be left alone, to contend with Brann.

"I won't leave you here," Collin assured me. "Though neither can I take you with me to meet Ian. I'll have to find some place safe for you."

I snorted. "*Is* there such a place in all of Scotland?" Instead of heading toward the door we had entered, I walked a slow circle around the room, part from curiosity, part half-wondering if there might be some clue we'd missed. "You don't suppose the dowry might be hidden here, do you?"

"I shouldn't think so," Collin said. "I doubt it's inside a building at all, given Brann's penchant for burning them down. If the money still exists, no doubt your grandfather took many precautions for it."

I stopped at the fireplace, so long cold that not even a trace of ash remained in the box. I studied the brick and pushed on a few that appeared loose, imaging how it would be if one concealed a secret compartment that held the missing money. At least some of our problems would be solved if it was found.

Collin pushed his chair back with a scraping of wood and rose, following me from the main room toward the narrow hall at the back. Two closed doors were on either side of it, and my curiosity peaked again.

"Maybe we should look in these rooms, just in case." I was eager to leave the dark cottage, but I also wanted to feel confident we'd done a thorough search.

The sound of snoring drifted through the broken window. Hugh, our guard out front, had fallen asleep an hour ago. *Some protection.*

"Go ahead if you'd like." Collin waved a hand absently as he studied a framed document on the wall between doors. "Sleeping quarters is likely all you'll find." He moved closer and lowered his voice. "We'll leave as soon as you're done. Is there anything particular at the castle you need? Or can we go straight away to the stables and leave from there—so as to avoid another encounter with Brann?"

I could hardly disagree with that suggestion, but I also wasn't eager to set off on another cross-country journey with nothing but the clothes on my back. "How far away is the MacDonald keep? How long will it take us to get there? What will we do when we arrive?" I didn't want to trade one threat for another without at least a semblance of a plan.

"There is a family there I trust with my life—and yours too." Collin spoke slowly, as if considering his words with care. "I'll leave you with them and go on to meet with Ian myself. I'll have a better chance reasoning with him alone."

"A MacDonald family?" I asked warily. "How can you be certain they won't object to hosting a Campbell?" The idea of being separated from Collin and left with potentially hostile strangers made me more than a little uneasy.

"They'll do as I ask. They're—" Collin broke off. His hand went to the back of his neck, rubbing absently as his lips pursed.

I turned the knob on the first door and paused. "They're what?"

"The closest thing to family I have. After your grandfather gave me my freedom, I realized quickly how good I'd had it with the Campbells. He sent me away, told me I was to take care of my own people for a few years before the time came for you to return." Collin sighed heavily. "I went home, thinking of what it had been before the rebellion."

"It was different?"

"Aye." Collin's head bobbed. "Very different. When I realized the state of the clan, when I learned all who had been lost, and what had happened in the years since—the failed crops and stolen animals, the English patrols harassing the people continually—it was like returning to the past and living the worst years all over again." His hand moved from the back of his neck to his hair, running troubled fingers through it.

"There was much of death and sorrow. Starvation and savagery. But I found a place I could be, a family who welcomed me. And that became my sanctuary. It can be yours as well. Gordon is of age now. He'll watch out for you and protect you if need be. And Mhairi and her mother are two of the kindest souls you'll ever meet."

Mhairi . . . my sanctuary . . . the closest thing to family. I felt as if I'd been struck.

What am I, then? I could not have heard Collin correctly. Still facing away from him, I spoke softly. "You want me to stay with the woman you kissed before me? The one who wanted to marry you?"

"Put like that it doesn't sound good, but I feel it wou—"

"What about how *I* feel? Have you considered that?" I pushed off the door and whirled toward him as it banged open. Any desire to continue the search for my dowry—to be given over to Mhairi and her family, for all I knew—had fled. I squared off with Collin, scarcely believing he had actually suggested that I might stay with them. Tears stung my eyes as hurt and anger battled for premier position. Collin was still stuttering for a response when I lashed out at him again.

"No. Absolutely not. I can't believe you would suggest such a thing." The insecurities of the first several days of our marriage resumed with vengeance. "You may know nothing about jealous females, but *I* do. My own sister turned on me, simply because I accepted an invitation to dance, just *once,* with her fiancé." He had not even been her fiancé at the time. I could only imagine what this Mhairi would do . . . Sink her teeth into me at the first opportunity? Strangle me in my sleep?

"Katie—" Collin stepped closer, his eyes wide.

Good. Let him see how upset he's made me—again.

He grabbed for me and missed as I stepped back, into the open room, beyond his reach. I felt equal parts incredulous and furious. I'd never wanted to hear Mhairi's name again, let alone meet her and have to stay with her.

"Katie, come here."

I could tell Collin meant his voice to be gentle, lulling, as if he thought that might somehow soften the blow he'd dealt me a moment ago. He held his hands out, coaxing me oddly, almost as if he was afraid.

He should be. Striving for calm, I breathed in deeply as I took another step back, widening the space between us. My back bumped into something, and I turned to see what it was.

"No, Katie!" Collin's tug on my arm came too late.

A face leered above mine, eyes bulging, skin blue, neck cocked viciously to the side beneath the rope encircling it. I'd backed into a corpse, putting it in motion. It swung toward me, dangling arms reaching out to ensnare.

Chapter Eleven

Collin's rough hand covered my mouth, stifling my scream almost before it began. "Don't look," he whispered as he wrapped his arm around me and backed us out of the room.

I scrunched my eyes shut, but that mattered little. The image was burned into my mind, from Edan's shock of white hair, to his bulging eyes and lolling tongue, to the rope descending from a rafter and cinched round his neck. He hung limply, above a floor littered with papers that I didn't need to read to identify.

We reached the hall, and Collin released me to pull the door closed. I turned from him, arms wrapped around my middle, trying to keep from retching, trying to stop trembling. My legs buckled and wanted to collapse, but instead I forced my feet to move, away from that room. I wanted out of this cottage, to be gone from the castle grounds and Campbell land, out of Scotland. I didn't think there was a place far away enough where I might forget or feel safe again.

Instead of following me, Collin caught my hand and tugged me into the shadow of the short hall. He gathered me to him, held me tight while murmuring soothing words. "It's all right. He cannot hurt you. I'm so sorry, lass. Cry if you must, only softly."

I wanted to be away but clung to him now instead, sobbing into the front of his shirt, shaking and terrified.

"Forget what you've seen. You must forget, Katie." Collin bent his head close to mine.

"Im—poss—ible." I couldn't block trauma as I somehow had as a child. I could no more forget the violent realities that had been my life here before than I could dismiss them now. I squeezed my eyes shut again, wishing I could.

If Brann had intended to frighten me, to threaten, he'd been entirely successful. I strained against Collin's hold, but his arms were like iron bands. "Please," I begged. "The only thing that will help is getting away from this place. We're not going to win."

"We can't leave—not now."

"What do you mean?" I ceased my struggling and lifted my face to better see his.

Collin brushed a tear from my cheek. "We should never have come inside. Brann made it too simple for us. I knew that—"

"I'm the one who is supposed to know of danger." Once again, I had not. My *gift* was both unreliable and unpredictable. Or was I expecting too much of it? I had felt something, a premonition of—certainly not this. Not the body of someone I had known, however briefly.

God speed, Edan and Liusaidh had said to one another. Almost as if he'd known. But if he had, then why had he helped me? Or tried to? *Another death—because of me.*

I didn't want there to be anymore. "Let's just go." I pushed down on Collin's arms, but still he didn't budge. "Please, Collin. Brann has made his message clear, and I don't want you to be his next target."

"Too late for that," Collin said, his voice grim.

"It's not," I insisted. He couldn't think it safe for us here, not now, after this. "We need to leave while we still can." If only we'd never come here, or had left during those days

Brann was gone. It wasn't difficult to piece together what he'd been doing during that time. Or what he might do next.

"I should have said something about the misgivings I felt in coming here this morning." I'd worried, but without a tangible vision, it was difficult to distinguish actual intuition from the constant buzz of danger surrounding us. With the discovery of Edan's body that buzz had risen to a fevered pitch, and I'd no doubt what our next course of action should be.

"That doesn't matter now. We've walked straight into a trap, and if we don't step carefully we'll not get out of it."

A trap. I'd had that very thought and ignored it. Why else would Brann not have acted this morning when he'd had both of us at his mercy? I'd been foolish to think my words alone had stopped him.

"He allowed us to come here, so he could accuse us—or me at least—of murdering Edan. The evidence will be ir-refutable. He'll be able to sway any of the clan who might have sided with us." Collin glanced toward the room we'd vacated. "No one else has been here, or so it has been made to appear. Everyone knows we've been searching for the dowry, and Edan is the man most likely to have had information about it."

"Brann will make it seem you killed Edan in anger." A moment ago I wouldn't have believed I could ever be more frightened, but I was now—for Collin's life.

"That I attacked Brann this morning will only bolster his claim." Collin's mouth turned down, and his eyes clouded. "I've no doubt that as soon as we leave this place, as soon as we step foot outside, someone will be upon us, ready to accuse and then to enact justice for Edan's murder."

The picture he painted was all too clear. Brann would lock Collin away—or worse—and I would be left alone and unprotected. I clutched Collin's arms. "What are we to do?"

"We're going to return to the table and books, before it's noticed we aren't there." Collin stayed behind me, as if to put a buffer between me and the body on the other side of the door. A sudden, horrid thought occurred to me when we reached the main room. "The second room," I whispered, too terrified to think of what—who—we might discover there. *Not Finlay. Please not Finlay.*

"I'll look," Collin whispered. "But not now." He led me to the table, where I took my seat with a minimum of chair scraping. Collin moved his hands, indicating that I was to open a book in front of me. I grabbed one from the stack and opened it carefully while Collin leaned around the side, peering through the broken window.

"Still sleeping," he said, his relief visible in the sigh of his chest. He took the seat he had had previously, across from me, opened a book of his own, and leaned his head close to mine. "I don't trust them." His gaze flickered to the window.

"Hugh and Donaid?"

Collin whispered. "We still don't know who helped Malcom try to take you on the way here. And Hugh seemed a bit too interested in hearing about Finlay's whereabouts."

I nodded, having noticed this too. Was it only a couple of hours ago that I'd been upset with Collin for his carelessness? Now I reached across the table and grasped his hand, both regretting our previous arguments and disregarding our agreement to avoid touching one another. In light of the circumstances we'd faced today, I wanted to hold onto him and never let go.

It occurred to me then exactly what he *should* do.

"You must leave while you still can." I squeezed his fingers in earnest. "I'll distract Hugh, and you can sneak away."

"And leave you here?" Collin shook his head adamantly. "Never."

"It's you Brann wants to be rid of. If you're not a threat to him, he won't harm me."

Collin's eyes darkened. "You're naïve and foolish if you believe that. He nearly ordered you killed this morning." Collin leaned even closer over the table. "I'm not going *anywhere* without you."

"I didn't say it would be long. Alistair could help me leave tonight."

"No," Collin said again. "I'll think of something else." Still grasping my hands, he lowered his head so that it appeared he was engaged in earnest prayer. I was, silently at least.

Help us know what to do.

Minutes passed. Another snore sounded from outside, followed by shuffling.

If Hugh still slept it probably wouldn't be for long. We'd been here close to three hours.

Collin leaned his head close to mine again. "I have an idea."

"Yes?"

"Better to bend than to break," Collin said.

"What do you mean?" The glint in his eye frightened me.

"It's going to be all right." He lifted one of the volumes from the table and hefted it in his hand. "We're going to take a leaf from Brann's book."

Chapter Twelve

I pulled the door to Edan's former residence and offices firmly shut, achieving the desired result when Hugh startled awake, jumping to a sitting position rather quickly for a man his size.

Paying him no heed, I made an exaggerated show of brushing dust from my skirts. "Oh," I exclaimed, looking up at the sky. "It is marvelous to be out of that place." Leaning my head back, I breathed in deeply, not at all embellishing my need for fresh air.

"Have you found what you were looking for?" Hugh asked while staring past me at the door, no doubt wondering what had become of Collin.

"No." I moved down the neglected pathway toward him. "But I cannot possibly look at another ledger. Collin will have to finish by himself. My head aches, and it is stuffy and filthy in there. Whoever this record keeper is—" my throat constricted, and I turned away quickly, bringing a hand to my mouth with the premise of coughing—"he is in dire need of someone to keep his house." Edan was in need of only one thing now—a decent burial—which he was not going to get.

"Are there many more ledgers to read? Maybe I should help your husband." Hugh heaved his oversized body from the ground.

"Please don't," I said. "Collin will insist that I return inside as well, if you're not out here with me. I do not believe I could stand another moment in there." That much was truth.

Hugh looked uncertainly toward the door. "All right—I guess."

I smiled my relief. My task was to delay and distract, which was proving difficult, given the current state of my nerves. But Collin had the far worse lot, and it was for him this ruse must be successful.

"Tell me more of your cousin Finlay." I moved farther from the house under the pretext of seeking shade from a nearby tree. "Has he always been a poet?"

"Aye." With a last glance toward the building which—if Collin's idea met with success—shortly would no longer be standing, Hugh joined me beneath the tree. "We descend from a bard. Used to be the lairds employed them for entertainment. But Brann seeks his diversion elsewhere." Hugh's gaze slid down the length of me in a way that sent an unpleasant chill down my spine and made me feel in need of a bath. "My lady would take care not to become such entertainment."

What he hinted at, on top of what I'd just seen, made me ill almost to the point of faintness. I pressed a hand to my stomach and leaned against the tree trunk.

"Are you unwell?" Hugh asked anxiously. "I did not mean to frighten you."

Hadn't he? I couldn't be certain if his words had been a warning or threat. "Aren't *you* unwell?" I stared at him. "How is any Campbell at all comfortable with what is happening here, on this land, the sacred home of our ancestors?" My voice rose to hysteria quickly, more of a reaction than Hugh had likely expected or was called for. It was the thought of what Collin was doing this very minute, and what he might find in the second room, that I found overwhelming. But Hugh must not suspect, so I continued my rant.

"Knives pointed at me and my husband. Families burned out of their homes." *Good men suffering a terrible death for trying to help.* "This isn't the way of things in the Highlands. Not for our clan." I brought a hand to my mouth, barely holding back a sob.

"I didn't mean to upset you so." Hugh took a step closer, then stopped when I flinched.

"You're right to be afraid of everyone. Finlay and the others should have never brought you back. There's nothing good for you here."

I searched Hugh's face, trying to discern his intent. He sounded genuine, yet I dared not trust him. "Collin brought me here to keep a promise he made to my grandfather."

"It will take more than a seer to help us. The clans, none of them, are what they used to be. Even if you stop driving people from the land, you'll find they'll leave anyway, eventually."

"Are you the seer now?" Who knew but that he was, given Finlay's startling revelation a few days ago.

Hugh shook his head. "Don't need to be. It's straw in the wind. Living off the land is no good anymore. The English have taken too much. A man barely has enough, and it is stolen from him. Brann does wrong by the people, but no more than would happen in time."

I shook my head. "You're mistaken. Grandfather wanted us to save our families. How can you not want that too?"

"What a man wants and what he is given do not equate."

That was true enough. I wanted a marriage like Anna's, one that provided security and opportunity, a roof over my head and food on our table. The blessing of children. Or at the least, a lack of danger. The possibility that my husband and I might live beyond the first month we were wed.

I had none of those things.

The scent of smoke drifted toward us, tickling my nose and nettling the back of my throat. It was not uncommon here, with the various fires burning, for everything from heating water for laundry to the fire of the blacksmith's forge. A miniature town existed within the walls of the keep, with both fire and water required to run much of it. Without moving my head, I cast a furtive glance toward the cottage. Was it *that* fire I smelled already? Would the stench of burning human flesh be noticeable?

"I only want to help," I said in a subdued voice, intended to calm our dialogue. For a few seconds I had forgotten that my purpose was to distract Hugh, and to learn as much as I could about him. Ten minutes into our conversation, and I still had no idea where his true loyalties lay.

"You should help yourself, then. Leave this place before harm comes to you." Hugh's face softened, and he clasped his hands together in front of him, as if begging.

A gentle giant? Words of genuine concern? I wished I knew.

"I would like to leave," I said, pushing off the tree trunk. I began retracing my steps toward the castle. The smell was stronger now, and at any minute I expected to see rising smoke. If Hugh saw it too, before the fire had consumed the contents of Edan's house, or at least that room, Collin's plan would not succeed.

Hugh sniffed the smoky air as he followed me. "Twenty shillings says the lads are up to no good again." He drew himself up even taller than he already stood, grabbed at the belt circling his wide waist, and hastened his steps—away from the cottage. "Burned my bog to the ground last week, they did," he muttered with a quick glance at me.

"Bog?" I queried as I ran along beside.

"My privy. Set it afire—and the stench! Not to mention I've no place to set now while . . . Never mind."

I pressed my lips together, holding back a smile.

"They're off their heads if they think I'll not catch them this time. Been setting fires all over the past month. I'll get them at their mischief, and I'll have their hides for it."

"It's more than mischief," Donaid shouted as he joined us, coming from the opposite direction.

How long has he *not been at his post?* I resisted the urge to look back toward Edan's house and counted myself blessed at this good fortune.

"The distillery is on fire." Donaid gestured for us to join him. "Did you not hear the explosion?"

"No." I must have been inside and Hugh asleep when it had happened. No doubt Hugh's snores had drowned out any other sound for him. *Some guards.*

We rounded the corner of the castle to a scene of utter chaos. Men and women with buckets shouted at one another as they ran to and fro. Children and animals seemed to be everywhere and underfoot, and a tower of black smoke billowed from the cluster of buildings in the farthest corner of the courtyard.

"The whole batch finished last night!" Hugh smacked his hoof-sized palm on his forehead. He and Donaid charged off to join the fray. With the threat of losing the distillery, and thereby the clan's source for spirits, clearly the importance of keeping guard over Collin and me had just plummeted.

On shaking legs I backed around the corner and began retracing my steps, sending a silent prayer of gratitude heavenward.

Saved by the memory of a burnt privy and some mischievous lads.

Chapter Thirteen

Though it was early afternoon and many people milled about—most heading for the distillery—I felt uncomfortably aware of my vulnerability as I hurried back toward what had been Edan's dwelling. At the least I was being watched. At most—

What if Brann's strategy all along was to separate Collin and me? What if it was he who lured our guards away?

I arrived at the cottage just as the matching window to the one Collin had broken exploded, sending a spray of glass into the yard.

Smoke poured out behind it, and flames shot up through the roof in the back of the house.

"Collin!" I ran toward the front door and reached it a second before it flung open and he emerged, coughing, sleeve held to his red face.

I threw my arm around his waist to guide him from the house. Heat scorched through my sleeve where it touched his back. We hobbled to the tree Hugh and I had spoken beneath. I paused, quickly assessing that my husband was not on fire.

He attempted to draw in breath with raspy effort as coughs wracked his body. I steered him toward the back entrance we had used this morning. Bridget would know what to do to help him.

We entered the kitchen, surprising only a handful of servants.

"I need water, quickly!" I eased Collin onto a bench as a

young girl jumped to do my bidding and fetched a dipperful from the barrel in the corner. Together we held it up to Collin's mouth, sloshing at least half down the front of his shirt.

We obliged three times more until Collin protested with a shake of his head.

"Upstairs," he managed.

I ordered a bucket of fresh well water to be brought up. Collin leaned on me as we ascended the stairs from the kitchen. His coughing had yet to cease, and his chest rattled with each attempt at breath.

To my immense relief, the hall was empty. I didn't know what might have happened had we run into Brann with Collin barely able to breathe, let alone defend either of us. The trip up the stairs to the second floor seemed to take forever, as I split my attention between assisting Collin and keeping a wary eye on the front doors below.

But no one entered, and I could only suppose that Brann was as concerned with the potential loss of the distillery as Donaid and Hugh had been.

Collin dug in his pocket for the key to our room. After a few attempts I forced it to turn and we were safe inside. Collin collapsed in a chair as the requested bucket of water arrived. I sent the serving girl in search of Bridget and then secured the bar.

Collin drained two cupfuls of water, and at last his coughing ceased. He leaned his head back, eyes closed, and worked at breathing normally.

I had a dozen questions but forbade myself from asking them yet. He was safe, and that was what mattered. He was safe, and Edan's body entombed in the burning pyre that had been his house.

With Collin out of immediate danger, I went to the window, peering down on the chaos below. Brann was at the forefront, seated on a horse and barking orders out to those scurrying about. The main fire of the distillery appeared to have been put out, but water was still being poured on it, and steam billowed from what had been the roof of the structure.

How long would it be before the fire Collin set was noticed?

Had it really been only mischievous lads who had set the first, and would they be blamed for ours as well? Or was something else afoot? Perhaps someone also trying to undermine Brann. Whoever it was, I owed them a debt of gratitude.

"Katie." Collin held his hand out, and I hurried to his side. His face, not so red now, was streaked with ash and soot. The shirt that had been crisp and white this morning was soiled now, burnt through in places.

"*Tsk,*" I teased, touching one of the holes. "It appears that I cannot keep you clean *or* well dressed."

"*Hmpf.*" From beneath his shirt Collin withdrew a packet of equally dirty papers—one of the copies of the deed entitling me to this castle—tossed them on the table, then pulled me onto his lap and held me tight, his face buried in the side of my hair. "Finlay was not in the other room. No one was."

"Thank heavens." I bent my head to his.

"He'll make it to Edinburg," Collin said. "And he has the other copy. I believe you're right and we've heaven's help."

"We must," I said. "Or someone else's, at least." I proceeded to tell him of the fire at the distillery.

Collin agreed that it had been fortuitous timing, especially considering his plan had taken him longer than he'd thought.

I listened—not because I particularly wished to hear it, but because I sensed he needed to tell me—as Collin described how he had cut a hole in the mattress and fitted Edan's body inside. He'd been careful, he said, to remove the rope from the rafter and all the papers from the floor. After dousing the bed with a bottle of whisky found in a cupboard, Collin lit the bed on fire and left the room, closing the door behind him.

"How fortunate," I said, in my best attempt at Scottish brogue and to keep from reverting to the state of hysteria I'd been in when we'd discovered the body. "That nary a house is to be found in all of Scotland without at least one bottle of whisky within its walls."

"There was only the one," Collin said. "So it took me longer than I thought to set the place ablaze. I had to keep returning to the room, carrying a book or chair leg or somewhat to catch that afire and then place it. It was on my last attempt—setting the books on the table to burn—that the smoke overcame me. The pile in the grate was blazing by then, but I'd shut up the chimney to keep the smoke in as long as possible. I didn't realize how bad it had become until it almost had me."

"I don't like the sound of that at all." I looped my arms around the back of Collin's neck and sought his eyes. "We have been twice blessed today, but we cannot expect such fortune to continue. Let's leave this place before it is too late."

"Aye." Collin turned his face to my arm and pressed a kiss there. "It will have to wait until tonight. We'll have to appear at hall and tell our tale of the fire someone started while I was yet inside working—and how it almost killed me."

"Quite a believable tale, given Brann's history. It was very clever of you." I kissed the top of Collin's sooty nose. "Would you like me to order water brought up for a bath?"

"Not yet," Collin said. "I want everyone at dinner to see me like this. It will strengthen my story."

"You should rest at least. I expect Bridget will be bringing up some herbs or other concoction for you shortly, and then I want you to lie in that bed and get your strength back." I attempted to rise from Collin's lap, but he kept his arms firmly around my waist.

"There's still the other matter to discuss."

"Yes." I sighed, conceding defeat already. Given the choice between Collin remaining here and in danger or my having to stay with Mhairi and her family while he dealt with Ian, I had to choose the latter. No matter how much it struck a spear of jealousy deep inside of me.

"I'll not bring you with me to see Ian. And there's only the one place I'll feel you are safe." Collin's rasping voice and labored breathing gave me little option but to agree.

"I'll go. I'll stay there," I agreed coolly. That didn't mean I had to like it.

Chapter Fourteen

ir. I cannot breathe. I could not see. Arms flailing helplessly in front of me, I stumbled around the small room, banging my shins on a chair and low table before I found the wood frame of a door set into the wall. My hands dropped lower, found the latch, and pulled. Air, still stale with smoke, but fresher than that I'd been confined in, poured into the space, and I gulped at it as I ran blindly.

Wait. Come back. Something was drawing me in, bidding me to stay in the burning cottage just a little longer. I hesitated. There was something I was supposed to learn, but I could see nothing, and to turn back would mean certain death. I fled.

Pitch black surrounded me as I bolted upright in bed, gasping, feeling suffocated by the tendrils of smoke circling my head.

"What is it?" Collin jumped up from his place on the floor. "What's wrong?" The bed creaked beneath his weight as he sat beside me.

Instead of answering I sucked in a mouthful of air and realized it was not smoky at all. My heart pounded as my eyes drank in the shapes in the shadowed room. *I'm not burning. I'm not blind.*

"Are you all right, Katie?" He found my hands and held them. "Was it a nightmare?"

"Yes. I think so."

Collin released me and leaned over to the bedside table

and the candle there. When he had it lit, I saw that all was as it should be. We were safely ensconced in my mother's old room, a barred door and presumably two guards between us and immediate danger.

"Better?" He brushed the hair back from my face with one hand and rubbed at his bleary eyes with another.

"You've done this before," I said.

A corner of his mouth lifted. "Aye. You were given to nightmares often as a lass." Collin stood and stretched then surprised me when he peeled the quilt back from the bed. "The difference is that now I can do something about it other than to pat your head and send you back to bed alone." He slid between the sheets beside me and pulled me down into his arms. "We'll not do anything but sleep, but I hope to be a comfort to you in that at least. Judging by the moon, we've an hour or so more before we need to leave."

"I think I shall have nightmares more often," I teased as I snuggled up against him. Collin's arm wrapped around me, and his hand came to rest over my stomach.

Someday. One day not too terribly far off, I hoped, we would lie together like this often. We would have only normal concerns then—of caring for our home and family. Not the weight of so many others and the constant threat to our lives. There would be no more nightmares. Only dreams fulfilled.

I closed my eyes, not particularly eager for sleep now that my husband was beside me. This was what I had wanted from him, the closeness I had missed since our arrival on Campbell lands. If I had only an hour, I wanted to savor every minute.

There was no smoke and no fire. We were safe. No one was burning.

Here.

But elsewhere—

"Liusaidh!" I threw back the covers as the details of my nightmare returned. "Brann is going to set her house on fire. I've seen it." I'd lived it, as if I had *been* Liusaidh, stumbling around in that smoke-filled room.

"Are you certain?" Collin's hand on my arm stopped me.

"Yes," I cried, twisting away from him, as eager to be gone from the bed as I had been to remain in it with him a moment earlier. "It wasn't a nightmare, but a vision."

I jumped up and ran to my mother's trunk. "Brann has learned we stayed there our first night back. He is furious about what happened at Edan's, that you foiled his plan. This is his revenge. I see it, Collin. Just as I saw him that day at the moor."

"All right." Collin had both boots on and was at the door by the time I'd jammed my feet into slippers and thrown a cloak over my nightrail.

"You should stay here," he said.

I shook my head and pushed past him into the hall. "We'll go together. I promise not to slow you down."

"A bit early yet, isn't it?" Alistair asked in a whisper as we left our room.

"Katie's had a vision." Collin took my hand as we headed toward the stairs. "Brann is going after Liusaidh."

"He's going to set fire to her house," I said.

"We'll come too," Quinn added from the other side of the doorway.

Together we thumped down the main staircase, not caring if anyone heard. Brann and those working with him had all gone to start the fire. No one here would bother us.

The waning moon provided little light as we left the hall and ran across the courtyard. While Collin and Quinn retrieved the horses, I shivered beneath my cloak and studied the sky. It must be nearing midnight. We had retired to our room early, giving the excuse that Collin was still recovering from his ordeal at Edan's house.

That much was true, though we had used the time to prepare for taking our leave in the middle of the night. We had planned to leave a little later than this, when Collin felt all but a few outside guards would be asleep. And now here we were, rushing toward yet another fire. *Please let us be in time.*

Quinn and Collin returned. Collin helped me up behind him, and we were off, racing toward the front gates which were, not surprisingly, open. The same old man who had called a warning to us upon our arrival stepped out from behind the wall as we thundered past. He waved and called to us as before, but his words were lost beneath the sound of hoof beats across the wooden bridge.

Quinn and Alistair edged ahead. We caught the road and started down it without interruption. It had taken the better part of an hour from Liusaidh's doorstep to the castle gates the morning we arrived. We were moving much faster now. I hoped it would be enough.

I bent my head against Collin's back and closed my eyes as the minutes passed, trying to picture her tiny home, but it wouldn't appear, almost as if it was already gone.

Why Luisaidh? I thought with anguish.

"Look." Still holding the reins, Collin inclined his head toward a plume of dark smoke rising in the distance.

"Oh no." My chest constricted, and I remembered the panic of my dream. "Wake up, Liusaidh. Wake up," I begged. Either way, Brann would have her. I saw it clearly now, saw her burning home, and saw that she had known this was to happen. Grandfather had told her as much when he'd brought her my mother's trunk years ago.

God speed, she and Edan had said to one another. They'd understood. They had each been told what helping me would cost, yet they had done it anyway.

I felt suddenly, violently ill. "Stop, Collin. We're too late." The back of my throat burned. *Liusaidh, dead. Because of me.* I placed my hands on Collin's arms. "Please. We must go back."

He didn't slow our pace. "We might be in time. Brann might have set fire to her shed first. Or she might not be home—"

"She's dead." I tugged on Collin's arms again. "Turn around. Please," I begged. "Brann has a bigger target here. He knew we would come."

Collin slowed the horse at this. "Has he an extra sense as well?"

I shook my head. "He *guessed* that we would come," I clarified. "He hoped for it, and again we have fallen neatly into his trap."

"Not yet, we haven't." Collin pulled hard to the left and turned us around just as the distant flames of Liusaidh's burning croft came into view. The orange glow reached skyward, stretching beyond the thatched roof. A cluster of men on horseback surrounded the house from a distance. *In case she had tried to get out.*

"Redcoats," Collin muttered. We broke into a gallop, heading back in the direction we had come.

"How can you tell from so far away and in the dark?"

"A particular talent of mine." Collin dug in his heels, urging Ian's horse to go faster. "I can spot one five furlongs away."

Alistair and Quinn were too far ahead for us to call back, but I had no time to worry for them.

I dared a look over my shoulder and saw that the circle had disbanded and appeared to be moving as one body toward us. I thought we could outride them. But I couldn't be sure.

"Collin, stop. Let me off. I'll hide, and you can ride faster. Get back to the castle, and I'll wait in the woods until you are able to get away again."

"Stop trying to have me leave you." Collin leaned forward, practically flattening himself over Ian's horse. I did the same. "I'll not do it, so quit asking."

Behind us I heard shouting and imagined that I felt the ground tremble as they gave chase. "Why are there soldiers here?"

"I don't know."

I stopped asking questions and began praying instead. And thinking. The castle was the safest place for us, wasn't it? If we darted off to a path in the woods, how easily could we be tracked? I didn't look behind to see how close the others were. The castle towers were visible in the distance above the treetops. It would be at least another fifteen minutes before we reached the gate. *Forever.* And Ian's horse seemed to be slowing. He'd carried us swiftly going out already, with no relief before we'd turned back. The Redcoats were rested from waiting for us.

As we rode I silently cursed my vision, my *gift.* It was worthless. Dangerous. I had been too late to help Liusaidh and had only put our lives in danger. I wanted nothing more to do with it.

"Almost there," Collin said.

I lifted my head just enough to see the gate was still open. Another quick glance behind, and I saw that the soldiers were a fair distance behind.

"We should be able to close the gates before they reach us," Collin said.

Burying my head again, I shut my eyes and clung to him, waiting to feel the change when we left the packed dirt to cross the weathered wood of the bridge.

"I'm going to dismount as soon as we pass through," Collin said. "Ride straight to the front doors. Leave the horse, go to the room, and lock yourself in."

"You can't secure the gate yourself," I argued, having no intention of leaving him. It had to take at least two grown men to move each of the two immense panels. And there was the matter of securing the doors once they were closed.

"I'll find help," Collin said. We hit the bridge at full speed, not slowing until we were within the wall's protection. He slid quickly from Ian's horse and thrust the reins at me.

"Not so fast." Brann emerged from the shadows on my other side, tugging them from my hand.

"You!" I kicked at his chest, and he grabbed my foot.

"Surprised to see me?" An evil grin split his face as he grasped my leg, pulling me toward him.

Behind me Collin shouted. I looked back to see three soldiers surrounding him. Brann yanked me from the horse, and I fell to the ground, legs spread painfully.

"What do you mean by this?" Ignoring the throbbing in my knee, I attempted to stand.

Brann's fingers tightened over my arm, biting into the skin as he jerked me to my feet. "What did the MacDonald mean by showing up here with an illegal weapon?" Brann marched me toward Collin and the soldiers—more Redcoats.

"He was holding it for me," I said loud enough that the soldier who had just removed Collin's pistol might hear. "It was a gift from my father before I left England. English citizens are still allowed arms, are they not?" I directed my question to the same soldier.

He gave me a look filled with disdain. "You're not even strong enough to lift this, let alone shoot it."

"You are mistaken, and if you will hand it to me, I will gladly prove it."

He laughed. "You take me for a fool."

"She's not lying." Collin spoke softly, in a tone I guessed was meant to diffuse the situation. "She shot my brother."

Now it was Brann who chuckled. He bent close, his hot, foul breath in my ear. "Is that true?"

"Yes." *Would that you were next.* If that opportunity was ever granted to me, I would make certain to aim better.

"Doesn't matter whose it was. It's mine now." The soldier tucked the pistol in the belt at his waist. "And as it was found in possession of a Scot, we'll be taking him."

"Where?" My eyes met Collin's. His gaze revealed nothing. *Act as if you do not care,* I imagined him saying.

I strained against Brann's hold and asked again. "*Where* are you taking him?"

"He'll have a short stay at prison. Then onto the Colonies with that lot." The soldier inclined his head toward the still-open gate, outside of which a line of downtrodden men, women, and children were being herded by a group of soldiers on horseback. The old man who'd tried to call out a warning to us was among them.

My worry for Collin expanded to concern for these people. A woman struggled along with a babe in her arms and a tiny child clinging to her hand. A man who had only one leg limped forward on a crutch. A woman about my age walked beside him and caught my eye as she passed. I read the panic in her gaze and felt her worry for the man—her father?

"What have *they* done?" I asked.

"They've done *nothing,*" Brann said. "Absolutely nothing. They turn no profit on the land allotted them, so they are being sent to work on plantations in the Colonies."

How? The very old, very young, or infirm seemed the poorest candidates for laborers in the Colonies or any place else. *They'll never make it.*

Brann knew that, as did the soldiers. And they didn't care.

"A nice purse for you in the bargain. This one, at least, will fetch a good price." One of the soldiers tossed a pouch at Brann. I lunged and caught it before he could, then turned it upside down.

"Give that—"

"You're despicable." Coins clattered to the ground as I shook the bag, flinging it to and fro out of Brann's reach. "You cannot sell these people. You don't own them."

"Who's going to stop me?" Brann shoved me to the ground. "You? Your husband? Pick those up." He pushed my head down, and I felt his knee in my back.

"Collin is not a Campbell, and that pistol is mine. You cannot ship him off like some—slave." The word tasted bitter. I pushed back against the weight of Brann's hand to plead with the English soldier. "Please. Take me as well."

He did not answer at once but looked over me at Brann, even as my eyes sought Collin's, still impassive, though I could see his mind was in turmoil—with worry for me. The silent pause continued, and for a second I allowed myself hope. *If we can but remain together.*

"Having the woman along might be just the thing to get this one to stay in line." The soldier nudged Collin with the butt of his musket.

"She stays here," Brann said. "With me."

"Very well." The Redcoat faced Collin. "You are hereby charged with having violated the Act of Proscription enacted the first of August 1746, which states that no Highlander may have in his custody, use, or bear a broad sword or target, poignard, whinger, dirk, or side pistol, or any other warlike weapon."

"It's for my defense," I shouted. "He's done nothing wrong. Almost every man in that castle carries a dirk."

Brann grabbed a fistful of my hair and pulled. Tears stung my eyes as my head jerked back. His other hand pressed my face to his leg. "Shut up," he hissed.

Collin lunged between the two soldiers and landed a punch to Brann's jaw before they restrained him.

"She'll pay for that," Brann said, still holding tight to my hair.

I winced but did not cry out.

"Let her go, or I swear I'll come back and kill you—even if it means returning from the grave." Collin's hands were pulled roughly behind him.

"Get in line," Brann said menacingly. "Katherine's mother already threatened the same. Yet I don't see her returned from the dead to save her daughter." He threw his head back. "No lightning strikes either." His dark laughter rang across the yard.

Tears spilled down my cheeks as two of the soldiers worked together to bind Collin with rope. *Don't hurt him.* I saw that they would. Just as Collin must know the same was true for me. There was no one to protect me from Brann. But I couldn't care about that right now and would have willingly done his bidding would they but free Collin.

I opened my mouth to say one last time that I loved him, but a brief shake of his head stopped me.

Don't give him more power. Whether my thought or Collin's, it was true. I was completely at Brann's mercy, and the more he thought he could hurt me, the more he would.

The soldier who had been speaking earlier cleared his throat. "You are hereby sentenced to be transported to one of his Majesty's plantations beyond the sea, there to remain for the space of fourteen years in servitude."

Fourteen years. We had not even had half as many weeks together. If by some miracle we were we both to survive, how were we to find one another again after so long a time? *Oh, Collin.*

The soldiers marched him through the gate to join the others being taken.

"Pick up those coins." Brann released my hair and thrust me forward. His boot on my back forced me to the ground. I gathered a handful of the gold, clutched it in my fist for a second, then flung my arm wide, sending coins spinning across the yard. Brann flipped me over and brought his boot down hard on my arm.

The sound of bone snapping coincided with my screams. His boot lifted again, hovered over me a second as we made eye contact, then struck my chest so hard the breath left my lungs.

Chapter Fifteen

The metal slot at the bottom of the door swung open, and in the sliver of light a tray pushed inside.

"Eat," a gruff voice ordered.

The flap swung shut, and I sat motionless, counting its movement back and forth, watching the slim band of golden yellow grow smaller and smaller on the floor until it was gone. Anything to distract me from the pain.

Behind me the rats came, scurrying over my legs and cloak in their haste toward the food I could not reach because it hurt too much to move. My stomach complained pitifully, with a desperate, gnawing hunger. I told myself I didn't care. If starving brought a quicker end to my suffering, I would be grateful.

Cradling my broken arm to my chest, I sat motionless as I listened to the rats enjoying their feast. *God is merciful* trailed through my mind continually. A sort of prayer as I remembered this scripture and begged for it to be true. *Mercy for Collin. Let him be spared.* And the others with him. I tried to have faith, but it was impossible to believe that many of them would survive long enough to be sold in the Colonies.

An odd squealing began from the rats, who had been my companions since I'd been thrown into the pitch-black cell. I'd fought them off at first, pushing them away and kicking whenever I felt one near. But the shooting pain caused by even the slightest movement soon overrode my fear and repulsion.

Eventually, I had consigned myself to the rats' presence

and continued attempts at sampling whatever parts of me were exposed. Before my arm had become too swollen to move at all, I had curled my legs beneath me and wrapped as tight as possible in my cloak to ward off their attacks.

I listened intently now at the frenzied noises coming from the crowd gathered at my plate. I couldn't see them, with the flap closed and the guard and his light moved on, but I imagined the rats in a tight circle surrounding the tin. Were they fighting over its contents?

My stomach roiled again, a phenomenon I found strange, considering its emptiness. Why should I feel nauseated when there was nothing within me to upset? I imagined what food might be on the plate. Oats? A bit of stale bread? A bowl of soup? I wouldn't have cared and would have gladly fought off the rats for my portion, if only I could.

The strange noises—almost shrieking, if that was possible from a rat—continued perhaps a minute more, then began to die off until total silence filled the cell. Puzzled, I listened harder for the sounds of eating or sleeping—something. They'd been rather raucous little pests since my arrival, squeaking, hissing and chattering, chomping and grinding their teeth.

This sudden, absolute silence felt unnerving. *Unnatural.*

I waited for their usual activity to resume and rested my head against the cold stone, eyes closed, arm and ribs throbbing, every breath agony.

Collin. I crawled into the deepest recesses of my mind, the place I still treasured, the only thing about me unharmed. As I had done countless times since my imprisonment, I recalled every minute we had shared over the few weeks of our marriage. From his first appearance in the foyer of my home to his happy declaration, just before he'd curled up beside me, that he was now able to do something about my nightmares.

If only we had stayed there, safe in the cocoon of our bed. Would the night have turned out any differently? Would we have made our escape later or been captured as we tried to leave?

I would never find out, but knew only that my foolish vision had a terrible cost. We were apart, possibly forever. I'd had ample time to revisit that night in my mind and recognized the critical error I had made in leaving my dream too soon. Someone had beckoned me back to that burning room, and I had refused to go. I had sensed there was something else, some important information I needed to know. But I had let my fear overcome me and had not listened.

And now the cost might be one or both of our lives. If I did survive, I would never forgive myself.

A drop of water landed on top of my head, then trickled down my forehead and nose. Anticipating that others would follow, I tilted my head back and opened my mouth. The water dripped from the kitchens above at certain times each day and was the only nourishment I'd had in all the time I had been here, however long that was. At least my parched throat knew some relief.

Hunger was another matter. The tray brought a while ago was the first I'd been offered in what I guessed to be days since I'd been down here. How long would it be before there was another? Would I even be alive then? *I must be.* Death tempted me every minute. I would have given much to leave the pain and cold and fear behind. But that would be leaving Collin. I had to survive for him.

More time passed. Ten minutes perhaps, or maybe thirty. Still the rats did not stir.

Are they dead? A chill swept through me, and I shivered, disrupting my anchor against additional pain. My arm was almost too much to bear; every breath I drew was agony. I welcomed the dark, if temporary, oblivion that had claimed me several times already. But first, I had to know if my inability to reach the plate of food had just saved me from being poisoned.

Slowly I unfolded my numb legs from beneath me. My movements were stiff and clumsy, followed by the feeling of a thousand needles poking my skin. Using my feet and legs, I painstakingly dragged the tin toward me. Still there was no movement or noise from the cell's former rodent population.

In increments I drew my knees up, until the plate was close enough for me to touch. I hesitated. Touching the rats with my slippered feet was one thing, but voluntarily reaching for them with my bare hand—

I have to know.

I drew out my movement, measured to cause as little pain as possible. If I moved too fast or it became too intense I would faint again.

At last my fingers brushed the coarse fur. It was cold, the body stiff as I picked it up. Bile rose in my stomach, and it was all I could do not to drop the creature. I set it down and ran my fingers blindly around the rim of the plate, over more rats, all of them dead. *Poisoned.*

The Lord is merciful. My heart raced at the realization of such a close brush with death and that I had been spared. For all my pain, for all I might have wished for death in my worst moments, it was not what I wanted.

How long before the guard returns? He would be expecting a dead body. Or would he even come at all? Would they just leave me down here forever?

I forced back the panic of that thought and tried to focus on what I should do. Brann had intended to poison me. The rats had saved me. He didn't know that. What if I could convince him that I ate the poison and was not killed?

He could try a second time, or simply leave me here to starve. He might use a more certain method to end my life.

Any of those were possible, though I doubted the latter. Brann had been frightened of me, or of killing me outright at least. *What exactly had my mother told him before she died?*

He'd had ample opportunity since my return and had not taken advantage of it. Poisoning was certainly a coward's way. If he believed his effort had failed, that I was not so easily done away with, might that not disturb him more? He had called me a witch, so what if I were to become one?

I reached for the rats again, grimacing with every move. *Stay awake,* I ordered myself, sharply. When the guard returned, he must not see the creatures. But where was I to put them? I could not move from my position on the floor. Any attempt, and I would pass out. With the foul rodent in my grip, I put my good hand behind me and shoved the body in the crevice of the wall where it met the floor. It took some maneuvering, but it was all I could think to do.

Four of the creatures fit there. The others I threw, one at a time, to the far corners of the room, hoping the guard wouldn't linger long enough to note that they were all dead.

The entire process took quite some time and left me with a cold sweat upon my head and pain thrumming in my chest and arm. I leaned back to receive a few drops more of the precious water when the sound of voices and feet disrupted the silence.

Using the last of my strength, I lifted the plate to my lap and waited.

Chapter Sixteen

The steps grew closer. I savored a last drop of water, then lowered my head so as to be facing the door when it opened.

"It's a dreich day. Especially down here." A man's voice echoed against the stone walls and carried to my cell. "What's the laird want us to do with her body?"

"Doesna care. Doesna even want to see it," a second, unfamiliar, voice replied.

"Seems a waste of a perfectly good lass," the first man said. "What harm did Brann think she could do with her MacDonald husband gone?"

"You'd be surprised," his companion said. "According to Brann, her mother was a witch." He hissed the word as if it were distasteful.

I'll show you a witch. Instead of being fearful of the men and what they might do, I anticipated the moment of our confrontation and what *I* would do. I hadn't much on my side, except the knowledge of Brann's fear.

Perhaps my mother really was a ghost, and he had seen her. If so, I wished she would visit me. I could use company other than the rats.

I'd been right in believing that Brann's earlier expressions had betrayed him. He'd kicked and stomped and beaten me out in the courtyard, but only to the point of great pain, not death. I'd worried he'd spared my life because he intended to use me—after I was broken.

Since being left down here this thought had warred with my instinct and will to survive for Collin. *Better I am dead than at Brann's mercy.* What might he wish to use my sight for? To know where other clans were placed and what their strengths and weaknesses were, so he might invade? Would he want to know when the English patrols frequenting the area would visit the Campbell keep—so he might assure all appeared as it should?

He would be disappointed in all of that, my sight being limited as it was. Perhaps he had realized this when Collin and I had walked neatly into his trap. Maybe that was why he

had tried to kill me. Not with his own hands, but a coward's way. His men had brought me down here. And now they'd been sent to retrieve what was left of me as well.

It was one thing to inflict cruelty in public, but quite another to be alone with me—if I was a witch—particularly in a place so dark and frightening as this. I could only hope his wariness would keep him far away for some time to come. Alone in a dank, musty cell was far better than with Brann anywhere else. My surviving his attempt to end my life might work in my favor.

Or, if I was wrong, it might not.

The key turned in the lock and the door swung open, its hinges whining terribly. The first man ducked his head and stepped inside the low cell. His companion followed, swinging a lantern.

"Hello." I squinted against the light and held my arm protectively as the men jumped back, the latter hitting his head on the low doorframe.

"What?" The first grabbed the lantern from his companion and held it up to me. "I thought you said she'd been poisoned."

The second muttered in Gaelic as he rubbed the back of his head. "She was. I saw it prepared. This is impossible." He crossed himself.

The first hit him in the arm. "Careful. If she is a witch, you've just marked yourself."

I was no more a witch than he was supposed to be Catholic. But I had learned that all at the Campbell keep was not as it seemed.

"What are we to do now?" the man with the lantern asked. His eyes were large and frightened. "I don't want to be the one to tell the laird."

"Then don't." The second, still rubbing the top of his head where it had struck the doorframe, stepped closer. He squatted in front of me and reached a tentative hand out. I flinched, anticipating the pain even the slightest touch would bring.

"She's hurt. Badly." He looked to his companion.

"So?"

"So she's Liam Campbell's granddaughter. We can't just leave her here." His words were concerned. He leaned toward me. "You're not a witch, are ye?" he asked kindly.

"No." Tears brimmed and spilled over. There was compassion in his expression. *The Lord is merciful.*

"I've a better idea than telling the laird." Looking at me, he asked, "Could you pretend to be dead, you think?"

I nodded. If they tried to move me the pain would be so great I would lose consciousness again.

"And just where do you propose to take her?" the first whispered harshly.

A smile curved my rescuer's mouth. "Somewhere the laird will never dare to look."

Heaven was a strange mixture of comfort and excruciating pain. My head rested on a soft pillow, and warm blankets covered me. But that was where the niceties ended. My stomach coiled in constant agony. I struggled for breath beneath ribs that felt crushed, and my arm throbbed and burned as if it was being wrenched in a medieval torture device.

I opened my eyes to ensure that wasn't actually the case and discovered that I was in my mother's old room. Four others were here with me as well, three women and one man. *No Collin.*

Light hurt too, so I squeezed my eyes shut against it, hating that I was powerless to stop the pain or the tears sliding down either side of my face.

A door opened, and footsteps padded almost silently across the floor.

"A fair blessing," a woman's voice whispered softly. "Gwen's bairn is on its way, and she's been tucked up in bed. Brann heard me send for the midwife, and he thinks I've come up to be with Gwen. We should be able to mask Katherine's screams. Anyone below will think it's the birthing, though that'll be hours yet."

"Good, good," another voice murmured. "Let's give her a bit more of the laudanum just the same."

I opened my eyes as a spoon was brought to my mouth. Bridget leaned over me, eyes crinkled with a look of deepest concern.

"Awake now, are you? Well, you'll soon wish otherwise. The healer says we must set that arm afore it's no good to you ever again."

Time rushed before my limited vision—the nightmare, the soldiers, Collin taken, Brann's cruelty, my prison. I tried lifting my head to look at my arm but hadn't the strength. Probably better, given how terribly it hurt.

I trembled at the thought of anyone touching it at all, let alone trying to rearrange the bones to set them correctly.

"Don't," I begged.

In response Bridget pulled down on my chin, opened my mouth, and forced some of the bitter liquid in. "Swallow it now. There's a good lass." She left my side, walked across the room, nearly silent in her movement again, then returned.

"Here." She placed something in my good hand and curled my fist around it. "That's one of your wee brushes. And you've paints over there just waiting to be used as well. But your arm must be mended first." Her tone might have been matter of fact, but her eyes were sympathetic. "I'll stay right here beside the whole time."

The other two women came forward. The man at the back of the room hovered near the door, twisting a hat in his hands. His face seemed familiar, and after a moment I recognized him as the one who had carried me from below the castle.

He looked over at me, and I caught his eye and attempted a smile. *Thank you.* My tongue felt too heavy to speak.

Bridget pulled up a stool near the head of the bed and settled on it. "Katherine, this is Mary Campbell—Alistair's wife and a rare fine healer and bone setter. You won't find better in Edinburg itself. She and her daughter are here to help you."

I understood that, but my heart pounded anyway. I'd never been so frightened, had never felt so vulnerable. Even out in the yard beneath Brann's attack I had been able to move at first, to fight back and attempt to defend myself. But now the pain was too great, and the medicine traveling through my body only added to the feeling of helplessness.

Mary rolled up her sleeves and took her position on one side of the bed while her daughter moved to the other. "I'll not lie," she said briskly. "This is going to hurt like the devil. We've to place the bone correctly and stretch the muscle around it." Looking up at Bridget, she added, "Be ready to hold her, though I doubt she'll stay with us long."

"Ready?" she asked, exchanging a look with her daughter. The young woman nodded, and two sets of hands descended.

I screamed until, blissfully, I could no longer feel.

Chapter Seventeen

"I'm sorry for the dark. We dare not use any candles. Even a little light coming under the door might seem suspicious." My companion, rescuer, and self-appointed protector—Earnan, I had since learned—stood stoically near the door for the long night ahead.

"I don't mind." After the gloom I'd endured belowstairs, the room did not seem very dark at all, with moonlight seeping through the louvered window.

"I should have brought you elsewhere. Being right under Brann's nose was perhaps not the wisest." Earnan studied the ground, as he tended to when he was embarrassed.

It was endearing, and had I been well enough, I would have given him a kiss on the cheek, as I had to Finlay before his departure. Though perhaps that would not have been the best idea, given that Earnan appeared much closer to my own age and possibly wont to mistake my gratitude for something else entirely.

"Why *did* you do bring me here?" My voice was returning in increments, my ability to speak short sentences coinciding with being able to swallow something other than broth or Bridget's tea. "Why take such a risk?"

"If we'd left the castle, someone might have seen you. That, and I didn't know if you could make it beyond these walls. When you fainted I thought—"

I was dead. I hadn't been far off.

"I owe you my life," I said gratefully.

Earnan shrugged and stared at the floor again. "It was fortunate Brann sent us to collect you in the middle of the night. Alistair and many others were already upset that he was holding you prisoner, so he did not want it widely known that you were dead."

"Which made it convenient for you to bring me here."

"Aye." Earnan stepped away from the door and nearer to the empty fireplace.

I wondered if he was cold. With the quilts piled on top of me I didn't miss the fire but felt guilty that those attending me might not be so warm, particularly in the chill of night.

"It was a good choice for other reasons too," he said. "Everyone knows Brann won't come into this room."

"I didn't know that."

"I don't suppose you would," Earnan said. "Not having lived here long. Many have heard the noises and seen the light coming from this room—when it had been both locked and unoccupied for months and then years."

"Did no one ever bother to see who or what was in here?" Not everyone in the Highlands believed in ghosts, did they?

"Liam claimed it was his daughter—your mother," Earnan added. "Said she was prowling the room, searching for you."

"And when my grandfather died, did this continue?"

"Aye. Right up until the time you came home."

I recalled the maids' reluctance to enter this room that first night Collin and I had stayed here. "If Brann believes it haunted, maybe we *should* have a lamp or two lit in here." Why would my mother not resume her search, if once more I was absent from this chamber?

Earnan shook his head. "I wouldn't want to chance it, m'lady."

He had already chanced so much. I felt contrite instantly. "I am sorry to suggest it, to worry you. I promise not to light a single candle." Not that I could, with my movement so severely limited. "I'll not scream anymore either."

Earnan's face split in a grin. "A good thing. And as well that Gwen's bairn was so large. When the midwife brought him down, no one questioned all the wailing they'd heard up here."

I might have laughed, had the effort of breathing and normal speech not already been pushing my tolerance for pain.

"Does it hurt much still?" Earnan nodded to my arm, encased in a wood splint and bandaged tightly.

"Not as much as it did." I didn't know anything about bone setting, but Mary Campbell seemed to have been very thorough in her work. My arm was gradually returning to its normal size and lay straight. It still throbbed, but the piercing pain of bone misplaced was gone. I'd even been able to wiggle my fingers a time or two.

My ribs were another matter, and breathing continued to be toe-curling labor. The less I moved, the better. Earnan was wise to be so cautious with light, noise, and anything else that might give us away. It would likely be many more weeks of hiding under Brann's nose before I would be well enough to leave this bed.

Weeks. I blinked back tears as I stared at the ceiling. Weeks before I might be well enough to make my escape from this place and begin the search for Collin. By then he might already be on a ship bound for the Colonies—or worse.

I tried not to think of that, of him and what he might be suffering right now. *Be grateful,* I reminded myself. *Patient.* It was nothing short of a miracle that I was alive. And if I had been granted such, why should Collin not be as well?

"I don't want any this morning." I turned my head from Bridget and her ever-present tea.

"It rests the body, and that will get you well sooner."

"Trying to be rid of me, are you?" I kept my face averted, not willing to give in this morning. Alistair was supposed to attempt a visit today, and if he chanced to be successful in finding a way up here without notice, I did not wish to be asleep.

"It's not that." Bridget clucked her tongue but at last removed the spoon and cup from my vision. "There's matters downstairs is all, and no sense in causing you worry."

"What matters?" My chest tightened, anxiety that we had been discovered adding to my already great discomfort.

"Brann's found himself in a spot of trouble is all." Bridget patted my good arm. "I've brought a book for you to read, if you'd like." She withdrew a slender volume from her apron pocket.

"Tell me." I turned my head to look at her. "What sort of trouble?"

"The sort he deserves," she muttered crossly.

I waited a minute, watching her inner dilemma as she worried her lip and wrung her hands. Bridget was not the sort to keep secrets from me. I had already learned from her, in the days following my nighttime conversation with Earnan, that it was she who had been responsible for the haunting of my room. It had been my grandfather's idea, and she had readily complied, trading off with him a time or two when he was still alive, so that no one would suspect either of them.

"It's not only Brann's trouble," she said suddenly, searching my face with a strange sort of plea. "Others may be harmed because of him. But you could—" She broke off suddenly and took up the cup again. "You need rest. Drink this."

At great expense to my pain level, I lifted my uninjured hand and pushed hers away. "I could what?"

"Nothing. It would only bring you harm." She moved away from the bed and went to stand at the window.

"How much worse can it be than what I've been through?"

"You tell me." Bridget's face was stony as she stared out the window. "The MacDonalds have surrounded the keep. Ian MacDonald says he'll attack tonight unless Brann sends you to meet him."

Chapter Eighteen

"A fine kettle, this," Mary Campbell, a formidable woman herself, squared off with Bridget, blocking my way to the door.

"I am *fine,*" I insisted, taking two steps to prove it. Thankfully, nothing was wrong with my legs. The sling Bridget had fastened from one of Collin's shirts held my arm in place nicely, so it was only the stabbing pain from my ribs that made me see spots with every move.

"If you couldn't keep your mouth shut, you oughtn't have tended her today." Mary shook a finger at Bridget, then swung around, pointing the appendage at me. "Back to bed, lass. You've no reason to be up."

"I've every reason." My gaze swung from Mary and Bridget to Earnan, standing tense at the window. "You cannot expect that I'll lie abed and let others be harmed when it's me Ian wants."

"Did he not try to kill you once already?" Mary demanded. "And did you not shoot him with a pistol since? You'll be going to your grave, and after Earnan risked his hide for you, and I've worked so hard to mend your arm proper. Was not an easy task, gone near a week out of place like that."

"I am grateful to you both." I took another shuffling step, and a cold sweat broke out along my forehead. "Which is why I have to at least try to appease Ian. If I can save even one Campbell from harm . . . "

"You're a braw lass, just like your mum." Bridget stepped

toward me, as if she wished to give me a hug, but I tensed and held up my good hand.

"And your ribs all mussed too. You ought to have told me," Mary scolded.

I hadn't been conscious to tell her when she'd finished her torture session with my arm. In the two times she'd come to check on me since, I had been too cowardly to mention it. I supposed I knew she might be able to do something to make the pain better. But I'd also guessed that the process of getting to that point would make things worse before.

"Will you fetch my cloak, please?" I asked Bridget.

Her face fell. "We burnt it," she said. "And all the clothes you were wearing when Earnan brought you up. "They were foul beyond cleaning, plus we wanted Brann to see their remains and to assume . . . "

That I had burned too. "Never mind the cloak." I took more halting steps toward the door. "A sheet will do, if you have one."

Bridget pulled one from the bed and tied it carefully around my shoulders, covering my sleeping gown as best she could. I'd declined her offer of assistance to get dressed, the thought of my ribs being encased in a corset or of moving my arm through the sleeve of a gown being simply too much.

"I'll help you down the stairs," Earnan said.

"No." My tone was sharper than I'd intended. "I don't want any of you coming out of this room. You're not to reveal yourself to Brann. Let him think I'm a ghost crawled from the pyre. I don't know what will happen out there, but I don't want any of you suffering repercussions for my sudden return to life."

"He ought to thank us," Bridget muttered. "If up to him, you'd be dead, and he *would* be facing Ian MacDonald on his own."

"It's tempting to let him." I reached the door and clung to the bar a moment, steadying myself. "If I believed for a minute that Ian would harm no other than Brann, I would not go."

That wasn't entirely true, but at least I also had an unselfish motive for sacrificing myself. I had no doubt Mary was right. There was every possibility Ian would end my life at first opportunity.

But somehow before, I would make him listen to me. If the MacDonalds he'd brought with him were truly as Earnan had described them, I had little chance of saving anyone here. My best hope was that Ian cared enough for his brother that he would go after him, and Collin might be rescued before a ship carried him far across the sea.

Bridget pulled open the door, and I stepped into the dark hallway. "Close and bar it," I whispered, then made my way over to the wood rail overlooking the hall below.

Brann and his council huddled around a table, arguing one with another about what must be done.

"Find another lass who looks like her, and send her to meet him," one suggested.

"There is no need for that." My voice was not loud, but carried nevertheless in the high stone chamber.

A chorus of gasps and a flurry of Gaelic sounded as the men looked up at me. I left the rail and started toward the stairs, moving carefully to spare my ribs, and with the draped sheet floating around me, as if I really was a spirit.

Perhaps I would be soon. Bridget, at least, would see that my brief legacy here lingered long after I was gone.

No one moved as I descended the stairs, my eyes locked on Brann's. His face had drained of color, and a tiny part of me gloried in the tables being somewhat turned, at seeing him frightened. But I couldn't focus on that for long. Just putting one foot in front of the other took all of my concentration, and beneath my thin nightrail it felt as if my heart might leap from my throbbing chest.

Facing one of the men who wanted me dead was terrifying enough. Facing them both made for impossible odds. I didn't want to die. But more than that, I wanted to save Collin. Ian was my best, my *only*, chance.

I reached the main floor and stopped, looking directly at the table containing the council and Brann. "Collin warned you," I said. "He told you his brother would come if you did not produce the dowry."

"Appease him," Brann hissed, rising from his seat, leaning forward. I saw through him, that he would not dare do more than that, not when he was unsure if I was real or spirit.

I held my ground. "There is *no* appeasing Ian Mac-Donald."

"Find a way, or there will be consequences." Brann's head tilted back, looking up to the stairs behind me and my room beyond, his eyes sharp with suspicion. It would not take much to confirm my timely resurrection had been aided by others.

"Because of you, there will be consequences for all of us," I said. "Prepare yourselves for battle."

I turned from him too quickly and paid for it in a wave of pain that temporarily blinded me. I continued walking, skirting the tables widely, hoping they wouldn't see the sheen of sweat across my forehead. No doubt I looked as white as the sheet cloaking me. I hadn't moved this much in over two weeks and each step was excruciating. It would be a miracle if I could make it all the way outside the gate to meet Ian.

Reaching the front doors without stumbling or crying out seemed a victory. At Brann's command, two men hurried to open them for me. I continued my gliding walk outside into a gloomy afternoon beneath a drizzle of rain.

More stairs. These were uneven and unkempt, with weeds growing up between. *Wet now too.* I wasn't certain I could manage without a rail to cling to. Alistair ran across the courtyard toward me, rubbing his eyes as if he, too, could not believe what he was seeing.

"What are you doing?" he whispered as he came up beside me.

I placed a hand on his arm for steadiness and took the first step carefully. "You were late. I came to see you instead." I attempted a jest, though neither of us smiled.

"This is madness," Alistair said. "You can't go out there. It will be suicide."

"Your wife said as much already." I made it down the second stair. *Two to go.* The doors closed behind us. Brann had let me walk away. *One evil man passed.* My odds at coming out alive were perhaps slightly better than they had been when I'd teetered at the top of the stairs.

"I need a horse. Ian's preferably, if it is still here." Or might that anger him more? A reminder that Collin and I had stolen it from him.

"And how are you supposed to seat a horse in this condition?" Alistair caught my elbow, keeping me from falling on my face when my foot missed the third stair but hit the fourth with a jarring step. I cried out and clenched my teeth.

"I have no choice." I turned to him, pleading. "You've seen what Ian is capable of. If I don't go out there, what might he do? And I can't walk that far."

"He'll do it anyway," Alistair said.

"I have to try," I insisted. "In my situation you would do the same."

"I'll come with you, then."

I shook my head, thinking of Mary upstairs and their pretty, red-headed daughter. "Just help me get on a horse."

"And once you're out there, what is your plan then?"

Nothing. "No plan. I've had no vision." That was what he was asking. Was there something I'd not told him that might make this decision less foolish than it appeared? "I have only my life in forfeit. It was me Ian asked for. Perhaps that will be enough." I could see by Alistair's sober expression that he didn't believe that anymore than I did.

I waited near the corner wall as he went to retrieve a horse. The usually busy yard and outbuildings were eerily still today, their occupants in hiding somewhere, waiting anxiously to see what would happen.

I thought of Ian when I had last seen him close up, face to face at the riverbank when he had held a knife to my throat, expecting me to cry out for Collin. *So he could murder him as well.*

Was I a complete fool to even hope Ian would attempt to save his brother from the English? Or would Ian simply be glad Collin, the obstacle in his quest to be laird, had been removed?

Why am I doing this? I glanced toward the castle doors, knowing there was no turning back now, not when Brann knew I was alive.

Alistair returned with Ian's black stallion. Seeing the beast brought strange comfort. I had last ridden him with Collin. This was as close to him as I might get.

Alistair helped me climb onto a low wall and from there to Ian's horse, sitting side-saddle instead of astride, and even that not without a great deal of tears and struggling on my part.

To my dismay, Alistair took the reins. "I'll go with you to the gate at least," he said.

"Thank you," I said, relieved that he would stay with me that long but would not endanger his life more than necessary. His presence was a comfort. I sat upright, as straight as possible, and cradled my arm against my stomach, my balance precarious at best.

We had no words until we reached the gate and waited for the guard to open the small door for us. All else had been secured—the first time I had seen it so since my arrival.

"This isn't right," Alistair said suddenly. "What kind of a man sends a lass out to face the enemy?"

"One whom the lass commands to do so," I replied. With great affection I looked down at him. "Nothing has been right here for a very long time, I think. If I am to shortly meet my grandfather and mother, I should like to be able to tell them that I tried my best to change that."

Alistair nodded and swiped the back of his sleeve across his eyes. "God bless you, lass."

"And you." I reached to take the reins from him and caught the glint of gold in a patch of grass.

"Look." I pointed. Alistair crouched and combed his fingers through the blades until he came up with a five-guinea coin. One of those I had thrown the morning Collin was taken? Alistair handed it to me, and I clutched it in my hand. It wouldn't be nearly enough to convince Ian to let me go and leave us in peace, but possibly it might entice him to follow the trail of the English, in search of treasure if not of his twin.

With a last look at Alistair, I entered the narrow corridor between the walls and heard the gate close behind. It took but a minute, and I came to the other side.

Out of the wolf's den to meet the lion.

Chapter Nineteen

My first glimpse at the long line of men encircling the castle caused my breath to catch in my throat, thick with sudden fear. The reins slackened in my hand, and Ian's horse paused, as if he, too, did not wish to proceed any farther.

I'd read stories of the bare-skinned, painted natives found in the Colonies, and had wondered if the authors of such articles had, perhaps, exaggerated the truth. The wall of half-naked men with painted faces spread out in front of me made me rethink my skepticism. *One does not have to travel across the ocean to see barbarians.*

The wild men stood frozen, then began to advance suddenly as one. At a signal from their leader they fanned out in a wide arc, moving steadily and heading straight for me, as if with intent.

For the first time in days fear overcame my pain. *I don't want to die.* Neither could I see how I would live. But for Collin I must, a little longer. Long enough to make a plea to Ian.

I pictured Collin in my mind, drawing on his memory for strength. *Fourteen years servitude. The Colonies.* Was he still in prison somewhere or already on a ship crossing the Atlantic? *Is he alive?* I hadn't had the courage to search my mind to see if I might know. But I found courage enough to urge the horse forward, and to beg Ian to seek out his brother.

I plodded across the courtyard, each step an agony of

body and soul. The rain continued, soaking through the sheet and my nightgown. Hair plastered to the side of my face and in front of my eyes, partially blocking my view, but I hadn't a free hand available to push it away.

Where are the English soldiers now? Though the MacDonalds were still far away and my vision clouded, I could see the outline of weapons—swords held high in the air as they advanced. These men had come for war. And at their head— Ian.

Heaven help us. I thought of Eithne and Gavin and prayed that they, and those like them living far from the castle, might somehow be safe.

And those inside . . . I couldn't think of that now.

The line of men stopped as suddenly as they had started, and Ian continued on alone. We drew closer to one another, on a path that would have us meet directly. Fear moved from my throat to my stomach, icy fingers of dread that spread as swift as the river's penetrating cold when Ian had tried to drown me.

The closer we came to one another, the more I could see that something about him was different—wrong. His long hair did not billow behind him as it usually did when he rode, but was bound tight to his head with a blood-soaked bandage.

A patch covered his left eye, reminding me again of a pirate, and his right eye had been blackened, with a wicked cut slicing across his cheekbone. When he stopped his horse beside me, close enough that our legs were nearly touching, I saw that matching, bloodied bandages wrapped around his hands. A fresh scar ran up his arm, with other vicious bruises marring his face to the point that it was nearly unrecognizable.

The Campbells were not to be his first battle since we had parted.

I brought my gaze up to meet the intense look coming

from his visible eye, as it scanned me from head to toe. His mouth turned down even more than it had been. "Who is responsible for your injuries?"

"Brann Campbell, but that matters not."

"The same who sent you out here alone, to beg for your people?"

"I came of my own will. I must tell you of Collin." Ian had expected me to scream at our last meeting. This time he wished to see me beg. I would, if it would make a difference. I held my hand toward him and uncurled my first, revealing the gold coin. "The English came nearly three weeks ago. They took Collin and intend to put him on a ship bound for the Colonies. They gave our laird a bag of coins like this in exchange. They had many prisoners, purchased as Collin was. It is probable the soldiers carry more gold with them."

"Put your coin away." Ian flicked his hand, dismissively. "Your money is no longer of interest to me. I've a better prize in mind." He raised his eyes and looked beyond me toward the keep.

"Please," I begged. "Collin is your brother. Won't you go after him?"

"And leave you here alone, with the man who treats you so cruelly." Ian reached a hand out toward me, and I flinched. His gaze hardened. "What else has he done to you, I wonder?"

"I—I will go with you, and do your bidding, if you will search for Collin."

"So easily she bargains." Ian scowled. "And yet she is not in a position to do so." He lifted a hand in the air and waved those behind him to come forward. "I've no reason to leave," he said. "With a castle and its fair lady here for my taking."

No. He must not refuse. My fist curled around the leather strap as I fought off the waves of nausea washing over me. "Please, Ian. Your brother—"

"—is no longer a consideration."

The row of men that had come up behind him parted, opening the way for a new procession, a dozen others who surged forward, hands hoisted near their shoulders, bearing a crudely made casket.

"Your husband," Ian said. "I have returned him to you."

Part Two

One for sorrow, two for joy,
Three for a girl, four for a boy.
Five for silver, six for gold,
Seven for a secret that must never be told.

Chapter Twenty

"Shh. Quiet now, lass." A finger pressed to my cracked lips.

I turned my head toward the voice and tried once more to speak my request. "Water," I croaked, or attempted to as I blinked in confusion, taking in my room and trying to remember how it was I'd come to be here—again.

Bridget held a cup out to me, her normally steady hand trembling.

An attempt to sit up confirmed the nightmare of the past several days as reality. I lay my head back on the pillow with a groan, feeling as if my insides had been split in two.

"Shh," she scolded again, in a voice barely above a whisper. "Take care for your bandages. You're bound up tight." She helped me lift my head, then brought the shaking cup to my parched lips. I parted them, and she poured her medicinal tea down my throat, heedless that most of the liquid dribbled down my chin.

"There now. Close your eyes again. You don't want him to know you're awake. Been in here a dozen times asking after you, prowling and raving like the devil himself."

"Water," I begged once more when the last of the tea was swallowed. Bridget obliged, and I gulped down as much as I could until I hurt too badly to keep my head up.

She cast an anxious glance at the half-closed door, as if she expected it to come crashing down any minute.

"Brann?" I stiffened. When had he discovered I was

alive? What had he done to those who'd aided me?

"Not him." Bridget clucked her tongue. "Brann and what others could get away took off as soon as Alistair said you were killed."

"I'm not, am I?" Heaven couldn't be this painful.

"Of course not." She patted my arm gently, and even that made me wince. "Not yet, anyway," she amended at my sudden intake of breath. "You only fainted, and the MacDonald caught you. Fell forward, right into his arms, you did. He brought you here, all slumped over like, as if you'd been stabbed or shot. We thought it so."

Her words, or one particular—MacDonald—lifted the fog from my mind. My clansmen often referred to Collin as the MacDonald. My heart soared with hope. "Collin? He's here?"

"Oh. Dearie." Bridget turned away, hand to her face. "Don't fret about any of that now."

About what? Apprehension unfurled in the pit of my stomach. "Is Collin here?" I asked once more, my voice rising in spite of her warning. If Brann was gone, then who was there to be afraid of?

Bridget's face was a stoic mask of sympathy. Her lips trembled along with her hands as if she either sought for or fought against the right words. "I thought you knew. Your husband isna with us anymore. It's the other MacDonald come for you. Your man is—dead."

I've returned him to you. Ian's face loomed in memory. With piercing shock, I remembered our confrontation.

Brann, gone. Ian, here. Collin, dead. I squeezed my eyes shut but not before tears started, leaking down either side of my face.

"O, ach bronach! Bronach," Bridget whispered with a

louder sniffle. "Oh, but sorrowful, sad news. Alistair told me they've laid him out in the hall, as proper as if he were the laird himself."

"He was." Collin would still be laird to the MacDonald clan if not for his promise to my grandfather and me. He would still be living, breathing, caring for his people who were now subject to the commands of his malevolent brother. My breath came in short, choppy gasps as Bridget prattled on, her hushed voice growing more anxious with each word and glance at the half-open door.

I turned my head away, not wanting to hear, but already picturing the casket on the table below, just as I'd seen in my dream weeks ago. Why hadn't I recognized it as a vision of the future? *I should have known. We should have left this place or never come here.* Crushing despair consumed me as it had then. Only this time I would not wake up. *Oh, Collin.* A sob tore from my throat.

Bridget pressed a finger to her lips and leaned over the bed. "You mustn't cry out so. I'm sorry, lass." Her head bent as she struggled to hold in her own emotion. "He seemed a good man. Your grandfather believed him so. But his brother—" She shuddered.

"Don't tell Ian I've woken," I whispered. "Please."

"Too late for that."

I turned my head toward the voice, as if he'd compelled me to his wishes already.

Ian filled the doorway, looking as battle-scarred and ferocious as he had when we'd met in front of the keep.

"Leave us." He stepped aside, and Bridget hurried to do his bidding, without so much as an apologetic glance my direction. He stopped her on the way out, gripping her arm tightly. "Tell no one she is awake."

Bridget nodded jerkily, looking like a frightened mouse.

She'd had no trouble standing up to Brann. But Ian was not Brann.

One does not argue with a pirate. No matter that he had not a ship to command. He had a castle at his disposal now.

Ian shut the door behind her and rammed the bar across, his anger rolling off of him in waves. I heard Bridget's footsteps as she hurried away, abandoning me. Ian stared about the room, like a beast on the prowl. It would not take him long to hone in on his prey. I looked at the bar thrust firmly over the door and knew that even was he to move from it and I to somehow reach it before he caught me, it wasn't likely I would be able to wrest it open in time. How ironic that the thing Collin meant to protect me now trapped me.

Collin. My chin trembled as I held back a sob.

I tracked Ian's progress across the room as he took one of the chairs before the fireplace, lifted it easily, as if it weighed nothing, and dropped it beside the bed. Only as he lowered himself into it did I catch his brief grimace, an indication that he, too, suffered. His many cuts and bruises perhaps indicated a deeper wound or wounds. I could only hope.

Once he was seated, his visible eye narrowed on mine. "Might you carry his child?"

I sucked in a quick breath and paid for it with blinding pain. Nothing, compared to what I suspected Ian could do. If I answered his question in the affirmative, would he kill me? My mind flashed to the casket downstairs, to Collin. What had I to live for? To tell Ian that I carried Collin's child could mean deliverance.

I spoke before I could lose my courage. "Yes."

With a howl of rage Ian jumped from his chair, lifted it over his head, and sent it crashing across the room. The pitcher on the stand came next, the porcelain exploding in dozens of pieces when he hurled it into the fireplace.

Inhuman sounds tore from Ian's throat as he rampaged the room, destroying everything he could move. He came to one of my mother's paintings, ripped it from the wall, then stopped suddenly, the canvas in midair about to be broken over his knee. He set it aside, almost reverently, and began pacing the room in long strides. The action, so reminiscent of his twin, and the shock of his brutal destruction forced another sob from my throat. Unable to move enough to roll away from him, I covered my face with my hand and wept.

"I'll kill him." Ian's footsteps turned to stomping. He kicked a log from the stack near the fire, and it spun across the floor.

I imagined a child being torn from my breast and knew a little relief that such a scene should never come to pass. There would be no child of Collin's. Watching Ian, I understood how right Collin had been in his unwillingness to risk a babe being conceived.

"Why wait until the child is born?" I asked. "Kill me now and be done with it."

Ian turned sharply to glare at me. "What?"

"If you allow me to carry the child, you risk my escaping, and Collin's son—with Campbell and English blood—someday taking your place as laird. Better to end my life now." My bold words came out in little more than whispers, my throat still swollen and dry. "Better to kill me than wait to end the child's life."

"I am not speaking of a child *or* Collin, but of your foul relative—Brann." Ian leaned over the bed, his face frighteningly close to mine. "I'll kill him for what he has done to you." He pulled a knife from his belt and held it up. Blood still stained the blade.

Collin's? I forced the horrifying thought aside, knowing it would haunt me later—if I lived long enough.

How had he died? I'd assumed the soldiers responsible, but if Ian had killed him, maybe any child of Collin's was no longer a threat. Then why should he care what Brann had done? My mind swam with confusion until it settled on one point of offensive clarity. *He thinks I've lain with Brann.*

Swiftly, and with an accompanying arc of pain, my good hand struck Ian's bruised cheek. I was certain the fury in my eyes matched that in his. "I've been faithful to your brother."

Ian's hand touched his face. "You just said—"

"I was speaking of Collin, not Brann. How dare you assume—"

"Collin?" Ian's brow furrowed. "You swear it?" He pressed into the mattress on either side of me, the knife still in his hand, brushing my arm. "You swear Brann didn't touch you."

"Only with his boot and his fist."

Ian backed up and turned away. Sheathing his knife, he resumed his circular march around the room, clutching his middle as if hurt. He dropped into the remaining chair and hunched forward, head in his hands, his shoulders trembling.

"Shouldn't have let him." His words were little more than mumbling. "I knew. I *knew.*" Ian shook his head as if arguing with himself.

I shrank into the covers, lying perfectly still and wishing I could disappear. Ian's fury I anticipated, but viewing him in this broken, seemingly confused state felt even more frightening. I'd no idea what he might do next. The bloody bandage still covered his head, and I wondered if his injury might be contributing to this apparent madness.

There was no one to stop him from completing what he'd attempted at the river, and I had given him reason to, yet he hadn't acted. *Why?*

Minutes passed. I lay tense and grieving, silent tears sliding down my face. I was afraid to die but didn't want to live.

At last Ian rose, then stood facing away from me several minutes more, one hand braced against the mantel, while his other swiped conspicuously beneath his nose.

Ian crying? I didn't believe it for a minute. This had to be some scheme of his, some ploy. But why should he want my sympathy?

Without warning he turned and stalked toward the bed, his eyes red-rimmed and wild and the bright stain of fresh blood seeping through his shirt front.

He is seriously injured.

"What are you going to do to me?" The foolish question fled my lips before I could call it back. My earlier bravery faltered with the reality of the bloody knife at his belt or the possibility of his hands on my throat. "What do you think another murder will gain you?"

Ian's sinister grin flashed briefly. "A great deal of satisfaction if it's Brann's." He strode past me to the window and flung the shutters open. "Miserable pile of stone," he muttered. "But it's yours. You've land the MacDonalds can only dream of anymore."

I tried but wasn't able to follow the conversation. How had we jumped to speaking of clan boundaries and all that had been taken from the MacDonalds?

He wants land. I could not give it to him, even had I wanted to. He had to realize that, as a female, I did not own it. If not land, what else was he after? Likely whatever he could get. He was here to collect on the debt of my undelivered dowry.

And when he finds nothing of value to substitute?

A new fear took hold of me. I had one thing of value, and

moments ago Ian had been furious thinking that Brann had stolen it. I would not barter with my virtue. Though it would not take much, weak as I was, for him to take it from me.

He was as far from the door as he could be and distracted by something outside. I would not get a better chance. With my good hand I flung the covers away and launched myself from the bed. An explosion of pain ricocheted through my chest, but I stumbled on, toward the door. If I could get to the hall and throw myself over the banister—

"What are you doing?" Ian grasped me beneath my arms, and I screamed.

He held me upright. "Are you *trying* to injure yourself?"

My vision blurred, and I feared I'd pass out again. "Everyone will know what you've done. Please just kill me."

He held my arms firmly and stared at me from the bruised slit that was his visible eye.

"First Collin's death." My voice broke on a sob. "Then mine. It was what you wanted."

Ian lessened his grip as if just now realizing what he was doing. I staggered backward and sagged against the bed, leaning onto the frame for support. Ian brought his hands in front of him, studying them as if seeing them for the first time.

"Katie." His voice, nearly pleading and so like Collin's, tore at my heart.

"I'm not going to—" Ian stopped abruptly at the sound of people outside my door. We both turned to look. When I glanced again to Ian it was to see that yet another instantaneous change had come over him, his scowl as fierce as ever. His eye narrowed on me, and he took a step closer, forcing me back so that I pressed into the side of bed.

"You think too little on your own life. You are far more valuable to me alive."

My pulse pounded in my ears as it had when he'd stood

over me at the river's edge. He'd not seen any value in sparing me then. What had changed?

"You've one week to rest." Ian ran a finger along the side of my face. "You'll be well enough to be of some use to me by then. I should know. I bandaged your ribs myself. They're only bruised, not broken."

My mouth opened and closed, too horrified to speak. My hand went to my chest. The sleeping gown I had worn outside to meet him had been removed, replaced by a clean shift, and beneath stiff bandages wrapped around me, holding me together. *Ian's doing.* Shame and humiliation washed over me.

There were worse things than death, Collin had once said.

Eye on the door, Ian spoke loudly. "Your dowry is gone, so payment must be made in other ways. Those with me will require shelter and food, clothing and heat throughout the coming winter."

"MacDonalds and Campbells at the same hearth?" I couldn't be hearing correctly. I remembered the tale of Glencoe when the guest Campbells had turned on their host MacDonalds and slaughtered all. Was that what Ian had planned?

"At the same hearth and with joint leaders," Ian said. "A Campbell and a MacDonald. Just as old Liam Campbell saw it would be."

Chapter Twenty-one

As with my nightmare several weeks ago, I awoke alone in the middle of the night and felt myself drawn to the great hall. I rolled from the bed, landing with a jolt on the cold, hard floor. I lay there a few minutes, panted, absorbed the pain as best I could, then crawled to the end of the bed and pulled myself up. Once standing, I waited, to see if I could remain upright.

When a minute passed without my collapsing, I began a series of jerky steps toward the door and out to the hall.

The journey from my bedroom to the room below was fraught with at least as many obstacles and as much difficulty as I'd experienced the night of my dream. My bare feet padded along the freezing floor, toes stubbing frequently when I stumbled. The bandages bound around my middle didn't allow for natural movement, but I dared not try to remove them.

I feared making Ian angrier than he'd been when he left my room earlier and discovered a handful of Campbells huddled outside of it, ready to burst in and attempt to save me. He'd knocked one of them down, nearly to the stairs, before an entourage of MacDonalds arrived to quiet the fray. Alistair had been among those roughly escorted away.

I had determined then that for as long as I remained, I must bear as silently and stoically as possible, whatever fate was to be mine. It might be the only thing I could do for Alistair and the others trapped here with me. But first . . .

I must see Collin. Just once more.

After a painstaking descent, I reached the main floor. The vast room was eerily silent and near dark, save for the embers glowing from the fireplace and a few, sputtering candles on the dais. These had burned low and barely illuminated the casket, casting its distorted shadow against the stone wall.

My chest and throat burned. *Not a nightmare.* I'd known it wasn't, but seeing the box that held Collin's body still sent a painful jolt through my already throbbing heart. My hand flew to my mouth, only partially covering my sobs.

"Collin." I cried his name aloud as I hobbled up the stairs to the platform.

The air was chill, and I shivered in my thin gown, gooseflesh springing up along my arms. I'd no fear of the dead, only the overwhelming sorrow that had wrenched me from sleep and propelled me this far. I'd wanted to be as near to my husband as possible, but the wood box brought no comfort. I touched its rough-hewn lid, then slid my fingers beneath and tried to lift it. *Just let me see his face once more.*

With both hands I pushed upward, but the lid didn't budge. I glanced down its length and saw that nails forbade it from opening. Whatever remained of Collin was to be kept from me. I would not even be allowed to look at him as I said goodbye. With an anguished cry, I bent my head to the casket.

A stream of tears matched my wailing as I relived every brief memory with Collin, from the past weeks to those that had come years before, right to this very place when my grandfather had joined our hands together. I had failed them both so utterly. I'd destroyed the future Grandfather had so clearly seen. And now the Campbells would fall because of it.

Collin is dead because of me.

"Enough, Katie. You'll wake the entire house."

I jumped, lifting my head and looking around warily, certain I'd just heard his voice.

"He doesn't deserve that kind of mourning." Ian leaned around from the head of the casket, the chair he'd been lounging in thudding loudly as its front feet made contact with the floor. He stood and started toward me.

I tightened my grip on the biting wood, as if it somehow offered protection. "What are you doing here?"

"Guarding." Ian inclined his head toward the box that held his brother. "Castle full of Campbells. It's likely at least a few of them wouldn't mind desecrating the body of a MacDonald."

"Oh." *The reason for the nails?* I hadn't thought of that but felt strangely grateful he had. There must have been at least some brotherly respect between them. I wiped the tears from my face and worried more were soon to follow and that it would anger Ian. Collin was certainly deserving of my mourning, but arguing with Ian would help no one.

I would find no comfort here. I turned away, hoping he might allow me to return to my room unhindered. I felt vulnerable, alone in the hall with him so late at night. As if he'd read my mind, Ian spoke a warning.

"It isn't safe for you to be here by yourself. Brann, or one of his men, might still be lurking nearby."

I nodded, thinking to myself that Brann was the least of my worries. It was Ian who threatened most now. He looked even more the part of a murderer with his bruised face and the bloodied bandages on his head and hands, and this only encouraged my panicked thoughts. Fear staved off my sorrow as Ian strode purposely toward me.

My faltering steps were not quick enough, and he met me as I reached the stairs. When he held a bandaged hand out, I felt I had little choice but to take it. His grip was light, just enough to see me safely down. But he did not release me when I reached the main floor. I glanced up, fearful of what his expression might reveal.

The dim light sheltered me from the worst of his horrors, but I longed to look away, just the same. His face appeared contorted, frozen in place with a permanent sneer. His piercing eye narrowed, as if considering his next course of action. I knew what I wanted mine to be. I wanted to flee.

I turned to do just that, but his other hand—bandage and all—was upon me before I'd taken so much as a step. "Not so fast, Mrs. MacDonald. Stay, though you cannot stand the sight of me."

First Katie, now Mrs. MacDonald. I didn't like all this name calling, not from Ian.

"We must speak of matters most important."

"Whatever you wish to say can wait until morning." I pried his fingers from me, noting his wince as he let go.

"Since you are awake—well enough to leave your bed—it cannot." His tongue darted out to lick dry, cracked lips. "We must speak of Collin."

The dagger in my heart wrenched again. For a few, strange seconds I had forgotten my sorrow. It returned forcefully now, in a rush that sent me stumbling backward to the steps. I sat down hard as tears surfaced and spilled over, falling unchecked down my cheeks. I held my broken arm beneath my bruised ribs and shook my head, my resolve not to anger Ian washed away in a wave of grief. "Don't say his name. Don't pretend to have cared. You wanted us both dead." For all I knew, the blood on Ian's knife *was* Collin's.

In the waning candlelight I saw that Ian's bruised face was smooth, a mask of calm. "You are correct. I didn't care for my brother as I should have. I have betrayed him in the worst way." Ian held out his bandaged hands as if pleading for my understanding or forgiveness. "But I also gave my word to protect you. *I swore an oath.*"

I sobbed harder. Collin wouldn't ask that of him. *He wouldn't.* But I was no longer certain. The last time I had seen Collin, Brann held me at his mercy. Was that enough that Collin would have extracted such a promise from his brother? I prayed not. But what would I have promised in those moments, to know that Collin would be safe? *Anything. Including my own life.*

"Did you kill him?" I demanded, looking up at Ian.

There was no short, harsh laugh as I'd expected. No boasting of the deed. "I did not," Ian said evenly, his gaze locked on mine. "Yet, I am responsible." Instead of pride or boasting, I read anguish, from the dark circles beneath his eye to the thin line of his mouth.

I believed him, though I wasn't certain how one could be responsible yet not have committed the act itself. I felt no better for his confession, if that even qualified as such. Collin was still dead, no matter who had ended his life.

"I release you from anything Collin asked," I said, still not believing Ian would have honored such a request from his brother to begin with. "You may leave this place and take the other MacDonalds with you."

This time he did laugh. "I can't do that." His tone was calm and even, frightening me far worse than when he was angry. I didn't know this Ian, didn't know how to react or what to expect of him. I shifted a hand to my pounding head that felt too heavy for my body. *I need you, Collin.* At the least I needed time—even a little of it—to grieve him alone.

"Go away, please." I was the one begging now.

Instead of heeding my request Ian came closer and sat beside me on the wide step. I drew my knees up and scooted as far away from him as possible.

"You're not the only one grieving," he said quietly.

I had no response. In the absence of imminent danger, sorrow washed over me again, seeping into every pore. My throat felt swollen, and a fresh batch of tears surfaced. I sniffled loudly in a vain attempt to hold them back.

"We can help each other," Ian continued. His voice dropped to a whisper. "If you'll but listen. Give me a chance to relieve your grief."

"Stay away from me." I stood as quickly as my sore body would allow.

He grasped the hem of my nightgown. "A bargain then, if you will hear me out." He was practically begging.

"What?" I asked coldly.

"Ten minutes in your room right now. I speak. You listen. Then I will open the casket if you still wish it."

To see Collin's face one last time. How could I refuse? But I would be wise about it. "Tell me what you wish right here. Now." I tried to pull my gown from Ian's grasp, but my limited movement would not allow it.

"It isn't safe to speak here. I am not well enough acquainted with this castle to know all of its hiding places and who might be listening. The watch will also be coming in soon."

What watch? "Then open the casket first. Grant me five minutes alone. I promise to go upstairs and listen to whatever you must say after." He had been in my room before and not done me harm. I would simply have to trust that this would be the same. He needn't have asked, for that matter, but could enter whenever he wished, given his command here.

He shook his head. "I must speak first—to prepare you."

"What is the difference? Then or now?" This was naught but a cruel trick. "There isn't any. You never intended to keep your word."

"I do intend to. You'll understand once—" He released my gown suddenly and stood, drawing himself up tall. "Go," he hissed, giving me a little shove. "Before you cannot."

I didn't need to be told twice but left him, moving stiffly across the hall. Behind me I heard the front doors open and close, followed by feet stomping and men's voices. I did not look back until I'd reached the stairs.

Ian stood surrounded by a cluster of MacDonalds.

"How was it, lads?" he asked.

"Nary a soul about," one answered. "We'll have no resistance from this lot."

"To conquest," another said, raising a flask.

"Aye, conquest," the others, excepting Ian, echoed. He was too busy watching me, staring as I groped my way up the dark staircase.

"To uniting our clans," Ian said, still not taking his eyes off me. He took the flask from the man and lifted it high. His toast was met by silence.

The men had to be thinking what I was, that he'd lost his senses. The Campbells and the MacDonalds would never unite. *He's gone mad.*

"Have ye lost your mind, man?" someone asked, echoing my thoughts.

"Entirely possible," Ian said, his voice turned suddenly cold and calculating.

Chapter Twenty-two

"Beneath the tree there. It will keep her dry." Hugging a quilt to her chest with one hand, Mary directed the men carrying me with her other.

The chair bumped to the ground, and she hurried to tuck in the quilts around me. I leaned my head back against the trunk of an old rowan, looking up through the leafy canopy to the grey sky above. A raindrop landed on my chin. Heaven wept for Collin.

Mary pulled up the hood of my borrowed cloak. "There now. You'll not catch a chill, at least." She pulled a clump of red berries from the tree and placed it in my hand. "To protect you from evil spirits."

Ian appeared behind her, first on the right, bearing the casket. He'd found a clean shirt for the occasion, and fresh bandages bound his head and hands, but his hair still hung limp and greasy down his back, and the patch covered his eye.

It would take more than berries to protect me.

Mary smiled kindly and patted my hand. "Take courage. Many a woman has been where you are today. And those less strong have survived."

I stared past her, not wanting to think about surviving or anything else.

The priest emerged from the kirk, and a humming began, made by the line of MacDonald men standing on either side of the casket.

Their tune was melancholy, a wailing lament, and the deep vibrations seemed to come from their chests.

Alistair crouched beside me. "We've not the pipes any-more, so this is the best the men can do."

Their combined efforts did sound pipe-like, and though they were MacDonalds and I knew none of them, I felt grateful Collin was getting a proper tribute.

The last of the mourners arrived—all MacDonalds, save Mary, Alistair, and myself.

The keening ceased, and the blessing and rain began in earnest. I curled my fingers around the edge of the chair and hung on, wanting it to be over, wanting to wake up.

"The sins of man do visit him in death," Father Rey began. "He is punished, who dared disrupt what was foreordained of God, that these sinful people be swept from the land and the earth cleansed with fire in their place."

"That's not true," I cried, struggling to rise from my chair.

Father Rey paused, sending a withering look my direction.

"It is the vengeance of Heaven come upon him, and you, his wife, will suffer as well."

"God does not intend these people to be homeless." I took a faltering step toward him. "Collin was a good man, honorable and brave."

"Well said." Ian moved to stand beside Father Rey near the open grave. "Perhaps you could start the service again. I believe the lady would like to hear something more—hopeful."

"I speak only truth," the priest said. "I warned them at their arrival. Damnation to any who presume to resist God's will. *You* have been warned now as well."

"Consider yourself the same." Ian clapped a hand on Father Rey's shoulder. "One warning is more than many are granted. But, as you're a man of the cloth, I'll be lenient." With a sudden shove, Ian sent him sprawling forward, headlong into the open grave.

My gasp echoed with others around me. Ian turned away from the shouting and cries for help from below.

"Now then," he said, looking around at those who'd gathered. "Is there anyone else who would like to say something about my brother?"

Chapter Twenty-three

*A*lone. *Finally.* I stared at the door Bridget had just exited, grateful Ian had been so demanding of her the past days that I was at last by myself, left to rest without anyone to watch over me. *Alone.* I raised my head to better see the table at the foot of the bed, near the fireplace. My heart raced with anticipation.

Bridget had left both the tray and teapot containing her poppy seed tea.

She'd given me a dose already, a bit more than the previous day, as I'd told her I required more to sleep now. I had gone from dreading the concoction to needing it desperately. Sleep was the only place I found escape from grief, the one pain I couldn't seem to tolerate.

With great effort I pulled myself from the bed. *The reward will be worth the temporary pain.* I crossed the room, eased into a chair, and reached for the kettle, careful not to tip it as I poured. If a spoonful or two made me sleep for a few hours, what might an entire cup do? *Eternal sleep?* It was worth the attempt. I brought it to my lips and drank.

Rhythmic steps fading in and out slowly lured me to wakefulness. I groaned, wanting to stay where I was, in a deep cocoon of non-existence.

"She's stirring."

The steps paused, then grew louder, marching, practically running. "Has she opened her eyes?"

Collin?

"Not yet."

"Leave us."

More footsteps, these lighter, just as quick. I listened, hovering between two worlds, one in which I felt nothing. One in which—

"Katherine."

My eyelids were peeled back and I stared up into a face I'd hoped never to see again. Ian hovered above me, his one eye roving over my face, the other hidden beneath the black patch. I felt an absurd desire to reach up and pluck it from his face. What was under there? Had he lost the eyeball itself? Or was it merely injured?

Instead I attempted to lift my hand, to move his from me, but my arm felt too heavy, and I'd no control over it. Ian took my unresponsive hand and pressed it to his lips in both a rough and tender manner. Gaelic rolled from his tongue as he looked heavenward, his eyes glistening. My confusion multiplied.

I took a deep breath to clear the mist from my mind and instead became reacquainted with the severe discomfort of my bound ribs, the return to reality shocking in more ways than one.

"Do you hurt?" Ian asked.

"Yes."

"*Good.*" His expression of prayerful gratitude slid into a scowl. "That means you're alive." He dropped my hand and pushed away from the bed with a jerk that caused another spasm in my chest.

"How *dare* you try to kill yourself, when my brother gave

his life for you." Ian's voice vibrated with quiet anger, so threatening that I almost wished he would shout instead. He towered over me, the hands that had been so tender a moment before now clenching and unclenching, causing fresh blood to seep from the edge of the bandages on them.

"Your week is up. You will get out of that bed, get dressed, and be in the hall at 5:00 tonight."

I sat in a stupor, shivering in a chair before the fire, awaiting the bath water that was to be brought up. It would do me little good. I would never feel warm or clean or whole again. Constant fear chilled my heart. Guilt ate at me and infused self-loathing. Grief's shadow was my constant companion.

My one chance at escape from all of it had failed.

I'd spoken truthfully when I had told Collin I could not see a way forward without him. Time had ceased from the moment I'd laid eyes on his casket. Nothing that happened now mattered. I hated myself and my circumstances. To feel, to breathe, to exist was to hurt, and I was weary of the ache.

Ian had said he was responsible for Collin's death. Yet, was I not as well? My incomplete vision led to his being taken. I'd failed at what Grandfather had expected of me, almost before I had begun.

And Collin . . . All those years he had waited faithfully to keep his promise. And it had ended with him bound and being led away, like a beast being taken to auction—or slaughter.

If only I hadn't told him of Liusaidh. Guilt twisted inside me. Collin's death was my fault, and perhaps Liusaidh's was as well. *If I had known sooner . . .*

What good was seeing something terrible was to happen only an hour before it did? And then, only knowing part of it? My sight was no gift, but the worst kind of curse.

The door opened, but I didn't bother to look up. Staring into the fire for endless hours seemed a much better pastime than acknowledging anything having to do with reality.

"He's sent a gown you're to wear from among your mother's things. Bit old fashioned, but quite pretty." Bridget's voice was falsely chipper as she bustled into the room. "He means to have a lovely bride."

He *has invaded the wrong castle then.* "I don't need a dress. Only more tea." My hand shook a little just thinking of it. It would dull my senses, the only way I could cope tonight. What I'd had yesterday hadn't been strong enough. Perhaps if she brewed another—

"Looking for this?"

My head raised at the sound of Ian's voice. He strode in the room behind Bridget, the familiar kettle in hand. He held it in front of me, tempting as he swirled the liquid around inside. A different kind of thirst clawed at my throat. I reached for it. "If you have any mercy at all—"

Ian snatched it away, walked to the fireplace and tossed it in, pot and all. The porcelain and its contents exploded in a brief, brilliant blaze of color.

"Next time just ask for your maid's head on a platter. It would be much simpler." He cast a withering look Bridget's direction. "*Never* touch a single plant in that garden again— or any other plant meant to harm."

"I didn't intend her to take so much. A little can be—"

"Leave us," Ian ordered. "Do not return here unless summoned specifically by me."

Bridget dropped the dress where she stood and hurried from the room, head lowered as if she truly feared his threat.

I'd no doubt she did. The past week had seen a string of Ian's temper tantrums, which had moved from the initial destruction wrought in my chamber to the use of force when necessary. I had heard that one Campbell had been beaten, resulting in the entire upheaval of the castle and courtyard beyond.

Ian's booming tone was oft heard echoing through the castle, issuing orders followed by threats if his demands were not met.

"Does my brother's life mean so little to you, that you would throw yours away?" He moved to stand in front of me, to tower over me, once more. "You've no idea what he—" Ian brought a fist to his mouth and turned away, head bowed. It was another of those rare moments that had me questioning. *Did* he care for Collin? Or *would* he have shot him that night in the clearing, had I not intervened?

"You're right. I have no idea, none at all what happened to my husband." I clasped my trembling hands in my lap, hating that they shook not because of Ian's presence, but because of something I had done. Ian's words had struck true. Collin would be both angry and distressed if he knew what I had attempted.

"Collin meant a great deal to me. I loved him very much." *I love him still.* Death had not changed that.

"Show that, then, by honoring his name given to you. A MacDonald does not stop fighting. A MacDonald does not give in, even when it seems everything is against him—or her."

"You never wanted me to be a MacDonald. You only wanted my dowry. Why have you changed your mind?"

"My brother gave his life to spare mine and in so doing caused that I should be in his debt. As are you," Ian added. "And a man—or woman—of honor does not go against his word."

So I had learned from Collin already. I would not have believed Ian a man of honor.

What did I really know of him? What had *I* promised that was left to be done? I'd married Collin, come to Scotland, laid claim to this castle and all the authority it entitled me to. Then I had lost Collin, this castle, and probably the good will of this people as well. I doubted very much they found living with MacDonalds much better than being burned out of their homes.

"How is it that he gave his life for yours?" How had they even come to be together, when Collin had been a captive of the English?

"I promise to tell you all of it, in time," Ian said.

"But not today," I snapped. Baiting him was foolish, but I didn't care. He had been angry with me numerous times over the past week and had yet to hurt me. Perhaps that made me recklessly brave. I did not feel there was much left to lose, or much that he would not take anyway, regardless.

"He has suffered, has done his part, and now we're going to fix the mess that our clans have become." Ian's hand swept the room, catching the still-open door and slamming it. "And we are going to do it *together.*"

His favorite theme. I'd heard it more times than I could count the past few days, since his proclamation, as he'd stood near Collin's casket that late night. Ian had acted as if he wished to take me into his confidence, to share with me something important, and foolishly, I had leaned toward trusting him.

I reminded myself that I must *not* trust him, that I must constantly keep my guard up, not knowing which Ian would appear next. The calm, seemingly rational man who inquired after my health several times each day, or the lunatic who'd beaten a man found to have loyalties to Brann? I never knew which one to expect, and so my nerves had stretched taut as the days wore on.

Until we reached yesterday afternoon, when Ian had declared that *together* would be more than a threat. I would be required to give my word, a vow of marriage, to him.

I thought it possible my ancestors would understand my attempted escape—the only one I could think of. Would being dead not be better than being forced to another's will?

But now there would be no escape and no help dulling either the physical pain or the emotional agony the future promised. My body felt slightly better for its week-long rest, but my soul remained shattered, the fragments scattered throughout me. It hurt to breathe, to swallow, to blink, to exist. And tonight everything only promised to get worse.

"Have your maid help you into this dress after your bath." Ian bent to the floor and picked up the discarded gown. He looked just as disheveled as he'd been when I'd met him outside the castle over a week ago, still wearing a repulsive, filthy cloth on his head and a patch over his left eye. Only now he held a gown draped over his arm. The sight was so incongruous that I nearly laughed. *Hysteria.* No doubt I'd giggle and sob my way through the evening.

I met his gaze head on. "Bridget is not my maid. She runs this castle. If you've any hope of keeping everyone fed and sheltered, you'll treat her kindly. And I *will not* marry you." Courage came easily when there was nothing to lose. Was Ian to threaten me at the river's edge again, I would gladly jump.

Yet again his reaction was not what I expected. Instead of showing anger at my refusal, he crossed the room, placed the gown at the foot of the bed and took the chair opposite me near the fire. "Are your loyalties so fickle that you would refuse me? Have you decided already that your people mean so little?" His uncovered eye pierced my armor, but only a bit.

"Do *you* not realize that harmful actions against any member of my clan will only hurt your cause? If you truly need us and our resources to survive the coming months, why would you jeopardize our cooperation with needless violence?"

"There need not be violence if we join forces."

It was a poor attempt at avoiding an answer to my question, and when I looked at Ian, I realized he knew that and saw that I did as well. He was toying with me as he had the first evening I'd known him, when he'd told me, at the inn, that Collin didn't want me. He'd been wrong then, and I wanted him to be wrong now. He was most definitely wrong in believing I could be easily persuaded.

"You cannot expect me to marry again when my husband is not even one week in the grave." We had buried him three days ago. Speaking of Collin like this, acknowledging the truth that he no longer lived, felt like a knife thrust in an already raw wound.

Ian flinched as if it pained him as well. "I didn't kill Collin. I tried to save my brother. And I gave my word that I would protect you. That is best accomplished if we are wed."

That isn't true, hovered on my lips, but before I could speak I saw—*felt*—that he was being honest with me. More than that, Ian was hurt by my rejection.

The devil has feelings.

I stared at him, confused by what I read in his anguished expression. Not only had he not harmed Collin, he felt remorse for what had befallen his brother—which was . . . Ian's thoughts closed suddenly, almost as if he'd sealed them off from me.

Strange. It had been only Collin's mind I could sometimes decipher, as a child and again shortly before his death,

as we'd grown closer. I had no desire to have a similar connection with Ian, to be closer to him in any way.

"I cannot marry you, Ian." My voice was gentler this
time, absurd given the monster before me. No doubt this was
some treachery of his to make me feel sorry for him.

"It is the only way I see to make this work." His voice was
quiet now, almost pleading. "Your clan will follow you. Mine
will follow me. Together they will follow us both. The
Campbells can keep the MacDonalds from starving this
winter. In return, we can protect you and your people from
Brann and those with him. We must do this—for Collin."

No. Not for Collin. He would never want this. How many
times had he told me to stay away from his brother? *Were you
to add horns to Ian's head . . .*

But Collin had also believed that Ian might be ready to be
a good leader. What if he'd been right? How could he be, given
Ian's irrational behavior on our journey? His erratic behavior
here? I brought a hand to my head as it began to pound.

Ian rose from his chair with swift movement, as if he
meant to mask both his physical discomfort and inner
turmoil. I noted them anyway and felt no sympathy. *This is
Ian,* I reminded myself again.

He was mad to think I'd agree to marriage. It was mad
enough that we were having this conversation. How had the
world turned so upside down? What could be done to right it
again? To make at least something better? *To help my people.*
The answer stuck in my throat.

"Bloody Scotsmen and their promises," I muttered
beneath my breath.

Ian chuckled. Surprised, I stared at him. His brow arched
and lip curled in a victorious, knowing way. It seemed I wasn't
the only one who could read minds here.

"Wear that gown tonight," he demanded in his usual,

terse voice. Oddly, it almost comforted me, having him act and speak as I expected.

"I tire of seeing you in your night clothes," he threw over his shoulder as he reached the door.

"If I am to be expected to wear finery, the least you could do is wash your hair," I shot back, ashamed at my state of undress. I'd not even a wrap over my thin nightgown. What had I been thinking to allow him in my room? *What choice did I have?* "Your hair looks as though it hasn't seen a comb in weeks. Who knows what might be living in it."

Ian gave a surprising bark of laughter. "You object to my hair?" He fingered the long, greasy strands hanging over his shoulder. "When we first met, you were wont to stare as if you fancied it."

I felt my face flush red, embarrassed that he had noticed. *Had Collin seen me staring at his brother as well?* Ian's hair *had* been fine to look at then, a source of pride for its owner, or so it had seemed the way he wore it, sleek and smooth, hanging straight down his back. He hadn't looked as many of the other MacDonalds did—with shaggy beards and roughly shorn locks. I supposed it was a testament to the trauma of whatever had happened with Collin and the English patrol that Ian had neglected grooming these many days.

"I do not fancy it, or anything about you. Just because I agree to dress properly and come downstairs this evening does not mean I will marry you."

He stood a long moment, his jaw working as if he fought with what he wished to say. "Handfast then. We'll do this the Scottish way. In the hall at five o'clock. Do not be late." The door slammed behind him, cutting off further argument.

My heart pounded loudly. *Handfast.* Was that better or worse than marriage? I glanced at the clock on the mantel. *Nearly noon.* Five hours before I had to face the devil again.

Chapter Twenty-four

"This will never do." I touched my hand to my cheek, pale from the weeks spent indoors, and noted that my hair had grown both longer and lighter since I'd left England. The gown Ian had chosen complimented both, the reflection in the glass proving more favorable than I had anticipated—or wished.

"It has to. The MacDonald will have my head if you don't wear this tonight. Besides, the gown's only a wee bit long. Nothing that can't be fixed." Bridget knelt before me, fingering the delicate lace of the trim. "Shall I remove this?"

"Yes, please," I said, eager to do any little thing to appear plainer. The gown fit well and hung all the way to the floor, unlike the plain, too-short, grey dress I had been married in. A heavy, deep rose fabric with a lavish imprint of flowers comprised the overskirt, while an inset bodice and sleeves of cream lace made it even more lovely. Too much so for such a somber occasion. *I ought to be wearing black.*

Once, years ago, beautiful gowns had been almost commonplace for Anna and me. But that time and place seemed far removed from today.

"Seems a shame not to use this," Bridget said as she picked at the stitching of the delicate hem. "Perhaps in your hair."

"No." I didn't want any more adornments and had almost refused the gown altogether, until Bridget told me Ian's ultimatum. If I would not wear it I was to be given nothing, not so much as a stocking or shift, but would be required to attend the proceedings just the same—even if he had to carry me down. The thought of appearing naked in front of a hall full of people was too mortifying to contemplate.

I suspected Ian's insistence would continue throughout the night ahead. If I refused to handfast with him, would he have my hand cut off?

"Oh, what a lovely sight you are to behold," Mary exclaimed as she entered the room. "And how is my patient this eve?"

Miserable. "Well enough." I mustered a smile for Alistair's wife. She'd been nothing but kindness itself, and her attentions had spared my arm and perhaps my life as well. I should have missed the former very much, though I could not say the same of the latter. In the face of what lay ahead, death still beckoned with considerable appeal.

"This was your mother's, I suppose?" Mary touched the elaborate sleeve as she took hold of my arm, her gentle probing of the bones beneath the splint making me wince as much from habit as from actual pain. Three weeks in the splint she'd fashioned had done wonders.

"It is well your sleeves are not longer," Mary said as she examined her handiwork.

"Had a devil of a time getting that contraption through them as it were," Bridget said.

"I remember when your grandfather sent away for this gown. It was a gift for your mother, to be worn on the occasion of a visit from some rather important *English* guests, if I recall."

Father? "Why would he have wished her to be present at all?" I asked, confused, given the horrendous acts the English seemed to perpetually commit upon the Scots. "I should think he would have wished to hide his daughter away and pretend he had none at all."

"One would think." Bridget finished with the hem and stood, a bundle of lace in her hands. "But Liam Campbell did not think like an ordinary man. He *felt*. And because he felt, he knew."

Mary nodded. "Pained him though it did, no doubt, your grandfather kent that his daughter was to marry an English-man. All he could do then was to make sure she met the right one."

"My father." He'd been a good man, though some of the things he'd done while in service to the crown were not admirable.

I thought of him and my stepmother, my sister Anna and my little brother Timothy. Would I ever see any of my family again? What would they say were they to see me now, about to wed—or handfast—my husband's twin, a scant week after learning of Collin's death and not even two months since our own marriage?

No doubt they would feel as appalled as I did. In addition, my stepmother would have been horrified by the state of the castle and grounds. Anna would perhaps have described my gown as quaint and charming, all while holding her nose and thinking herself above wearing anything so antiquated. Timothy would have thought it terribly exciting that I was marrying a pirate.

I smiled at the thought.

"There now, lass. That's it," Mary said. "Smile like that for the MacDonald, and you'll melt his heart fine."

"The man doesn't have a heart." Bridget spoke my very thought.

"If that were truth," Mary mused, "why did he not come here and slaughter us all? He might have, you know."

"Perhaps he prefers to toy with his prey first," Bridget grumbled.

I'd had the exact suspicion about Ian and found it even more discomfiting now that someone else had voiced it.

"I've never met a man who hasn't a heart somewhere," Mary said. "Even the fierce ones. Sorry I am that the task of taming this one falls to you, Katherine. But we're counting on you, just the same."

"What do you mean?" My eyes met hers in the reflection of the glass.

"The MacDonalds are here to stay. They've settled in right as rain and are not intending to go anywhere till next spring, at least. Ian MacDonald means to govern us all, and you're the only thing standing between the clan and his temper." Mary patted my arm softly. "Do what you can, lass."

"All the more reason for a bit of lace." Bridget stood behind me and began gathering my hair. "He'll not let me serve you after tonight if anything goes wrong. He's told me as much already."

I didn't want my hair done up fancy but held back my protest. It seemed almost selfish, given what Mary had just shared with me. What I wanted ceased to matter—if it ever had.

I stared at my reflection again. From the moment I'd put on the gown, I'd felt equal parts dismayed and bolstered in spirit, as if my mother knew me and the peril I faced and would be beside me in my trials. It was a feeling near to what Collin had described to me once, and what had seemed strange then, felt comforting now. If the spirits of the dead lingered in this place, I welcomed them and whatever help they could give as I stumbled blindly into a frightening future.

"A bonny bride you are, that's what." Bridget stood back to admire her work. "A shame you're marryin' the devil."

"I'm not a bride." I turned from the glass and the woman I saw there about to betray her husband.

It was Collin for whom I should have looked pretty. Collin, who had never seen me in a gown this fine, or with my hair arranged as it was now.

When Alistair came to my room a few minutes before five my face was already wet with tears. He didn't appear well either, with dark circles beneath his eyes, and hair not much tidier than Ian's.

"Are you well?" I asked with concern. Ian had kept Alistair a prisoner only one day after the Campbell vigil outside my door, but I'd not been allowed to speak with him at all.

"Ah, lass." He patted my hand affectionately. "As well as can be. Better than you've been, I hear." His reproachful, downcast expression made me squirm.

"I've never been more proud than when I saw you ride out to face Ian Campbell with your head held high. And I've never been more disappointed than when I heard you'd tried to take your life. It is a sin serious enough to keep one from Heaven," Alistair reminded me gently.

"I know," I whispered, too ashamed to look at him. "But how am I to live without Collin, and *with* Ian?" More tears. Would they never cease?

"I've no answer for you, save to tell you that you *will*," Alistair said. "It isn't in your nature to back down from a challenge. I could see that the first time we met. Then, when I found out you'd come with us on so little notice and without any recollection of your past, I knew you'd a rare courage. Then *and* now," Alistair added. "That much hasn't changed."

I swallowed and nodded. "I didn't remember Collin then, so how is it that it feels like I've known him my entire life?

Three weeks feels like three decades. I never knew anything could be so powerful." *Or so crippling when it is gone.*

"That is the blessing and curse of love." A wistful smile broke through the untamed scruff of Alistair's beard. "Would you have given up those three weeks to avoid feeling as you do now?"

"No. Of course not."

"Well then, there's your answer, lass. When you gave your heart to Collin, you knew what might be required. He did as well. And you cannot have only part of the bargain."

I clasped my hands, still clammy and shaky from the tonic, together beneath my chin. My legs felt weak as well. "But Ian—"

"Ach." Alistair clucked his tongue disapprovingly. "It's a dangerous game the MacDonald plays at, though I must admire his strategy."

"What do you mean?"

Alistair moved nearer the fire and held his hands before it, warming them. "Have you not heard the tale of how he came to take the castle?"

"He had an army and we did not?"

Alistair chuckled. "The sorriest force anyone has ever conquered with, no doubt. Made of women dressed as men and children perched on tree stumps and bearing wooden swords. The MacDonald *army* was naught but an illusion, a ruse meant to frighten. In reality they'd barely enough fit men to do battle with the council, had they stayed. Mostly, we are hosts to MacDonald women and bairns."

"So you don't believe Ian intends a repeat of Glencoe, only the other way around?"

"Bah." Alistair swatted the air in front of him. "You may put that worry from your mind."

With a sigh that strained my bound ribcage, I did, grateful to have one less thing to fear.

Alistair turned away from the fire and then angled his backside toward the heat. He gave a sigh as well, one of comfort and satisfaction. "I only wish I could be there to see Brann's face when he realizes he was ousted by a group of bairns." Alistair chuckled again. Then his lips puckered in seriousness. "But it is a dangerous game the MacDonald plays. He has been allowed to stay thus far, simply *because* he's rid the castle of Brann. But that doesn't mean the Campbells are pleased to have MacDonalds in their keep."

"I should think not," I said. I doubted any Campbells were in favor of hosting an enemy clan all winter. "Has something else happened?" I didn't want to worry over one more thing. What I wanted was to be left alone with my grief, to mourn Collin instead of worrying about his brother's behavior.

"Some of the MacDonald men left the night before last. They aren't in accord with joining with the Campbells as Ian intends. He's worried they'll ally with another clan or even Brann's group to bring us more trouble. As such, the MacDonald has set extra guards round about, particularly out in the fields with the beasts. After two nights on the watch, I'm needing a bit of sleep is all."

"It's only a matter of time, isn't it?" I bit my lip. "Before something terrible happens." My something terrible had already happened, and while I didn't think I could hurt more than I did now, neither did I wish harm to come to anyone else. "Ian doesn't really believe the Campbells and Mac-Donalds can coexist, does he? He must have something else planned."

"He doesn't, lass. Strange though the whole affair seems. He's convinced this is the only way. I near am too," Alistair added quietly, then offered his arm. "Shall we? Best not be late."

I placed my hand on his sleeve but held back. "You were there at the river when Ian tried to kill me. How can we even contemplate joining forces with him? Is there *nothing* else we can do?"

Alistair's weariness melted into compassion as he placed his hand over mine. "It seems impossible now, but I do believe this is the best chance—for all of us." He turned to face me, looking me in the eye as he spoke slowly. "Ian is not the same man he was at the river."

I swallowed back a sob and nodded bravely. "I know. Something's happened to him. But that doesn't mean we should trust him."

"We've no choice but to." Alistair led me to the doorway. "He's given me his word he will not harm you." Alistair paused. "Nor touch you unless you desire it." He cleared his throat uncomfortably as we stepped into the darkened upstairs hall.

I felt grateful Alistair could not see the doubt on my face. *A promise given to Alistair is all I have to keep me safe.* I didn't believe for one minute that I was protected.

Chapter Twenty-five

I n contrast to the dark upstairs, the room below was a blaze of light. Warmth from the many bodies crammed into the space radiated upward, making me feel even more faint than I did already.

What am I doing here?

The first time I'd faced a MacDonald before a much smaller crowd had been hard enough. But to make any sort of bargain or promise with one who loathed me and in front of this many strangers seemed the worst sort of idea. But I'd run out of alternatives.

"Courage, lass," Alistair whispered as we descended the stairs. It seemed he was out of ideas too. "Bear up. Perhaps it will not be as bad as you think."

The crowd parted at the foot of the stairs, and Alistair left me to walk the distance to the dais alone. I hadn't looked up there yet, but I knew Ian waited. I could feel him again, could feel his tension. For entirely different reasons, his nerves were stretched as taut as mine. This was to be a symbolic joining of our people. It would not take much objecting to go terribly wrong.

Just one illegal weapon decently aimed. I looked up sharply at the crowd and felt an equally sharp pain in my ribs as this thought—Ian's—struck me. He was worried someone, a displeased MacDonald or one of Brann's followers, might hurt me. As if I hadn't enough to be afraid of before.

I gathered my skirts to ascend the steps, and a bandaged

hand appeared to help me up. I took it, and the fingers closed gently over mine. I looked up at Ian—his disfigured face, eye mask, and frighteningly *bald* head. A gasp parted my lips, and I pulled back.

His knowing smirk appeared at my open-mouthed stare. "You objected to my hair, did you not?" He helped me up the stairs and leaned closer, whispering so only I could hear. "Couldn't have you displeased with me already, could I?"

I didn't answer. My eyes were too riveted to the right side of his head and what the bandage had been hiding. A thick, ugly red line curved from his forehead over the top of his skull. It had been stitched neatly, and that thought alone made me shudder.

"The work of a claymore," Ian said, turning his scar my direction, as if to show it off. "Would have split my head in half, had I not already been falling backward. It knocked me to the bottom of a ravine between granite cliffs. Nearly broke my neck in the fall, but it saved my life. Redcoats supposed I was dead and didn't bother to follow."

"I thought swords of any kind were outlawed."

"They are." Ian scowled. "But the English like to play with the ones they confiscate."

"That scar doesn't look like anyone playing." I raised up on tiptoes, to better see it, strangely drawn to its gruesomeness.

"True," Ian said. "At least one of us was not having fun."

"Who mended it for you?" I walked behind him, trying to see how far it went. *Nearly to his neck.* I suppressed a shudder.

"My brother stitched it," Ian said. "Not a bad job, considering the circumstances."

Which were? I imagined Collin tending Ian with care. *Part of the debt incurred?*

"Wishing he hadn't done quite so well?" Ian asked. "Or perhaps wishing to see my other injuries." He stuck a finger beneath the mask as if to pluck it from his face.

"No," I said quickly and shuddered, imagining a vacant socket where his eye had been. *If his head is this bad . . .*

"When did Collin tend your wound? Where were you? Where were the soldiers who took him?"

"I will tell you all, but not now when we've other matters to attend to."

I pressed a hand to my stomach, feeling queasy. Not only because of Ian's gruesome injuries but because of the reminder of what lay ahead. In a haze of distress I allowed him to take my arm and lead me to the center of the dais where Collin's casket had been laid out just a few days earlier. All evidence it had been here was gone, but I could not so easily forget.

Collin. Collin is my husband. Not Ian.

Ian seemed determined to change that. He was dressed in finery equal to my gown, his shirt freshly pressed beneath a narrow-cut surcoat. Dark breeches tapered to tuck into the polished black boots I remembered from the day I had wed Collin. Then Ian had seemed intriguing and perhaps a little dangerous. Now, with his bald head, hideous scar, bruised face, and eye patch, his appearance was both revolting and sinister.

It inspired fear. Words—not so quiet as those speaking likely intended—filtered through the hall.

"The poor thing. Glad I'm not her."

" . . . pains me just to look at him."

"Have you ever seen anyone so wicked?"

"All her grandfather's doing, this. Brann was right to distrust the old man."

I scanned the crowd in a vain attempt to see who harbored such feelings, who among us still sided with Brann. But the sea of solemn faces packed into every corner and crevice of the room was blurred and unfamiliar.

Ian turned us to face the hall, and a hush spread quickly over those assembled.

"MacDonalds and Campbells have a long history of foul blood between them," Ian began, in a loud voice. "My own hatred for the Campbells has run strong and with good reason. My father was betrayed by them and then killed by the English. Collin MacDonald, whom many of you remember was recently sold to the English by your own laird."

Murmurs rippled through the crowd, and by their faces I began to see more clearly who might be a MacDonald—and *for* Ian's plan—and who might not.

"My brother has made a great sacrifice that I might be here today—with the people of my clan and the people of yours—Katherine's. Liam Campbell saw this day. He saw the demise of the Highlands, except her people. Even sworn enemies such as are here tonight should band together in such circumstances."

Ian took my hand in his bandaged one before I could object.

"At great personal expense Collin brought Liam's granddaughter home to you, though the dowry promised him for such service was not delivered. In lieu of that, the MacDonalds will winter here, among you. All will work. All will share. Any who disagree or do not feel to do their part may leave. While I yet live, I vow to do mine to assure our lives as Highlanders continue. That Scotland, her people, are not driven from this land and lost forever, as was attempted here already by Brann Campbell, when he took your homes and kept for himself what was meant for all."

Murmurs of agreement passed among the crowd. For all his frightening appearance, Ian spoke well, and it seemed his words were winning them over. I would not have guessed it possible.

"As a symbol of our commitment to this cooperation and to our people, Katherine and I will handfast."

My panic flared as he turned toward me.

Already we had reached the end of his pretty speech. Had it been Collin who'd spoken those words I might have felt a swell of pride or at the least an eagerness to stand at his side and support him. With Ian I felt nothing but distrust. I was a pawn in whatever game he played. I didn't like it but could see no choice but to play along. He'd known it would be so. For all my recent thoughts of dying, there was a hall full of people who needed me to live.

Alistair and another man joined us, the latter unwrapping one of Ian's bandaged hands. I braced myself for more atrocities beneath and saw I was correct when the red, raw skin of recently burned flesh was revealed.

My nausea doubled. The hand was not healed, not nearly so, and had both blistered and bled recently, given the pink tinge of the inner bandage when it was removed.

My questioning gaze flickered to Ian, but he stood still and focused, pain etched deep in the lines of his forehead. "To be binding, our skin must touch."

His brief explanation did not make me feel any better.

"Join hands, please," Alistair said, though he had to realize it would cause Ian discomfort.

I didn't want to touch him, and for several seconds my good hand remained at my side, twisting in the folds of my gown.

"Katherine." Ian spoke between clenched teeth.

I swallowed back my repulsion and fear and slowly raised

my hand, placing my palm against his. Our touch was light, made less so when a white cloth was wrapped around our clasped hands.

"Well done," Ian whispered. His uncovered eye flickered to mine as I felt the pressure of his fingers against my wrist. I shuddered and tried not to think of my hand against his or the feel of his charred skin on mine.

"White for purity," Alistair said loudly as I fought for calm.

"Blue for loyalty." A second cloth was added.

My breathing evened. *This is not a wedding.* It was a way to protect the Campbells, nothing more.

"Red for love."

Red for bloodshed would have been more accurate.

A crimson band covered the others. Like the first ceremony I'd participated in with a MacDonald, this felt like far too much—too many assumptions, too much pageantry, and too false for this circumstance involving strangers who could barely tolerate one another.

We were asked questions then. Not so many as when Collin and I wed, but enough—more promises than I cared to be making. I made them anyway, all the while refusing to look at Ian. I wanted this nightmare to be over, but these words were only the beginning of it.

I am promising myself to a pirate.

Ian looked down on me with his one eye. With courage I met his gaze, trying not to cringe. Without his hair, and with that angry scar crossing his head, he was horrifying to look upon. It was as if the evil inside him had come to light, and all could see what he truly was. Before, his beauty might have hidden his nature.

Except that his appearance didn't seem to be all about him that had changed. I'd have expected a speech like the one he'd just given to have come from Collin, not Ian. And the words he spoke next, as he knelt in front of me and bowed his scarred head over our joined hands, *had* come from Collin.

"I take you to my heart at the rising of the moon and the setting of the stars. To love and to honor through all that may come, through all our lives together."

Not love. Don't speak of love. My heart had known Collin, even when my mind had not remembered him. But I didn't have that connection with Ian. I didn't *want* that connection. Tears fell from my eyes onto our joined hands.

"In all our lives, may we be reborn, that we may meet and know, and love again." His hand tightened over mine. "And remember."

Remember me, Katie. It was Collin's voice in my mind, and in my heart only Collin to whom I spoke the promise.

"I will."

Chapter Twenty-six

"Give me your knife," I demanded of Alistair the second our hands were unbound.

"Planning to murder me already?" Ian winced as the last cloth stuck to his tender flesh.

I ignored his jibe. "Hold still." I pricked his thumb with the tip of the blade, then did the same to mine. "Your words were very pretty, but I require a blood oath in front of all these witnesses."

His brow arched as if impressed. "What do you want me to swear?"

"That you will not harm a single Campbell while you are here—or for a year after you have left."

Ian shook his head. "No."

"Then I do not wish to handfast."

"Too late." His smile was positively sinister.

"Probably best I hold this." Alistair took the knife from me.

I glared at him, wondering whose side he was on. Whispers had started again in the hall below, ripples of question about what we were arguing over.

Ian took my thumb and pressed it to his. "Best do this before we have to use the knife again."

"You just said—"

"Compromise." He turned to the crowd and spoke loudly. "The lady would like a blood oath for her safety and that of her people, and so I give my word. So long as the

MacDonalds, myself included, remain on Campbell land, no Campbell shall be harmed or killed by the hand of a MacDonald—save for two exceptions," Ian added with a sharp look at me. "Should I have opportunity to meet Brann Campbell at any time, I may do with him as I please, as retribution for the lady's injuries. And, should anyone attempt further harm upon Lady Katherine, he or she will answer in kind."

A cheer of approval rose up, as Alistair raised our hands together. Blood trickled down the side of my thumb, and I felt a little faint from that and all else.

"Let the celebration begin," Alistair declared. Another cheer went up, and the ale began to flow. He released our hands and turned back to me with a smile.

"Braw lass." He patted my shoulder. "And wise as well." He seemed particularly pleased with how things had gone. "You've only to sign the document now."

I followed Alistair to the table and read over the brief paper. "One year and one day." *Forever.* Somehow I would get through it—untouched. Ian had given his word, and I prayed he would keep it. I signed below him, noting his signature was little improved from when he'd signed as witness at my wedding. At least he had an excuse now, hands bandaged as they were.

I turned to find him already accepting hearty congratulations from his clansmen. It appeared that I was the only one feeling bereft, as if I had just betrayed both my best friend and my family as well.

It was during the celebration and feasting afterward that I realized what month it was.

"August already and half the fields yet untouched. Even with help, how will we get it all done? What's to become of us if we don't?" a group of Campbell women lamented in hushed tones. They had gathered near the table laden with meat pies, slabs of venison, and trays of bread and sweets. Anyone looking at the generous offerings would not have believed that either Campbells or MacDonalds were in any danger of starving.

But apparently—according to their worried conversation—we were.

August. In two months I would be twenty. *A widow already. Soon-to-be owner of one castle, crumbling to the ground a piece at a time. Alone in a strange land that was once my home. Handfast to the devil.* Twenty promised to be a fine year.

I'd been born on All Hallows' Eve. Growing up in England, this had meant little to me, other than an extra hour or two sitting quietly in chapel—during our more religious years—to honor this hallowed or holy evening.

But in Scotland, and particularly the Highlands, October 31st held much more meaning. Collin had told me that Samhain or Hallowe'en, as it was known here, was a time of remembering the deceased and even welcoming their return. Being born on such a day, along with the fact that I was Liam Campbell's granddaughter, was seen as a great omen.

Not only was I to see the events of the future unfold, but it was my link to the past that would allow them to do so. *My connection with the dead.*

With Collin? A sort of hopeful fear shivered down my spine. Might I somehow possess the ability to communicate with him still?

"This was needed." Ian's voice in my ear and his hand at my elbow startled me. I'd wandered away from him, amidst the sea of well-wishers, but had been aware of him tracking my movements the past several minutes. Unfortunately, I'd allowed my guard down enough that he'd managed to come near again.

"*Everyone* needed this," he said. "MacDonalds and Campbells alike. Each have been too long without hope."

"Some of us are still without hope," I said miserably. I was surrounded by strangers and pledged now to the strangest one of all. I lifted my cup to my lips for another fortifying drink, while Ian looked on disapprovingly. He held his hand out. I surrendered the cup and waited as he first sniffed it then sipped.

"Water?"

I nodded. "I've been thirsty all day. And shaky. From the tea," I admitted as I held out a trembling hand. Not to mention my headache, nausea, and dizziness.

"No more than you deserve," he said without sympathy and gave the cup back to me. "It is fortunate you were not subjected to Bridget's poppy seed tea overlong."

I nodded, though a fair part of me yearned for it still.

"If you care not for your welfare, care at least for hers," Ian urged. "If so much as another drop of that concoction reaches your lips—or anyone else's—she will be banished not only from this keep, but from Campbell lands entirely. How well do you think a woman of her years would do, alone in the Highlands, with winter coming?"

"It is not within your authority to send her away," I said, challenging him. "You are not the owner of this castle and therefore cannot order its inhabitants from it."

"I'm as good as married to its owner." A wicked grin curved Ian's mouth. "I believe you'll find that affords me quite a bit of authority. I would not test that by drinking more tea if I were you."

I folded my good arm across my middle and turned away.

"You needn't be upset," Ian said, his tone less arrogant than a moment ago. "I don't intend to lord anything over you—unless you insist on acting foolishly."

Wanting to get away from you wasn't foolish.

"Uniting our people will be hard. Surviving winter, possibly even harder." Ian moved around me so that we faced each other again. "But if we work together, it's not impossible." He tipped my chin up gently so that I was forced to look at him. "The worst may be having to look at this, aye?" He drew a circle in the air around his face. "Everyone here already believes you a braw lass, just for standing up with me tonight." His mouth quirked in a smile I found all too reminiscent of Collin, as his eye roved over me in a way I found far too possessive. "You look bonny tonight, Katie. Thank you for wearing the gown. It's the kind of dress you ought to have had on your wedding day."

"My name is Katherine. Henceforth, if you wish me to respond when you speak to me, you will please call me that and nothing else." No endearments, and certainly not Katie. My eyes smarted. "I would also ask that you do not speak of the past or of Collin. Looking at you is reminder enough."

"Is it?" Ian asked curiously. "Even with my scars and shaved hair?" He smoothed a hand over his head.

"What hair? You haven't any." A half-sob, half-laugh escaped my throat. I wasn't jesting with him, merely trying to keep grief at bay a while longer. I could fall apart later, when I wasn't surrounded by a hundred or more people.

One side of Ian's mouth twisted. "I did this for you." He angled his face to and fro, showing off all sides of his head.

"Thank you for—" I waved my hand at his head "—removing your insect-laden hair."

Ian laughed outright, eliciting curious looks from several

people around us. No doubt the MacDonalds were not accustomed to such a sound coming from him. And the Campbells could only feel as disturbed as I when looking upon him.

"There were no insects," he said. "But anything—for you."

I lowered my chin almost into my cup. "What do you want from me, Ian?" This wasn't the place to ask that question, or perhaps it was, as it was certainly safer among so many. His reaction would be careful and calculated here. I braved a glance at him. "What do you *really* want? What game are we playing at?"

"No game." He shook his head slowly. "Too many lives at stake for that." He caught my gaze and held it. "Use your gift when you *really* want to know."

Chapter Twenty-seven

It was near midnight when I ascended the stairs to return to my room. The celebration below didn't seem to be ending anytime soon, but I'd no desire to be a part of it.

The week of profound grief and tension had left me exhausted, and I was still feeling the effects of Bridget's special poppy seed brew, though nearly two full days had passed since I'd consumed any.

I'd done my best tonight to meet members of my own clan and to welcome the MacDonalds, doing my best to act as the lady of this castle and my clan. The last I'd seen of Ian, he and a group of men had been headed outside, presumably for the watch. As before—the first time I'd wed—it seemed I was to be granted a night to myself.

I opened my door and stepped inside, then turned to secure the bolt behind me. When it was in place I pressed my forehead to the cool wood and released a weary sigh.

"Was it that awful?"

I whirled to find Ian lounging casually on the bed in the near dark—legs crossed, hands behind his bald head. A low fire burned in the grate, and two glasses stood beside a tall bottle and a tray of bannocks on the table.

"You hardly ate anything tonight," he said, following my gaze. "I thought you might be hungry."

"I'm not."

"In that case." He lowered a hand and patted the spot beside him. "Change out of your gown and come to bed." It was an order, not a request.

"I'll do no such thing. Not with you." I reached behind me for the crossbar.

Ian's brows rose. "You prefer sleeping elsewhere? With someone else?"

"The man I preferred is dead."

"Be that as it may," Ian said. "It is within my rights to order you to come to bed with me."

I stared at him blankly, doing my best to conceal my fear beneath a mask of anger. "I need not stay with you."

"True enough," Ian said. "In a year's time you may choose to end our agreement. But until then . . . "

I was as good as wed to him and subject to his law. I'd just hoped he wouldn't care to impose it quite so soon. *So much for his promise to Alistair.*

Ian uncrossed his legs, and I caught him wince. His injuries still pained him. There was something in my favor at least. My fingers closed over the bar, and I pushed it up.

"Change and come to bed, Katherine." He spoke more sharply than before, as if he had guessed my intent. "If you try to leave this room, I'll only come after you. And neither of us ought to be chasing about while we're still healing. Not to mention that I doubt you'd like putting on a show for the crowd downstairs."

And no one will dare to help you, he might have said. Bridget the brave feared him, and Alistair had bade me to do Ian's will. What closer allies did I have? I let the bar fall and crossed the chamber to the dressing screen, grateful for what little protection it offered. At least I wouldn't have to look at Ian for a few minutes.

Or a few hours . . . a few days. It would probably take that long for me to figure out how to get out of this gown myself, one-handed as I still was.

I stood in the dark, hugging myself, shivering with cold and trepidation and trying to calm my racing heart.

Even if Bridget wasn't in bed already, I doubted Ian would allow me to call for her. Why had I come upstairs? Why had I imagined for a minute that Ian would be the gentleman his brother had been?

"Head up."

I startled at and instinctively obeyed Ian's command, looking up as a bundle of cloth fitted over my head and slid to my shoulders. I reached up to touch the fabric and realized it was my sleeping gown. At the feel of Ian's hands on my waist I started to turn.

"I wouldn't do that," he warned. "Unless you *want* to be facing me when your gown is loosened and comes free. Hold still."

I did as he instructed, hardly daring to breathe as he worked awkwardly at first the buttons and then the laces of the gown, petticoats, and corset.

"Fool bandages don't help," he muttered.

"What happened to them—your hands?" When our tricolor of wraps had been undone after the handfast, it was to find that the first, the white one, was bright with spots of his blood. Ian's soft voice and eloquent words had belied the pain he must have felt during the ceremony, but his white face and set jaw revealed it fully afterward.

"Wasn't it obvious when you saw my hand tonight?" Ian asked. "They've been burned."

I rolled my eyes, exasperated with his response. "Yes, but how?"

"Fire," he said in a droll tone. "It's very hot."

I attempted to glare at him over my shoulder before remembering my ribs and their aversion to movement. *Fine.* I would play along. If nothing else, his annoying banter was keeping me from being completely flustered. Perhaps it would prolong the inevitable as well.

"Let me guess . . . You were cooking over a fire and in your ravenous state forgot that the kettle was hot. The aroma of stewing oats became too much, and you clasped your hands around the base, scalded them terribly, and sent a pot full of mush skyward."

"That's better than the truth." He paused, then quieter. "I like you—Katherine. I am looking forward to many lively conversations."

"Don't," I warned. "No platitudes or niceties. We know each other too well for that already. I am the means to an end for you. That's all. Nothing more."

"What end would that be?" he asked, all humor gone from his voice.

"Revenge. Conquer. Taking what is ours and making it yours." I shrugged.

"If this was about revenge, why did I not simply remove or murder the Campbells that remained when we came?"

"With your army of women and children?" I scoffed. "You are fortunate the Campbells did not do away with *you.*"

"Possibly. Though I choose to believe they did not fight because I brought hope. Is it not better now that Brann and his followers have gone? Or would you prefer I leave and allow them to return?"

I didn't answer. What was I to say? What I truly wanted I could not have.

"All done." Ian braced his hands on my shoulders.

I tensed and clutched the front of my gown.

"Believe what you will," he said. "Time will prove you right or wrong." Ian stepped away. "Hurry and finish now before you catch your death of cold."

I waited, listening to his retreating footsteps and the sound of wine being poured into two glasses.

The dress slid from my shoulders and, with a bit of tugging to get the sleeve over my splint, fell in a silent heap on the floor. It was all I could do not to follow. Our polite, almost friendly conversation unnerved me more than his angry ultimatums. His kindness confused and left me even more wary.

I stepped from the petticoats and leaned forward, letting the corset drop on top of those. The nightgown he'd placed over my head slid in place to cover me with little effort on my part, and I felt the slightest bit of gratitude at his small courtesy. With nothing more to delay me, I stepped from behind the screen.

Ian crouched by the fireplace, a pained look upon his face as he carefully picked up wood, one piece at a time, and added it to the fire. "Come warm yourself."

A chair by the fire being an obviously safer choice over the bed, I complied with his suggestion and slid into the closest one. There were two again now, the one he'd broken having been replaced sometime during my sleeping episodes.

With a groan Ian stood then backed into the other chair. He took one glass for himself and handed me the other. Looking at me, he held his aloft. "To Mrs. and Mr. MacDonald, lady and laird of the Campbell keep."

"To peace between our clans," I added, not quite agreeing with the titles he'd assigned us.

Our glasses clinked briefly before we brought them to our lips. Ian drank deeply while I took only the tiniest sip. It had been one thing for me to seek refuge in sleep, but it seemed quite another to not be in possession of all my faculties for the night ahead.

I stared at the fire for some time, aware that Ian studied me instead, until I could ignore him no longer.

"Hasn't anyone ever taught you that it is rude to stare?"

"Is it?" He poured more wine into his glass and swirled it around. "I thought it rather complimentary. At all costs, you avoid looking at me, hideous as I am with these scars and bruises. But I cannot seem to keep my eyes from feasting on you. Your hair, your face—the effort it takes you to stay angry, the intensity in your eyes when you are, the way your lips pucker and your eyes squint when you are puzzling something out. I find you utterly fascinating."

"Pity the feeling is not returned," I said coldly. "I avoid looking at you in attempt to forget your face as it was at the river, when you nearly ended my life." I slammed my glass on the table and stood more quickly than I should have. Spots swam in my vision, and my first step away was unsure.

He was at my side instantly, one hand on my arm, the other at my back to catch me if I fell. Silently I cursed my bruised ribs and my own foolishness with the tea.

"You can let go of me," I said after my vision had cleared and the room steadied. "I'm not going to fall."

"You're right," Ian said. "I won't let you. Don't move." He released me, then crouched down, reaching for a folded blanket on the floor near the fire.

"You're still cold." He shook the quilt open and draped it over my shoulders, then proceeded to wrap me snuggly in it. "Better?"

I nodded, unable to deny the soothing effects of warmth. He startled me then when he stepped closer, close enough to put his arms around me. Too late I realized mine were pinned helplessly beneath the blanket. Panicking, I tried to squirm away.

"Shh," Ian said as if he was soothing a little child. "I only

228

want to get you warm. You've had a terrible week. Give yourself a moment. Just one. To be comforted." With a gentleness reminiscent of his brother, Ian pulled me gradually closer.

I stood stiff and unmoving, more off balance than when I'd stood too quickly. What were his motives?

"A minute of comfort. That is all." His hushed voice sounded so like Collin's. A wave of anguish broke over me, tears falling before I'd felt them gather. Grief-filled sobs wracked my fragile body. Ian cradled my face against his chest, and I allowed it. He held me tightly against him, a solid block of warmth in the chill night. I felt powerless to leave his grasp and more powerless yet to cease my wailing. Anyone listening outside our door would either think me the greatest coward or that Ian was torturing me—possibly both. But I had no care for others or Ian or even myself.

"Cry it out," he whispered. "You'll feel better for it tomorrow."

I wouldn't. Not ever again would there be a better day. Not with Collin gone. I couldn't bear it. With my eyes squeezed shut, I imagined it was *his* heart beating in my ear. Collin telling me that everything would be all right. Collin holding me in his arms. *Collin . . .*

Chapter Twenty-eight

"Good morning to you." Bridget waltzed into the room in seeming good cheer, or better than I'd seen since Ian's arrival. She set a bowl on the table near the fireplace and went to the window to pull back the curtains and open the shutters.

Squinting against the sunlight, I turned my head away and saw with relief that Ian was gone. *How long?* Had he even stayed the night here with me? I vaguely remembered him sitting on the bed beside me, after my minute of comfort had turned into a half hour. *And then?*

The quilt he'd warmed near the fire was still wrapped around me, my sleeping gown entirely intact beneath. I pondered my curious good fortune at having survived the night unscathed, as well as not having to face him this morning. Maybe he really would be true to the promise given Alistair.

Bridget bustled about the room, filling my basin and laying out clothes.

"Thank you," I said, not wishing to seem ungrateful. "But I would prefer to sleep longer. Would you mind coming back in a few hours to help me dress?"

"I wouldn't mind, but I daresay the MacDonald would."

"Oh?" I followed her with my eyes as she laid out stockings and a sensible pair of shoes I'd not seen before. "Has he other duties for you?"

"Not me." Bridget arrived at the side of the bed and

looked curiously at the quilt rolled around me. "That's one way to keep a man out, though I'd not count on it to work for long. I hear there was a fair amount of wailing coming from this room late last night."

"*You* hear?" Had she, or someone else, been eavesdropping in the hall outside my door?

"Not me, personally, but—" She pressed her lips together. "Never mind. Isn't any of my business."

It wasn't, and though I was fond of Bridget, I didn't feel the need to confide any of what had and had not happened last night. Ian the monster hadn't swallowed me whole or murdered me in my sleep. That much was apparent. What wasn't, and what I wisely deemed no one else should know, was Ian's temporary show of compassion. For both his reputation and mine, that would remain our secret.

"He wants you up and about now. You've been assigned to help in the shearing shed."

"What?" I cringed as she helped me sit up and unwrap myself from the quilt.

"Everyone has been assigned a task," she explained. "Yours is to carry the wool from the shearing to those who will be washing it. When you've finished that in a week or so, you'll be carrying it from the wash room to those who are carding. And when that is done, you're to bring the carded wool to the castle for spinning." She helped me out of my nightgown. "Everyone's to have a task—the MacDonald's orders."

"I don't suppose there is one involving a paintbrush," I asked, my voice muffled as I pulled a clean shift over my head.

"What?" Bridget helped me into a petticoat.

"Nothing." I hadn't painted in so long I worried I had forgotten how. My arm wasn't healed enough yet. What if I never had the chance again?

"The wool should be fine for you," Bridget said, as she

fastened my simple frock. "You're mending well and look a fair sight better than your man."

"He isn't my man." *Collin is—was.*

"Aye, well, think what you like, but after last night, he most assuredly is. And if you set yourself to one task in the coming weeks, it ought to be keepin' him content. I've a feeling much depends upon that."

It wasn't the speech I wanted to hear first thing in the morning, but I held my peace, knowing Bridget was probably right. I wandered over to the table, feeling more of an appetite than I had in days. Maybe all that crying had done a little good.

"Did you bring him oatmeal as well?" I asked, scrunching my nose in distaste as I noted the contents of the bowl.

"That I did. Beginning today, a half dipper of oats is the ration for breakfast—man, woman, or child. Unless you're carrying a bairn, then you get a bit more. Are you?" Bridget asked casually. "If so, I'll have another portion sent up."

"I most certainly am not." I spoke as though offended at the suggestion, but the truth was that I would have been happy to be carrying Collin's child, to have something of him to continue with me.

"Not yet, anyway." Bridget said, with a sideways glance.

It was so near to what Eithne had said about Collin the day we had visited and helped with the soap that I felt like I'd been struck. I stepped backward and sank heavily into the nearest chair. *To have that day back again.* I would willingly suffer what I had since all over again, if only to have one day more, another hour even, with Collin.

As if one poignant reminder was not enough this morning, the singular aroma of steaming oatmeal wafted toward me, an assault on my already struggling senses. The scent spoke of Collin and his infernal supply of raw oats. Memories of our days spent alone in the Highlands, struggling to stay alive, enjoying the pleasures of budding friendship and becoming acquainted with one another, filled my mind and tore at the raw wound on my heart. My eyes responded with their usual course, flooding with their seemingly endless reserve of tears. I pushed the bowl across the table.

"Take it away, please. I can't eat it."

"Are you certain you're not with child?" Bridget's speculative gaze roved over me. "It could be too early to tell proper."

I shook my head angrily and angled my body away. "Leave me."

Bridget did as I asked, taking the offensive oatmeal with her. As soon as the door had closed behind her, I fell apart, allowing the tears to fall freely, head held in my hand as my not-so-silent sobs filled the otherwise quiet room.

My respite did not last long. Bridget's voice returned, accompanied by Ian's.

Tattletale, I thought crossly.

Their footsteps stopped outside my door, and a hushed conversation I could not decipher ensued. I briefly considered rising to secure the bar but desisted. Angering Ian first thing probably wasn't the best idea.

The door opened a few seconds later, and he entered, bowl in hand. I stared past him, at the dying fire, until he pulled the other chair opposite me, sat, and blocked my view.

"Is starving yourself your next course of action?" His tone was neither angry nor amused, but a forced calm I sensed would not last long.

"I have an aversion to oats. I can't eat them without being ill."

"Bridget believes you might be with child. Is that possible? Were you telling me the truth when we spoke about Brann?"

I finally looked at him. "Why should that matter to you?"

"Because he would have—*will have?*" Ian's voice slipped "—taken something from you that was not his to take."

Because it's yours now? "There is *no* child. It is impossible. No man has touched me." I admitted to him what I'd feared would come to light last night. I feared it, not only for what Ian might do, but because I felt he would take some absurd delight in the fact that it would be he, not Collin, who had the privilege.

Ian leaned back, hand moving across the stubble along his chin as he considered me.

Debating whether I've told the truth?

"Thank you for telling me," he said at last. "We'll not speak of it again. Now, then." He scooted the chair closer and took a spoon from the table. "I've tasks aplenty to do this morning, but if you'll not eat on your own, I'll see that you do."

"I'll have something else," I said. "One of Bridget's bannocks or—"

"Flour is precious. It is no longer to be used for breakfast, but for a ration of bread with our main meal. If we are not wise with our resources, they'll not last the winter." He held a spoonful of oats out to me. "Parritch is a fine breakfast. It will stick to your ribs, and yours could use some paste, aye?" A corner of his mouth lifted. Mine remained closed tight.

He changed tactics. "Would your grandfather want you starving yourself? Would Collin?"

Would Collin want me to be here, with his pirate brother? I glanced briefly at Ian, the brow of his visible eye arched in a question I didn't want to answer.

I vow you the first cut of my meat, the first sip of my wine. Marriage vows Collin had taken seriously, though it had been the first cup of spring water and the first bite of fish—or oats—

235

for most of our brief marriage. He had kept me safe, and then given his life.

I gave a sigh of defeat, closed my eyes, and reached for the spoon. Ian handed it over. I closed my eyes and parted my lips. The texture and flavor of cooked oats transported me back to a forest glen as I knew they would, and it was with some difficulty that I swallowed.

Ian handed me a cup of water, which washed the taste away, though not the memory.

"There's a good lass," he said, treating me as a child.

I held my hand out for the spoon. "I can feed myself."

"Promise that you will?" He placed it in my hand but did not let go.

"Yes."

With that he stood and left the room. I ate my ration quickly, trying to be grateful for it, guessing I would need my strength for the day to come.

"Ian is having me *watched?*" I faced off with a man I'd never seen before who stepped in beside me in the upstairs corridor after giving the brief explanation that he was to accompany me wherever I went today.

"Not watched so much, as *watching out* for those who would do you harm."

Like many of the other MacDonalds I'd seen, this man's eyes were hollow, his frame gaunt. He stared at me with as wary a look as I likely cast at him. He appeared to be near Earnan's age, which I had guessed to be close to my own.

"Name's Gordon." He stuck his left hand out. I had only my right hand, my good one, to offer in return, which made a handshake impossible. Gordon covered the awkward moment by taking my hand and bending over it with a brief kiss. He released me and stepped immediately back, to my vast relief.

"I'll see to it that no harm comes to you, my lady."

"Oh, good," I said with false cheerfulness. *You'll keep me safe from Ian then.* Ignoring my unwanted escort as best I could, I swept toward the stairs while taking in the room below where a great deal of activity was already underway. The tables had all been pushed to the side, and several women were vigorously scrubbing the floor. Buckets and barrels were lined up on the benches, and children carrying baskets overflowing with vegetables came in through the front doors and headed toward the kitchen. An elderly woman marched up the stairs, her arms laden with bedding.

She stopped before us and sank into a curtsy. "My lady." Beneath her burden her gnarled hand reached out to mine, grasping it briefly. "Thank you for your sacrifice."

"You're welcome?" I said, bewildered at her greeting.

With a nod she continued up the stairs.

"Your grandfather's rooms and most of the rest have been taken o'er by the MacDonald widows," Gordon explained. "More bedding is being brought up for them."

"That woman—she's a MacDonald then?"

"Aye," he said. "One of many whose husbands died in the Uprising."

"And she's—grateful to me for the use of Grandfather's rooms?" If I considered that Ian might have stayed there instead of with me, it was a sacrifice.

My escort moved ahead of me on the stairs. "I am sure she is, but that wasn't why she thanked you just now. She's one of the women—the whole lot of them—who are grateful to you for being willing to join with their laird, temperamental man that he is. They think it'll go better for them, now that you're warming his bed."

I grasped the railing, appalled that the whole of the castle, apparently, believed Ian and I had been intimate. "Are you suggesting that before now he, Ian—made use of the widows for—" I couldn't even say it.

"Entertainment?"

I nodded, feeling worse than I had a minute ago.

"It's not that," Gordon said. "Ian MacDonald is known, among other things, for his rare temper. In the past he's been volatile and unpredictable toward everyone."

The past? As in yesterday?

"Somewhat the opposite of his brother," Gordon continued. "It often took Collin to rein him in."

I remembered as much from our journey here.

"We weren't certain what to expect when Collin married you and Ian became laird. A short while ago he didn't seem capable of leading a hunting party, let alone an entire clan, and even more, joining them with another."

"It's unprecedented," I said. *If he succeeds.* I still didn't know if Ian truly wanted this coexistence to endure long, or if he was just using the Campbells to bring in the harvest.

"His behavior is what's unprecedented," Gordon continued. "Since Collin's death Ian's been rational and just, and focused, for once, on the good of the clan and making this mad idea of his work. A lot of people think you're at the root of this change, that you've influenced him toward becoming the leader Collin was."

It was more credit than I deserved or wanted the burden of. "It wasn't me," I said quietly. "But losing Collin. If Ian is truly changed, it is because of his brother's death."

Two more women passed us, each curtsying as the first had. I responded in kind, feeling more unsettled by the minute. Save for a handful of people, my own clan had barely acknowledged my return.

"I'm to help with the wool," I reminded Gordon. "Will you take me where I'm to go, please?" Engaging in work of some sort, in any ordinary task, held sudden appeal.

We crossed the busy hall while Gordon explained that Ian had asked for an accounting of everything from the dishes to the sheets. "He has all but the youngest children working in the gardens and fields, harvesting every last root and stem."

So he'll *have plenty to eat, and know what the Campbells have of value?* I still couldn't trust that Ian intended to spend the next several months living peaceably with us. Last night, speaking in front of everyone, he'd sounded genuine, but in the light of day I imagined his words were merely meant to appease us into submission.

Just like Brann. It seemed so clear to me, I wondered how it could not be to the others, especially to those like Alistair, who'd known Ian before. I couldn't be the only one feeling this way. And if I wasn't, what were we to do about it? What would Collin have done?

I thought back to that morning at the inn when I'd upset Ian. Collin had spent the following two days cooling his brother's temper and keeping him away from me. Perhaps that was the only approach I could take right now—to keep Ian's temper under control, and to cooperate and encourage others to do so as well, while somehow, secretly, we would need to plan for the eventuality of his betrayal.

Gordon led me through the courtyard, as bustling with activity as the hall had been. A cartload of timber was being wheeled in the direction of the burned distillery, and the sounds of saws and hammers alike filled the air.

We passed the stables and left the main yard, coming upon a grouping of sheds I'd not seen before, just inside the east wall.

Gordon pointed to them. "They're shearing in that first

one, so the women will be nearby, collecting the wool for washing and carding. Someone there will tell you what to do. I'll be there as well, helping with the shearing."

"Thank you—I think." I regretted my initial rudeness already. He was only doing Ian's bidding, and having someone around to talk to me might prove a nice distraction from my melancholy.

In the distance I saw the millhouse wheel churning—the first time I'd seen it going since my arrival. A cleared path, free of mud and debris, led between the castle and the various outbuildings. How had so much been accomplished in little over a week?

Halfway to the sheds I paused, staying back to avoid a collision with a dozen MacDonald men walking toward the gate. Each wore a bulging pouch, and the two bringing up the rear were on horseback, pulling carts behind them. I watched as they exited the courtyard, heading in the opposite direction that Collin and I had gone the night of Liusaidh's fire.

The last time we had gone anywhere together.

"They're off to see to the barley we left behind." As he had in the hall last night, and in my room, Ian appeared suddenly. "We cannot risk losing it."

"Of course not." I hugged my arms to myself, in attempt to ward off the lingering chill in the air. "Whoever heard of surviving a winter without whisky?"

"No one in Scotland." Ian's tone was light, jesting almost at my intended barb. "But it's about more than having it ourselves. It'll fetch a high price and provide a good barter for some of what we're in need of."

"Which is?" I turned to look at him, expecting him to struggle with an answer as I caught him in the elaborate lie he was building. Instead his mouth turned down, and his forehead wrinkled.

"Nearly everything." He began ticking items off on his fingers. "More grain. It's our greatest deficiency. Neither clan planted enough. As it stands now, we'll run out in January. We'll need meat as well, though we can hunt that ourselves, into winter if need be." He held up a third finger. "Shelter. Not everyone fits in the castle, and I'm worried for those who live far from it. They're easy pickings for Brann. I'll feel better if, once the harvest is complete, we can move everyone in close, so at least they're safe, though we've not near enough food to see either clan through the winter. I think it was Brann's intention to starve those he'd not burned out already.

"Then there is the matter of care for those who've been living in the wild since Brann took their homes. They've need of a place to stay and clothing and shoes as well. Half the bairns have scarce of either. If they don't starve to death they'll surely freeze." Ian ran a hand across his stubbled chin. For a second his troubled expression almost convinced me that he truly cared. He tugged at the cap covering his bald head, and a worried sigh escaped his slightly parted lips.

I stared at his mouth, so like Collin's, a second longer than necessary, and Ian took notice. His eye met mine briefly, and I tensed, waiting for some false accusation or coarse remark, but thankfully he let the moment pass.

"The Campbells are hardly better off than the MacDonalds," Gordon said, reminding me that we were not alone. "I'd not expected that, given the land and resources you have."

"Then why not leave us and simply worry about providing for you own?" I addressed the question to Ian.

A corner of his mouth rose. "And would you be coming with me, if I did go?"

"Of course not."

"There you have it," Ian said smugly. "I cannot leave you.

My brother's suffering won't be for naught. I'll be staying here to look after MacDonalds and Campbells alike—particularly *one* Campbell."

Chapter Twenty-nine

I could hear the sheep bleating pitifully long before we reached the sheds. Ian had left us again, headed to some other task. He seemed driven, filled with purpose as he'd never been on our journey here. Maybe Collin had been right, and Ian would rise to fill his brother's role of leadership. Or was I, like most everyone else here—like the MacDonalds at Glencoe had been—being lulled into false security?

We reached the sheds, and Gordon opened the door to the first one for me.

"Isn't it a bit late in the year for shearing?" I asked.

"Aye," he said but offered no more. For all his talkative nature earlier, he'd grown silent since Ian's departure.

"Won't the sheep freeze without their coats? They can't grow back that fast, before it's truly cold, can they?"

"They could freeze," Gordon said. "But these sheep won't make it through winter anyhow. Many of the pastures near the castle have been stripped already, and Ian doesn't feel it wise to be sending shepherds out on the high moors in search of winter grass—too easy for another clan, or your previous laird, to take the sheep and murder those tending them."

"You mean they're going to starve?" I paused just inside.

Gordon shook his head. "We'll slaughter them first, for the meat. As soon as the ground's too frozen for them to feed well—or sooner if we need them."

Dismay at the animals' unjust fate—and ours—filled me. "In the spring the Campbells will have nothing," I protested.

"But hopefully you'll all be alive. Without the meat from the sheep, that's doubtful."

I let this sink in a moment while Gordon pulled the door shut behind us.

"Thank you for your escort," I said belatedly. "I'm Katherine, by the way. You may call me that if you'd like."

"I know who you are," Gordon said. "Spent the better part of six years listening to Collin tell tales of you."

"You did—*he* did?" Gordon had spent years with Collin, while I'd had only weeks.

"Collin spoke of you often. First, as a reminder to my sister that he was spoken for, then later because we would ask him for stories."

Sister? "What could he possibly have told you? I was a child when we parted." It would be just like Ian to have me work alongside the other woman who had cared for Collin.

"Aye, but what a lass you were." Gordon smiled, no doubt remembering some tale of my mischief. "Then later Collin spoke—to me, anyway—of his imaginations of the woman you'd grown into. I do not think he was disappointed."

"Thank you," I whispered, grateful for this unexpected gift and sorry again for my earlier rudeness. Being around Ian kept me testy and on edge. "Will you tell me sometime?"

"Aye. Though I doubt all that Collin told us was true. Tales about you hanging from the rafters like a ghost . . . "

"That one *is* true," I muttered.

"Well then, we'll have to talk more sometime. I expect I ought to help now." He inclined his head toward the far side of the shed and the sheep gathered there, awaiting their turn with the shearer. "My sister will show you what to do." He looked past me.

I turned around slowly and came face to face with one of

the most beautiful women I had ever seen. Her hair reminded me of Ian's when I first met him—long and shiny, black as midnight. What man would not want to run his fingers through it? *Had Collin?*

In contrast to her dark hair, her eyes were a pale blue, set in a flawless face, with creamy skin that accentuated her other features. I had the brief thought that Collin might have been happy with her, had my grandfather not previously bound him to me. If not for me, Collin might have been both happy and alive.

"My lady." With simple elegance she held the side of her ragged gown out and sank into a curtsy worthy of greeting the queen.

"Hello." *Mhairi.* I returned the gesture, feeling it was I who ought to be falling at her feet, apologizing. Even if she hadn't loved Collin, he had been her laird, and I had taken him from her. "Please, call me Katherine." I extended my hand.

She shook it. "Mhairi."

I followed her to the opposite end of the shed, to an enormous table with women seated around it. Each had a blade in hand as they bent over a pile of wool, cutting out what I gathered must be the impurities, given the bowls in the middle of the table, piled high with bits of hay, burrs, and feces.

"This is Katherine," Mhairi said. "She is here to help."

Only two of the women bothered to look up from their work.

"Did the MacDonald do that to ye?" the younger one asked, pointing to my arm in its sling.

"No," I said. "Of course not." Though Ian was definitely capable of hurting me, he had not to this point since his arrival. It wouldn't do to have needless fear and rumors being spread about. "Brann—the former Campbell laird—is the one who hurt me," I explained. "Ian MacDonald rescued me."

The truth sounded strange, yet that was exactly what had happened. If not for Ian, I could still be suffering, a captive of Brann or possibly even dead by now.

"Brann's an evil one, that's certain," another woman said. "But the man you're stuck with now, is he any better?"

"I don't know," I answered truthfully. "He was unkind to me in the past." A slight understatement for Ian's attempt on my life. "But since coming here . . . " I swallowed painfully, this truth even more difficult to speak than the last. "Since my husband's death—Ian's brother's death—" I clarified for those who were not MacDonalds—"he seems changed. I think losing Collin has affected him in ways I wouldn't have predicted." My eyes shifted anxiously around the table. I had no idea which women were Campbells and which were MacDonalds and could only hope to offend neither.

"It has affected us all," Mhairi said, a sadness in her voice I recognized all too well. "Come. I'll show you what to do." She retrieved a half dozen baskets from the floor behind the table.

"Fill one at a time with the shorn wool, then bring them to us. Keep a few out for us to put in the pieces we've picked through, then take those to be washed. Keep the bowls on the table emptied—they can go right to the fire beneath the kettles."

"All right." That didn't sound too difficult, but the humblest of tasks perhaps. Had Mhairi's curtsy been mocking? I didn't think so, but it was difficult to tell. She had every right to hate me. I glanced wistfully at the table and the women seated there. *Why wasn't I to be allowed to work with them?*

"The laird was thinking of your arm when he gave you this task," Mhairi said, as if she'd discerned my thoughts. "It would be difficult for you to use scissors with that arm and near impossible to work the carding brushes."

"I suppose you're right." I took up two of the baskets and made my way toward the bleating, soon-to-be-naked sheep.

A gate separated the animals and shearers from the women's end of the shed. I opened this and moved inside what was clearly men's territory, with giant shears snapping in quick succession, shouting, laughter, and Gaelic flying back and forth among them. The smell was stronger here too.

Gordon beckoned me over, pointing to the ground. "I'm sorry, but you'll have to gather the wool off the floor. I'll toss it to the middle as best I can. Will you be able, with your arm?"

It was tempting to say no, to make my excuses and return to the refuge of my bed chamber. But what would I do then, except to think of Collin? Better to stay here, to listen to the chatter of the women's gossip and the sheep's sad bleating. *Better to be of use in some small way.* Even if it was not what my grandfather had intended.

"I'll be fine," I said, to myself as much as to Gordon. Dropping to the floor, I began gathering the wool. I quickly found it all I had expected—dirty, smelly, unpleasant.

Glancing at Mhairi, seated at the table with the others, I felt that I deserved no less.

Chapter Thirty

"Arguing already and not even a fortnight since we handfast." Ian removed one of his boots and dropped it to the floor. Propping one leg over the other, he began to massage his foot. "Doesn't bode well for years of happily wedded bliss. Were you this difficult for Collin?"

His comment didn't deserve a response, other than a reminder not to mention his brother's name. I ignored it and stayed focused on the more pressing matter at hand before my courage failed me. Literally on the edge of my seat, so I could move quickly if need be—if Ian's temper flared at my audacity to challenge his decision—I plunged headlong into my objection.

"You *cannot* kill all of the Campbells' sheep. Like it or not, that is much of their livelihood now. Take that away, and they'll surely perish—or perhaps that was your plan all along. Feast on mutton throughout the winter, then leave us in the spring with barren fields and no livestock."

"I can appreciate your sympathy toward the sheep." With a grimace, Ian removed his other boot. "But mine tends toward people over animals. And I'd prefer not to live another winter watching children and adults near starvation. The sheep can help solve that problem."

"It's cruel," I protested. "Many of them aren't even a year old yet."

"I'm not asking you to be the one to slit their throats,"

Ian said. "And if you want to know what cruelty is—to both animals and people—spend a winter surviving by bleeding cattle and mixing their blood with oats. I'll not subject the MacDonalds to that again, not when there is meat to be had right in front of us."

"It isn't yours to take," I said, but my argument held no sway. What he'd just described was appalling. I could neither imagine participating in such horrors nor eating the spoils to survive. *And if I'd a child dependent upon such . . .*

Ian drew his chair closer to mine. "I'm not going to abandon you come spring. Many of the fields have lain dormant and even been burned the past year or two, but that does not mean they cannot be planted again. The rest will likely have done them good, and crops will grow in abundance, as I'm sure they once did here."

"I don't remember that time." I looked down at my lap, feeling defeated in more ways than one.

"You might if you tried," Ian said quietly. "Collin believed you'd extraordinary abilities to see both the past and future but that you were afraid to use them, that you did not trust yourself."

"The last time I did—" I broke off, unable to finish.

"The last time," Ian prompted.

I shook my head. "The *last* time," I amended. "There will be no more seeing the future or recalling the past." I'd managed that fairly well over the past few days, shutting out any thought of how or why I'd come to be here and what had come before. Hard work was the antidote for nights haunted by the past. Being too tired to even remove my clothing—as I had been last night—made falling asleep easy. Existing in a state of numb exhaustion was better than the alternative of suffering with feelings so deep they caused every breath to hurt.

"It is unfortunate you refuse to access your gift. It could be helpful."

"For what? Discovering the whereabouts of my elusive dowry?"

Ian shook his head. "No. For finding your elusive Campbell laird and his followers." He made no move to return his chair to its previous location but instead leaned forward, taking my hand in his.

I tensed. We'd not touched since the night of our handfast. Ian had not even stayed in this room the past three nights, having taken his turn at the watch rotation. I had to admit he was fair in that, at least, and in the sharing of the workload that was suddenly ours. In spite of hands that were still healing, and his many other injuries, he'd been busy with everything from shearing sheep to unloading sacks of grain. I'd not spoken to him in days but had seen him frequently, not only giving orders but working alongside those he gave them to.

"This will never do." His thumb passed over my red, chafed skin.

"It's from washing the wool." Five hours plunged repeatedly in tubs of warm, dirty water had done my hand no favors. I tugged it away with a vain hope that its roughness repulsed him enough to leave me alone.

Ian frowned his displeasure, then stood and left the room without speaking another word. The door closed behind him, and I collapsed against the back of the chair and only then realized I was trembling again. *This* would never do. I could not spend my life in constant fear of my husband's brother. Which was how I still regarded Ian. Not as the man I'd handfast to, not as the one who'd appointed himself leader of both his MacDonald clan and my Campbells. He was just Ian,

Collin's pirate brother, willing to do whatever it took to get what he wanted.

He won't have me. Such brave determination was easy enough with him gone from the room. But I knew that I could only refuse him for so long before there were consequences, either to myself or others. With these troubled thoughts swirling around in my mind and the hypnotizing firelight making my eyelids heavy, I curled up in the chair and drifted off into a restless sleep.

"She's a bonny little lass." Ian held a bundle out to me, and I took it eagerly, staring down into the tiny, precious face of an infant not an hour old.

"You'll be a fine mother to her," Ian said as I shook my head in confusion and held the child closer to my breast, covered only by a sleeping gown. I glanced up and saw that I was seated in bed, with Ian leaning over me, an almost tender expression on his face.

A single candle sputtered in an otherwise dark room. It was the middle of the night.

I glanced at the child again, eyes closed, faint lashes lying serenely against pale cheeks. A dainty nose and perfectly rounded chin. *How did this happen? Will he allow the child to live?* I remembered promising myself that Ian would not touch me, that I would evade him as long as possible. And now, I'd not only broken my vows to Collin but had born his brother's child as well?

"Give me your hand, Katie," Ian said.

"No." I shrank from him. "You'll not harm her."

"I'm trying to help." Ian's tone held the exasperation I

was becoming familiar with. I looked up and gasped at his face so close to mine. He sat in the chair before me and held my hand in his as he rubbed something onto it.

I tried to pull away as I looked around the room to the still-made bed, illuminated in the firelight. There was no infant anywhere. "Where is she?"

"Who?" Ian continued working over my hand.

My baby. She'd been in my arms a moment ago, and I had been in bed wearing a nightgown. But now—I was still in my day clothes, seated in a chair as I had been only this evening. Ian had looked different as well when he handed me the child. His hair had grown back, not to its full, glorious length, but a shaggy mop of dark had swept low across his brow the way Collin's used to. Had I been dreaming of Collin?

Had I been dreaming at all? Everything had seemed so real. I remembered the smell of the baby, the soft feel of her skin.

Ian paused his ministrations to search my face. "Are you well, Katherine?"

"I fear I am not." Perhaps if he believed me ill, he would leave me alone tonight. I met his one-eyed gaze and remembered that a moment ago, when he'd stood at the bedside and handed me the infant, he'd also worn the eye patch.

Not a dream of Collin then.

Disappointment, followed swiftly by fear, wrapped around my heart. I could not have Ian's child.

"What are you doing?" I demanded, tugging at my hand once more.

"The lanolin will help your skin." He began rubbing a small mound of the greasy substance over each of my knuckles. "Ironically, it comes from sheep's wool. Not much of it is set aside for lanolin," Ian explained. "It requires boiling the wool for several hours, after which it's no good for spinning. But a few of the women have been making it. Its healing properties are many."

"Mmm." It *was* soothing my hand. For just a moment I allowed myself to close my eyes and enjoy the comfort of feeling cared for. I remembered Collin's hands on my shoulders at the inn the second night after we were married. The way he'd torn his carriage apart so I could ride in it without being afraid. How he'd held me close after Malcom's attack. I missed that comfort and feeling of security. I missed him.

Ian is a poor substitute. Once more I reminded myself of his crimes and forced my eyes open, letting his touch cease placating, in light of the face before me. Ian's heart was as scarred as his face, and I would do well to remember that. He released my hand, and I drew it almost shyly back to my lap.

Wounds heal. Scars remain. They changed a person's appearance, but could they change a man himself? I didn't want to consider that. But I couldn't deny that my hand felt better already. Ian's touch had been gentle, his act caring.

"What about *your* hands?" I heard myself asking. Before I'd thought through what I was doing, I reached for the one he'd held mine with. I turned it over and began unwrapping the bandages. Beneath the last layer I found the same red, raw skin I had seen the night of our handfast. It had continued to heal but would never be as it once was.

"This must hurt you terribly."

He shrugged. "Not as much as before."

"Will lanolin help them as well?"

Ian shook his head. "I don't think so. Alistair's wife has been treating them with vinegar and linseed oil. Best to keep to her methods, I should think."

"Yes," I agreed, relieved that I would not need to rub his hand as he had done mine. I released him, sorry that I had touched him at all.

"Repulsive, are they not? Like the rest of me?" There was a sadness to his voice as he stared down at his hands. "Little wonder you avoid me." A fleeting smile curved his lips, then vanished almost as quickly as it had appeared. His eye fixed on me, a long-pained look of yearning.

Occasionally over the past weeks I had sensed within him tender emotion and, each time, been surprised at the depth of it. The afternoon before our handfast, when I had refused marriage to him, Ian had been hurt by my rejection. He was feeling that again now. It was as plainly written on his face as if he had spoken the words to me directly.

Confusion must have been evident on mine. If I had found Collin a difficult man to decipher, Ian was impossible— a complete mystery. *He is a pirate—cruel, cunning, ruthless in the pursuit of the treasure he seeks.* I could no longer convince myself this was entirely the truth. He might be all of those things, but he was others as well. At the moment he seemed merely broken.

Desperate for my acceptance and approval. At the very least.

"It is not a man's appearance, but his actions that make his measure—make him desirable." I added the last with hesitation, not wanting to give him false hope. I wasn't certain there was anything Ian could do that would make me desire him. In those moments I had felt a connection with him, a breaking down of the barriers between us, I had been thinking of Collin. *Always.*

The sad smile reappeared just as briefly. "Do you know that it is impossible for you to lie? It is all right to say you find me hideous. I read it in your expression every time you do chance a look at me. It is as if you are hoping to see something else and are disappointed each time."

I swallowed with difficulty, unsettled that he had read me so well, and surprisingly guilt-ridden that I was hurting him. "Your voice reminds me of Collin. Sometimes I forget . . . "

"It would be best if you could."

I gave a tight nod, the familiar sting of tears threatening. "I know."

"We have now been handfast almost as long as you were married to him."

"Yes." I paused, gaining control once again, calling back my tears. I suppose I was making progress. "That doesn't seem to make it easier. It was different with Collin, as if our hearts had known each other all those years between."

There was a subtle shifting, of both Ian's body as he leaned back, settling more fully into the chair, and of our conversation. We had both admitted to vulnerable points and were well aware the other could use those against us, inflicting even more pain than we felt at present.

Ian unrolled his shirtsleeves, tugging them down to cover the worst of his scarred arms and hands, then began unwrapping his other hand. It was the same routine he followed every night, and for the first time I realized that it was meant to spare me from seeing any more of his burned flesh than necessary.

"Mary says the skin must be allowed to breathe. If not, I would keep my hands hidden from you."

"You can't wear bandages forever."

He shrugged. "They are still necessary. While we heal."

His inclusion of *we* intrigued and concerned me. Did he hope that I might someday be able to both overlook his scars and to forget my affection for Collin?

Ian was watching me again. "As a book left open, to the very line. And I thought you were the one who was able to read minds."

"I hardly ever know what you are thinking," I admitted.

"Well—" His mouth twisted in a grimace as one of the bandages stuck. "Some of us are very good at hiding things."

A warning? That I was not to trust him?

"You never finished telling me what happened to your hands," I reminded him.

"They became rather busy that night you first asked, didn't they?" His teasing was suggestive, as if he had done something other than hold me wrapped tight in a warm quilt while I succumbed to grief.

"Tell me," I said, refusing to acknowledge his inference. I settled more comfortably into my own chair, expecting a story.

"There was a fire. Set purposely by the English." His mouth twisted once more as he flexed his stiff fingers. "It's no wonder some of the Scottish lairds have taken to the same tactic. Learned it from the English. If there is something or someone you don't like, just set fire to it."

"What didn't the English want, in this instance?"

"A Scotsman telling them what to do. They intended him to give them his horse. He felt to keep it himself. The dragoons don't take kindly to being told no. They took the animal anyway then set fire to the man's barn."

"That's horrible. How can people be so cruel—so wicked?"

"They don't see *us* as people. Because we are not like them we are somehow less. Little better than vermin, I've heard them say."

"That is so terribly wrong." It was this treatment of the Scots that my English father had opposed and lost his commission for. The treatment I had both witnessed and received from the English myself since coming to Scotland made me want to take up his cause.

"How did you become involved? Was it a MacDonald barn and horse?"

Ian shook his head. "Not even on our land. Before the tinder was struck the soldiers threw a man into the building. There was some commotion, a woman shouting that he wasn't dead and the soldiers restraining her. The fire was started, and they did not wait around to admire their work but moved off, taking the woman with them."

"And you—went in after the man?" I remembered the heat blazing from the fire at Edan's house, and how I had not been able to stand being anywhere close. What kind of courage had it required for Ian to step inside that barn?

"What else was I to do?" He shrugged. "A burning beam had fallen across his chest. I tried to lift it. Another fell and struck my head and eye." His hand brushed the patch. "That is all I remember of my adventures with fire. I awoke in the farmhouse with my hands and eye bandaged. The farmer had rescued me."

"I am glad of it," I declared.

"Are you?" Ian sounded skeptical. Little wonder, given our past discord.

"Yes," I said quietly. I was still wary of him, still mourning Collin, still uncertain about many things. But at this moment I felt strangely grateful for his companionship.

I watched—with a mixture of disgust and sympathy—as Ian worked at stretching his hands. "They're wont to curl if I don't do this," he explained as he painstakingly straightened each finger, one at a time.

Our chairs were still quite close, and I had the impulsive thought to help him, that my touch might be less torturous than his own. I leaned forward and held my hands out, palms up.

It took him a few seconds to notice. Then he raised his head slowly, his eye meeting mine.

"I'll be gentle." *Trust me.*

After a moment's hesitation Ian scooted to the edge of his chair and placed his hand in mine. His trembled slightly, and I felt his fear—not that I would hurt him physically, but that I would find touching him too abhorrent after all. More than anything, he feared my rejection.

Who is the open book now?

I began with his thumb, running my own along its creased flesh, slowly pushing down to straighten it. "Thank you for telling me what happened to you."

"Someday I should like to tell you more of what transpired before I came here."

"More of Collin?" I wasn't sure I was ready to hear.

"Aye." Ian's eye closed, and he leaned his head back. "When the time is right I will tell you about Collin."

"I will hold you to that promise." I'd not push him for more tonight. I wanted to know and felt I must out of respect to Collin and for my own peace, but I was loath to disrupt the tranquility that had settled over us. There was nothing the least romantic in our contact, yet we *were* touching. And speaking civilly to one another—a significant improvement over our initial, raging standoffs.

I moved onto his index finger, unbending it slowly, massaging the muscle beneath the taut skin. His hands had repulsed me the night of our vows, still blistered as they had been. The skin felt closer to normal now, though fragile, and it seemed the scarring was here to stay.

Ian gave a sudden shudder, and I stopped, afraid I was hurting him. "I'm sorry."

"Don't be. From you, it is a kind of sweet torture."

I didn't like what he implied, but neither could I bring myself to stop helping him. My own injuries had been both real and severe enough that I understood what it was to suffer. I continued bending and stretching his hand, one finger at a time, then moved onto his palm, pressing my own flat against his to hold it in place.

"*Tada gan iarracht,*" he whispered. The scar on his head bulged with tension, though with his hair growing back, it was already not as visible as it had been.

"What does that mean?"

"Nothing done without effort." Ian let out a breath of relief when I released his hand.

"Not so fast," I said, as he started to pull away. "What about your wrist and arm?" I took the edge of his sleeve to pull it back.

"Not tonight." He drew away swiftly. "You have done enough. I thank you for your kindness."

"I am sorry if I hurt you." Perhaps I hadn't been as gentle as I'd thought.

"You did well," Ian hurried to assure me. "Truly." His smile was more an unconvincing grimace. "And your arm?" he asked, nodding to it. "How does it fare?"

"Better. Mary has been tending it as well." Carefully, I straightened it, and showed him my hand could open and close. "She says it was a clean break and should heal fully."

"Enough for you to paint again?"

"Perhaps. I suppose I shall try when the splint comes off." I didn't want to think of that now. I had painted the future before without even realizing it. What was to keep me from doing the same, was I to pick up a brush again? And if I did, what would I see?

I'd been afraid of doing harm to anyone else with my visions, and tonight I realized a new fear. If to see the future meant to know what kind of man Ian really was and what he intended for us, I wasn't sure I was brave enough to know.

Chapter Thirty-one

The following days became a repeat of the same pattern. I hauled and washed the wool and took it to those who did the carding. At last, after weeks of work, the wool was ready for spinning. The Campbell women in our group taught me how, and I took my turn alternately on one of the two big wheels in the sunny upstairs solar adjacent to what had been my grandfather's rooms. Eight of us labored there, using hand spinners when it wasn't our turn with the wheel. I'd never done any sort of work like this before but found it satisfying. It was the nearest to creating I'd done since leaving England.

It was also a good place to hear the latest gossip and discover what both Campbells and MacDonalds alike thought of our new, shared, arrangements.

"Clayton and Maggie are moving into their new house today," Mhairi announced on Friday morning.

"It's finished already?" another asked. "Cannot be much good if it was built in less than a week."

"It's a fine, simple house," Mhairi declared. "At least as good as what they had before. No less than ten men spent the better part of three days on it, and now they're onto building the next—that one is to be for a Campbell, of course." Her gaze strayed to the three Campbell women seated across the room. I was not next to them this morning, having purposely seated myself in a different chair, every day this week, in an effort to get to know all of the women, Campbells and MacDonalds.

"Campbells helped build the last house, did they not?" one of the three asked.

"Aye," Mhairi said.

"Then it is only fair that they should get the next house," I said, striving to keep the conversation civil. "We are working together to help *both* clans."

"Who would have ever thought such a thing?" A Campbell named Ellen clucked her tongue. "MacDonalds among us."

"My grandfather, Laird Campbell, thought of such a thing," I said firmly. All eyes were on me now. I set the spindle down and looked at each of the women in turn. "He saw this day. It was why I was betrothed to Collin MacDonald when I was only four years old."

"That was done in secret," Ellen said. "Had many of us known, there would have been objections."

"And have you objections now?" I asked. "To what is being done here?"

"I don't like it," Ellen said boldly. "And I suppose you can tell your husband that if you'd like and have me beaten for it."

"My husband is dead." I tamped down the stab of pain that accompanied this statement. "Anything told to me in this room will not be repeated to Ian MacDonald." I hoped that wasn't a foolish promise. "Women need a safe place to speak their minds and share what they feel."

"Aye," several chorused as their heads bobbed.

"Ian MacDonald and I are handfast, working together for this year, doing our best to save our families. Neither clan was likely to survive the winter without each other—or his leadership," I added. "Had we continued under Brann's rule, Campbells were likely to be extinct before another five years had passed."

"Because of your laird," Mhairi said. "Your land is not to

fault. You've so much of it can be tilled. And you've forests and rivers, lochs, mountains, and moors. MacDonalds have scarcely any. You have it all." It was the first bitterness I'd heard from her.

Had it all? I wondered if she was referring to more than land and crops. *To Collin.*

"For now, at least, you have as much as we do." *I lost him too.*

I directed my next words to the Campbell side of the room. "The MacDonalds have been here only a short time, and already look what has been accomplished." Collin had been right. "Ian *is* a good leader." His tactics were at times harsh, but I could also see that some of that was needed here.

I looked at Ellen again. "What don't you like? What would you see changed?"

"Aside from the MacDonalds leaving?" she asked.

"New homes would not be being built, but burned, if not for the MacDonalds," I reminded her.

"True. But it's not natural them being here. Can't trust 'em."

"It is the Campbells who cannot be trusted," another of the MacDonald women spoke up. "How are we to be certain you won't murder us in our beds as was done at Glencoe?"

Always their arguments return to the past. Feeling a headache coming on, I rubbed my temples. "You cannot let the past govern your thoughts and actions today," I argued. "None of us were there. We are not *those* Campbells or MacDonalds. We are better than that, and we are here—together—fighting to keep our country and the Highlands alive."

"Little you know," Ellen said with a *harrumph.* "You've not even passed a season with us yet."

"She knows plenty," Mhairi said, surprising me with her

defense. "Anyone who can tame Ian MacDonald deserves our respect." She glanced at me. "He is not the same as when he left with Collin to fetch you from England. Ian's changed into the man his brother believed he could be. I only wish Collin was here to see it."

"Thank you." I smiled my appreciation, grateful to feel I had perhaps one friend here, and a MacDonald at that.

As had become custom, I retired to our chamber as soon as we had taken our evening meal. Ian followed a short time later, and I could not entirely fault him, the tension in the great hall being what it was these days. Collin had years of earned trust and had become a respected friend to at least some Campbells; but Ian was seen more as an unwelcome interloper and I his accomplice now that we had handfast. Though I could see his efforts and others surely could too, it was going to take a great deal more time and no few miracles if the winter of Campbells and MacDonalds together was to be a success.

Life had become complicated and wearying, and the line I balanced upon that much more tenuous than before. Only now I was more invested in it. I was developing a genuine concern and love for my mother's people—*my* people—and I would not be driven from them. Perhaps not surprising, given the feelings I'd had for Collin, I felt the same about the MacDonalds. Ian's chant of together did not bother me as it had two months ago. I was starting to think he might not be as mad as I'd believed him to be.

And that was terrifying for its own reasons.

I glanced up from my mending to see him openly staring

at me from his chair on the other side of the room. He'd brought several pairs of boots up with him tonight and sat working over them by the lamp, leaving me the better light and warmth near the fire.

And the better light for him to watch me in. I had caught Ian's eye on me too many times to count the past weeks. It never ceased to unnerve me, and on those few occasions I had allowed our gazes to meet . . . Those feelings did not bear thinking about. In spite of being surrounded by numerous people daily, I was lonely, still very much a stranger in a foreign land, and still mourning Collin. All circumstances to recall in moments I felt weak. Ian undoubtedly sensed this weakness and would pounce given the first opportunity.

That he had not done so yet no longer surprised me. I'd come to understand that he intended to keep his promise to Alistair. I sensed I'd become a challenge to Ian. His quest to win me over became as personal as his dealings with the clans during the day tended toward impersonal and methodical. His judgments were swift, commanding, and largely impartial. I'd seen him grant and withhold from Campbells and MacDonalds alike.

But with me it was different. He'd not had another outburst since the incident of the tea. Ian's voice, while loud and unrelenting by day as he oversaw all manner of work—pushing all to do the most, the best, and what at times seemed impossible—turned quiet and reflective during the evening hours we spent together. His questions were meant to draw me out, his many kindnesses meant to woo.

I fought off his advances as I would have had they been of a physical nature. For were I to forget and give in even once, a child might result and I would be *his*, to order about, to MacDonald lands or beyond, as he saw fit. It was a danger I could not risk.

Outwardly, he might appear to have softened, but I could not allow myself to be deceived. His eye, so like Collin's, was merely calculating when it looked upon me. And his actions, no matter how considerate, might still be a ruse, a means of gaining trust before the axe that was the MacDonald clan fell upon us.

"What is wrong?" Ian asked, setting a boot aside. "You're brooding tonight."

"You're a fine one to speak of brooding," I muttered, stabbing the needle into the cloth viciously.

"True enough," Ian admitted. "But it does not become you. Tell me what is troubling you. I've a hunch it is I, so best be out with it and let our quarrel be done with sooner rather than later."

"I've no wish to argue." *It's not like that, anyway.* There was nothing palpable that we could argue over. Ian made me feel uneasy—unsettled in his presence—and I was not about to admit that.

"I'll guess, then. You're upset because I've cut meals to two per day, except for children under twelve."

I understood exactly why he'd done that. I'd been present for the final tally of the harvest and knew how the larder would have to stretch to feed all in the coming months. Still, he had not made the decision I would have. "What of nursing mothers, or those expecting a child? They ought to be favored with the children."

Ian's gaze slid to my belly. "Might you wish that included you after all?"

"Only if it was Collin's."

"So you would have extra meals? I ought to give them to you anyway. You've yet to recover fully from Brann's mistreatment."

"No." I frowned, realizing Ian was baiting me once more,

yet unable to hold back my retort. "So I might have something of Collin to remember."

"You have me." Ian tilted his chin toward the ceiling and struck an exaggerated pose, his lopsided grin somehow more amusing than sinister tonight.

He appeared so ridiculous that I bit my lip to keep from laughing, even as I realized what he was doing and felt a flare of anger. Would that Collin and I had enjoyed nights like this to jest with one another.

"Not that, then." Ian abandoned his effort, unaware of how close he'd come to breaking my stony exterior. "You're angry I ordered the Campbell men out to hunt and kept the MacDonalds here."

"Shouldn't I be?" That had made me, and the rest of the Campbells, more than a bit wary. What more perfect opportunity might there be for MacDonald men to take advantage of or outright murder the women and children left behind?

"You do realize that I armed those Campbell men with nearly everything we have," Ian said in his defense. "The Campbells know this land far better than the MacDonalds. It made sense that your clan should hunt. And had they wished, it would have been far easier for them to turn on us, slitting throats or filling us with lead. At the least they could have easily shot *me* or slit *my* throat." Ian brought a hand to his neck, and I knew a moment of panic, imagining him killed. This was followed immediately by alarm that I actually wanted him to stay alive and safe. How could I possibly feel this way?

Ian leaned forward, staring at me intently. "What is it, Katherine?"

"Nothing. You should stop looking at me like that."

"Like what?" He continued to stare and sounded far more innocent than I believed him to be.

"As if I'm a tasty dish you cannot wait to devour. It's unholy."

"Is that why you're angry with me? Because I enjoy feasting my eyes upon you? But you do look tasty." Ian's mouth crooked in a smile that I would have found endearing from Collin.

"I've no intention of devouring you," Ian continued. "I should miss your company too much. You must forgive me the indulgence of taking in a lovely sight. It is about the only pleasure left to me." He flexed his hands, free at night of bandages, but scarred enough that movement was still restricted. His black eye had long since healed, and so largely had the other cuts and bruises on his face and arms. Yet I knew he suffered.

Often in the evenings I would notice that his mind seemed to be in another place, one that caused a grimace of pain or his lips to be pressed together as if holding in deep sorrow. I wondered if he was thinking of Collin, or if some other, bitter memory haunted him. Either way, I did not feel sympathy. His behavior, prior to coming here, had been deserving of misery.

"I am not your pleasure," I said, bristling at such a term. "And even were I—Collin never looked at me that way."

"Then he is an even bigger fool than I believed." Ian wiped his hands on a rag and tossed it aside.

"Don't," I ordered, a fragile quiver to my voice. "Don't you dare criticize him. You've no right."

"I've more right than you'd believe." Ian stood and ran a hand through his regrowing hair, making it stand on end. "He brought you here and endangered your life."

"He brought me home," I corrected.

"He spent much-needed MacDonald money on travel when it wasn't going to be replaced."

I stiffened in my chair, the subject of my spent dowry still a sore one. "Neither of us knew the money was gone."

"He left the MacDonalds floundering and stirred up the pot with the Campbells—not exactly doing his part to save Scotland."

"That is quite a lot of responsibility and blame to put upon one man." I looked down at the shirt spread across my lap. It had belonged to Collin. And I was mending it for Ian, who—like the rest of the MacDonalds—had arrived with very little. "Collin was a good man, but I doubt even he had it in him to save Scotland."

"Aye, well the old Campbell laird believed he did." Ian's words were so soft I almost missed them.

"My grandfather believed in me too. If you think he'd be disappointed in Collin, I imagine it is nothing compared to what he would feel about me."

"Collin said your grandfather had this astounding faith in both of you." Ian brought a hand to his forehead in a gesture that *was* familiar. During the short time I'd been married to Collin, I had seen him take this same stance many times, and on each occasion I'd thought he looked as if he carried the weight of the world. It seemed that weight had been transferred to Ian's shoulders now. I wouldn't have thought it possible.

The Ian I had known on our journey to Scotland had been cold and calculating, with vision only for himself and perhaps his own clan. The Ian I'd witnessed since then seemed to waver between ruthless and compassionate, depending upon whose company he was in. An improvement, to be sure, but still . . .

The irritation I'd felt just a few moments before melted away as I looked at him—physically altered, yet I dared not hope internally changed as well. If only I might trust that was so, I would take his scarred appearance and changed heart any day over the striking figure he used to pose.

"I've almost finished with this shirt," I said, holding it up to show him. Our conversation had grown too serious for my liking, and I feared allowing my own heart to soften anymore toward my self-proclaimed protector. *He can protect me from Brann, but that is all.* I would not be safe in any way if I allowed myself to get close to Ian or to trust him.

"Thank you." His brief smile appeared again, and he returned to the pile of boots. He'd ceased wearing his old ones, complaining that they were no longer comfortable, since his foot had been recently stepped on by a horse.

"How many pairs do you need?" I asked, only half-teasing.

"These aren't for me." Ian held up a shoe, dangling it from his fingertips. "What do you think?"

I blinked, making sure I was seeing correctly. The shoe was small, much too small for a grown man, and appeared to be cut from the leather of Ian's old boots.

"Is it for a child?"

"Aye." He turned the shoe over, holding it between his knees, and resumed his work. "Winter is coming, and too many weeuns in bare feet." He inclined his head toward the pile of shoes and boots on the floor beside his chair. "These weren't being used by anyone. The Campbells are a lazy, wasteful lot."

I took umbrage at this, mending a shirt for him, as I was. "So who are those to be for?"

Ian looked up at me, a sly grin on his face. "MacDonald bairns, of course."

Weary of our conversation, I said nothing but put the shirt down and retreated to the safety of the screen, to change from my gown. My composure was slipping, and sooner or later I *would* laugh—or possibly lunge at him—because of something he said. Better to hide in the refuge of sleep.

With the longer strings Bridget had found for tying my corset, I had the process of undressing down to a few minutes. Ian knew his assistance was not needed and thankfully stayed away.

But this night when I went to get into bed I found him already there, shirt off, sitting on the edge, as if waiting for me. My breath caught as my eyes riveted to a recently-healed cut zigzagging across his midsection. It marred an otherwise perfect torso, one that brought to mind Collin when he had removed his shirt the evening I pushed him in the water.

A corner of Ian's mouth lifted. "Not entirely indifferent then, are we?"

"I'm looking at your scar," I said a little too quickly. "You're one big mess of them. I'm amazed you survived whatever happened before you came here."

"Perhaps it is time I tell you what happened."

"Maybe some other evening." I didn't trust myself to more conversation with him tonight.

"How long are we to continue this way?" he asked.

"Another nine months and twenty-three days," I retorted. I kept careful track, lest he attempt some trickery at the end of our term.

"And then—after that—will you acknowledge me as a person?"

I dropped into a chair. "I acknowledge that now. You are the person who pointed a pistol at his own brother and who tried to drown me. You are the man who raged at me in this very room and destroyed many of its belongings like some savage animal. You are the person who had a man beaten almost to death, because he was Brann's follower. You are the man who would have banished an innocent woman for her part in trying to help me. You are someone to be wary of."

"I see we have slightly different points of view," Ian grumbled. "And I must say yours is skewed rather dangerously. The man was beaten because he threatened you. He was found on the stairs in possession of a knife. That he confessed to working for Brann only confirmed what I had guessed. And he is fortunate to have escaped with his life, considering his intent was to end yours."

I had not heard that part of the story before and realized, with some consternation, that if Ian spoke the truth, then my Campbell relations had purposely omitted it.

"As for Bridget, her mistake was grievous. Had there been but a little more of her brew, you would not be here now, but beneath the ground. Again, I believe I curbed my anger and expressed my displeasure in a rather contained manner, given the circumstances."

"Be that as it may, there are still the incidences before your arrival," I reminded him and myself as well. *A good man does not force someone into a river at knifepoint.*

"You mention only my faults," Ian argued. "How about acknowledging the good I've done here and that a man can change?"

"Once broken, trust is difficult to repair."

"But not impossible?" There was a small bit of hope and a great deal of uncertainty in the question.

Two months ago I would have said with surety that it was impossible Ian MacDonald might ever be considered trustworthy, least of all by me. A month ago we wouldn't have been having this conversation. But now . . . I was either the biggest fool for starting to believe in him, or perhaps a man really could change.

He was asking me to give him hope, yet to do so seemed

it would only walk me that much closer to the edge of the cliff. And if I fell, I wasn't certain whether he would catch me or laugh as he watched me tumble to my death.

"Earning my trust will take at least another nine months, and even then it's doubtful." More in question was whether I could continue that long in these strained circumstances. If, after only two months, I found it increasingly difficult to reconcile the two Ian's, how was I to feel when three or six months had passed? A year? Was I handfast to the pistol and knife-wielding Ian, or the Ian who, this very day, had stopped to lift a crying child from the mud and carry her to her mother? I wasn't certain who he was anymore. And worse, he made me uncertain who I was and what I wanted.

To believe in him, to trust him and begin to care for him, felt like betrayal to Collin. We might have had only three weeks together, but a promise of nearly fifteen years had bound us, its pull stronger than anything earthly. There was no such promise with Ian, no otherworldly forces binding us together. But what if Collin *had* trusted Ian in the end?

"Katherine." Ian's touch was light on my shoulder. I gave a little jump anyway. Since the night we had tended to one another's hands, we had gone out of our way—or I'd gone out of mine—to avoid touching each other, so it was unnerving when we did. He removed his hand, then crouched beside my chair so that we were nearly eye level. "We can't go on like this. I need your forgiveness—your understanding. I can't bear to see you still grieving so. The things I've done—they're eating me inside. I need to tell you—" He broke off suddenly at the sound of angry voices outside our door.

Ian stood and walked over to it, pressing his ear to the wood. His face drained of color, followed at once by a hardening of his jaw. "Impossible." His whispered words sounded shocked—and fearful. He turned a quick circle, scanning the room, his eye lingering a moment on my dressing screen before settling on the bed.

"Get into bed," he ordered,

I held my ground. "What? Why? Who is out there?"

"Quiet." Two strides and he was before me again, then scooping me from the chair. I shrieked as he walked to the bed and practically threw me on it. The voices outside were louder now, accompanied by pounding on the door. I scrambled away as Ian pulled a knife from his discarded boot and stuck it in the back of his belt. "Cover yourself as best you can. Don't speak. If you've the chance to get out, take it. Find Alistair or Gordon—Earnan. Anyone who will protect you."

"From who? What is going on, Ian?"

"*Katie.*" He gripped my shoulder so hard that it hurt. "Trust me and do as I say." More than his words or the threat in his touch, it was his pleading expression before he turned away that convinced me.

A woman's scream on the other side of the door made my hair stand on end.

"I know you're in there, Ian!"

I scrambled beneath the quilt a second before Ian undid the bar and lock. He jumped back as the door flew open, the heavy wood stopping only when Ian's hand shot out to catch it. Mhairi appeared in the doorway, her head wrenched back by the man behind her.

I gasped. Ian's accomplice from the river stood only a few paces from our bed. He took his attention from Ian long enough to look over at me. Recollection sparked in his eyes and flared his nostrils.

"I'm sorry," Mhairi cried. "He threatened to kill Greta's bairn if I didn't take you to him."

"It's all right," Ian said in a soothing tone. "You did well."

"It's true." Niall's gaze flickered between me and Ian.

"You've really done it—taken your brother's bride and her clan."

"Their laird left them in a poor state," Ian said nonchalantly, not quite bragging, yet neither clarifying the particulars of the arrangement and the tenuous peace he'd worked to establish between MacDonalds and Campbells.

Where are his pretty words now?

Niall's gaze slid toward me once more. "And with Collin out of the way—"

"Aye." Ian cut him off. "What do you want, Niall? I'm a bit busy." He inclined his head toward our bed.

"Seems we both are." Niall sniggered, the same menacing laugh he'd had at the river's edge when his knife had been pointed at me. Holding Mhairi by the hair, he forced her to face him, then pulled her close against the length of his body.

"Let her go," Ian's voice was deceptively calm, while his stance was as a wild cat ready to spring. The muscles in his neck stood taut, his scar bulging beneath his new growth of hair. "Your quarrel is with me, not her."

My eyes flickered to Mhairi. *I must help her.*

"True." Niall released Mhairi, then slapped her face, rocking her head to the side. "But she is a family friend, no?" In a flash of steel Niall's blade was out and slashing the air in front of Ian's face.

Ian ducked to the side just in time, pushing Mhairi out of the way. He reached behind him, and then his own knife was raised, matching blow for blow with Niall's.

I clutched the covers, thinking madly what I must do. *What would Collin have done?* "You deceived me." Niall stabbed the air, only narrowly missing Ian's shoulder. "Left me for dead."

"Should have made certain you were." Ian attempted an undercut, but Niall moved faster, slicing the tip of his knife across Ian's forearm. Ian gave a shout as blood trickled down his arm and the fight continued.

Mhairi scooted her way toward the door, but Niall was still close enough that he might reach her. I gave a slight nod as I caught her attention, then grabbed the pitcher on the night table and slowly raised to a standing position on the bed.

"Suppose you thought you'd enjoy the spoils here on your own without me." Niall struck again, barely missing Ian once more. I screamed as loud as I could. Both men turned toward me, giving Mhairi precious seconds to flee.

"S'alright," Niall said, catching sight of her. "I'm more interested in you," he said to me. "I'll have my turn in a minute." He grinned, showing off an array of filthy teeth.

I threw the pitcher at him, and he ducked easily, the porcelain shattering on the floor behind him. Niall's blade met Ian's flesh again. The fighting continued, far more barbaric than sword play, at such close contact.

I leapt from the bed, but kept pressed against the wall, looking about for anything that might be used as a weapon.

Niall surged forward, backing Ian toward the chairs and fire. I shoved the one I'd sat in out of the way just in time to keep him from tripping over it.

"Get out of here, Katie," he yelled.

"Aye. Run and hide." Niall sneered. "Makes the game that much more fun."

I backed toward the fire, banked now for the night. Hands behind me, I grabbed the poker just as Niall leapt, shoving Ian backward against the wall and sending his knife spinning across the room. I swung the poker as hard as I could, slamming it into the back of Niall's neck instead of his head as I'd intended.

He shouted, looked over, and missed Ian's fist coming at him. Ian's aim was better than mine, and Niall stumbled backward, tripping when I caught him behind the legs with the poker.

Ian pounced, straddling Niall's torso, fist already raised. He brought it down savagely, pummeling Niall's face. By the second punch blood spurted from Niall's nose.

"You ruined my brother—nearly destroyed him!" Ian lifted Niall by his shoulders, then slammed him back onto the floor repeatedly. "If not for you, he'd be here. He'd be alive."

If not for—What did Niall have to do with—

He shoved Ian from him, and they rolled across the floor. I jumped back. Ian gained the advantage again, shaking Niall, as the latter slowly raised his arm, knife poised.

"Ian!" I lunged forward as Ian shifted his weight, not a second too soon. In a fluid movement he jumped up, stepped on Niall's arm, then wrested the knife from him. Instead of throwing it away, he raised it above Niall's chest.

I turned away, but not quickly enough to miss Ian lunge, the blade sinking into Niall's chest. The man's brief scream blended with mine as I felt myself sliding to the floor. I backed away, curling myself into the corner.

Ian jerked the knife from Niall's body and raised it to strike again.

Bile rose in my throat as I half sobbed, half gagged. Ian turned toward me, his expression murderous. Our eyes met, his bulging with fury. He jerked back, as if surprised to see me there, then threw the knife aside and stepped away from Niall's lifeless body.

"Katie—" He held bloody hands out to me, pleading.

I shook my head and tried to make myself smaller. "Stay away."

He stared at me a long second, anguish contorting his face. Running footsteps pounded in the hall. Alistair burst into the room, Mhairi and two other men close behind.

"What have you done?" Alistair's eyes were huge as he looked from the body to Ian.

"Murderer," another man, also a Campbell, said.

"Aye." Ian turned from me and faced them. "I am a murderer. You would do well not to forget." He poked at Niall's corpse with his foot. "And not to cross me."

Chapter Thirty-two

A late October wind swept me along as I held my shawl tight and hurried toward the castle. Earnan, my guard today, was unaware of my errand, and I needed to be back before he or anyone else noticed my absence. It had been my good fortune to be sewing with the other women in the solar when the midwife had joined us, requesting hazel and bog myrtle from Mary, who lived outside the gates. I had eagerly volunteered to fetch the herbs, the opportunity to be outside and to enjoy a visit with Mary too good to pass up and well worth the risk of being caught.

In the month since Niall's death, Ian had not allowed me to leave the castle at all, and I felt near to going mad with confinement. He claimed it was for my safety, that he didn't know how many others out there might be our enemies and only too eager to harm me. I felt the real reason was that he feared I would try to escape, interfering with his grand scheme to control the Campbells.

He needn't have worried. As much as I wished to be free of his company, I suffered no illusions about my abilities to survive on my own. At the least, venturing far would only be an invitation for Brann to find me. He was out there—somewhere. I'd dreamt of him twice, seeing him each time near the old rowan I'd sat beneath in the kirkyard when we'd buried Collin.

I wasn't certain of the dream's significance and had mentioned it to no one. Would I meet Brann there? Did it mean he was soon to die?

The smell of woodsmoke filled the chill air at the end of the newly completed row houses, simple squares all connected to one another, built in a row along the castle wall.

They had been Ian's idea, requiring the least lumber possible, as close to the castle as possible, and housing as many families as possible. The wall behind them, he had explained, would offer protection from the elements. And were we to be attacked, those living there would be able to quickly come inside the gates for additional protection.

His plan had been presented in one of many nightly meetings, for both Campbell and MacDonald leaders and open to anyone else who wished to attend. My presence was always required. And on that occasion Ian had added, with a pointed look my direction, that I, with my abilities, would be able to alert the families in plenty of time before any attack.

"Katherine will know," he'd stated vehemently. I'd not disagreed. I didn't dare. We'd barely spoken at all the past weeks, since Niall's violent death. His body had been removed, his blood scrubbed from the floor that very night. But I could not forget Ian towering over him, first viciously beating him and then plunging his knife into Niall's chest. I dreaded being in my room and dreaded Ian all the more. The only consolation was that he had not slept beside me since the incident. He slept on the floor now, or didn't come to bed at all.

I could only feel grateful that I hadn't succumbed to any of my doubts concerning him. I'd almost believed he was changed, that he was not the same man who had so violently threatened both Collin and me last summer. But seeing Ian's transformation when fighting Niall was a reminder of his true nature. To cross him was to die. And yet . . .

I still saw glimpses of humanity. He knew I was afraid of him and stayed away. When it came time to slaughter the sheep, he'd spared the youngest of the flocks. Over half of the MacDonald barley had been ground for flour instead of all being taken to the new distillery to be made into malt. He'd been solicitous in all his behaviors since that dreadful evening. So much so that I felt myself wanting to trust him again. At least enough for the two of us to have a conversation.

There were things I wanted to ask. What, specifically, had Ian sought my forgiveness for the night of Niall's murder, and what had been his and Niall's involvement in Collin's death? It was time I knew, and I had deemed tonight, my twentieth birthday, the night for answers.

It was nothing I looked forward to, and there had been little to find joy in the past weeks as we all worked toward sustaining our fragile existence. But this afternoon, beneath the blue sky and amidst the trees boasting red and gold, I felt a bit of freedom and happiness and determined to treasure both as long as possible. It was all I could do without canvas, paints, or brush to capture and preserve the memory.

Near the last row house closest to the gates, a group of children stood around a fire, each with an apple on a stick roasting over the low flames. A woman pulled laundry from the line, and a man lifted his hand in a friendly wave as he rolled past with a wagon of firewood. To any passerby the scene might have appeared completely ordinary.

They would not have known that every other house sheltered a MacDonald family and those between a Campbell. They would not have realized that both Campbell and MacDonald children stood at the same fire, laughing and talking together as any children might. I realized all this and appreciated it for the miracle it was. My grandfather truly had been a seer, his vision come to pass regardless that those he'd expected to carry it out had failed.

I stepped through the open gates, onto the hard-packed road that led directly to the front doors. The mud that had met Collin and me in July had been scraped away, along with the scraps and debris that had lined the paths. On either side of me people hurried to and fro, engaged purposefully in work of all sorts. I felt the heat of the blacksmith's bellows as I passed, while only a short distance farther a group of young boys worked together rewiring a large pen of swine. The last of the MacDonalds and their livestock had safely arrived a few days before.

There were now more cows for milking, an additional three wagons of chickens, and numerous other animals added to the barns and sheds. Still not enough, Ian had mused. But better than what we'd had before.

I reached the castle and entered, sorry my hour of freedom was over. I stopped briefly to speak with Bridget and ask that water for a bath be sent to my room. Then I headed directly for the stairs, eager to divest of the evidence in the basket over my arm. When I knocked on Grandfather's door—as I still thought of it—a young girl answered. She appeared troubled, and the moans of agony from within left no doubt as to why. A woman was birthing here. *MacDonald or Campbell?* It might be either, as we'd only the one midwife between us, a MacDonald. The Campbell midwife had been one of those run off the land the previous year.

I handed the girl my basket of herbs and made a hasty exit, saying a silent prayer for the mother and thinking of Anna. I'd posted a letter shortly after Collin and I had arrived at the Campbell keep. A few days ago one had arrived in return. It had included a drawing from Timothy and a note from my mother telling me, among other things, that Anna was with child.

Better her than me. My troubling dream of bearing Ian's child had not returned, and I could only feel grateful for that and our increased distance since Niall's death.

Telling myself yet again that Niall's ghost did not haunt here, I entered my room slowly and stood just beyond the doorway listening. *Foolish,* I silently berated myself. But I could not help the ripple of fear every time I came into the room. Death had visited here—unexpected, violent death. Whether a spirit lurked here or not, the events of that night replayed frequently in my mind.

I rubbed my arms, warding off the chill that had little to do with temperature and everything to do with my imagination, taking flight now as my shadow danced along the wall. *Some seer I am, afraid of my own shadow.*

In the dim light I also made out the tub set before the fire, already partly filled with water so warm steam rose from it. *Bless you, Bridget.*

I dared not bathe in the evenings anymore, lest Ian come to our room. And in the mornings I was expected to be up and at my tasks at first light, along with everyone else. This left only the occasional afternoon, when my work was finished early, to delight in the pleasure of soaking in a warm tub.

I dropped my shawl on the closest chair and retreated to the screen to undress. The simple work gowns I wore now were easy to get out of on my own. I required no help from Ian or anyone else. Compared to my first few days of travel in England, when I had needed assistance with nearly everything, I had grown quite independent—in many ways.

And lonely. Collin and I had needed each other. Without him I felt bereft, a stranger in a land that, while somewhat familiar, was also not what I had known.

A knock sounded at my door, and Bridget entered with two other women carrying buckets. They poured more water into the tub and left, Bridget promising to lock the door and that she would return to wash my hair.

When the door had closed again I crossed the room quickly and stuck a toe in the tub, testing the temperature. *Deliciously warm.* I climbed in eagerly and sank into the depths, letting the warm water lap beneath my chin as I closed my eyes. The scent of lavender wafted around me, and I silently thanked Bridget for her thoughtfulness and Eithne for her hard work. I should have liked to help her again, if only Ian would allow me to visit her.

"I see it is an afternoon for indulgences."

My eyes flew open, and I jerked upright, then at once sank lower as Ian looked over at me. He leaned casually against the door he'd just closed, the key dangling from a ribbon in his left hand.

"Please leave." My shaky command sounded anything but authoritative.

"You should have barred the door," he scolded lightly, then fixed it himself. "What if I'd been Brann?"

I ignored his question as he'd ignored my request. "Bridget is to return in a minute to wash my hair."

"She's been called away to more pressing matters. I assured her I would assist you." Ian hefted a bucket from the floor behind him. "Your rinse water, milady."

"I don't need your help. Please leave," I said again, my voice firmer, more desperate. Beneath my pounding heart, full-fledged panic erupted.

"Why should I leave?" Ian drawled, walking farther from the door instead of out it. "This is my room as well."

"Because a gentleman gives a lady privacy." I drew my knees up to my chest in an attempt at covering myself.

"But I'm not a gentleman." Ian crossed the room—on the

far side, away from my bath. "We both know that. I'm the devil. Wasn't that what you told Collin?"

My lips parted in surprise. I frowned at this revelation of confidence breached. What else had Collin told him?

Ian laughed. "Collin shared your opinion of me that morning at the inn, after you'd insulted me—something about not believing I could read, if I recall correctly."

He did remember. And he was the devil. No more so than at this moment, toying with me as a cat might play with a mouse before pouncing.

"Why *can* you read?" I asked, grasping for anything to prolong this conversation, to distract him from me. "Collin said you'd been treated poorly by the Munros. It does not seem likely they hired a tutor for you."

"I was fourteen when I was taken by them," Ian said, not acknowledging his father's part in the process. "I was the son of a laird and had been educated as such. I was literate in far more than book learning—schooled in everything from how to govern a clan, to fighting, to the keeping of accounts." He leaned forward and put out one of the two lamps. "There may even have been a lesson or two along the way regarding the washing of a woman's hair."

"You are worse than the devil," I muttered, hugging my knees to my chest and keeping as low as possible in the water.

"Undeniably." Ian made his way around the bed to the second lamp. "I believe you'd another name assigned me as well. What else was it that Collin said . . . " Ian tapped a finger against his lips contemplatively. "Ah yes, I remember. You thought me a *pirate* the first time we met." Ian snarled, and twisted his face such that his eye patch moved up and down. "And you know a pirate would definitely *not* leave if there was a beautiful woman bathing in his bedchamber."

I turned away from him with a huff, attempting to mask the fear shivering up my back.

The room darkened as the second lamp went out. I tried to think through a defense and—as had been the case at the river—came up with none. If Ian wished to finish what he'd started there—

"Let me help you."

I flinched at his voice, so close behind me.

"No." I sat in total darkness, my heartbeat frantic as I tried to remember where the towel was and if I'd be able to get to it or the door before he reached me. "You promised Alistair you wouldn't touch me unless I wished it."

"What do you think I am trying to do?" There was a definite smirk in his voice.

"Frightening a woman is not the way—"

"You're frightened?" The teasing was gone.

"How can I not be after you tried to drown me once already?"

Ian swore softly. "I'm sorry. I did not think that you might suppose—didn't think about the water. I mean you no harm today or any other."

I couldn't believe him, not with the horror of Niall's death so recently added to my own experience. It wasn't only that Ian had killed him so brutally but in the days following, still brimming with fury, he had insisted Niall's body be displayed in the courtyard as a lesson to any who might think to cross him. *I* was crossing him now, refusing his advances.

"I don't want you to be afraid of me," Ian continued. "Though I cannot blame you. I've no excuse for my actions at the river. I, too, was a wicked man and deserve all the suffering that has come my way since."

"What about Niall?" I sniffed and realized I was crying,

helplessness and dread spilling from my eyes in a most cowardly manner. "The way you killed him—"

"I've no regrets there," Ian said. "Only perhaps that you were witness. Niall delighted in hurting women. When he set his sights on you—well, perhaps I went a little mad. After what he'd already done to my brother, I could not let him hurt anyone else—*especially* you."

"Was Niall responsible for Collin's death?" This wasn't how I'd imagined our conversation to go, yet here we were. Keeping him talking might be my only defense.

"Not directly," Ian said. "But were it not for him, I cannot help but think my brother *would* be with us today."

Niall was wicked. We are safer with him gone. I believed that perhaps a bit more now. Collin had killed to protect me too. I had felt only relief that morning at the cave when he'd stabbed Malcom. Were Ian's actions really so different?

"Enough talk of the past," Ian said. "I cannot undo what has been done, but I give you my word that it will not be repeated, or added upon. I promised that I would keep you safe, and so I will. And I will do my best not to frighten you along the way. Here—use this."

Something landed on the water in front of me.

"Cover yourself with the towel while I wash your hair," Ian said.

"You still insist when I've told you I would not prefer it." I grabbed the sodden fabric and did my best to drape it over me.

"Aye." He stood directly behind me now. "Just as you insisted on walking outside alone today when I had told you I did not prefer that."

"Punishment. That's what this is about?" After tucking the towel around me, I twisted around in the tub to look at him.

Ian shook his head. "I wouldn't call it that. But as you were given to dangerous indulgence this afternoon, so am I. For my endangerment, I choose washing your hair." He placed his hands on my bare shoulders and turned me from him.

"I hardly see how that is dangerous to you."

"I don't suppose you would." He raised the bucket over my head. "Lean forward."

Water began cascading over me. Left with no choice, I complied, but attempted once more to dissuade him. "You are not my husband," I spluttered. "We have an agreement, and it does not extend to things of a personal nature."

"Let's discuss that agreement, shall we?" Ian placed his hands on my head, and I resisted the urge to lean away from his touch. *Better his hands on my head than anywhere else.*

"I have agreed to protect you from Brann. I've promised to keep my clansmen here under control, promised that no more Campbells will be driven from their homes. I have, in fact, been busy rebuilding many of those homes and working tirelessly to ensure that all have what they need to survive the coming winter. In return you have promised me . . . Hmmm. I can't seem to recall. What is it I am getting in exchange for my services?"

"The MacDonalds are benefitting from this arrangement too," I reminded him.

"Little good that does me personally." His fingers began massaging my head.

"You are free to leave at any time." *Goodness.* "I would not hold you in breach of our contract." *This feels divine.*

"Is that what you truly wish?" Ian's hands stilled. "Should I leave you to your own defenses against Brann?"

That I required Ian's protection had already been proven. Had Brann been the one sharing my chamber these past weeks instead of Ian, I'd no doubt my situation would be very different. For all of Ian's talk of being a pirate, he hadn't truly acted as one. He'd left me mostly alone—until now.

Did I want him to leave? What would happen if he did? A repeat of my time spent belowstairs was too much of a possibility. I didn't necessarily want Ian here, certainly did not want him so close to me at this moment, but I *had* been safer with him around.

"You are taking a very long time to answer," he said.

"No," I whispered, reluctant to share the conclusion I'd come to. "I do not wish you to leave. Neither do I wish to be intimate with you. My feelings for Collin—"

"—are abundantly clear," he muttered beneath his breath. "I will keep to my word not to touch you as a husband might. But I *will* wash your hair, taking my pleasure as you took yours outside." His hands began moving again, working their way from the top of my head to the back of my neck, then lifting strands of hair, working the soap into their lengths.

I closed my eyes and pursed my lips, not trusting them to contain a blissful moan. *What sorcery is this?* His hands worked their magic, mesmerizing me much as Collin's had the night he'd braided my hair. After a few minutes I ceased worrying about Ian taking his pleasure and worried that I was taking mine. His touch was surprisingly tender, and I felt myself relaxing, responding to his gentle ministrations, savoring the contact with another person—and hating myself because I did.

Collin. I strained to hold onto him and our past in my mind. I grasped at images that passed by fleetingly, only to be replaced every time by Ian, with the dark fuzz of his newly-grown hair and his pirate patch.

Pirate devil. Devil pirate. That's what he was. A murder-er. A thief, coming to Campbell land as he had and taking over. But as with my attempts to keep an image of Collin in my mind, the image of Ian as vile would not hold.

A pirate would not have comforted a frightened woman as Ian had comforted Mhairi the night he'd killed Niall. The devil did not whittle toys or fashion shoes for children by firelight each night. A pirate would not stop to join in their games during the day. He'd not give up his chair for an old woman to sit in. Yet Ian had done all those things and more since coming here. But that still couldn't change who he really was at his core. *What he's done and once tried to do—to me.*

What he was doing to me right now. He'd as much as declared his intent to make me willing, and here I was falling victim. I couldn't see that this was danger for him, but a very real threat to me. I sank lower in the tub, scarcely remembering to keep hold of the towel as well as to hold in a sigh of delight as Ian massaged the top of my head once more.

This is wrong. I must not dishonor Collin. I pressed the towel tighter across my torso and legs as I simultaneously prayed Ian would stop and wished he wouldn't. This wasn't the Ian I knew, or that I had known. If I continued seeing this other side of him, the side so like his twin, I feared I'd go mad. I *would* desire his company, and where would that lead me?

Chapter Thirty-three

"He *still* refuses to see me?" I craned my neck, trying, to no avail, to see over the heads of the two MacDonald guards stationed outside my door.

"Aye," Gordon said apologetically. "We're not to let you set so much as a toe from your room."

"Not unless we're wanting the same fate as your last guard," Bryce, the other one, added.

"And you don't want that for us, do you?" Gordon asked, not unkindly.

"No. Of course not." I stepped back inside the room and closed the door softly behind me. The reminder of what had happened to Earnan six days earlier still weighed heavily. For his carelessness in letting me slip outside the gates alone, he had been given fifteen lashes—one for every three minutes of the forty-five I had been outside the walls unchaperoned.

Afterward he had been made to stand out in the rainy courtyard for as many hours. I had watched all this from my window, having discovered the night before—shortly after Ian had left me to finish my bath alone—that I was not permitted to leave my room. Earnan had not deserved such punishment, not when it was I who had disobeyed. Not when he had once saved my life and had only served me well since.

I'd written a note expressing my regret and apology and given it to Gordon, then asked him to give it to his sister, hoping she would see it safely to Earnan's hands. Since the night of Niall's death, and our shared trauma, Mhairi and I had become friendlier to one another.

Staying in my room had been bad enough but was made that much worse by the lack of human contact the past week. Aside from the few, brief conversations with the guards posted at my door, I had not seen or talked with anyone since Ian had washed my hair. I felt certain I was soon to go mad from it.

Could loneliness and boredom drive a person insane?

I crossed the room and returned to my post at the window seat, where I might at least look to the courtyard below and see that other people still existed. In particular, *one* other person—*Ian.* He'd driven me mad in an entirely different way the night of my birthday, then left me troubled and simmering and *wanting* his company—of all things.

That evening—after I had been denied the privilege of going down to dinner and had mistakenly guessed this meant Ian would be joining me and we would dine together in our room—I had dreamed once more that he brought me a child. I'd noticed, this time, that I didn't seem upset by this, only a bit confused perhaps when he handed me the baby. When I awoke from the dream, I wasn't as panicked as I had been previously. Being handfast with him, what other choice did I have for a family of my own? *Would bearing Ian's child not be better than a life alone, with no child? No husband?*

Before I'd had time to explore these newly-developing feelings he had crushed them. The fragile trust he'd earned by keeping his promise, even to the point of washing my hair without touching any other part of me, had vanished with the first crack of the whip against Earnan's back. The desire for Ian's company had doused as quickly as it had flared to life, replaced by a boiling fury.

I couldn't wait to see him. The words I would speak, the anger I'd convey—How dare he punish Earnan because I'd visited Mary. How dare he lock me in my room overnight.

How dare he leave me here alone for *days*, with nothing

to do and no company and no control over anything to do with my life. How I hated Ian MacDonald, and I could not wait to tell him.

If he believed all this time alone would cool my temper, he was sorely wrong. It was fortunate for Ian that I didn't have a pistol at my disposal. Because I would have shot him again, and this time I would have had better aim.

Dusk settled outside the castle, quickly shrouding the east-facing room in darkness. I did not bother to light the candles. There was nothing I required light for, and I feared using them, doubtful Ian would grant me more.

A faint sliver of a moon appeared in the sky, and I recalled Father's words, wondering, sorrowfully, where he was and if that same moon still shone for him. An ache for home and family, all that was familiar, swelled within me, and I found myself crying once again, tears of frustration, loneliness, and despair. Was I to spend the rest of my life shut up like this? Did anyone outside my door even care?

Do I care? I tracked the moon's slow progress and contemplated this. Three months ago it hadn't mattered to me whether I lived or died. Collin's loss had seemed too great to overcome. There was no going back to the plans we'd had and the promises made to one another and my grandfather. There would be no one to replace Collin, not even his brother. I had to forge a new life without him and had been doing so blindly, stumbling along, focused solely on getting through one day at a time. That had been working fairly well until the afternoon of my walk and Ian's untimely visit.

The numb had almost left me then, had been in jeopardy of being replaced with feelings of a more hopeful and tender nature—a sure way to have my heart crushed again. Perhaps Ian had done a good turn in leaving me alone these many days.

But I could not continue doing nothing. Therein did lie the path to madness.

If only I had a canvas. I still had the charcoal, paints, and brushes Finlay had saved for me. What if, after so many months without painting, I had forgotten how? The thought sent a fleeting panic, followed almost immediately by sheer determination. I left the seat and went to light the candles.

Once the room was illuminated I began a thorough search. I had plenty of walls to choose from, most of the artwork having previously been taken down, after Ian's initial wreckage, but the stone was too rough and dark to paint on directly.

A half hour later I had spread a sheet on the floor and knelt over it, charcoal in hand as I sketched the limbs of a tree, the rowan from my dream. Perhaps if I painted it exactly as I'd seen, it might give me some clue to the purpose of its repeated appearance.

We might even find Brann.

Maybe then Ian would deem it safe for me to enjoy the freedoms granted to a normal person.

Some hours later my back ached—though I had no intention of stopping. My door opened. A shadow fell across my work, and I knew without looking up that it was Ian. His footfall sounded different from others, as he slightly favored his right foot since the incident with the horse. The length of his shadow, uniform and rigid, save for the bottle hanging from his fingertips, stretched to the wall.

Come with apologies, has he? I didn't much care. Once started on the painting, I'd found I worked with a fever. Whether from being so long denied my passion or whether it was because this tree truly was important, I didn't know. Only that I must finish it.

"Gordon said you wished to see me."

"He was mistaken." I still didn't look up but dipped the brush in the lighter of the paints for shading. Painting may have soothed in other ways, but it had not taken away the anger I felt toward Ian.

He set the bottle on the table and crossed the room. "What are you painting?"

"If you cannot tell, there's no point in—"

"*Why* are you painting a tree?" He stepped over the sheet to grab my arm and haul me to my feet.

"What does it matter to you?" I met his one-eyed gaze and felt all the emotion of the last week rush forth. "What does anything matter to you? Is painting against the rules? Will you have me lashed for ruining the sheet?"

"Earnan put your life in danger. He deserved his punishment—worse actually. It was only the thought of your tender emotions that kept mine in check."

"I'm so flattered." I pulled myself from his grasp and walked away. "And I suppose I deserve being locked in this room the rest of my life."

"If that's the only way to keep you safe, then yes."

I whirled to face him. "I took a *walk* to see Mary, to fetch some medicines for the midwife. The castle was in view the entire time."

"In view isn't good enough." Ian stepped around the rest of the painted sheet and moved close to me once more.

With the bed behind me and the wall to the side, I had no choice but to stand my ground and face him.

"Brann has had the castle in sight too. He's been spotted no less than three times in the past two months, all within little more than a stone's throw from here."

"I wasn't truly alone," I argued. "There were always other people around."

"And would they stand up to you against Brann?" Ian edged closer. "Would you have had even a chance if he'd seen you?"

"How do you know he didn't?" I lifted my chin higher in an attempt at indifference when, really, I felt shaken by the knowledge that Brann had been so close. Gone from sight, gone from mind may not have been working so well in helping me to adjust to life after Collin, but it appeared to have been working with regards to Brann. I'd mostly succeeded in blocking him from my thoughts and had all but convinced myself that he was somewhere far away now and would not bother me again.

"You wouldn't be here if he'd seen you." Ian pulled me near enough that I could feel his breath on my face. "I've kept you locked up all week to teach you a lesson. But apparently a week isn't long enough. So we'll revisit this conversation in a month."

He released me and turned to go.

"I *hate* you," I said, equally hating the tears that sprang to my eyes.

He paused, then slowly pivoted to face me again. His expression was no longer angry as it had been just seconds before, but a challenge hovered there. "No you don't—hate me."

"I do—"

He grabbed both my arms this time and wrenched me toward him. I looked up a second before his lips covered mine, silencing my protest before it could begin.

There was nothing tender in his action, the way his mouth moved over mine, punishing, dominating, and somehow insinuating that I should be pleased.

I wasn't and tried to move away, when suddenly he changed tactics. His grip lessened and his arm slid around me, resting his hand in the small of my back. His other hand moved behind my neck, his fingers playing in my hair.

The fierce possessiveness of his mouth yielded to a softer approach. His lips moved over mine, searching and teasing their way. I could have easily bitten him. My eyes fluttered shut in a second of indecision. Hate melted into need. And what I needed was him.

Perhaps sensing this, Ian's hand at my waist tightened, pulling me closer. My hands were on his chest now. *Perfect for pushing him away.* Instead I slid them up around the back of his neck and pulled his head closer to mine to deepen our kiss. His lips were surprisingly soft.

And warm. Warmth radiated off his entire body onto mine. I couldn't decide if I liked that the best or his hand caressing my neck, or the way he murmured my name when at last we broke apart.

Breathing heavily, I lay my head against his chest, feeling only comforted and safe as he held me. Long seconds passed. I began emerging from my kissing-induced coma and sensed repercussions on the horizon.

"You don't kiss like a woman who hates me." Ian chuckled, sounding only amused, not evil as I'd thought so many of his other laughs were.

"I hate you all the more for that," I said quietly, still not moving—loath to leave the comfort of his embrace. "I hate that you can make me desire you. But that is all that this is. Nothing more. I will *never* feel for you as I did for Collin."

Ian stiffened, releasing me as if I'd the plague. With a wince he stepped away. I wondered if he had a new injury.

If so, deserved, no doubt. I rubbed my arms, feeling a definite chill, denied the warmth and comfort I'd felt in his arms.

"I don't believe you." His gaze still challenged.

"You should." Never mind that I wasn't entirely convinced either. I dug deep for the words and emotion I'd kept bottled all week. "Where Collin was kind, you are cruel. He showed compassion; you are unsympathetic. He was loving, and you are harsh. Where he was tender, you are cold." I paused for effect. "He was handsome. You—are hideous." I regretted the words the moment they fled my mouth.

Ian's lips pressed together, and raw hurt flickered in the depth of his eye.

I didn't mean it, I wanted to say, but those words, the good ones, stuck in my throat. What I had said wasn't even true. His bruises and cuts had healed, and his hair was growing back and mostly covered the scar across his head. Save for his eye patch, physically he might have passed for Collin.

But there was no stopping what I had started. Ian had been correct. I didn't truly hate him. But I'd no doubt he wanted nothing to do with me now. I added my final barb with vengeance. "I know the color of your heart. It is black and does not bleed. And for that I will never, *ever* care for you."

Wordlessly, he turned from me and made his way across the room, still taking care not to step on my painting.

It was a hollow victory. The words I'd rehearsed in my mind and waited so long to say were finally out, and I felt worse instead of better for having said them.

He reached the door. "I can never be Collin." He sounded both sad and weary and as if he had just reached that conclusion.

"Exactly." My tone held no sympathy, though his had wavered between resigned and pleading. "You shouldn't bother trying. It won't work. Not with me. Not for us."

"Collin was too soft, too weak to ever accomplish what I've done here. We—none of us—would have had a chance."

He reached inside his coat, and I waited, breathless, expecting a weapon. Instead he withdrew a folded paper and tossed it at me.

"Keep this, then. Remember Collin on that pedestal all you want, though it was he who left you here, unprotected, to suffer at Brann's whim, while it was I who saved you—and countless others. Believe me, it would have been far easier not to. But we MacDonalds keep our promises. I'd been led to believe that the Campbells did too."

Chapter Thirty-four

I hugged my arms to myself to ward off the chill in the room. It was silent, frighteningly so, since Ian's abrupt departure.

I knelt to pick up the paper he had tossed to the floor. Though I already knew what it was, with a trembling hand I opened it and pressed it flat across my lap.

Collin stared up at me, with the same, serious expression I'd witnessed the night I'd sketched this—our wedding night. I recognized that expression now. It belonged to a man who carried the weight of the world—or at least a clan or two—on his shoulders. It belonged to Ian.

We MacDonalds keep our promises. I'd been led to believe that Campbells did too. What had Collin told him about me? That I would be loyal and perhaps eventually loving? That I would do my part, as I had tried to when Collin was alive, to search out answers and solutions and work with Ian—together? That I would try to use my gift to help, that I would listen and take seriously what he said? I leaned against the wall, drew my knees up to my chest, and pressed my forehead to them, ashamed.

The parallel of my life and Collin's seemed suddenly clear. Had he once not been in a similar situation? With a father who had given up his life for his son, and a foreign clan—enemies—with which to live and adapt to?

Collin had not wasted many days doubting or hating. He had embraced his new life—including me—and had lived up to his promises, until it was he giving up a life.

But that was where our similarities ended. I had spent the past months doubting Ian, even when both instinct and evidence proved him a changed man. I had not embraced anything, but remained curled tightly within myself, seeking any excuse to remain there, and away from the man who had taken his brother's place as my protector. I had ignored his requests and my own visions. I had not helped but hurt him repeatedly.

My eyes were too dry for tears, my self-loathing too complete for any sympathy—particularly my own. There was no fixing what I had done tonight. My words had been too cruel, too final, striking Ian where I knew him to be most vulnerable. No doubt it would be him now, counting down the months until the period of our handfast was over.

A feeling of utter helplessness prevailed. There was nothing I could do to make this better. *Not one thing.*

Except paint.

I looked over at the sheet and the partially completed rowan tree. What secrets was it hiding? I closed my eyes, reaching out to the future, practically begging my gift to work. *What is it I am meant to see? Show me.*

I crawled across the floor toward my brushes and leaned forward, reaching for one. The floorboard beneath my hand flipped up suddenly, nearly hitting me in the face. Stunned, I sat back, then leaned forward, more carefully this time, and pushed.

It raised slowly, revealing a hole beneath the floor that was too dark to see into clearly. I jumped up to retrieve a candle, heartbeat skipping, wondering if my dowry had been hidden right beneath us all this time. I carried the candle over to the hole and peered inside. The space was empty, save for one very dusty pistol.

Wary of spiders, I reached in and retrieved the weapon. Had I found this earlier, I might have used it on Ian, I'd been so angry with him. Or so I had believed.

I blew some of the dust off the barrel, wondering how long the gun had been there. Were there other loose floorboards? Had I perhaps stumbled onto something that might lead me to the missing dowry?

And if by chance I had, would its discovery be enough to earn Ian's forgiveness?

Carefully, I slid the pistol back into its hiding place and replaced the board. Showing it to Ian would not change anything; neither would finding my dowry. Money was good for only so many things in this world, and absolution was not one of them.

Chapter Thirty-five

I returned to spinning wool. A guard escorted me to the solar each morning, and another to my room each evening, where I took my meals alone, while listening to voices and even laughter from the hall below. The latter intrigued me, and so I found myself inquiring, during a spinning session, about the general state of affairs between clans.

"How are the Campbells faring these days?" I asked Ellen one morning when we found ourselves side by side at the large wheels. I'd taken care that it should be so earlier, when I'd chosen my seat in the circle. I knew she was one who would talk freely.

Ellen lifted an eyebrow at me as she looked down her nose. "Wouldn't have to ask if you'd come amongst us once in a while."

"It is not my choice to stay inside," I said, reminding her of what I'd told the others already, minus the particulars of my disagreement with Ian. Others knowing the extent of our discord would likely only cause trouble.

"Leave her be, Ellen. Laird keeps her in so she can see her visions. Without them we wouldn't be safe," Aila, the eldest of the women, said.

"What do you mean?" I looked past Ellen to Aila.

She frowned. "Hasn't he told you how much your suggestions have helped? Moving those living on outlying crofts closer, building the enormous sheds to house all the

305

animals together—your ideas that have saved lives. At least one family has been spared, and who knows how much livestock. Brann and his council cannot hurt us when you're one step ahead of them."

"Oh," I said, taken aback by both the news that Ian gave me credit for his preventions, and that Brann was not only lurking about, but apparently still attempting harm as well.

"Ian didn't tell you?" Mhairi looked suddenly suspicious.

"Don't suppose he would," Aila said. "Seeing what is to come requires a clear mind. You cannot have that when it's filled with troubles. Isn't that right, Katherine?"

"Aye." I answered with more enthusiasm than I felt. What was Ian playing at here? Why had he told these women—and presumably others—that I was having visions? I wanted to tell them the truth and set matters straight but sensed that might do more harm than good. Certainly I would have to speak to Ian about this.

If he ever chose to speak with me again.

"You see why I ask after the Campbells—and MacDonalds," I added, for the benefit of those women seated across the room. There was still a definite separation between the women of each clan, yet it seemed to me the conversation flowed more freely between them now.

"Campbells are becoming accustomed to the arrangement, though I can't say we favor it," Ellen said.

"Most of us are *grateful*," Aila corrected her. "Seeing how we've no more fear of being burned in our beds, and our children have roofs over their heads, food in their bellies, and even shoes on their feet."

"My lad's wearing a pair of shoes cut from the MacDonald laird's own boots," another Campbell woman added.

I recalled the many nights Ian had labored over tiny pairs of shoes—and led me to believe they were all for MacDonald children. I raised my foot and let the spinning wheel slow, then turned to the other side of the room. "And what of the MacDonalds? How are the lot of you feeling and faring?"

"About our laird? Well enough," one of them answered curtly, with a pointed look at me.

"And what of the kinsman Ian killed?" I pressed, anxious to know if that event bred resentment or discord.

"Niall wasn't a kinsman; he was an animal," Mhairi declared. The other MacDonald women around her added their agreement. "Ian saved at least your life and mine that night. No one faults him that."

"And Earnan? How is he?" I looked to Mhairi again.

"He is healing well," she said.

"He feels badly he let you out in harm's way. Hasn't forgotten how you were when he found you belowstairs, near death yourself." Ellen reached over and tapped on my wheel, as if to chastise me for slowing it. "The laird did fair by him."

"There is no lasting harm," Mhairi added.

"Niall was a disgrace to the name MacDonald," the woman who'd spoken a moment ago said. "He deserved what became of him. As for the one beaten—we don't blame the laird none for that. We blame *you*. Had you done as you ought and not left the castle alone, there would have been no thrashing. We were only glad to know you had yours as well. Though it was rather cowardly, staying shut up in your room all week to recover from it."

I opened my mouth to correct her, to explain that Ian hadn't laid so much as a finger on me—only lips—then changed my mind and returned to spinning, head down as I focused on feeding the fleece. My face warmed as I recalled our kiss, my pink cheeks no doubt confirming I had indeed been beaten. I tried not to think about the kiss, and what all these lies from Ian meant. My foot found a good rhythm and was soon whirring as steadily as my mind.

The Campbells were coming to think of Ian as their champion. The MacDonalds thought well of him too. But neither clan realized that I was not the woman they believed me to be. Ian had been giving me credit for what he had done. He had made me out to be better than I was.

Lies. All of it.

Lies that sooner or later, I felt certain, would be revealed for what they were.

A full week after Ian's visit I had not seen him again, but routine broke when four jars were delivered along with my evening meal. Curious, I opened them as soon as the shy maid had taken her leave. I hadn't seen Bridget at all in the past two weeks, not since my exile from the hall. My spinning sisters, as I'd come to think of them, assured me she was well, and I consoled myself with that at least.

The jars opened somewhat easily, and I could not contain my cry of delight as I looked down at them, lined up on the tray, a different color contained within each. *More paint!* I clasped my hands like a child being handed a particularly delightful toy. Beside the silverware were two brushes, one medium-sized and which appeared to be made from horse hair. The other was more fine, the bristles softer and smaller. The hair forming each had been carefully trimmed and shaped before being lashed to a smoothly carved stick.

I held each in turn, then brought the softer of the two to my face, stroking my cheek with the fine hairs. *Ian did this.* I closed my eyes and imagined—or perhaps saw—him laboring over mortar and pestle, grinding plants for the colors, then mixing those carefully with animal fat. I envisioned him shaving the rough edges from the sticks that formed the brush handles and patiently grooming the hairs that would top them.

Why? I'd given him no reason to show kindness. This left only one possibility for his generosity. He must sense—as did I—that my partially completed painting was in some way significant. I had done what I could with it to this point, but the additional colors and brushes might make it possible to complete.

Though his gift only added to the guilt I felt for my horrible behavior, there was clearly nothing to be done but use the brushes and paint.

My evening meal remained untouched as I unfolded the sheet, anchored it between various pieces of furniture, and began filling in the detail I'd been unable to before. Evening turned to night. I lit several candles, noting that more had been added to my stack. Light spilled onto my makeshift canvas as warmth flooded a corner of my barren heart.

I will *thank Ian. I will somehow fix everything I've done and make it up to him.* I forged on, filling the sheet with color as though my life depended upon it.

Nine days later I returned from a day of spinning and found the completed painting had been hung on the wall. *Ian again.* I noted with disappointment that he was not in the room. Guilt and a sort of desperation propelled me toward the bed, which I flopped across in acute melancholy.

My fingers strayed to my lips, as they had so many times the past two weeks. If I closed my eyes I could relive the moment of our kiss, every torturous, wonderful second. The last I would likely ever enjoy.

To distract myself from absolute despair, I pulled a chair

up before the painting and studied it from a new perspective. Aside from the stately tree, the scene now had other details, the brittle grass beneath and the headstones pressed therein. The rickety fence that surrounded the kirkyard, the kirk itself in the distance. And closer up, the initials on the tree, engraved by Collin so long ago.

KCM + CIM

1747

The scene was still missing something. I closed my eyes, seeing the kirkyard in my mind, then opened them once more and stared at the painting. *What is it?* I repeated the process, this time focusing on the tree, as that had been my starting point. Brann's name floated before my eyes, then settled on a rounded grey stone to the left of the rowan.

His gravestone.

Chapter Thirty-six

"Katie, wake up."

The candle on my night table flickered to life as I opened my eyes to Ian's face hovering above me.

"What is it?" I sat up quickly, pushing myself back into the pillows, away from him.

Ian's smile tinged with sadness. "I've brought you a bairn. She's a bonny little lass." He held a bundle out to me.

As I had in my dream I reached out, taking the child and staring down into the tiny, precious face of a newborn infant.

"You'll be a fine mother to her," Ian said as I looked around the room in confusion and then down at the baby. Faint lashes lay serenely against pale cheeks. A dainty nose, rosy lips, and perfectly rounded chin confirmed his words. She was bonny. She also wasn't mine. Relief swept through me. *I didn't bear Ian's child.*

"Whose is she? Where did you get her?" I pulled my gaze from her face long enough to glance at Ian and catch the gentle curve of his mouth and the tender gaze in his eye. A new thought struck me. "Is she *yours*?"

Ian's head came back as if I'd slapped him, reminding me not of the time that I had, but of Collin's reaction the morning at the carriage when I had all but accused him of planning to leave me to be with Mhairi.

"I see your opinion of me has not improved." The tenderness was gone, replaced with a scowl. "Her mother died in childbirth but, in the moments before, asked that the babe be given to you."

"And the child's father?" I didn't believe a stranger would simply give his child to me. *To us.* Ian was the laird. Perhaps the parents had been thinking of that when they'd made such a decision.

"He'll be along shortly to see the lass. He's with his wife now, paying his last respects."

My heart throbbed, a swift, anguishing pain. Over the past months Collin's death had faded to the dull, constant ache of loss, but imagining this child's father at his wife's side, holding her limp hand and brushing a kiss across her still forehead, hurtled my own grief to the surface.

At least he has the opportunity to say goodbye. I doubted that lessened the pain of his loss.

"Surely he won't be all right with this arrangement." My arms tightened possessively around the infant even as I argued against keeping her.

"Brian has four bairns already, the oldest but five and the youngest not yet two." Ian sighed as if imagining such a burden. "He cannot take on the care of a newborn in addition, not on his own."

Silently I agreed and felt a swell of compassion for the other, now motherless, children. "Isn't that for him to say?"

"Aye," Ian said. "And what will he?"

"That the child belongs with me—with *us.*" I looked up at him. In accepting her as ours, I would be accepting Ian as well, long past our year and a day. "I saw this night—the moment you handed me the child—in a dream weeks ago. Only I believed—"

"You thought it would be *our* child."

"Yes." Using the back of my finger, I traced the baby's

soft cheek, almost wishing she really was mine. *Mine and Collin's.* It was startling, this pull I felt toward her.

"What else have you seen?" Ian settled on the edge of the bed beside me.

"Brann, twice. Near the tree in the painting. And just last week, his stone. Look there." I raised a hand, pointing at the grave marker I had painted to the side of the tree. "The headstone on the left, the plain one, is Brann's."

"You've seen his death?" Ian turned his head sideways, facing me instead of the painting.

"Not exactly." The babe stirred, and I wondered that our conversation had so quickly gone from her miraculous presence and the tragedy that preceded it, to Brann. "I saw that stone with his name on it, near the rowan in the kirkyard. I don't think the stone is there—yet. But the tree is real."

Ian nodded. "I remember it from the day of the burial. You sat beneath it."

Not a pleasant memory. "It was also the place Collin and I played as children. Brann was frightened of the spirits in the kirkyard, so we felt safe there." I smiled, vaguely recalling the days of Collin and me chasing around the stones. "It was also the place we were found by my father when he came to take me to England."

"Would that I knew where Brann was to be found," Ian muttered. "I'll set men out to hide and keep an eye for him near the kirk."

"I can't imagine why he would come there." I brushed a finger along the fine hairs sprinkled across the baby's head. "Not when he knows this land well—better than you and the other MacDonalds who have only just come to it. There must be plenty of places to hide."

"Brann doesn't want to hide. He wants to take back what he sees as his."

"But we have the castle." I smiled at Ian, truly smiled at him, for once feeling no animosity between us. Whether it was because of the late hour and my half-awake state, or the wonder of the child he'd placed in my arms, or simply that somewhere between allowing myself to recognize all the good he had done here—and that perhaps it was starting to outweigh his former wrongs—I had decided to earnestly try letting go of my fear, doubt, and animosity.

I'd had ample time to think these past evenings alone, and I realized that more than being afraid of Ian or even mistrustful of him, I'd been angry—because he had returned instead of Collin.

"Little good this pile of stone will do us come spring when we've crops to plant in the fields and have men and women and livestock about on the land." He leaned forward, head in his hands. "At present we are doing little more than biding time."

Hesitantly I placed my hand on the back of his head, drawing my fingers gently down his soft, dark hair. It had come in rich and thick as it used to be. Not yet long again, but covering much of his scar nicely. "You plan to be here, come spring? You would not wish us to go elsewhere?"

He turned sideways to look at me. "If you are here, this is where I will be."

My heart squeezed with the dual emotions of both relief and anticipation. As horrid as I had been, he was not going to leave me or my people.

"Ian." My hand slid from his hair to rest lightly on his arm. "I am sorry for what I said the last time we spoke. I was angry. I didn't mean any of it."

"I think you did." He looked away, as if afraid to confirm that. "You have every right to be angry, to hate me as well."

"I don't." I pushed the inkling of unease caused by his

words to the back of my mind. *What has he done now, that I don't know of yet?* Just for once, for tonight, I didn't want to worry. The tension of months of arguing and constant fear had worn on me.

The baby stirred again, one tiny hand freeing itself from the swaddling. I placed my finger beneath the outstretched palm, as I recalled doing with Timothy when he was a newborn, and the tiny fist curled inward, grasping onto me.

"She's so perfect," I said, feeling an overwhelming sense of awe and responsibility at the same time. I looked at Ian, certain my expression reflected the panic I felt. "I don't know the first thing about caring for a baby."

"I imagine you'll learn quickly enough," he said. "If you want her, that is."

If you want me? he was also asking.

"I do." I nodded, still utterly astonished at the immediacy and strength of my feelings. *Would I have felt so strongly for this child had I not seen her before in my dreams?*

"There's a wet nurse arranged already," Ian said. "Another MacDonald woman with a bairn and milk to spare. Though she's asked you only bring the child when she needs to eat. She's not up to caring for another, beyond feeding that is."

He's given me a MacDonald baby.

I eased back against the headboard. "Will you stay with us a while?" I felt almost shy asking, when we had seen each other so infrequently the past weeks and had parted on such poor terms. Whether he had been staying away as part of my punishment, or simply to avoid another outburst like my last one, it had resulted in my wishing for his company.

He hesitated, indecision written in the lines creasing his forehead.

"Please," I added softly. *I really am sorry.*

"For a while," he conceded. "I could do with some sleep."

Ian leaned forward to remove his boots, and I studied his profile. Dark circles rimmed his eye—he really was tired. Where *had* he been sleeping during his absence? His jaw was rigid, set in that stubborn MacDonald way, and there was a sorrow there that seemed to have developed since our last encounter.

Little wonder. My words had been so cruel. I really had hurt him. The tenuous peace we'd established since our handfast had been shattered. We would have to return to the very beginning and start over if there was to be any hope of accord between us.

Ian lay back, keeping on top of the quilts, then rolled on his side facing us. He touched the top of the baby's hand where it curled around mine. "I don't know much about bairns either, seeing as it was just my brother and I."

There was the tiniest catch as he mentioned Collin, but to me it seemed as if a curtain had been drawn back, revealing a stage showcasing Ian's grief. In his still expression I read yearning for the mother he had not known. Guilt, still after all these years, that his father had sacrificed his life for him. Self-loathing that easily matched and even surpassed my own, as he held himself responsible for his brother's death. There was loneliness too, and a feeling that all was lost and the future bleak indeed.

My chest ached with the depth of his sorrows. I had not known, would never have guessed that he had been suffering so.

I extracted my finger from the baby's fist and placed my hand over Ian's on the bed. "You're not alone. You have me."

"Do I?" He gave a derisive snort meant to mask the hurt I'd glimpsed, and the metaphoric curtain closed swiftly. He pulled his hand from beneath mine. "I think not, Katherine. It is Collin whom you loved, whom you will always care for."

Denial formed on my lips but did no more. Ian was right. Anything I said to the contrary he would realize as a lie.

He sat abruptly and collected his boots from the floor.

"Ian—" I held a hand out to him. "Because I continue to care for Collin does not

mean—"

"It is not your fault," he said. "But mine. I should have realized before I came here. Should have thought it through better, more thoroughly. If there had only been time. If I hadn't felt your life hung in the balance."

"What could you have done differently?" My pulse fluttered, guessing, dreading, half-knowing already that he was headed toward some kind of confession. *If he really did kill Collin . . .* How could I ever care for my husband's murderer? If Ian deserved all the guilt and self-incrimination I had glimpsed within him, what was I to do?

"Many things might have been different." Ian lifted his shoulders in a helpless shrug. "Which would have impacted many lives. I thought this was best, I truly believed . . . I swear I was thinking of your safety." He reached the door and leaned his head against it.

"Tell me," I said, raising up on my knees in the bed, the baby still clutched to my breast. "Tell me what you were going to the night Niall came to our room. I want to know everything about Collin's death."

A tiny wail followed my demand. My escalating voice had woken the child.

"I'm sorry," I soothed, looking down at the bundle in my arms. "Shh. All is well."

It was a far cry from it, and both Ian and I knew that.

"Tell me," I said, softer this time. "Not knowing is perhaps worse."

He turned from the door to face me. "You don't really believe that, do you?"

"No," I whispered. I was already fearing the worst, and the fierce look in Ian's eye told me he was going to confirm it.

"It doesn't matter how my brother died. Remember Collin as you do. It is better I leave you with that at least."

Part Three

Were it not for hope the heart would break.

Chapter Thirty-seven

"Down there is where the horses are kept." I angled Lydia toward the stables, just visible from our room. Standing at the window to ease her fussing was one of many tricks I'd learned over the past month. I bounced lightly and continued speaking to her in a soothing voice. "Your father has a fine horse. When you are older, we will have to ask him to teach you to ride." The image of Ian as I had first known him in England came to mind. I remembered him in my yard, seated upon his stallion, the black mane matching his own sleek locks. Both animal and rider tall and proud.

"You won't need to ask."

I turned to find Ian in the doorway, his expression tender as he looked on us. "May I come in? The door was open."

I beckoned him. "Bridget has gone for more nappies and water to bathe Lydia, since she insists on soaking through her clothing at least three times a day."

"I believe most bairns are wont to do that." Ian crossed the room. I met him halfway and handed Lydia to him.

"There now," he hushed her crying before it could begin. "Da's here." He settled in the rocker that had been added to the room since her arrival. I began removing her clothes from the line strung before the fireplace, stepping carefully around the cradle Ian had finished just last week. Behind me, his soft crooning began, soothing Lydia as nothing else seemed to during these evening hours.

Oh rowan tree, oh rowan tree,
Thoul't aye be dear to me.
Entwin'd thou art wi' mony ties,
O' hame and infancy.
Thy leaves were aye the first o spring,
Thy flowr's the simmer's pride:
There was na sic a bonnie tree,
In all the country side.
Oh rowan tree.

How fair wert thou in simmer time,
Wi' all thy clusters white.
How rich and gay thy autumn dress,
Wi' berries red and bright.
Oh thy fair stem were mony names
Which now nae mair I see,
But there engraven on my heart,
Forgot they ne'er can be.
Oh rowan tree.

It was my favorite of the melodies Ian sang, and I looked to the painting on the wall, the rowan beneath which Collin and I had played as children and upon which our love had been engraved. I wondered suddenly if the song had meaning to Ian too.

"How old are you, Ian?" I asked, turning from the painting to watch him cooing over Lydia. Though he was Collin's twin, I realized I'd never learned when their birthday was.

"Twenty-nine. Thirty come May. Why?"

"Was there ever a woman you fancied? Have you never been in love or thought of marriage or children?" His adoration for Lydia was apparent. Not a day had gone by since he'd brought her to me that he had not come to see her—to hold her and sing to her. I'd spent more time with Ian in the past month than I had in the three previous, simply because he wanted to be with the bairn. It occurred to me that I had no idea what his life had been like before I met him. What if he'd had a home and family? What losses had he suffered that I was unaware of?

"There was someone—once." A wistful smile curved his mouth.

"What happened? Why are you not with her?" I felt a nudge of jealousy as I posed the question. *Absurd.* My feelings for Ian were not of a romantic nature. Still, we were handfast, and now we had a child to care for. We'd reached a state of cooperation and peace, notwithstanding our continued wariness of one another.

In accepting Lydia I had accepted Ian as well. The child had been given to *us*, not to me alone. What I had dreaded—being somehow beholden or bound to Ian beyond the period of one year—I had willingly chosen.

"It was some time ago," Ian said. "As fate would have it, we were parted from one another. When we were reunited she was not able to love me for who I had become."

"She would now." I looked at him, his scarred hands cradling Lydia's head so gently, a tender version of Ian MacDonald I would never have envisioned when we were first acquainted. If the woman he loved had known him then, it was no wonder she found him lacking. But now . . . I felt myself very fortunate to count him mine. *Mine.*

"Who is to say?" Ian's gaze remained focused on Lydia, for which I was grateful. He had said he could read my every thought, and I was certain my last one would have been apparent.

"But this will do, aye?" The rocker squeaked as he picked up speed. "You've not had to suffer my touch, and we've a bairn—a child to love who will love us with no condition."

"Yes." I turned away quickly and continued pulling Lydia's clothes from the line. *Tiny clothes. Tiny changes.* Dozens of little things were adding up, changing my heart toward Ian. *What more will it take for us to love each other with no condition?* I wasn't ready to answer that yet.

But for the first time, in a very long time, I felt hope.

A tickle across my cheek woke me. I opened my eyes to find Ian close, a feather in his hand.

"Haven't you anything better to do than wake people who are sleeping peacefully?"

"Nothing better." Ian grinned, then ran the feather across my forehead quickly before setting it on the night table. He lay back on the bed, hands crossed behind his head. "I believe you summoned me."

"I wanted to show you Lydia's new trick, but I guess we both fell asleep." Lydia lay between us, her sweet face blissful.

"I'll wait," Ian said, his own eyes closing. "It's too wet outside to work much right now anyway."

It was almost always wet in the Highlands, but the rain outside did sound heavy. I pulled a quilt over all three of us.

Ian rolled on his side to face me, or rather, Lydia. He touched her head almost reverently and gazed upon her with equal parts tenderness and protection. "Have you figured out what your new painting means?"

"No," I said, frustrated I hadn't a better answer for him.

"I've no idea why I'm painting a seascape now. Maybe it means Brann has sailed far, far away."

"We can hope," Ian said, sounding as if he believed it no more than I.

"She's waking," I said excitedly. "Lydia love," I cooed at her. "Watch this, I'll get her to smile. She's done it three times today."

"That's not new. She's been smiling for me for weeks." He ran a fingertip along the side of her mouth, and it curved.

"That's reflex, not a *real* smile." I leaned forward on my elbow and made eye contact with her. "Lyd-ia," I said in a sing-song voice. Her mouth curved again, and stayed that way as I continued to engage her. "See."

Ian tried it and, after the third attempt, earned a smile of his own. "There's a sweet lass." He glanced from Lydia to me. "Kath-er-ine," he sang in the same voice.

"Amusing," I said, secretly finding it so. We so rarely had any light conversation between us.

He tried again, and I couldn't hold back a silly grin.

"Aha, it worked," Ian exclaimed. "I've discovered the secret to making you smile." He picked Lydia up and lay her on his chest.

Maybe he had. I looked at them both, feeling my heart swell.

Chapter Thirty-eight

M hairi nudged me with her shoulder, jarring the needle out of place and making me lose my concentration for the fifth time in as many minutes. The first four had been because of Lydia, content at last in the basket near my feet. Since Lydia's arrival over a month ago, Mhairi had been cold to me, parting quickly from the course of friendship I'd felt we were on. But purposely disrupting my knitting when I was already struggling with it—a fact she was well aware of—was simply mean.

"The laird wishes a word with you." Mhairi lifted her head toward the doorway of the solar where Ian stood, taking in the scene with an air of satisfaction.

As well he might, I thought irritably, blaming him for my current predicament. The wool had long since been spun and the former spinners, myself included, had moved on to knitting. Or some of us had, anyway. *Pity the poor soul who ends up with my socks.*

He beckoned me, and I stood, only too glad to abandon my post. I scooped up Lydia and crossed the room.

We stepped into the hall, and he closed the door behind him.

"Yes?" I asked, bouncing the baby, wishing as I had before that I wasn't reliant upon the nurse to feed her. If up to me she would be fed more often and not made to wait so long between.

"I wondered," Ian began almost nervously, "if you might

327

like to walk in the kirkyard with me. To visit your mother's and grandfather's graves? It isn't as cold today, though possibly the last pleasant day we'll have for a while. Clouds coming in."

Shock delayed my answer by several seconds. Then concern over his motives was won over by the prospect of both leaving knitting for the afternoon and getting outside the gloomy castle. "Let me fetch my cloak and find someone to watch Lydia."

"Bundle her up and bring her," Ian suggested. "I can hold her, if you'd like."

"All right." I smiled, as much cheered by his presence as I was by his invitation.

When we were both bundled well, Ian with Lydia tightly swaddled against his chest, we headed outside. It was a beautiful December day, cool and crisp, with sun shining and high clouds.

"Were your tasks today as dreary as mine?" I asked, still finding it odd he had taken leave of his responsibilities in the middle of the day. No one worked harder than Ian. In the nearly five months he had been here, he had earned the respect of MacDonalds and Campbells alike.

"Not particularly. There is a matter I wish to speak to you about, and the kirkyard will afford us some privacy."

Our room would have done so as well. Uneasiness nudged away some of my enthusiasm for our walk. "What matter?" I looked at him, expecting further explanation, and received only one of Ian's rare smiles, usually reserved for Lydia.

"Patience," he admonished, and we continued our stroll.

The kirkyard was quiet today, but not eerily so. Both Earnan and Gordon were at their posts on either side of the yard, visible only because I knew where to look for them. We would be safe here. Open fields surrounded fenced yard on three sides, with the kirk on the other. If Brann was to come, we would see him long before his arrival.

Instinctively I wandered toward the rowan. Ian followed, and when I paused beneath it, he stopped as well. Cradling the back of Lydia's head carefully, he crouched to trace the carving near the base of the tree.

"Do you remember this?" he asked.

"Very well." I tilted my head back, looking up to the high branches. "I'd been hiding in the tree for quite some time. Collin couldn't find me. And when he did—when I at last alerted him to my presence—he refused to come up and get me, but began carving this instead."

"It must have taken a long time." Ian stood once more but continued to stare at the initials. "And much patience."

"More with me. I'd given him a scare hiding so long and so well."

"And so high," Ian added, looking up to the limbs of tree.

"That too. Like you, Collin was very patient with me." I touched the wedding band on my finger, the other symbol of Collin's love that still remained, and one that had taken him much longer to create.

"I was thinking about patience the other day at the forge," Ian said. "When young Jeremy Campbell spooked a horse, scalded three men in succession, and set a corner of the roof ablaze in his haste to be rid of the shoe he'd removed from the fire. All because he was afraid of getting burned."

"What has that to do with patience?" In the knitting room I'd heard tell of the verbal thrashing Ian had unleashed on the boy and could only imagine a physical punishment had followed.

"Well, I did not kill him outright," Ian boasted with a teasing smile. "I in fact kept his father from doing the same when I put a stop to the thrashing after a dozen strokes."

"Good of you." I rolled my eyes and turned away from him, showing I was less than impressed.

"The thing is," Ian continued, "the boy was afraid of being burned. Because of his fear he hurt others and himself in the end." Ian took my arm and gently turned me to him.

"I have been afraid—still am," he admitted, "of hurting you more than I already have. Of bringing harm to the people who depend on us."

On you, I silently amended. I had done very little. I loved our little lass fiercely, and she did depend upon me—if not for her actual nourishment, for me to at least see that she received it. Everything else I did for her, and I loved her for it.

I tugged the cap covering Lydia's head a bit lower to cover her ears. She gurgled a complaint, apparently not caring for the wool pressing upon her head.

Ian bounced her gently. "I've been afraid for myself, what you will think—or not think of me—when all the truth is known. I've realized I'm no better than Jeremy at the forge. I've been swinging about wildly, as if with the hot tongs and shoe in my hand, and it's you who has been hurt most."

I failed to completely follow his analogy, but he had my attention and curiosity. *For Ian Campbell to admit fear...*

"Go on," I urged.

"I don't want to live separate lives. I want us to be more than cordial with one another. There are still things between us—secrets that need to be told. I'm prepared for the consequences of those."

I wasn't certain I was, but I'd been lonely enough to grasp at what he offered. "All right. Tell me."

"I will. But first walk with me."

We covered the short distance to Collin's grave. I regretted that I'd not had time to gather a posy to lay over the top. The grass had not yet regrown, and the bare mound of dirt seemed a stark contrast to the rest of the yard. We stopped before it, and I started to kneel. Ian's hand on my arm stopped me.

"Don't."

I frowned as I shrugged from his grasp, then knelt and pressed my lips to the ground.

Collin. I felt him here, in this place that had been dear to us both. We'd never lived in fear of the dead, only those living who would do us harm. I rose and looked up at Ian, chastisement ready. "I will always kiss his grave. It is a sign of respect. I think Collin is deserving of that much, at least."

"Would that you feel the same an hour from now," Ian said.

"What do you mean by that?" Did he think to convince me that Collin had done something to deserve his death?

"You'll understand soon enough." Ian sat on the ground beside me, careful to hold Lydia the way she liked. "I thought, with Hogmanay, it would be a fitting time for a new start for us as well."

"That seems a good idea," I said warily, still upset by his suggestion that I would somehow come to think less of Collin.

I settled more comfortably beside Ian and worked to cool my irritation. I *wanted* us to get along. Collin had been gone five months. Ian and I needed to figure this out. Lydia needed both a mother and father. As much or more than that, *I* needed Ian, and I believed he needed me. We were not each other's first choice, but I had made peace with that.

I believed I could care for him—the man he had become. He had already shown he could care for me. But there was still something holding each of us back. *Someone. Collin.* Every time we gained a little ground he was there, his ghost between us. Maybe Ian was right and knowing the entire truth, all his secrets, was our only way forward.

"I told you how I burned my hands." He held one out, and I took it, fearful suddenly, irrationally, for both of us. Whatever he was about to share with me had already happened. *It is only how I react that matters now.* The cost, Collin's life, had already been paid.

"I need to tell you what led me to that barn, and why I risked my life—and yours—going inside." Ian's fingers curved over mine. "Hold onto me while I tell it. Please listen, and don't let go."

"I won't let go," I promised, enjoying the feeling of my hand in his. It was the comfort I had craved, the physical connection with another human being. Caring for Lydia had helped to fill some of that, but even the sweetest bairn could not replace the affection I had enjoyed with Collin. Was it so wrong that I was beginning to feel something similar for Ian? Collin had sent him to me, had bound him by oath to protect me. *To care for me as well?*

It seemed a hundred years had passed since I had declared to Collin, with all the giddiness of first love and newly discovered passion, that I loved kissing. How childish that seemed now. When what I felt for the man beside me was so much more.

More? With a start, I looked up from our joined hands. *More, or simply different?* Ian was my protector and the Campbells' too. He was hard and stubborn, given to fits of melancholy and temper. But he was also kind, thoughtful, fair, and forgiving. He had been more than patient with me.

The last of my own stubborn pride gave way as I allowed his many acts of kindness to sift from the list I had catalogued in my mind, to fill the corners of my empty heart. A soft and subtle joy filled me with sweeter hope than I had believed possible.

I leaned forward and placed a hand upon Ian's cheek before pressing my lips to his. "Whatever you must say to me, it will be all right. *We* will be all right." When I pulled back, it was to see tears swimming in his eyes.

He squeezed my fingers, as if to say, "hold on," then took a deep breath.

"The man in that grave is not Collin."

Chapter Thirty-nine

"**W**hat?" My exclamation coincided with Lydia's piercing cry. Her mouth opened, and pained wailing filled the kirkyard at the same time she soaked the front of Ian's shirt.

He added his own oath as he held her quickly away, though it was too late. A foul, pasty yellow mess stained them both.

"How does a bairn so small make such a mess as that?" His wrinkled nose would have evoked laughter under other circumstances, but I felt too close to tears already.

"Hand her to me," I said, my hands outstretched.

Ian shook his head. "It's all right. No need for both of us to smell this bad. I'll take her in and get Bridget to help. Stay and visit your mother's grave. I'll return as soon as I can."

I gave a terse nod. I stood and turned away from Ian, rubbing my arms briskly.

Cold. So cold. Not Collin—here? Where? What *happened? I kissed* Ian.

I felt dirty, as if I had done much more than that. He still stood behind me, I sensed. "If not here, where is Collin? *Who* is in that grave?"

"The half-dead man the English tossed into that burning barn rests there," Ian said. "I need more than a minute to answer the rest of those questions. Will you wait for me to return?"

Lydia continued her wailing, but my instincts to care for her grew numb.

"Just go," I said, her incessant crying only increasing my agitation.

"I'll be right back. Stay in the kirkyard," Ian warned. "If you decide to leave before I return, ask Earnan to walk you to the castle."

"Fine." *Don't tell me what to do.*

The sound of Ian's feet crunching over leaves faded. I followed him as far as the rowan, then crumpled to the ground once more, a mess of tears and confusion. I had promised to listen. I would. But what could he say to fix this? What reason could there be for his deception?

I pounded my fist on the ground in frustration and struck something much harder than dirt. With a cry, I clutched my hand to my chest, rubbing it in attempt to make the throbbing stop. The edge of a stone peeked out from the grass in front of me. I reached down, parting more, to reveal a narrow stone pressed deep into the ground.

Per Mare Per Terras

By sea or by land. There was no name or date, not that the stone was big enough to include those. It was certainly too close to the tree for anyone to be buried here. *By sea . . .* A chill passed through me, as cold as if a ghost had. *My painting?* Could there be a connection? I flattened the grass over the top once more and stood, looking around uneasily.

No longer quite as comfortable as I had always been in this place, I hurried over to my grandfather's stone. Not surprisingly, it was the largest in the yard. I knelt before it, pressing my fingers first to my lips and then to his name. "Help me, Grandfather," I whispered. "I'm so confused about what I am to do and feel."

Only silence answered my plea. Silence, then a whistle I'd heard once before. *Donaid?* If it was him, who or what was he watching out for this time?

The double doors leading to the kirk swung open, and Father Rey exited, only a slight limp to his walk, the lingering reminder of Ian's previous *warning.*

Had he seen me and come to lecture? *Not today.* I was already kneeling, but instinctively ducked, so as to be completely blocked from his view.

He was joined a few minutes later by Donaid. The two began speaking with much animation, leading me to believe their conversation was of some importance.

I relaxed a little, trusting Donaid would rescue me from a lengthy sermon if Father Rey chanced to see me. Word that Ian had pushed the priest into the grave had traveled quickly among the Campbells. To my pleasant surprise, most had applauded Ian's action. It seemed the good father was rather unpopular.

It was starting to sprinkle, and I considered my options—make myself known and endure at least a brief confrontation with the priest, or remain hidden and hope they left soon before I became too wet.

Their steps and conversation drifted closer.

" . . . insisted Collin is not dead," Donaid said. "Or not of three weeks ago, at least, when they put him on the *Ulysses,* bound for the Colonies."

I gasped. Both men turned their heads my direction.

Collin—alive? Was that what Ian had been about to tell me? *And I kissed him!* If Ian knew his brother was alive, what kind of new beginning had he believed this might be for us? There would be no *us* if Collin still lived and breathed. Anywhere. Even an ocean away.

My impulse was to make myself known and demand that Donaid tell me what he knew. Common sense kept me in place, tense and waiting until their conversation had resumed. *Why is Donaid telling this to Father Rey instead of to me?*

"You're certain that is what the Redcoat captain said?" Father Rey asked.

"Aye," Donaid insisted. "They put Collin aboard with other fugitives near three weeks ago. The MacDonald *had* escaped earlier and was quite severely wounded when recaptured. But he was successfully retrieved and had been convalescing in prison until deemed healthy enough to sail. He was quite a bit of trouble, apparently, but still worth the price he fetched. The captain was not pleased to learn the usual lot of prisoners from us was to be indefinitely delayed."

"Nothing we can do about that at present," Father Rey said. "The captain is positive the man was Collin? Those soldiers aren't always the smartest," Father Rey intoned.

"I inquired to that," Donaid said. "They assured me it was the same man. Collin had a scar earned from the captain's claymore the day after they took him from here. Ran across the top of his head. Had to have nearly killed him."

Ian's scar? What were the odds both brothers had the same injury? My mind spun. What could this possibly mean? Ian was here, and Collin was—*Alive? Alive.* My heart gave a jolt as if it had just restarted after a very long time. Tears mingled with the rain on my cheeks. Besieged with emotion, I slumped against my grandfather's stone. *Collin. Alive.*

"Who have we here, then?" Father Rey nudged Collin's gravestone with his toe. "It was blasphemous enough to bury a MacDonald here. But now who knows what we've put in our hallowed ground. We'll have to dig it up."

"That's not the body I'm concerned with," Donaid said. "But the MacDonald at the castle. What are we to do with *him?*"

I was going to wretch. *Donaid. This whole time.* Covering my mouth with my hand, I bent over, parallel to the ground, praying they would go away. *Collin. Alive. On a ship to the Colonies, but alive. Ian—in danger.* And Donaid, the traitor who'd schemed with Brann and Malcom to take me from Collin on our journey from England.

The answer to my prayer came as the clouds broke loose, increasing the drizzle to a steady downpour in a matter of minutes. Donaid and Father Rey returned to the kirk. I dug my fingers into the wet grass, hanging on, waiting for the world to right itself. When they had been gone several minutes I staggered to my feet, hurrying the opposite direction. Earnan met me at the gate, white-faced and tight-lipped. "You weren't supposed to leave the yard."

"I didn't. I promise." I looked at him so he could see the truth in my eyes. If Ian was right, and I could not lie, Earnan should see as much as well. "I was kneeling at my grandfather's grave when Father Rey came. I hid because I didn't want him to see me. He lectures so."

"Aye, that he does." The tension eased from Earnan's face. "Just the same, next time I'll accompany you."

"Of course." I didn't think there would be a next time. I didn't want to come here again, but I did need to warn Ian that I had ferreted out at least one of our enemies. Or was Donaid only *my* enemy? Ian had known Collin was not in that grave. *He knew he wasn't dead and lied to me.* Was it possible Donaid and Ian were somehow connected, though the conversation I'd just overheard made it appear the opposite? My head ached with the effort of trying to figure it out, and I shivered beneath my wet cloak.

"We had best get you inside before you catch your death of cold." Earnan offered his arm. "What was the laird thinking, to have you out in this weather? In the kirkyard, no less?"

"I'm sure I don't know." *What* was *Ian thinking? What are his plans?*

I felt the oddest mix of confusion, disappointment, hope, and anger. If what Donaid had said was true, Collin was alive, while the man I had begun to trust, and even care for, had lied to me in the most grievous manner. My heart felt broken all over again, as hope for the life I had planned with Ian seemed all but lost.

But Collin, the husband I had worked to forget, might yet be mine.

Chapter Forty

"There, now." Bridget finished tucking a sprig of winter berries through the curls perched on top of my head. "Right festive you look. No doubt the laird will take notice, and you won't have to suffer as the barren bride much longer."

"Is that what I am called?" I looked in the mirror at her reflection behind me. "Are people saying I'm barren?"

Bridget clucked her tongue and had the decency to look abashed. "I thought for certain you'd heard, given the company you keep each day with those gossipy women. It's them who're saying it."

"Ian and I have only been handfast five months," I said, to myself as much as to Bridget.

"Aye," she said. "And you married near a month before that—half a year with a man to warm your bed. Plenty of time to get a bairn of your own growing in your belly."

Plenty of time if one was intimate with the man she was pledged to. A status I had reached with neither Collin nor Ian—would never reach with Ian if what I had learned this afternoon was true.

And if it isn't? Would I be devastated all over again? I had thought of little else but Collin the past two hours, through the hot bath that had taken away my chill, while caring for Lydia, and while waiting for Ian. He'd never come to finish our conversation but had sent Gordon to tell me there had been an accident at the well and he was needed there.

Instead, I'd spent the time remembering the exhilaration of riding with Collin, our long conversations, the many attempts he had made to teach me how to catch a fish. Sleeping beside him, confiding in him, our declarations of love. How had I thought my relationship with Ian to be more? Yet this afternoon, before, it had seemed so. There had not been much joy between us, only work and strife, with the common thread of our love for our people—and now Lydia—binding us together. What I felt for him was different than what I had felt for Collin. Less romantic, more intense. A friendship borne of necessity rather than want.

If I was being honest, and someone here needed to be, a part of me would feel relieved to find out nothing from this afternoon was real. I would not have to give up the connection I'd formed with Ian or revisit the devastation of losing Collin.

I love Collin, I reminded myself again, as I had over and over this afternoon. Going in search of him would mean leaving Ian. I couldn't love them both.

"Are you well, lass? Shall we add a spot of color to your cheeks?" Bridget's hands appeared in my peripheral vision, her large thumbs flexing, ready to pinch in the name of beauty. I ducked just in time.

"No. Thank you. I'm tired is all. Lydia hasn't been sleeping well."

"Well, smile then at least tonight, so as folks will think you're as pleased with your man as they are. I'm not saying the gossip is true," Bridget prattled on. "But if you were to show the MacDonald a bit of affection this eve, it could go a long way in dispelling the rumors."

"Rumors that I cannot have a child?" I didn't see the connection.

Bridget shook her head. "Those that say you're frigid." She lowered her voice to a whisper. "Some say you don't allow the laird to touch you." Her lips turned down disapprovingly. "Terrible fate to make a man suffer. They say he lets you alone so you can have the visions, but still . . . "

I opened my mouth in surprise—as much at her knowledge of our situation as at her reasoning. A few months ago she'd scurried away like a frightened mouse anytime Ian was near. The night I was handfast she'd pitied me, though she'd urged me to do what I must to appease the MacDonald's temper. But now, he was her laird? And she was siding with him on this, of all issues?

"I am not frigid," I returned in a glacial whisper. "My husband *died*. Was I supposed to forget—and allow his brother to take his place in our marriage bed, just like that?"

"Aye," Bridget said, matter-of-factly. "That was exactly what you were to do."

"I don't love Ian," I said, defending myself while wondering if I perhaps did, just a little.

"But he loves *you*, lass. There's not a woman in this castle who does not see it—except perhaps you." Bridget began gathering the leftover berries and ribbon.

He doesn't. Love me. "Take care to throw those away," I said, thinking of Lydia's siblings who liked to frequent the room to visit their little sister. "They may look pretty, but they're poisonous."

Bridget scooped the berries into her hand and poured the lot into her apron pocket. "Well, that's something," she said. "You may not love your man, but at least you've no plans to poison him."

He loves you. The three simple words were wreaking

havoc within me, every bit as much as Ian's declaration that Collin didn't want me had in the early days of my marriage. Every bit as much as Donaid's revelation that Collin might still be alive. *Alive. An ocean away. But alive. And mine.*

Had Collin, knowing he was to be gone fourteen years in the Colonies, sworn Ian to an oath to come here and protect me? If so, had he also encouraged the faking of his death? Or, had Ian come up with that on his own? If any of my conclusions were true, I didn't know what to do. I also didn't see how Bridget could be right, how Ian could feel more than the mutual attraction I'd grudgingly acknowledged the night he kissed me. Desire was one thing. But love . . .

I hadn't given him any reason to love me, nothing in return for the many things he had done for me, the kindnesses he had shown. Nothing, save harsh and unkind words.

Lydia squirmed in her blanket and started to cry, as was her pattern most evenings. I began swaying, hoping to keep her satisfied in Ian's absence.

"There, little lass. It's all right. Mama's here. I love you."

I did love her, though she had never given me reason to either, unless you counted crying and wet nappies. From the first moment Ian placed her in my arms, I'd felt the tug of motherhood, that magic of coming to know and falling in love with a child entrusted to you. I hadn't expected anything in return for her care, but I'd received it anyway—an increase of love greater than I had ever imagined. It seemed the more I did for her, the deeper my affection ran.

The list of things Ian had done for me since Collin's death was long. If the same principle of care and service equaling love worked between a couple, then perhaps he really did— love me. Which left my own, confused feelings for him an even more jumbled mess.

I didn't want to think about it but couldn't seem to help

myself as I subtly attempted to both avoid Ian and follow his progress around the hall at the clan's Hogmanay celebration. He'd arrived late—all the talk of the evening was of the child he'd rescued from the well—and was currently lingering with a group of MacDonald and Campbell men near the table filled with clootie dumplings. Dinner had been mutton stew, served in trenchers of fresh baked bread, along with ale and kegs of the MacDonald whisky, brought up from the cellar. Now the sweet smell of the dumplings filled the hall.

I watched as Mhairi offered Ian a particularly large serving along with an overly warm and inviting smile.

Or was that just my imagination? Instead of moving closer, I drifted away, speaking with a few of the women from our spinning group—the best I could do, at present, to mingle. I felt adrift, an observer more than a participant in the night's festivities. My mind was elsewhere, circling endlessly around my heart's dilemma. I lingered in the background, using Lydia's fussing as an excuse to avoid conversation.

Ian did not appear to be suffering under the same inner turmoil as me and seemed more than comfortable and on good terms with everyone in attendance, moving with ease among the various groups of both Campbells and Mac-Donalds, men and women. What a difference from last August, when the MacDonalds had been uncertain of his ability to lead and the Campbells had mistrusted him outright.

Lydia fussed in my arms, and I realized she needed to be changed again. The dancing was to begin soon, and it was expected I would dance the first with Ian.

Let them say I am frigid, I thought angrily and marched from the hall to my room, grateful for the excuse to avoid being close to him. I would stay up here until the dancing was well under way.

"There now, sweet lass," I cooed as I unswaddled Lydia.

Legs that had grown chubby churned in happy response, and her smile melted my heart. "There's my pretty girl." I could tell already from her delicate features that she was going to be beautiful. Her older sister shared the same face, along with a head full of curls. I waited eagerly for Lydia's hair to grow, hoping she would be similarly blessed.

When she was dry and bundled again I settled in the rocker and sang to her, the steady rhythm and lullabies doing as much to soothe me as her. Music and the sounds of making merry drifted from the hall below. I contemplated not returning to the festivities at all but worried Ian might come up to fetch me himself. I'd no desire for an emotional scene in front of everyone else. What must happen between us could come later, when we were alone.

Taking Lydia, I returned to the hall to find the tables had been pushed aside and the musicians for the *ceilidh* up on the dais. Sets for the next dance had formed in the middle of the floor, including one with Ian facing Mhairi. I wended my way through the throng gathered around the dancers.

I watched as he whirled about with a smile on his face, seemingly ignorant of the fact or having forgotten that he had altered my world this afternoon. My anger burned brighter, that he should be so carefree after perpetrating such deception.

Lifting Lydia to my shoulder, I faded farther into the crowd, patting her back and bouncing in time with the lively music. The steps and style were vastly different from any I'd seen in English ballrooms, and it seemed the participants—particularly the men—enjoyed the dance a great deal more.

Someone nudged my shoulder. "You ought to be out there, lass."

"Gavin," I exclaimed, overjoyed to see both him and Eithne standing beside me and looking well. The day Collin and I had spent with them remained one of my sweetest memories.

Ian had gathered them, and what others would come, close to the castle as promised, providing them living quarters to see them safely through winter.

"I'm afraid my years away from the Highlands have left my dancing skills lacking. I don't know this one." I repeated my rehearsed excuse.

"Not much to the Reel of Tulloch," Eithne said. "Excepting the bounce in your step and knee, and the turnabout. They say it was invented by a group of parishioners trying to stay warm while waiting in the cold for their tardy priest to unlock the kirk."

"Those dancing certainly look warm," I remarked. In particular, Ian's partner appeared rosy cheeked.

"Aye, well it isn't as good a dance as it used to be," Gavin complained. "Breeches don't make the flap a kilt does."

"Not nearly as exciting for the womenfolk," Eithne added with a playful wink.

I wondered how much of their banter was meant to soothe over the fact that Gavin could dance no more. Walking itself appeared difficult for him. Even if he'd remained stationary and let Eithne dance around him, his gnarled hands would not have been able to grasp hers as she turned a reel.

"Life is certainly different than it used to be," Gavin agreed. "No plaid, no pipes."

Much pain and little movement. I felt for him and Eithne and so many others with their daily struggles.

Yet looking around, it was undeniable that those in attendance seemed happy. The Campbells, in general, appeared happier than when I had first arrived. Were we not, with this dance and meal, celebrating our hard work and continued improvements, the preserving both the people and the way of life as Grandfather had wished?

In the briefest of speeches given when he arrived, Ian had reminded both clans of all we had accomplished—together. And that our new year would only be prosperous and happy if it began with joy and the continued break from the tradition of past animosity between our clans.

Looking around the hall, I noted that most were well on their way to starting the year full of joy—and spirits. After weeks of careful rationing, this was one night when resources were flowing literally and liberally, for all to enjoy.

Mhairi was still Ian's partner, and when his hand wrapped around her waist lightly in the turn, I felt a flare of something discomfiting take hold in me. I *should be dancing with him.*

I wondered how many people were looking at me, standing here by myself, and were pitying either me—the barren wife—or Ian—handfast to a woman who showed him no affection. I fidgeted with the blanket covering Lydia, self conscious in the midst of so many, not wanting their sympathy or judgment, but wishing suddenly that Ian *would* notice me—as he hadn't seemed to all evening. I moved in more closely, until I had worked my way to the front.

Knees bouncing, Ian turned toward me, one hand raised in the air, palm forward, his scarred hand held high for all to see. His other hand pushed the hair from his eyes, and I caught the sparkle of sweat across his brow.

Alistair joined me at the edge of the crowd. "You haven't danced once tonight, lass."

"Ian seems rather in demand, and Lydia has been *demanding*."

"Mary and I will take the bairn," Alistair offered.

"For the night, if you'd like," Mary said, joining us. "We'll be staying here until morning."

"Truly?" The thought of getting actual sleep was tempting. Not to mention Ian and I had many things to discuss, later, after all had quieted here.

Mary nodded. "It would be our pleasure."

I hesitated a few seconds more. "She's sleeping now, but I'm not sure how long that will last." I passed her into Mary's outstretched arms, then reached to rub my aching shoulders.

"You're still rocking, lass," Alistair chided teasingly.

I realized he was right and with some effort stopped the continuous motion. In some ways it felt like I had been dancing all night.

"She'll need the wet nurse in about two hours," I said.

"I'll see to it she gets fed. You enjoy the rest of the night. I know what it is to have a bairn—or eight." Mary laughed.

"Eight," I said faintly. "You have my undying admiration, Mary."

She laughed again and moved off, taking Lydia to the quiet of their quarters for the night. I watched her go, feeling the angst I did each time Lydia was out of my sight. I felt so grateful for the respite, yet I missed her already. Did all mothers feel this, or was it just me, because of the circumstances by which Lydia had become mine? Given the way the evening had gone thus far, it didn't seem likely I was ever to know what it felt like to have a child of my own flesh and blood.

Collin—possibly alive, and an ocean and fourteen years of indenture separating us. Ian—unforgivably deceitful.

He made another turn around the floor with Mhairi on his arm. I wavered between attempting to get his attention before the next dance or simply going up to bed. I could at least get sleep tonight, if not the answers I sought. Maybe our conversation would be best tomorrow, when I might more rationally process all that had come, and was yet to come, to light.

"Is that the lass you were worried about on our travels here?" Alistair inclined his head toward Mhairi, her head thrown back, her beautiful dark hair swinging about as she laughed at something Ian had said.

"Yes." I bristled. Was Alistair trying to make me feel worse than I already did? "She cared for Collin a great deal, I think."

"Appears not much has changed."

"What is that supposed to mean?"

"All is not always as it seems." Alistair gave the same cryptic warning he had before, on the occasion I had been overwrought with jealousy, believing that Collin loved someone else.

That someone else was now dancing with the man I was handfast to. And though my feelings for Ian were rather jumbled and precarious at the moment, that still did not take away the fact that he had given his pledge to me.

If Alistair is suggesting that Mhairi has developed feelings for him or he for her—

Ian rotated another quarter turn toward me, arm raised once more, his face flush beneath the lanterns swinging overhead. For a fraction of a second the light shone on his raised hand, illuminating its imperfections, including a thin sliver of white barely visible as it trailed from his palm to his wrist. *An older scar—a perfect line.*

I blinked, and he turned again, and I couldn't be certain of what I'd seen.

Collin? My own wrist throbbed as a whisper of the past cut through me.

Don't leave me. Don't let me go. I was five and begging him not to let the English soldiers take me.

I won't. Collin's hold was fierce, even in the face of the weapons pointed at him.

Keep her hand, then, if you're so fond of her. We'll take the rest.

Searing pain. Collin's release. Blood spilling on my gown.

"Are you well, Katherine?"

My head snapped around to see two of the women from the spinning room watching me closely, as I backed into the crowd and fumbled toward the wall.

"Was it a vision?" Ellen asked.

I nodded, still too stunned by that glimpse into the past and even more by what I thought I'd seen just before, right here in the hall. *A minute ago?* It felt like much more time had passed, but Mhairi and Ian still circled the floor.

"Would you like us to fetch the laird for you? Or perhaps Mary?"

"No. I'm well enough," I lied, though time seemed to have suspended and then reversed. As when it had happened previously, I was left weak and reeling.

"Excuse me," I said, and began making my way toward the stairs. I needed fresh air but dared not go outside alone. My room would have to suffice. At least I could be alone to think. There were too many people here, and it was stifling.

It was only my imagination. The hour was late, and I had been tired even before the evening began. *It is only because I heard news of Collin today, only because I am hopeful he is yet alive.*

I turned my hand over, staring at the faded scar running down my palm.

Chapter Forty-one

By the time Ian staggered into our bedchamber, some time after one in the morning, I'd both gathered my wits, having formed a semblance of a plan, and worked myself into an emotional frenzy. He closed the door, leaving the room in complete darkness, as I stepped from behind the screen, pistol leveled at his chest.

"Don't move."

He startled and swore an oath but did as I said. "What are you about, Katie? It's black as the Earl of Hell's waistcoat in here."

Katie again. "Light the lamp." I spoke through clenched teeth.

He took a step, then hesitated. "Are you alone?" He sounded wary, fearful.

Not for himself, but for me. His concern didn't sway my determination. In other circumstances I might have felt guilt at having worried him. But the emotions raging through me now were about as far from guilt as one might be. "No one else is here. Do as I say."

His tension expelled in a long breath. "You might have lit a candle yourself instead of scaring a man half to death."

You think that *was frightening?* Perhaps when he saw the expression on my face and that I'd a pistol pointed at him, he might begin to appreciate the gravity of the situation.

My ears followed him as he stumbled about the room, muttering in Gaelic.

"You weren't there for the first footing," he said, sounding hurt, of all things.

"I was tending Lydia. You brought me a bairn to care for, remember?"

"Aye. And has it softened your heart toward me? Not a whit."

If he only knew. Until this afternoon my heart had been steadily progressing toward forfeit to him. After five months of struggle against that very thing, I'd been perilously close to giving in.

Light flared, followed by a soft glow emanating from the corner of the room. Ian put the cover on the lamp, then turned to face me. His lips parted as his gaze came to rest on the barrel of the gun.

"Where did you get *that*?" He eyed the pistol with a wariness that bordered on respect. "Whatever this is about, seems you've thought it through." He took a step toward me.

"Stay back," I warned, even as I moved to accommodate his nearness.

"I wasn't planning to attempt a New Year's kiss, if that's what has you riled." He gave a derisive laugh. "You didn't even allow me one dance tonight."

"You weren't lacking partners."

"No," he agreed. "Only the right one." His eye hadn't left the pistol. "Somehow I doubt jealousy is the reason for your sudden desire to shoot me. You're angry about this afternoon. I wanted to explain, but I'd no sooner found Bridget than there was an accident at the well. I had to—"

"Remove your breeks." What he'd told me this afternoon was only the beginning of all that had me distressed.

Instead of hurrying to comply, the tension slid from Ian's face. A lazy grin replaced it as he took a confident step toward me. "There's no need for weapons. If you're wanting more from our marriage, you need only ask."

"We are *not* married." *Are we?* I didn't know what—or even who—we were anymore. Who the man I'd spent the last five months with really was.

"A conversation like this does give a man hope," Ian drawled.

"Take. Them. Off." I moved my finger over the trigger, careful not to touch it. I'd no idea if the pistol actually worked or was even loaded. But he didn't know that. I angled the gun lower, toward his leg. "Show me the scar on your thigh where I shot you."

This stopped him for a second. Fleeting surprise and then concern flashed in his eye and sobered his expression. "Wanting to check your aim before you give it another try?"

"That depends."

"On what?" he asked, advancing another step. I held my ground, though just barely.

"On what I see." I sucked in a breath. "On who you really are."

"Who I—" The lines of worry returned to his face, lingered briefly, then transformed into a look and sigh that sounded part weary resignation, part relief. "Ah." He removed his belt and tossed it aside on the bed. Next he untucked his shirt. I noted gratefully that it fell to mid thigh. I would be spared seeing more than necessary.

He leaned forward as if to remove a boot, then lunged at me instead, knocking the pistol from my hand. Before my scream had fully formed, Ian had my arms pinned behind me.

"If it were Brann here instead of me, he'd have taken your weapon and used it on you by now. In the future if you plan to shoot someone, best go through with it right off." He released me as suddenly as he'd grabbed me, and I stumbled forward, only just catching the edge of the bed with my hands and avoiding a fall. Hot tears of humiliation and anger flooded my eyes.

I'd lost my weapon, but I was still ready to fight. Face burning, fists clenched at my sides, I whirled to face Ian. "I hate you."

"So you've said before. No doubt you'll mean it before the night is through." He retrieved the pistol and examined it.

"I mean it now. You lied to me."

"Next time you hold a man at gunpoint make certain the gun is loaded as well." He tossed it on the bed, then moved to stand before me, close enough that I could strike him if I wished. "That was the *last* lesson you'll ever receive from me as Ian MacDonald." His lip wobbled slightly, and his voice dropped to a whisper. "There is *no* scar on my leg." He pushed his sleeve up and turned his arm over, palm up. "Only this."

My focus riveted to the thin white line descending below his newer scars. Even in the room's low light, it was plainly visible. I hadn't really believed it before, certain my tired eyes had been playing tricks on me. I couldn't quite trust it now. I felt as I had in the kirkyard, only worse, and sank against the bed, clutching the post for support. *Collin?* "Why?" *Why would you be so cruel?*

Instead of answering right away he removed the patch from his face, revealing an eye that seemed whole and functioning, with only a slightly puckered, pink scar along the top lid.

"Regardless of what happens in the next hours, I shall not miss this." He tossed the patch on the bedside table behind him. "Once my eyelid healed, I kept the patch off a great deal of the day when I was outside, but it seemed you found my other scars revolting enough, so I kept this one covered when I was around you."

"I didn't ask you to do that."

Was this one of his actions that had led to others believing me an unkind wife? *Frigid,* Bridget had said I was called. *Just wait.* I was feeling positively glacial right now, and the evening had just begun.

With the patch removed, gone was the pirate I had been starting to love. Yet it didn't feel as if the man I *had* loved was returned. I had neither. I searched this stranger's eyes, *Collin's* eyes, for some explanation, some reason I could not possibly fathom, for his elaborate and prolonged deception. *Why* had he hurt me so? Why lead me to believe he had died? Why masquerade as his brother?

"God knows you've every reason to hate me," he said. "And I'm about to give you more. But one thing I tell you first, and swear under heaven it is truth. I acted as I did for your safety. I meant to save your life, and I did. And I would do it again thrice. I've made a muck of things since, but in the end, if it allowed you to live, I stand by my decision."

My chest still heaved with anger, while grief—equal to that I had felt when I'd believed him dead—poured over me, a deluge of lost trust, tainted memories, and a betrayal so deep I'd no hope of ever recovering from it. I struggled just to breathe but wanted to scream. My pulse pounded in my ears, wild and erratic, and my head spun so that I could barely remain upright, reminding me of when the pain of my injuries had been so great I had lost consciousness. Would that I might do so now and then wake to find this had all been some sort of terrible, lingering nightmare.

"You don't look well. Come sit." He offered his hand.

I leaned away. "Don't touch me." *Ever again.*

"Come seat yourself then," he said, unfazed, as if he had expected my rejection. "It is apt to be a long night."

It had already been a long day and night, but I followed

him to the set of chairs at the foot of the bed and waited as he laid the fire. I tried but could not put a name to the emotions crashing over me, submerging me repeatedly with their relentless pounding, much like the painting I had started, of a tempest at sea. If I did not make some sense of my erratic feelings soon and find my footing, I'd no doubt I would drown.

He finished at the fire and took the chair opposite mine. "At least there was an easier way to answer your question—one that didn't require removal of my clothing."

We agreed on that. I could be grateful we were not having this discussion with him sitting here, half-naked.

"What if we had—" *Been intimate before.* I couldn't say it. "I would have seen your leg."

He held his hands up as he shrugged. "You would have known the truth that much sooner."

"So this is *my* fault?"

"No. Of course not, Katie. The blame is mine." He turned his hands over in front of him, studying their many scars. "It was fortunate a little of the old skin was left as proof of my identity. I was starting to forget, myself. Also fortunate my hands mended so well. Mary is a fine healer."

"Does *she* know?"

"Who I am?" Collin shook his head. "Only Alistair does, and I imagine Mary will tell him he's off his head, when he tries to explain the truth. Mhairi is aware of my identity as well," he added quickly. "Since the night of Lydia's birth."

"You trusted Alistair and Mhairi, but not me?" I was jumping ahead with my accusations, still not knowing why Ian—*Collin*—had even constructed this lie to begin with.

"It was not a matter of trust." Collin leaned forward, elbows on his knees, head in his hands. "Telling Alistair became necessary. Mhairi found out quite by accident. She, too, noticed my scar. "

That explained the hostility I'd felt from her the past several weeks. I hated that she'd recognized Collin before I had, and that she knew him well enough that his scar was familiar. *The scar he gained protecting me.*

"My deception began as a means to rescue you from Brann, and then to keep you safe a while longer," Collin said.

"And then?" Was *longer* the rest of my life?

"I did mean to tell you today, in case that matters," Collin said. "I started to. I tried."

"Why should I believe you? *I* found out." I pointed to my chest. "First in the kirkyard, and then when I noticed your scar as you danced."

"In the kirkyard?" His brow wrinkled. "I'm the one who told you it wasn't Collin in that grave. " He gave a shake of exasperation. "I *was* careless in leaving my bandages off tonight, but I think a part of me hoped you might notice when *we* were dancing, or later when I raised my glass for the first toast of the year."

"You believed this conversation would go better if I'd a bit of ale in me and was surrounded by a hundred people?" It was going worse by the minute, Collin digging himself deeper in the proverbial grave. Which wasn't a good analogy at all but brought forth the memory of when I *had* believed him in a grave—forever. Tears rolled down my cheeks as I fought to maintain some semblance of control. *I hate him. I love him. I can't. Ever again.*

"Just get on with it," I demanded. "Before it is morning and Lydia is returned."

"I did not think it would go better downstairs," Collin said. "I believed only that if you noticed my scar it might be a way to begin to tell you the truth. I've tried a dozen times before, and always my efforts were thwarted, or my courage failed. The night of Lydia's birth I decided to give it up altogether. To remain Ian, your *pirate*." Collin rubbed the scar over his eye. "I thought having you tolerate me as Ian was better than not having you at all. I feared this very thing—that telling you the truth would ruin any chance we had to return to who we once were."

He was right, on both counts. I had begun to care for him as Ian. I had come to the place where I felt that was better than loneliness. *Better than this.* For a few brief seconds I wondered what would have happened if I didn't know the truth but had continued on in contented—if not blissful—ignorance. That was no longer possible and hadn't been, since the crippling moment in the kirkyard when I had heard Collin's name.

There was still that matter to discuss as well—why that other man was in that grave, and who was on that ship. Those questions had set this entire chain of events in motion and had far greater implications yet. But even those would have to wait until later.

"Supposing you were going to tell me, what changed your mind to that course—after all this time?"

"You." Collin turned his head to me. "I couldn't be in a room with you without wanting to call you Katie, to claim you as mine and take you in my arms. Neither could I be near you and not feel stricken with guilt for my dishonesty and the torment I had caused. It was destroying me a day, an hour, a minute at a time. I decided that at the New Year I would make a new start—or try to anyway."

"Try, then," I said. "I agree to listen at least." Understanding and forgiveness remained to be seen.

"I thank you for that." Collin straightened in his chair. "I will tell you everything from the beginning, from the moment I left you the night of Liusaidh's fire." He took a drink from the glass on the table, braced his hands on his knees, and began.

"The English walked us nearly until dark that first day, herding us along like animals. Every step was a step farther away from you. Your screams still echoed in my ears. I thought of nothing else all day but how I would escape and return to you. At nightfall they made camp. The prisoners were all tied to trees—except the women, who were expected to cook the meal."

"They wouldn't attempt escape on their own?" I would have.

"You wouldn't have," Collin said, as if he'd read my mind, "if it meant leaving Lydia behind."

"Oh," I said softly. That possibility brought fresh tears. "They couldn't leave or their children would be killed."

"Aye." Collin nodded solemnly. "Very effective method of containment—and all else the soldiers wished," he added bitterly. "There is little a mother will not do for her child."

Or a father for his son. I thought of Collin's father. "How did *you* escape?"

"The English had searched me right off and found the dirk in my boot. But they are lazy, and they did not think to look in the other boot as well. I'd a shorter knife there, the one I use for carving—one given to me by your grandfather long ago."

Our eyes met for a brief moment before I looked away. But I had seen what he was thinking, and he likely knew my thoughts as well. Grandfather had not given him that knife merely for carving. He had known that one day Collin would need it.

"I'd helped an old man to walk throughout the day, allowing him to lean on me, when he would have been whipped—or perhaps shot—by the soldiers. He'd a daughter with him, and she came to me at the night to bring me a bit of water and bread. I convinced her to fetch my knife and cut me loose. She did. Before I left I had to tie her up, with a gag as well, so come morning the soldiers would not suspect that she had helped me."

"Why didn't you set her and the others free?" It was a fine story of escape, but I could not help thinking of those left behind.

"I had asked, did she want to come with me, but she would not leave her father, and we could not take him, slow as he was. As for bringing the others—none of us would have made it away." Collin's face pinched, and he shook his head, looking aggrieved. "I did feel badly leaving them. But it was to you I'd sworn my oath, you I had pledged to protect and had failed. Nothing weighed stronger than returning to you."

"That was the first day. You didn't return for almost three weeks."

"The longest three weeks of my life." Collin chanced another look my direction. I answered it with one I hoped was closed. I was intrigued by his story, that was all.

"I returned the way we'd come, walking the entire night through, staying clear of the roads, lest the soldiers came searching for me. I had nothing, save my knife. They'd given me little to eat or drink the whole of the day before. At sun up I could go no farther but found an old foxhole and curled up in it, covering myself with leaves. It was a fitful sleep, for I heard your screams in my mind, and then I heard the soldiers in the woods around me. It seems the coin they'd given Brann was a pittance compared to the price I'd fetch as a servant in the Colonies, and they were not about to let their income be lost."

"Fourteen years of labor ought to be worth something," I muttered, my ties to the English and soldiering leaving a bad taste in my mouth.

"Aye. It is—to the English, anyway. They came too close.

I left my hiding place and ran farther into the woods. A particular brutish soldier took to cutting through the brambles with his newest toy—a claymore confiscated from one of the other prisoner's homes. The soldier was close. I heard him thrashing about, but I did not think he saw me. I ran on, ducking between bushes and around trees. Until I came around one, lost my footing, and my head met the side of his claymore. I fell as it struck, off the edge of a precipice, into a deep ravine."

I gave a start, almost feeling the fall myself. *Oh, Collin.* I started to reach for him but stopped myself just in time. "Go on," I said in a choked voice.

"It was dark and freezing when I woke again. My head hurt something fierce, and I felt faint with the loss of blood. But I was blessedly alone and had landed on my side, my head literally stuck in the mud. The fall kept me from the Redcoats and stopped up my wound—though I cannot recommend mud as a treatment in general." Collin grimaced.

"I wrapped my shirt around my head tightly then trudged on, walking in a cold stream to both keep myself awake and to cover my scent. I found a dead fish and ate it raw." A corner of Collin's mouth lifted as he glanced at me.

"Dead fish aren't so bad after all?" He had teased me terribly once, on our journey through the Highlands, when I had speared a fish, only to discover it had been dead for some time. Remembering that morning together, and thinking of him alone and bleeding with naught but a raw, dead fish to eat, softened my heart a little more.

"They *are* bad," he confirmed. "I ought to have chosen starving. The next day I heaved out my guts—and the fish's too."

"Ugh." I clutched my stomach, feeling ill myself.

"Somehow I survived that and kept going."

"Somehow?" I didn't want him leaving any detail out. I wanted to know everything that had transpired. It was the only way I might come to a proper conclusion.

"Because I had to," Collin amended. "Every step brought me closer to you. Every minute longer I was gone gave Brann more time to hurt you. I was close to the Campbell keep. But I'd no idea what I might do when I arrived—no weapon, save a wee knife. No strength to speak of. Going there as I was would have provided Brann the perfect opportunity to kill me—before your very eyes. As much as I wanted to charge in and save you, I couldn't."

"You went home instead," I guessed, remembering the clan map showing the border we shared with MacDonalds.

"I started to." Collin rose from his chair and began pacing in front of the fireplace. For months I'd believed it a habit of both brothers, when really he had been here, right before my eyes. Why hadn't I seen it? *What kind of wife does not know her own husband?* One who had been married all of three weeks, perhaps.

"I'd not yet reached home when I discovered that my clan was coming to me—or to confront the Campbells. They were camped on the border of our lands, and Ian had wasted no time preparing them as if for war—men, women, *and* children. He'd armed them with everything he could think of—wooden swords, tines formed from antlers, pitchforks—a broomstick." Collin gave a short laugh. "I might have found it amusing, except that it was rather brilliant. By use of disguise and props, Ian intended to make it appear the MacDonalds were greater in number and decently armed. When I realized what he had accomplished in so short a time, I saw him for the leader he could be—if only his motives were well aimed."

Collin stopped his pacing to roll his neck and shoulders.

I sensed this was not a tale easily related. But so far, I did not doubt the truth of it.

"I'd not made myself known to Ian or the MacDonalds yet. I wasn't certain how they would receive me, and I needed time to plan what I might say to persuade them from their course. If not, there could be both bloodshed and repercussions. I had to persuade them—all of them, but especially Ian—to help me.

"I lingered far enough away from their camp not to spook the horses, but not so far as to have them out of my sight. About an hour after most had gone to bed, there was a commotion. I'd dozed off and woke to see Ian and Niall in a heated argument on the rise above the camp, parallel to my hiding place and only a short distance away. I crept closer and overheard them arguing over what to do when they arrived on the morrow. Niall wished to seek me out straight away and kill me. But Ian—" Collin brought a fist to his mouth and bowed his head.

I remembered another moment I had seen him thus, when speaking of his brother—when I had believed him to be Ian, speaking of Collin.

I ached for him—ached to go to him but couldn't. *Not yet. Not ever?* I reminded myself that I was angry. *Furious with him.* He had lied to and hurt me. All things that should not have been difficult to remember. Yet I was struggling to remember already and wanted nothing more in this moment than to stand and wrap my arms around him. Instead, I slid my traitorous hands beneath my legs. We had much more territory to cover.

Collin regained his composure and continued. "Ian said he would *not* kill me, and he forbade Niall or anyone else from it, stating that he would personally see to it they suffered a gruesome death if they even attempted as much. Niall argued that if Ian was to have any chance as laird, I needed to be dead. Elsewise, the people would not follow him. 'Let them follow whom they will,' Ian said. 'I'll not kill my brother.'"

"He seemed keen enough to do it before," I said.

"So we believed." Collin favored me with another smile. How I had missed those—and him. He seemed different already, less formal and guarded, more comfortable in my presence, already transforming in the past hour from the man I had believed myself handfast to, into the husband I had loved.

"You've one thing in common with my brother," he said.

Before tonight I would have said we had much more than that, like the shared love for the child bequeathed to us. "Which is?"

"You are both good at bluffing."

It took me a second to understand what Collin meant. "That night in the clearing, Ian's gun was empty too?"

"Aye." Collin took his chair again, angling his body toward me. "It was all show for Niall, to appease him. Ian did want to send you back to England. He *was* against our marriage. But murder had never been his plan."

"But at the river—"

"He meant to scare you. That was his first idea, to frighten you enough that you'd ask to go home. Ian knew I'd take you if you asked it of me."

"He held a *knife* to my throat." I was the one standing now, bearing down on Collin. "He *pushed* me in. I nearly drowned."

"He wasn't expecting anyone to come upon you so sudden. He became spooked and lost his head."

"I nearly lost mine and everything else that night. I don't believe it." I crossed my arms and turned away from Collin.

"How did you find all this out, anyway? You couldn't have learned so much listening to that one conversation."

"I didn't learn any of it then. Only that my brother did not mean me harm from that point on. Which was enough that when Niall rose up and tried to kill Ian, I did what I must. I flung my knife into his back then ran forward and bashed his head with a rock."

I shuddered. *Violence. Always.* Would Scotland ever know another way?

I faced Collin again. "You didn't kill him."

"I believed I had. We rolled his body down the opposite side of the hill and left it.

"No wonder you were surprised when he showed up here."

"Surprised. Angry. Frightened for you. I'd no choice but to finish what I'd started and kill him that night. But I was wrong in acting out of anger." Collin expelled a breath, as if letting that same rage go once more. He took his glass from the table and lifted it to his mouth before discovering it was empty.

"I had learned, by then, all the harm Niall had done Ian. It was Niall who convinced Ian that both my father and I had abandoned him on purpose. Niall had twisted my words and actions, to make it seem as if I hated my brother. All that and more, leading Ian away to a depth of misery and toward hell itself—when he had practically been there so long already, during his years with the Munros—and yet Ian had still refused any attempt to take my life. When I saved his, Ian realized Niall had been wrong. About many things."

I let all of this settle for a minute while Collin left to find us drinks and something to eat. All-night revelations apparently made for great hunger and thirst, as I was experiencing a considerable amount of both. *A good sign?*

When we had started this conversation I wasn't sure I'd ever be able to eat or drink or do much of anything ever again. *Utter devastation* seemed too light a description for what I'd felt when Collin had pushed back his sleeve. Enough that I had wanted to curl in a ball and never move again.

Two hours in, and I was doing all right. *Breathing without pain, anyway.* As of yet we had skirted the main topic, the actuality of what had happened to cause Collin's deceit. But I believed him so far and felt more open to empathy than I would have said possible when we began.

I sat once more and brought my hands to my head, pounding for some time now with an incessant ache—all the crying, no doubt. No wonder I was thirsty. Since leaving the hall I'd probably shed enough tears to fill a small bucket.

There would undoubtedly be more before the night was through.

Is he worth it?

At the kirkyard just hearing Collin's name and the possibility that he was alive sent my heart soaring with hope, though I'd believed an ocean and months or even years separated us.

What was so different now? Five months of deception, heartbreak, and mistrust made up the chasm between us. I hung my head back and sighed.

Crossing an ocean might have been easier.

Chapter Forty-two

ollin set his drink down and pushed the plate toward me. "Have the last bannock."

"Thank you." I left it for later, stifling a yawn, wondering how long it would be before we finished here.

"You've been patient," he said. "Not many would have been so. I'll get on with it, so you can rest your head a bit."

I nodded, doubting very much I would be able to rest anything, even if given the opportunity, before Lydia's return. My mind was too consumed with the tales of the night and the man beside me, whom I had believed lost to me forever.

Collin cleared his throat and began once more. "I'd no sooner helped Ian move Niall's body than I collapsed, near death myself from blood loss and sheer exhaustion. We couldn't even make it the distance back to camp, but Ian found a crevice in the rock and carried me to it. Fearing I would be dead before he returned, he ran all the way back to the main camp and grabbed what he could to help me. I had presence of mind enough to tell him not to let anyone know I was there. With the English patrol still about, it was safer for both them and me if no one was aware of my presence."

Collin refilled his cup and drained it quickly.

"Over the next three days Ian shared his whisky and stitched my head." Collin grimaced. "Made me wish I was dead—as much from the poor drink as the stitches. But it was no small miracle I'd survived to find him, and he did not intend I lose the battle from there. As I tried to regain my strength he told me much of what I have shared with you already. For the first time, since we were fourteen, Ian and I were truly brothers again. I came to know the true measure of him, to see that he is as good a man as our father was."

As good as you are. My eyes were watering once again, imagining what such a reunion must have meant to Collin. I thought of Anna, our estrangement the past few years, and how I had been hurt by it. How much greater had Collin's loss and sorrow been?

It was easier to believe Ian of good character than I would have imagined, probably because I had spent the past five months reinventing the monster Ian into a man I thought I could love and trust. I wondered how I would feel if ever we met again.

Collin continued his story. "While Ian had been caring for me, a few of the MacDonald men grew restless and raided one of the neighboring clans, the Menzies, catching the attention of the Redcoats still in the area."

"They were *still* looking?" I gripped my cup tighter.

"Aye. A few MacDonalds rode out to distract the patrol, while Ian had the others pack up and make haste toward home."

"What would the patrol have done if they had found you all?" I thought of the MacDonald women here who had become my friends. Of the families, the children, the men and women who had assimilated among us—with gratitude, if anything.

"I do not like to think of it," Collin said. "Armed as we were, even with our crude weapons, it would have meant a great deal more people headed to the Colonies. But the English are careless with life, and particularly the Highlanders' lives. If they had come upon the body of camp when all were there, I fear the MacDonalds would have been ripe for slaughter."

"It was then I came to my decision." Collin paused, then

leaned closer, hands open in front of him, pleading in the depths of his eyes. In it I saw the pain and self-loathing I'd witnessed weeks ago. Whatever had happened next, he hated himself for it.

"I told Ian I must turn myself in or the clan would suffer for it. I reasoned that if the English had me in their possession once more and believed me responsible for the trouble with the Menzies, they would leave. I knew that if I went with them, I'd not escape again, and that meant leaving you alone to suffer what you would with Brann. It tore my heart out. I did not know how I could do it, yet how could I not—and save many?"

"Leaving your entire clan in the way of an angry English patrol was not an option," I agreed. I could not fault him his decision. "How did you come to be here? And the Mac-Donalds too?" I breathed easier, reminding myself that they *had* all come here. *Except Ian.* My gaze flickered to Collin's stricken one.

He nodded slowly. "You have guessed already, I see. Ian and I followed the patrol, staying safely away until we were far enough from the MacDonalds. Ian asked that I wait a half hour before I turned myself in, to give him time enough to rejoin the clan. I agreed.

"Before he left, he swore an oath to me that if you still lived, he would see you safe. Since we had not a Bible to swear upon Ian took his knife and cut his hair off as a symbol of his vow as had Paul of old."

Ian's beautiful hair. "Oh, Collin." This time I did reach out to him, grasping his hand firmly. He responded in kind, holding to me as if he needed strength to tell the next.

"I thought him so serious because he wished to ease my mind about you. And it was eased, somewhat—more than it had been since I left you. I had seen that Ian possessed leadership and strength, and a cunning mind, the likes of which he would need to save you from Brann."

Collin pressed his lips together. His eyes shone with a flood of grief that hovered, and the dam holding it back seemed soon to burst.

"Ian bade me a tearful farewell. I had the thought to detain him, to call him back and insist that I leave first. But I ignored it, not knowing my brother was about to use that cunning mind—" Collin turned away so that I could not see his face.

I waited, letting him struggle on a tide of angst. But I held on to his hand. I would not let it sweep him away from me. A minute or more passed.

It ebbed, and he could speak again.

"I watched Ian walk toward the MacDonald camp—the opposite direction of the patrol—until I could see him no more. Then, only minutes later, a shot rang through the grove, and I heard shouting below. I scrambled from my hiding place to see what had happened. Ian had doubled back and lay sprawled on the ground, unmoving, with a soldier holding a pistol above him. Another hauled Ian to his feet, but he could not stand on his own. I was close enough to see the blood running down his head."

I sucked in a breath and clapped a hand over my mouth. What had Donaid said yesterday? *Collin had a scar earned from the captain's claymore. Ran across the top of his head. Had to have nearly killed him.* The hair hadn't been enough. Ian had cut himself so there could be no mistake that he was the man they sought, that he was Collin.

Collin's hand was gripping mine so tight it was painful. A tear rolled down his cheek.

"It wasn't an accident. He meant to do it."

"So you could return to me."

"Aye." Collin drew in a shaky breath.

"He had all but told me what he planned. Had Paul not once been Saul? It was one of the stories our father shared when we were growing up, always telling us that a man could change and become better than he was. With the cutting of his hair and that most solemn vow, Ian intended the same—to become better than he thought he was. To become *me*. I should have realized. I even had the thought to call him back, and I didn't!"

Collin released my hand suddenly, stood, and began pacing again, his steps faster, agitation apparent in every part of his body. The muscles in his neck showed taut in the firelight, and his scarred hands clenched and unclenched at his sides.

"They dragged him to a horse and threw him over the back. Blood seeped from his shirt, in a bright red circle. I felt paralyzed, as utterly helpless as when I'd heard your screams the night the English marched me away. My brother had just given his life for mine—for yours."

Collin turned sharply toward me, his eyes widened with rage, nostrils flaring. "I didn't *ask* him to do that! I didn't need him to be my father all over again. But he had done it anyway, all so I might come to you as I had the first time, all those years ago." He flung his hands wide. "Always the Campbells. Always you. First, your grandfather had told me. How right he was." Collin laughed bitterly, then spun away from me and gripped the mantel as if he wished to tear it from the wall.

The man whose wrath had destroyed this room and frightened me months ago had returned. This time I did not fear him but understood the reason for his anguish. His anger directed at me wasn't entirely unjust. Unaware of the sacrifice that had been made for my safety, I had acted only with the goal of self-preservation, which included avoidance of and disdain for him these many months.

"You were angry with me when you came," I said.

"Furious," Collin conceded. "It wasn't fair, and I ask your forgiveness for it now. But yes, I blamed you in part for my brother's death."

I thought of all I had done in the time he had been here— the rejection and rebukes, the dismissal of his feelings, the angry words spoken between us . . . *Attempting to end my life.* I was filled with deep shame and remorse. It was I who needed to beg forgiveness, as much or more than Collin.

Minutes passed, and neither of us spoke. Again I wanted to go to him, to wrap my arms around him and soothe his suffering. I refrained now not because I was angry, but because I did not feel worthy to offer comfort.

Gradually his breathing eased. I glanced at the window, trying to judge how much longer we had before Lydia was returned. I needed to hear the rest of the story, and Collin needed to tell it. Only then could we begin the work of bridging the gap between us.

"When did you decide to pretend to be Ian?" I asked, breaking the silence that had become oppressive.

"Not then. I railed against my promise to your grandfather—to you. Instead of coming straight here I tracked the English patrol, following them from a safe distance for an entire day and night. Ian was still with them, still unmoving. I'd overheard one of the soldiers shouting to the others that Ian was not long for this earth. The woman who had helped me escape was tending him."

"You might have been recaptured yourself," I said, feeling anxious at the thought of him being so close to the patrol.

Collin nodded. "I was careful, as much or more than they

were careless. Now that they weren't looking for anyone, they stayed to their camp, never bothering to see if an area was secure. The second afternoon they arrived at a farm—and shortly after set the barn on fire."

"Oh no." I knew this part of the story.

"Aye," Collin said. "The man I went in after was my brother. But I did not come out with him. When I left that farm five days later, hardly able to seat a horse, I carried Ian's remains with me—charred bone and ash, wrapped in a cloth.

"I had a long journey back to the MacDonalds. A long time to think and plan. My brother was lost to me. Perhaps you were too. I could no longer be Collin MacDonald. He had died at the hands of the English. But I *could* become Ian. If I didn't, if the soldiers somehow discovered that they'd been duped, then Ian's sacrifice would have been in vain."

Collin's expression was slack, his eyes dull. We were practically to the end. I recognized sharp pain blunted to the constant ache of loss. I'd been living with it myself for months.

"Being Ian had other advantages," Collin said. "I had been taken forcibly from here and was no warrior or threat to Brann. No hero. But Ian MacDonald had a reputation that preceded him, that of an unpredictable, unmanageable, and ruthless foe who was not to be denied what was his. Pretending to be Ian allowed me to find out quickly whether you lived or had died. When the gate opened and I saw you seated upon that horse—" Collin broke off, trying to look away again, but I caught his face in my hands and held it between them.

"You were so battered," he said. "Had been so close to death. I'd left, and you suffered."

"We both did."

"And then I had to hurt you more. When you saw the casket and fainted, I thought I had killed you."

"Alistair did too," I said drily. "Your coming then was

enough to make Brann abandon ship. Pirate," I added softly. I released Collin's face and brushed my finger across the scar on his eyelid. "This must have hurt very much."

"Nothing compared to believing I had lost you."

"Or losing Ian?"

"Aye." Collin leaned back in his chair, his expression far away. I needed to tell him what I'd overheard at the kirkyard, but I feared raising his hope. If Ian had been thrown in that burning building, how was it possible that he might be alive?

"I have many things to apologize for," Collin said. "The first being that I broke my vow to protect you. I should never have put you in jeopardy as I did, coming here."

"Collin—" How good it felt to say his name. "We had little choice but to come if we intended to keep *our* promises to my grandfather."

"Second," he continued as if he had not heard me. "I ask your forgiveness for not returning to you straightaway when I had made my escape. I allowed myself to think of others first."

"Thinking of your brother and the many families dependent upon you was not wrong. I would never fault you for that decision. Especially when it was my failing that led us to being separated to begin with."

"What do you mean?" He raised his head to look at me, though his shoulders remained hunched, such was his burden of guilt.

I told him of my incomplete dream, how I had left the vision early when I had sensed there was more I needed to see. "Had I the courage to remain, I would have seen it was a trap, meant to take you from me."

"That would have only postponed the inevitable." Collin sighed. "Brann had summoned the English, and he knew I had a pistol. I would have been arrested either way. Naught but my own foolishness to be blamed."

"Arguing about who is at fault will do us no good," I said.

"Aye," Collin agreed. "I only meant to begin to apologize for the many ways I have hurt you."

"There is but one that matters—that I don't understand. Why did you not tell me, once you had come? Why not trust me with your secret?"

"I planned to," Collin said. "I had to arrive as Ian, and remain so to others. But I planned to tell you as soon as your health could endure the shock. I tried—the night you came to the hall to see the casket. We were interrupted, and I decided that was best, that it would be better if you believed me Ian the night of our handfast."

"You tried to tell me then as well." I recalled the way he had knelt before me, repeating the same vows of our wedding, asking me to remember.

"I did," Collin said. "You were so obviously repulsed and frightened by my appearance, and by the time we went up to bed, I had convinced myself it might be better if Collin had died. I did not think you would believe me if I attempted the truth. You wouldn't *want* to believe that the monster before you could be your husband."

"You ought to have given me the chance." I wanted to believe better of myself, to know for a fact that he was wrong. But I *had* been appalled and frightened by his appearance. At first. "There were other times?" I asked.

"Many. It was a constant thought and guilt that would not be appeased. After a while it seemed you might be growing used to my appearance, that you might be able to overlook it, and that brought worries all its own. Ian was dead. Brann was gone, though still very much a threat. I was weak—in my desire for you. Having you believe I was Ian, having you mistrust and outright dislike me, made it easier for me to stay away from you. I ask forgiveness for that as well."

"For keeping your word?"

"For using my deception as a means to keep it. I ought to have been strong enough to be honest with you *and* to stay away from your bed."

"All this wasted time," I said sadly, remembering the way we had been before all this had happened, when I had wanted him in my bed. "Nearly half a year of our marriage."

"I know," he said. "And I'm sorry."

We sat in silence as I absorbed all he had told me thus far, the reasons he'd had, the forgiveness he had asked for. Some things were easier to forgive than others. I knew it would have to all be forgotten, his wrongs absolved, if we were to have any hope from here.

"The night Niall surprised us I came close to telling you," Collin said. "But then the way you looked at me after I killed him—more terrified of who I was than my scarred appearance—I knew it would never be the same between us. You would never believe I wasn't Ian."

"I really am an open book." That was exactly how I had felt that night. I looked down at the floor where Niall had died. It had been scrubbed clean, but the memory still disturbed me.

"Even now you are doubting," Collin said.

"No." I looked at him, denying the accusation. "It is only—"

"I do not seem the same man you married."

"In some ways you are not." How could he be, given the experiences he had lived through and the loss he had sustained? As surely as his outward appearance was changed, scars remained inside as well, marking him in ways he had not been previously.

I hugged my arms to myself, feeling chilled again, and unsteady. I had answers now but didn't know what to do with or about them.

Collin built up the fire again, and I returned to my chair after taking a blanket from the bed and wrapping myself in it. I'd not realized how cold the room had become. We had been so intent in our discussion that the hearth had grown cold, even as daylight had stolen into the room.

"Mary will be bringing Lydia any minute," I said.

"She won't." Collin turned from his work to look at me. "After I left you at the kirkyard I found Alistair and asked if he and Mary could keep Lydia until this evening, so you and I would have the time we needed. To talk," he added. "I really did mean to tell you."

"I believe you," I said. "I believe everything you've told me."

"Well, there's something," Collin said.

It was a start. That first solid plank on a bridge requiring many.

"You're tired," he said, observing the way I was curled up in the blanket. "I'll hurry with the rest. There is not much more to tell."

"I'm listening." I'd laid my head against the back of the chair and closed my eyes but a few seconds and would have been asleep in a few more. We had waded too deep into the waters of the past to stop now. Sink or swim, we had to continue to the other side.

"Everyone thought you were Ian, and you could not tell them otherwise." *Could not be yourself.* And I thought I had been lonely.

"Everyone except Alistair. I needed his help to make this work, so I'd no choice but to take him into my confidence. You'll recall that before I did, he and the other Campbells were ready to break down your door and fight me to the death for you. Had I not told him, there would have been bloodshed."

"I remember. Every hour of those very dark days."

"They were dark for me too, Katie. I needed you as I never had before, and I could not have you and had caused you even more pain instead." Collin turned from the fireplace, his shoulders hunched once more.

I stood, hesitant to come any closer, not because I hated him or was afraid, but merely because I didn't know how to bridge our gap. I didn't know if he wanted me beside him, or wanted me to stay here—only a few paces away but with an ocean of suffering between us.

"I don't hate you," I said finally, quietly. *Please let him believe me.* "I didn't hate you before when I thought you were Ian. I just didn't understand you."

"You may not even now. Sometimes I feel I don't know myself . . . " His voice trailed off, leaving a suggestion of hopelessness in the air.

Tell him. "Collin." I touched his sleeve. "There is something I must tell you."

"Aye." He turned to face me. I took a step closer.

"Yesterday after you left the kirkyard, I heard Donaid and Father Rey speak your name. Donaid had seen the English captain of the patrol that took you. He'd been surprised to hear that you were dead and buried in the kirkyard. The captain said that you were yet alive and had been put on a ship bound for the Colonies just three weeks ago."

"He was mistaken." Collin shook his head.

"I don't think so." I took Collin's hand and led him back to his chair. We sat, and he leaned forward, head cocked attentively.

"The captain said that you *had* escaped but were then recaptured a few days later. They knew it was the same man, as you'd had a particular head wound and you still had it when they seized you again."

Collin's shocked expression reflected what my own must have been when I'd overheard their conversation.

"Ian *alive?* Impossible."

"Did you *see* Ian's face when they put him in that barn? Are you positive it was him?"

"No. I heard the woman screaming that he wasn't yet dead. I thought it must be Ian, but I never actually saw his face. Inside the barn smoke made it difficult to see, and the beam covered him."

I leaned forward excitedly. "It could be true, then. Ian might really be alive."

"Aye," Collin said, wonder in his voice. His gaze flickered to the painting on the wall behind me, the unfinished seascape.

I turned to look at it with him. "I don't know what it means. I rarely do." I still hadn't deciphered what had prompted me to paint the tree in the kirkyard in such vivid detail.

"No matter," Collin said. "If Ian is on a ship bound for the Colonies there is little I can do about it."

I faced him again. "You can hope."

"I am already," he admitted. "You have not shoved me out the window or told me to leave your room and never return."

"I did plan to shoot you," I reminded him with a smile.

"With an unloaded gun," he replied, offering his own, tentative grin.

We sat staring at one another, inane smiles upon our faces. It felt like we were seeing each other for the first time, after a long time apart. Though really, there had been very little. I reminded myself of all we had shared together, from meals and work, to arguments and that one, passionate kiss. And lately, quiet nights with Lydia in the bed between us.

I didn't know what to feel and even less what to say or do

when, a second later, Collin slid from his chair and knelt before me.

"I have made peace with the loss of my brother, though it pains me still. Will you tell me now, if I must do the same of my wife? Or might it be that you may someday forgive me?"

I closed my eyes, shutting out his face, still beautiful to me, and tried to summon my anger of last night. It was a heavy emotion, requiring much effort to maintain and eclipsing all others. I couldn't find mine. It was gone, burned out in the hours between, as light as the ashes that lay piled below the grate. Later today those would be swept up and tossed away, or possibly given to Eithne to be made into soap.

Something old turned to something new. Collin didn't need to beg my forgiveness. He had it already and would a hundred times more if it came to that. We had been bound once by promises neither of us had been old enough to understand. What connected us now had become much more powerful. An old promise to be faithful had given way to a new promise of love today, tomorrow, and every day forward— even though we were both imperfect, though we had both made grave mistakes.

"Not someday," I said, taking his face in my hands as I looked at him. "Today. Now. You are forgiven."

Collin buried his face in my lap as a sob tore from him. His shoulders shook, and he wrapped a length of my gown in his fist, as if hanging on for dear life.

I placed a hesitant hand on his head, stroking his soft hair, offering what comfort I could, though I felt in great need of it myself.

Perhaps sensing this, he raised his head, then scrubbed at his eyes with his shirt sleeve. He stood and pulled me up with him and wrapped his arms around me. My own twined around his waist, holding tight. I never wanted to let him go.

We stood thus, gently swaying in a tender embrace, until my head nodded suddenly in sleep.

Collin pressed a kiss to my forehead, swept me up, and carried me to the bed. He slipped the shoes from my feet, covered me with the blanket, and sat beside me. "A song for sweet dreams?"

"Yes, please." I snuggled deeper into the quilt.

> *Should auld acquaintance be forgot,*
> *Tho' they return with scars?*
> *These are the noblest hero's lot,*
> *Obtain'd in glorious wars.*
> *Welcome, my Varo, to my breast,*
> *Thy arms about me twine,*
> *And make me once again as blest*
> *As I was lang syne.*

He kissed me gently. "Happy new year, Katie."

Chapter Forty-three

I woke sometime late in the afternoon to the sound of the rocker, its steady rhythm familiar and comforting to my otherwise confused mind. I watched the man seated there, the tender expression on his scarred face and the gurgling laughter of the child who so readily accepted him.

My grandfather's face had been scarred as well. But as a child, I'd hardly noticed his appearance. His kindness and love made him the great man he was. *Much like—*

"Collin?"

"Aye?" He raised his head and looked at me, a tentative smile curving his lips.

Relief and a kind of giddy joy swept through me, chasing away the lingering cobwebs of uncertainty. *It wasn't a dream. He is alive. He's here.*

I sat up and pushed the quilt from me, feeling shy when I realized my gown was bunched about my legs. Collin politely averted his gaze as I struggled to fix it.

"I'm sorry if I woke you," he said. "I missed the lass, so I asked that she be brought to our room."

"I don't mind."

"I also thought there less chance you would try again to shoot me, if I'd the bairn in my lap."

I laughed, my heart lighter than it had been in months.

"That is a sound I've not heard in a long while. I have missed it." Collin pulled his attention from Lydia to me, perched on the edge of the bed.

As tired as I had been last night, there had been no late-night laughter. That I had found it so quickly this morning and felt a happiness I'd never thought to know again seemed the greatest of blessings.

"For all your generous words last night, I was not sure how you would awake," he admitted.

As erratic as I'd found his behavior as Ian, mine had been just as bad, if not worse. We had each forgiven, but the bridge back to one another also required steps of trust. I gave him one now. "You are still and forever forgiven. Furthermore, I promise never to point a gun at you or your brother ever again."

"Ian would be relieved to know that."

"I have missed *you*," I said, still confused and with many questions about the past months and all that had been and not been between us. It was going to take some time to recover from and to figure out how to move forward from here. I doubted we'd had our last discussion or argument about it. Regardless, one thing I knew.

From the very depths of my soul, to every corner of my heart and mind, with every fiber of my being, I was grateful Collin had returned to me.

Though spring was months away, this morning the world seemed fresh and new, life alight with possibility.

I moved nearer to the rocker, my heart swelling as I looked down on the two people I loved most in this world.

Collin held his hand out, and I placed mine in it. Such a simple thing, and the greatest of luxuries at the same time. I wanted to hold onto him and never let go.

He began singing again, the same melody from last night, or rather this morning, when he had tucked me into bed.

Methinks around us on each bough
A thousand Cupids play,
Whilst thro' the groves I walk with you,
Each object makes me gay.
Since your return, the sun and moon
With brighter beams do shine,
Streams murmur soft notes while they run,
As they did auld lang syne.

"You fell asleep before I even made it to the second verse."

"We were up *all* night. Go on," I urged. "I'm listening now." The words were certainly an apt description of my feelings this afternoon, and it seemed, perhaps, Collin's too. "Lydia likes it as well."

Her eyelids were fluttering in almost sleep, the way babies do, fighting it as long as they can.

"Aye, well, perhaps the rest should wait until later." Collin's gaze shifted from mine, but not before I caught the slightly abashed look in his eyes.

"Mmhm. Just what sort of words are you singing to our child? Ought I be concerned?"

"Possibly," he admitted with a grin and squeeze of my fingers. He stood, then crossed to Lydia's cradle and laid her in it, rocking it gently and humming until her breathing deepened and she succumbed to dreams.

I went to the basin to wash my face and attempt to rid my hair of tangles. My reflection in the glass confirmed that Bridget's creation of berries and curls had most certainly not been intended to last through the night.

Collin backed away from the cradle with silent steps. "We've more to discuss, but I don't want to wake her. Would you mind very much if we slept a bit ourselves?"

"I just woke," I reminded him. "How long have you been up?"

"I haven't slept."

Our eyes locked in the mirror. "Not at all?" I'd been so exhausted this morning that even having my husband miraculously returned to me had not been enough to keep me awake.

"I wanted to look at you awhile," Collin said. "In case you'd had a chance to think about things and . . ." His voice trailed off, and he shrugged.

And I wanted you to leave. I set my brush down, turned, and closed the space between us, stopping directly in front of him. "If I was starting to love the man I believed to be Ian, it was because I saw you in him." I stepped forward, wrapping my arms around Collin's waist and laying my head against his chest. He pulled me close and nuzzled his face close to mine.

"Katie."

My name sounded like a prayer on his lips. I'd missed that and everything else about him, about *us.*

"I wanted to dance with you last at Hogmanay last night," I confessed. "But I was so confused. I couldn't think why *Ian* had lied to me about his brother's death when really he was alive and—" *Ian is alive.* The proof was hanging on our wall.

"Look." I pointed to my partially completed painting. "Ian is why I painted the ocean. What if that's the ship he's on? Or . . . if I paint *our* future, then maybe that is the ship we are to sail on—to find your brother."

Stunned silence from both of us followed this possibility. Collin's eyes traveled from the painting to mine, no doubt reading what I felt, what I somehow *knew.* The tempest-tossed ship I'd painted was not Ian's, but ours.

"How can we leave?" Collin whispered. "What will become of everyone here?"

I hadn't an answer for him and was still lost in my own shock. *Marry in June when the roses grow, and o'er land and sea you'll go.* Finlay had known long before me.

The sounds of excited shouting and some sort of commotion reached us from the hall below. Whatever or whoever it was ascended the stairs rapidly, based on the sounds outside our door.

"I'll head them off before they wake Lydia." Collin hurried to the door, opened it, and stepped into the hall. I continued staring at the painting of the ship tossed upon the water. When were we to go? And how? We were managing all right here, but we'd no funds to speak of for travel or anything else.

The bedroom door opened again, and Collin reentered and stepped aside, making way for the man behind him, nearly unrecognizable beneath a scraggly beard and filthy clothes.

He nodded to me and spoke in a familiar voice. "Good to see you, lass."

Finlay had returned.

"Brann has been granted both the keep and the Campbell lands." Finlay paused to rub his hands before the fire as Collin, Alistair, Mary, and I exchanged looks of dismay.

All we have worked for here.

"There's more." Finlay's mouth pressed into a grim line, and he leaned forward, hands braced on his knees, as if standing upright was painful. He appeared far older than when he'd left, and I wondered what he'd gone through the past months, in both delivering the documents and staying to fight for their acknowledgement. That he had made it safely to Edinburg and back again was no small matter.

"The adjoining MacDonald lands are forfeit to Brann as well, for grievances put upon him by Collin." Finlay paused, straightened, and spoke as if quoting someone. "The MacDonald traitor having been shipped off to the Colonies for indenture is no longer entitled to said lands. A reward of twelve pound sterling is offered for the capture of his twin brother, Ian."

I slumped in my chair, grateful I was already sitting. Collin appeared too agitated to even pace. He stood, unmoving, his mouth set and gaze distant.

"What are we to do?" I asked.

"Leave," Collin said. "And quickly. We've no choice. It was one thing to oppose Brann, but you've seen firsthand we cannot withstand the English."

"You've a little time," Finlay offered. "At present Brann is a guest at court in Edinburg. The New Year festivities there are to continue another three days. Supposing he left then, or even before, you should have another week to prepare."

"Unless he is already on his way here."

Everyone turned to look at me.

"Katie, do you know something?" Collin asked.

"Only a vague unease that I feel we should trust." The last time I had such a feeling we had discovered Edan's corpse.

"I'll need your help, Alistair," Collin said. "We must gather everyone that we can. We'll meet in the hall at seven tonight to discuss what is to be done."

Chapter Forty-four

"A moment, if you please, Katherine."

I turned from changing Lydia to see Finlay lingering in the doorway after the others had gone, Collin included, to alert as many as possible.

"Of course. Come in." I lifted Lydia to my shoulder.

Finlay stopped a few paces into the room. "I've something for you," he said in that same endearing way he had months ago.

"More paint?" Once I would have welcomed such a treasure, but the time for painting anything was far gone. I knew without asking that we would be able to bring only the necessities.

"Something better." Beneath his shaggy overgrowth of beard, Finlay's smile was barely visible. As he had before, he reached in his sporran. I leaned forward, eager for whatever gift he bore.

"A letter!" I exclaimed as he withdrew the parchment. Anna's familiar script spanned the front, and I felt a sudden longing for home and the sister I had loved. "Thank you, Finlay." I didn't kiss him this time, being uncertain whether or not I could find anything to kiss beneath all that hair. But I squeezed his hand appreciatively after I had taken the letter from it.

"Glad to bring a bit of happiness," he said. I stepped back, expecting him to go, now that he had delivered his gift. Instead, he took another step into the room. "May I?" He nodded to the paintings.

"Yes, of course." I lingered where I was, bouncing Lydia, as he crossed the room.

"Fascinating," he said when a minute or more had passed in which he had studied both paintings intently. "Where all planted therein doth not grow. Of course," he murmured, trailing a finger below the bottom of the picture with the rowan. "I'd no idea what that meant when I said it, only that it was a key to the future."

His hand moved to hover over the seascape. "Per mare per terras. Not an easy journey, I think. But survivable." He turned abruptly.

"Your gift and talent are remarkable, both in vision and execution. Good day, Katherine. I shall see you in a few hours at hall."

He left me speechless—at my own stupidity. What we sought had been right in front of me this whole time. I had painted it, had pounded my fist upon it. The letter slipped from my fingers, forgotten, in light of what I finally understood.

The ground was frozen. Had I put my mind to this more earnestly when Finlay had first given me the clue, I might have been digging in soft soil beneath the summer sun. Instead I huddled beneath my cloak, the hood pulled up to keep out the falling snow. My hands were numb already, and only one narrow end of the stone had budged at all.

"Look high and low where all planted therein *doth not grow.*" Finlay's words to us last July. They'd made no sense then, but now seemed a most logical clue. *A kirkyard, of course.* How had I been so blind? Bodies planted in graves definitely did not grow.

Per mare per terras. By sea or by land. We had crossed the land. Now it was time to sail the ocean. The dowry Grandfather had left was going to make that possible. If only I could reach it.

I wrenched the knife beneath the loose side once more, pressing on the handle with all my weight. With a sudden pop, it released from the earth, revealing the hole I had been expecting beneath. Pushing the stone aside on the snow-covered grass, I reached inside. My hand closed over a bag—one of many. I withdrew it, feeling the heavy weight and hearing the jingle of coin. Kneeling beside the tree, my cold fingers fumbled with the string until I'd opened the sack, revealing the sparkle of gold. *Sovereigns.*

"Merciful heaven." I dug my hand in, letting them sift between my fingers.

How many were there? *Fifty? One hundred? In each pouch?* The siphoned money from how many years? Grandfather might have been giving some of his wealth to help displaced Jacobites, but it seemed he'd been stashing quite a bit away as well. We were saved.

Thank you. I raised my face in gratitude to the clouded sky and saw instead Father Rey's leering eyes and flapping jowls.

"Stealing from the church. *Tsk. Tsk.* You know the penalty. Which hand would you like cut off?"

"It isn't stealing. This is my dowry." I dropped the bag in the hole and reached for the stone to cover it. Father Rey's shoe came down painfully over my fingers.

"It's in my kirkyard. It belongs to the church."

I shoved his leg back with my free hand at the same time I yanked the other from beneath his foot. He stumbled backward, grabbing at the remnant of my Hogmanay curls to keep his balance.

I screamed. My eyes blurred, my stinging scalp all too reminiscent of Brann's treatment. "Let go!"

"Do as she says. For now." Brann's voice was more than a memory. The same boots that had broken my arm and bruised my ribs appeared in my peripheral vision. He looked just as I had seen him in my dream.

Father Rey thrust me away. I clung to the tree for support and pulled myself up.

"I admit you have surprised me, Katherine. How fortunate for me you did not die after all." Brann knelt and retrieved the bag I had dropped. He opened it, and the light of greed flashed in his eyes. "When Donaid reported to me that Malcom had taken you without any trouble, I doubted that you'd any ability to see the future. Since you've managed to find this, it appears I was wrong, and there might be some value to keeping you after all."

"I will not be kept," I said defiantly. "Neither will any of that gold—by you."

"Still foolishly brave I see." He smirked. "No worries. I am a patient man. Between Father Rey and myself, we should be able to purge you of those traits."

As the two men exchanged evil smirks, I snatched the bag from Brann's fingers. The tree behind me blocked any quick escape, and he yanked me to him before I'd taken two steps.

"Which arm did I break last time? Shall we try it again?" He twisted my arm behind my back, forcing me against his chest. The sack dropped to the ground as I struggled then stopped at the feel of cold steel against my throat.

I closed my eyes, shutting out Father Rey's sinister expression and fighting through the blinding pain in my arm and the terrifying prospect of it being broken again.

It came to me, as it had many times before, that this was not what Grandfather had intended for me. It was not what he had *seen* my future to be. Too many times I had been here before, in similar circumstances, at another's mercy. My strength was no match for a man's, but my words ... My *gift*.

"If you kill me, or even harm me now, you will lose your life as well."

"Not likely, when you are here all alone. They won't even know what's become of you. I could have you in that grave with your husband, and no one would ever realize."

"I'm not alone." I'd Ian to thank for that lesson—that it was unwise to go alone in search of anything, be it water or gold. "The kirkyard is filled with MacDonalds and Campbells."

"Aye, dead ones." Brann gave a harsh laugh, though I noted Father Rey appeared uneasy as he craned his neck, looking for evidence I spoke the truth.

"You are not to die today," I continued. "I've seen the date of your death, inscribed on your gravestone, in this very yard."

"Enough." He wrenched my arm tighter. I bit down on my lip to keep from crying out.

"I even know exactly what will claim your life on the eleventh of March 17—"

"Silence, witch," Brann hissed in my ear. The tip of his knife pierced my skin with a sting. I felt the trickle of blood down my neck. "No more of your foul preaching."

"It's of the devil, as is she," Father Rey cried. "She ought to be burned for such blasphemy. Excepting the Lord, no one knows when—" He crumpled suddenly, revealing Alistair standing behind him, a good-sized stone in his hand.

"Your *sermons* are of the devil," he declared.

Brann stepped back, hauling me with him. "Stay away," he warned. "There's an English patrol not far behind me, and they'll—"

"1774," I cried. "That's when you are to die. Not today. Not even here, though they will return your body to this place." I flung my head back, smashing into his chin and jarring his arm. A bullet whizzed past our heads, and Brann thrust me away from him. I dropped to the ground seconds before the next one struck, this one in his arm as he ran. His knife fell, and I snatched it from the ground.

A cry of rage filled the air as Collin and a dozen other men of our clans leapt over stones and ran from behind bushes to hurl themselves at Brann.

I fell back against the tree, panting and shaken, but alive and mostly whole. Collin dropped to his knee beside me.

"Are you all right?"

"Yes."

"Never again." He pressed his lips against mine swiftly in a kiss meant to reassure us both that I was safe. "Never again will you be bait for Brann or anyone else."

"Agreed." I pressed two fingers against my neck to stop the bleeding.

It had not all gone as smoothly as I had hoped, or as I had promised Collin it would when I'd told him I had seen what must happen in order for us to get both Brann and the gold. But then, I hadn't really seen it at all, or known Brann's date of death, for that matter. I'd acted in faith, with only the past dreams of Brann near this place, and the knowledge that the dowry was buried here to guide me. Collin need never know of my deception.

He wasn't the only one who could lie to keep the other safe.

Chapter Forty-five

A sense of urgency prevailed the next morning. Though Brann, Donaid, Father Rey, and the council had been safely deposited in the cells belowstairs, there was the threat of the roaming English patrol soon to arrive and the price on Collin's head. The keep was a flurry of activity, both inside and out, with almost all packing to leave for some destination.

A dozen or more families had gone already, choosing a life in the towns or elsewhere in Scotland over a long ocean voyage to a new land. I wondered if the idea would have tempted Collin or I, had there not been Ian, and Grandfather's knowledge of where our future lay, to consider.

The pile of coins on the table grew steadily lower as each family came forward and declared their intentions. Those remaining in Scotland were given two guineas, no matter how large their family. It wasn't exactly a fair distribution, but it was more than either the Campbells or MacDonalds would have received under past circumstances.

Those going with us received nothing today, as those bags containing sovereigns exclusively had been set aside for provisions on our journey and crossing the ocean. We would spend them carefully as needed for all on our way. We did not yet know what the passage would cost, or even when we might sail. Only that we would and would live to see the new land, this new Scotland Grandfather had written of on the back of the stone in the kirkyard.

Per mare per terras, I had learned last night, was the MacDonald clan motto. Had I known that earlier, or had Collin seen the stone himself, we might have guessed it as both a message from and the hiding place of my grandfather.

"By sea or by land, we will go," Collin had declared, after telling his clan that what little land they'd had left had been forfeit.

The stone itself rested on the table in front of the piles of coin, so each who came before us might see for himself my grandfather's last edict, that our people remain together and strong—not here, as we had believed—but across the sea in a New Scotland, ùr na h-alba, Nova Scotia.

It wasn't the castle or even the land that Grandfather had wanted us to preserve, but the people themselves. He'd not bothered to restore the keep but had fortified the members of his clan instead, instilling within them knowledge and a deep, abiding faith that good would prevail and that God had a hand in their lives—and not the hand Father Rey had preached of.

Between bouncing Lydia, I recorded the ledgers while Collin—still known as Ian to most everyone else—distributed the coin. Alistair and Finlay were on hand to assist as well, lest anyone become insistent about taking more than his share.

"My family and I will not be joining you." Brian Mac-Donald stood before the table, battered hat in his hand, his motherless children huddled around him.

No. I had come to love this little family, especially the youngest two, who seemed to visit our room as eager for my attention as they were to see their little sister. *Lydia will not know her siblings.*

"My parents' and now my wife's bones lie in Scotland," Brian said. "I'll not leave them to risk a journey across the sea." He paused, then looked over at me. "Neither will my daughter."

It took me a few seconds to realize what he meant, before his pointed stare at the squirming bundle in my arms finally reached me.

I stepped back, clutching Lydia to my breast. "You *gave* her to me. You can't possibly care for her along with your other children too." I glanced at Collin, his expression grim as he stood.

"Think carefully what is best for the bairn," he said to Brian. "Katie loves her fiercely, as do I. We will see that she is safe and raised well. Lydia needs a mother."

"She'll have one." Brian plunked the hat back on his head. "We're to be married as soon as we can, by proper clergy, which is a mite better than your own arrangement."

"Ian and I will marry," I said. Keeping Lydia was worth false witness before God. Considering our circumstances, I felt certain he would both understand and forgive.

"No need," Brian said. "My wife will take care of the bairn. We'll go to the coast and work the kelp." Brian didn't make it sound any better than it was—an arranged marriage born of need, and perhaps desperation. But who here felt desperate enough to agree to staying *and* taking on the care of another woman's five small children?

"Whom are you to marry?" Collin sounded as dazed as I felt.

"Me." Mhairi moved from her brother's side, farther back in the line, to stand at Brian's. Her gaze met mine, challenging.

I stepped back and sat down hard in the chair, startling Lydia. She began to cry, and I bent my head close to hers, whispering soothing words.

"Why would you do this?" The back of Collin's hands grew white as he leaned forward, pressing into the table. "For spite? It's cruel to bring a bairn into it, and Katie's done nothing to you. Your quarrel was with me, and it has long passed."

Mhairi edged closer, speaking low so only we could hear. "Nothing—Collin? Your wife has everything I ever wanted, and she doesn't even appreciate it. She didn't even recognize you when I did. She can't love you as I do." Mhairi made to come around the table. "Hand me the child," she said more loudly.

"Her *name* is Lydia." I closed my eyes and pressed my cheek close to Lydia's, inhaling her sweet baby scent. *This can't be happening.*

"Katie." Collin's voice was choked. He knelt beside me and placed a hand on the back of Lydia's head. "I'm so sorry."

Our eyes met, each bright with tears. "She's *ours*," I whispered. "He can't simply take her back—not after all this time."

"I'm afraid he can." Collin stroked Lydia's soft curls. "To try to stop him would mean a fight—bloodshed, either his or mine. Either way it would only hurt all of his children more. You know as well as I we've little time as it is to get everyone safely away. Better Lydia is away with them, than delayed here in harm's way."

"*We* love her. He hardly knows her at all—never comes to visit. Mhairi won't care for her either."

"That is not for us to judge." Collin reached to take Lydia from me.

"We love her," I repeated. Tears coursed down my face as he pulled her from my arms.

"We always will," Collin said. "It is because we love her that we must let her go."

"Wait." I leaned forward, pressing a kiss to her forehead.

Collin pressed his own to mine. "Courage."

My hands shook as I unpinned Lydia's clothes from the ever-present line in our room. I held each to my chest, the tiny garments I had sewn for her, imperfectly made, but created with a perfect love. It had never mattered that she'd not been born of me. She'd been my baby, my daughter. The idea of a world without her in it was incomprehensible. I ached to hold her already.

Can I have no happiness?

"I am beginning to think you really do love Collin. He tells me you have forgiven his deceit."

I didn't need to look up to know that Mhairi stood behind me. I hadn't bothered closing the door, certain I would fall to pieces the second I was alone.

"You really *don't* love him," I threw back. "Or you wouldn't hurt him like this."

"You both needed to know what it feels like to love someone you can't have."

"You think we don't understand loss and yearning?" I ripped a nappie from the line. "When did your mother die—a few months ago? I lost mine when I was *four*. I've wanted to be with her my whole life. I can't because she was murdered in front of me by the man who has now returned to lead this clan and who would happily kill us all. Knowing this, Collin and I came here and faced him—and nearly lost each other and our lives in the process." I tossed the clothes on the bed and marched across the room, stopping only when I was toe-to-toe with Mhairi.

She had Lydia with her wrapped snuggly, more so than she liked to be these days. Mhairi stood with feet planted wide, one hand on her hips as if ready for battle. I was too.

Doing my best not to look at Lydia—and cry—I forced my attention to Mhairi's face.

"Collin's father gave his life for him. I left my family behind in England to come here, to be with Collin and to try to help. I *know* what it is to love—and lose. Collin and I both do."

Spent from my speech and all else from the past few days, I sank into the rocker and brought a hand to my throbbing head.

"This isn't just about that," Mhairi said. "About a cost to you and Collin. You lived only months believing he was Ian, with the constant reminder of the man you loved and believed dead. *I* have lived *years* watching Collin, hoping, having him right *here* in front of me but unable to claim his as mine." Her eyes were bright as she shook her head. "I can't spend the rest of my life watching you both, seeing what I can never have. Leaving Scotland was never an option for me."

"So stay." I kept my head down, not wanting to see Lydia or the hurt reflecting from Mhairi's face. *She* was hurting *us*—and Lydia. I brought my clasped hands to my mouth and breathed deeply, battling both sorrow and anger as I had the night Collin confessed his deception.

"Why marry Brian? There are other men here." Those who weren't mourning a wife and who didn't have five children already. "I thought you liked Earnan."

"I do. But he is leaving to go with you, and I've just told you why I cannot."

"*Five* bairns, Mhairi. Do you realize how much work that will be?" I faced her again. "Caring for Lydia takes all my time, and she is but one."

"*Took* all your time," Mhairi corrected. "Now you will have more to devote to your husband. While I fill my days caring for Lydia and her siblings. God willing, they will exhaust me. I ask nothing more of my new situation than to be able to fall asleep at night without thinking of your husband."

She was throwing her life away. Caring for motherless children was noble, but Mhairi wasn't doing it for them or their father or even for herself. It was to make Collin and me suffer as she did and with the hope that she'd work herself into oblivion. I hoped she would.

I sniffed loudly and brushed the tears from my cheeks—a pointless effort, as more followed. Perhaps if I begged, her heart would soften. "Four children will be plenty to both occupy your mind and exhaust you. Lydia knows only me as her mother and Collin as her father. We love her. We would do anything for her."

"*Anything?*" Mhairi's voice was unusually high. "Would you give each other up for her? If I said you could have Lydia, would you leave Collin and return to England?"

My breath caught, lungs refusing to expand or contract. I'd been wrong about Mhairi's reasons. There was one more. She'd come up here to force me to a choice. It was her last chance, some ill-thought, absurdly planned attempt at winning Collin. No matter that I was already married to him and that she, too, had given her promise to another man.

I closed my eyes, tears squeezing from them. Lydia would probably be resented, or at the least ignored because I had loved her. How could I let her go, knowing this?

An innocent child.

I stood and moved close to Mhairi once more. I pulled back the corner of the blanket and touched Lydia's soft cheek, remembering the night Collin had first brought her to me.

"You were the one spreading rumors—calling me the barren bride."

"Aye," Mhairi admitted easily. "And frigid. We all knew you wouldn't let Collin touch you. He deserves more. He deserves *me*."

"It's true that I wouldn't let the man I believed to be Ian touch me. But the few times he did, it was as if a flame leapt up between us. The same that existed between Collin and me. I didn't want to feel that for anyone else. I didn't want to be disloyal to my husband, no matter that we'd been married only three weeks and I believed him dead."

Mhairi scoffed. "You did not even recognize your own husband."

"You knew Collin years to my weeks. Little wonder you recognized him first." I touched the soft curls beginning to show on Lydia's head. "You could give her to someone else," I suggested. "Someone who wants a child."

"You want a child. You want her," Mhairi insisted.

"I do."

She pushed Lydia toward me. "Take her then. And go."

Lydia. Collin. The imaginary scale in my mind would not equal. Just as he must always consider me first, I had promised the same to him.

My eyes fastened on Lydia's innocent face one last time. Tears blurred my vision as I stepped back and shook my head. "My love for Collin began before either of us walked this earth." I still could not imagine my life without him. I didn't want to. I wouldn't. Ever. We were meant to be together. "I would never do anything to hurt him."

Bless Lydia and keep her safe. "I will *never* leave him. My answer is no. A thousand times no. I will never give up Collin."

Chapter Forty-six

I turned a slow circle, taking a last look around the room ... the fireplace where the man I'd believed to be Ian had shattered a pitcher in a fit of rage, the bed I had slept in mostly alone, my mother's paintings and my own. I appreciated them for what they were now, not so much perfected works of art, but glimpses of the future, given to us for guidance in a tumultuous world. So much had taken place here these past months. Much of it had been fraught with tension, yet I still felt a sorrowful tug at leaving.

Then there was Lydia. I fingered the soft wool cap in my hands. My first attempt at knitting had not been spectacular, but she had looked darling in it, and I had been sad when it no longer fit her growing head. It was all I would have to remember her by, the first child of my heart, if not my womb.

"Udal Cuain," Collin remarked, casting a dark look at the ocean painting.

"What?" I took a careful breath and tucked the hat inside my satchel.

"To be tossed about or have distress at sea. It is what I would call this painting," Collin said. "I wonder, will you ever paint a picture of good things to come?"

"I painted Bealach Druim Uachdair," I reminded him. Our afternoon on that mountainside had been one of the sweetest of my life.

"So you did," Collin said, a thoughtful expression on his face. "We should go. Alistair will have everyone in ranks by now. I want to leave ahead of them."

We were not going to be traveling with the others, given the price on his head. Nearly everyone here still knew him as Ian, and Collin worried about endangering them with his presence as well as the temptation the offered reward presented for those in desperate circumstances.

Alistair, Finlay, and Gordon had been entrusted with the rest of my dowry, with Collin and me keeping enough for our own passage as well as for necessary funds when we arrived.

He headed for the door, and I followed, pausing for a last lingering glance from the hall.

The room looked much as it had when we'd arrived, save for the addition of the rocker—and the envelope mostly hidden beneath it. "My letter," I exclaimed, rushing back into the room.

"From your family?" Collin asked, joining me.

"From my *sister*." I'd had no hope of her ever writing to me, parting on poor terms as we had. But that didn't lessen the pain of our estrangement. I broke the seal and unfolded the parchment. My eyes eagerly scanned the lines, then stopped at the unexpected news of my stepmother's death.

"Oh no." I brought a hand to my mouth, unable to speak what I had read out loud. Collin took the letter from me, looked over it quickly, then pulled me into his arms.

"I'm so sorry, Katie."

On top of everything else from the past few days, I found this news made me simply numb. I'd no more tears to cry; I'd spent them all on Lydia.

"Anna wants me to come."

"Aye. I read her words," Collin said.

"I'll have to send a letter explaining when we get to Glasgow."

"A letter would be a good idea," Collin said. "So she'll know when to expect us."

I leaned back to better see his face.

"Anna lives near London."

Collin shrugged. "Ships leave from England as well."

"We would have to cross the border." With the price on his head—or Ian's, as it were—we needed to avoid any confrontation with the English. "We wouldn't be sailing with the others?"

"Probably not," Collin said. "If we are fortunate enough to enter England undetected, I shouldn't want to risk another trip north. Alistair, Finlay, and Gordon are capable. They will do well enough without us for now." He pulled me close again, his hand stroking the back of my head. "Besides, if we can sail across an ocean and traipse through the Colonies in search of my brother, a week or two to visit your sister seems more than fair."

Chapter Forty-seven

Had I known the Highlands better or had any sense of direction, I might have realized that Collin led us northwest instead of south. We didn't talk much that first afternoon of riding. I was too grief-stricken with Lydia's loss, and Collin seemed much the same. We camped without a fire that night. Too exhausted to care about anything except sleep, we curled up together to keep from freezing.

The second day we skirted a settlement, and only when I'd noted Collin's continual craning, as if trying to spot something or someone in the crofts below, did I ask what it was and where we were.

"The MacDonald land, or what used to be," he said. "I thought you knew where we were going."

He hadn't mentioned it, and I hadn't asked, but I could not fault him for needing his own goodbyes. I puzzled further as we passed the keep and the buildings clustered around it and scattered beyond in the valley below, riding until the afternoon sun sparkled off a loch to our west.

"Where are we going now?" I asked.

"To the home of my ancestors. There is an old castle there that will provide us shelter for the night and where I do not think anyone will bother us. Even have the English arrived at the Campbells', they'll likely follow the main body south. Or, if they think to look for me on MacDonald land, it will be in the places we passed earlier."

I rested my head against Collin's back and savored the

sight of the peaceful loch and the ruin growing closer. It seemed familiar, though I was certain I'd never been here before.

Perched on the edge of a bluff overlooking the water, the keep was still grand, though on one side the walls had been battered, exposing the castle's innards to the elements. I sat up, studying it closer, thinking I should like to paint such a scene, when it occurred to me that I *had* painted it, years ago in England.

"This place—" I leaned around Collin, noting the cornerstone detail was exactly as I had drawn it, as was the low stone wall that ran in front of the keep along the bluff. "One of the canvases I brought with me, the one the soldiers destroyed on our way to Scotland, it was this place. Do you remember?"

"Aye." Collin guided us beneath an arch and brought Ian's horse to a stop in front of what must have been the main entrance. "I've wanted to show it to you since. This may be our only chance. Once we leave Scotland . . . " He shrugged.

"We won't ever be coming back."

"I don't believe we will." Collin slid from the horse, then helped me do the same. I turned from him, looking out at the water.

"That's Loch Linnhe. If you follow it long enough, it leads to the ocean."

"It's beautiful." I shrugged from my cloak, which smelled strongly of sweaty horse. It was warmer here, near the coast. Snow-capped mountains rose up far away, on the other side of the inlet lake, but here the sun warmed the earth and my back. It felt restorative. I crossed the narrow yard and walked along the wall, imagining the people who had once lived here and what might have happened to cause them to leave such a lovely place.

After he'd seen to the horse, Collin joined me. We walked alongside each other for a time, without talking or touching. My mind was a jumble of mixed emotions, from all that had been hurled at me the past few days. I hadn't had time to process any of them yet, from my reunion with Collin, to Brann's knife at my throat, to losing Lydia.

"You're wearing the gown we handfast in."

"Yes." I fingered the skirt, somewhat worse for wear after a day and a half on a horse, the incident at the kirkyard before, and being slept in. "It was the best I had for Hogmanay, and I haven't had a chance to change since." Clothing had been the least of my concerns as we'd prepared to leave. If I'd thought of it at all it had been to make sure that Lydia's went with her.

I brought a hand to my chest at the pang of sorrow accompanying that thought.

"You look bonny in it," Collin said. "And your hair, too, left unbound like that."

I touched the back of my head self-consciously, wondering if the last of the berries had finally blown away. "It is a tangled mess."

"You can tame it with this later." Collin withdrew my mother's silver brush and comb set from his sporran and held them out to me.

"You brought those." I found a smile of gratitude for him. "Thank you." I touched his sleeve. I'd been too distracted and distraught to think of bringing much, practical or otherwise.

"And these." Collin tucked the brush and comb back in his pouch and withdrew my paintbrushes. "And this." He pulled the carved horse free and set it in my hand. "Someday we'll have another child to give this to."

"It should have gone with Lydia. She never had a chance to play with it." A choked sob tore from my throat. I hadn't cried since we left, but the tears came freely now, the first splashing on the horse's perfectly carved mane.

Collin took it from me and tucked it away again. "May I touch you?"

I nodded, expecting the comforting weight of his hands on my shoulders as he had offered so many times before. Instead they found my waist and pulled me close.

"I would give anything to take this hurt from you." He bent his head close to mine and wept his own grief into my hair. We clung to each other, our embrace sustaining as nothing else might. The sounds of our weeping filled the vacant courtyard, and his tears wet my hands when at last I leaned back and held his face between them.

"We will survive this. What I couldn't have survived was if you'd never come back to me." I reached up to kiss him, but his lips were already on mine, soft and slow and filled with tenderness. There was nothing passionate in the exchange, but I felt love flow from Collin to me, its power restoring, even in light of all that we had lost.

"I love you, Katie MacDonald." He held my face close to his heart.

"And I love you, Collin Ian MacDonald. In whatever way you come to me."

He lifted me in his arms and started for the castle. "No evil spirits tonight. We've sacred work to do."

"Work?" I nestled my head against his shoulder.

"Aye," he said seriously. "Our bairn may not grow up in Scotland, but he can begin here, in the land of our ancestors."

Before the first streaks of dawn pinked the sky I lay awake, nestled in Collin's arms, my head on his chest, our skin touching. For a while, an hour or more perhaps, I remained content, relishing in luxuries too long denied us. We were safe and warm, well fed, and together. Loved. These things alone were all I needed, and I would have been perfectly happy to remain here forever, carving out a life for ourselves on this bit of land. But it was no longer Collin's to claim. Like so many other things, he'd lost it because of his love for me.

It seemed the price for his loyalty, for promises kept, climbed higher and higher. He'd suffered physically, with wounds that had nearly killed him and scars that would remain forever. His lands had been forfeit, a child we loved taken from us, and soon Scotland would be lost to him forever. And the ultimate cost . . .

His brother.

Collin still slept soundly, but I found I could not. Wrapping one of the blankets around me, I slid from our snug cocoon and crossed the chill floor on bare feet. I stopped near the window, or where one had once been. I peered instead through the gaping hole in the stone wall, out to Loch Linnhe below, thinking of the sea beyond, the vast Atlantic we were shortly to cross.

I felt slightly ill when I thought of the journey that awaited, as if the waves tossing the ship about were already making me seasick. It wasn't only the actual crossing that worried me, but what awaited upon those foreign shores. We were leaving Brann and all the danger he presented behind, but we would be going toward the unknown. Where were we to live? How were we to find shelter, employment, food—for the entire company?

And Ian . . . What were the chances that we might actually find him? And if we did, what would that mean? I could not imagine that an ocean voyage and months of interment and hard labor had done anything to soften his heart toward me.

Yet find him we must. I feared Collin would never be whole if we did not.

"Are you mad, woman?" Collin's voice, still gruff from sleep, interrupted my worried thoughts. "You'll catch your death of cold before we even set foot on that ship."

"I'm plenty warm," I murmured, recalling the heat he'd ignited within me only a short while ago. A deep blush toasted my cheeks as the details of our intimacy played out in my mind.

"You've not a stitch of clothes on," Collin muttered, throwing aside the other quilts, revealing he was in very much the same condition. "Not so much as a stocking."

My blush deepened as I turned quickly away. Last night had been dark, but the light already filtering through the gaps in the stone illuminated our chamber quite well, even at this early hour. "This blanket covers me sufficiently."

"That's what you think." Dragging his own wrap with him, Collin stumbled toward me.

"Careful," I admonished. "You don't want to pitch face first out the wall."

"No," Collin agreed, his footing regained by the time he reached me. "Wasn't what I had in mind when I said you were near to killing me." He pulled me back against the solid wall of his bare chest, wrapping an arm securely around my middle. "See that you take care yourself. What is it that has so captured your attention this morning? I've been watching you stand here a good, long time."

"I didn't realize how long it had been." I lifted an ice-cold foot and rubbed it against the side of his leg. "I guess I am a bit cold."

"A bit?" Collin snorted. "You're a regular block of ice."

"That's not a very kind thing to say of your wife," I scolded.

"You didn't let me finish." Collin lowered his chin, nuzzling the blanket from my shoulder. "Beneath that frosty facade is a heart that beats the warmest blood you'll ever find. Fire and ice, that's what my Katie is." He pressed his lips to my shoulder, then swept my hair aside to trail kisses along the back of my neck.

I sighed blissfully. "I could stay here forever."

"Your feet would freeze." Collin's lips continued their progress to my other shoulder, pushing the blanket dangerously low. I clutched it to me, holding it firmly in place. I *would* freeze without it.

"I didn't mean here, in this spot. I meant *here*." I swept one hand in front of me, indicating the land below. "I can see us out there in the yard, me chasing around after the chickens while you're milking the coooo." I dragged out the syllable, exaggerating the Scots' pronunciation of cow, then felt a catch in my throat. "How can you not hate me for costing you all of this?" *For the loss of your home and country, your father and now Ian?*

Collin paused his kisses. "I might, if you don't come back to bed," he teased.

"I'm serious." Tears filled my eyes. *Would I never be done with crying?*

"You think I wasn't?" He began pulling me away from the wall and back toward the bed we had made. "Besides, this old castle would be a bit drafty come winter, and far too big for just the two of us."

"We could have built a little house, right down there." I pointed to an outcropping near the loch. "Or, if you'd been set on rebuilding this place, we would simply have had to fill it with children."

Collin placed his hands on my shoulders and turned me to him. "*Children*? You realize what's required if you wish more than one bairn." His brows arched in question, the one with the scar slightly askew.

I smiled through my tears, suspecting where he was going with this. Cold as I was, the idea of crawling between the blankets with him again was more than appealing. "Generally, bairns come one at a time," I reminded him. "No matter how much effort—"

"Not always," Collin said, a wicked glint in his eye. He swept me into his arms and carried me back toward the center of the room. "Don't forget, I'm a twin."

NEXT FROM

MICHELE PAIGE HOLMES

A Hearthfire Historical Romance

The Promise of Home

A final note,

Thank you for reading *A Promise for Tomorrow*.

I continue to appreciate those who take the time to read my stories and those who post reviews as well. You make it possible for me to continue doing what I love.

If you would like more information about my other books and future releases, please visit www.michelepaigeholmes.com. You can also follow me on Twitter at @MichelePHolmes.

Happy reading!

Michele

About Michele Paige Holmes

Michele Paige Holmes spent her childhood and youth in Arizona and northern California, often curled up with a good book instead of out enjoying the sunshine. She graduated from Brigham Young University with a degree in elementary education and found it an excellent major with which to indulge her love of children's literature.

Her first novel, *Counting Stars*, won the 2007 Whitney Award for Best Romance. Its companion novel, a romantic suspense titled *All the Stars in Heaven*, was a Whitney Award finalist, as was her first historical romance, *Captive Heart. My Lucky Stars* completed the Stars series.

In 2014 Michele launched the Hearthfire Historical Romance line, with the debut title, *Saving Grace. Loving Helen* is the companion novel, with a third, *Marrying Christopher*, followed by the companion novella *Twelve Days in December*.

When not reading or writing romance, Michele is busy with her full-time job as a wife and mother. She and her husband live in Utah with their five high-maintenance children, and a Shitzu that resembles a teddy bear, in a house with a wonderful view of the mountains.

You can find Michele on the web:

http://MichelePaigeHolmes.com

Facebook: Michele Holmes

Twitter: @MichelePHolmes

Acknowledgments

A Promise for Tomorrow was months (years, in some ways) in the making, and I have many people to thank for their help in getting it from the initial ideas in my head to its final form on paper.

I am grateful to Brekke Felt for the beautiful photography for the covers of *Yesterday's Promise*, *A Promise for Tomorrow*, and the upcoming *The Promise of Home*. Her ability to capture the Highland countryside (right here in Utah!) was much appreciated. I am also grateful to Rachael Anderson for her continued talents producing each of the beautiful Hearthfire covers. Thank you for putting up with my pickiness!

Cassidy Wadsworth Sorenson and Lisa Shepherd have become two of my favorite editors. They are both so thorough, and they excel at finding mistakes and ways to improve my stories. I am so grateful to each of them for making me look better than I am.

I am particularly thankful to Mindy Holt and Heather Moore at Mirror Press. These two ladies are on top of their game and keep trying to get me to be on top of mine (please don't give up on me yet!). I am grateful for their brain power and know-how, for the time and effort they spend getting my books into the hands of readers. Their intelligence and hard work does not go unnoticed, and I continue to aspire to share even a portion of their abilities.

Finally, I owe a continued debt of gratitude to my husband and children. Some books take longer to write than others. *A Promise for Tomorrow* definitely fell into that "longer" category. Thank you, Dixon, for the weekends you sacrificed to my laptop, the nights you went to bed alone because I was up late writing. Thank you for covering the school carnival, homework duty, and basement finishing because my writing consumed so much of my time. Thank you for putting up with the never-ending pile of laundry (someday I hope to actually sort it and put it away), simple dinners, and a wife who's always walking around with half her brain in another world. Being married to me cannot be easy; thank you for your patience, for roses when I finish, for being more romantic than all the heroes I write.

Thank you, Hannah and Andrew, for mostly doing your homework on your own, for putting up with a mom who can be a little distracted when she's in the throes of drafting a novel, for being self-motivated and responsible kids. I hope you grow up knowing that hard work pays off in fulfilling your own dreams.